The Second List

Max Bridges

A Jeunive Publishing Book

TheSecondList.com
MaxBridgesAuthor.com

Facebook: facebook.com/maxbridgesauthor
Instagram: instagram.com/maxbridgesofficial

Published by
Jeunive Publishing, LLC, Irvine, CA
www.jeunivepublishing.com

Printed in the United States

Author's Note
The Second List, in its entirety, is a work of fiction. All names, characters, businesses, institutions, places, events, and incidents in this book are either the product of the author's imagination or used in a fictitious manner. Certain business organizations, institutions, agencies, and public offices are mentioned, but the characters involved, not limited to their actions and opinions, are wholly imaginary. Any resemblance to actual persons, living or dead, actual events, and/or institutions and businesses is purely coincidental. The opinions expressed are those of the characters and should not be confused with the authors.

ISBN: 978-1-7368040-1-8

For Dad,

in humble debt of your unconditional guidance,

support, and generosity.

For Susan, Ciena, and Cheyenne,

the three most important people in my life.

"Three may keep a secret, if two of them are dead."

–Benjamin Franklin

Prologue

January 27, 1945—11:23 PM (CET)
Mount Pilatus, Central Switzerland

"How much farther?" Tom shouted through the hauling bitterly cold winds, unsure if his words reached the man ahead of him. Walking through the deep snow was taking its toll. He looked around to get a hint on their progress, but everything around him was pitch black except the fast-swirling snowflakes and the snow-covered, steep railroad track underneath his feet, both faintly illuminated by the beam of his lantern. A few steps ahead, the light carried by his companion seemed to disappear into the storm.

In addition to the usual low winter temperatures, an arctic front was moving over the Swiss Alps, its wind chill factor causing conditions below the already life-threatening averages. Ice had been building up on Tom's unshaven cheeks, his ears and feet felt numb, and he had given up on wiping the constant drip off his nose. Now nearly up the mountain, he cursed himself for insisting on the excursion. He took off his gloves in a desperate attempt to blow some warm air onto his freezing fingers, but the exposure to the frosty winds made them even worse. Despite the strenuous ascent, his entire body was shivering, and he wondered how much his core temperature had dropped.

+ + +

It was only a few hours earlier that Tom had stepped into the local restaurant and stomped the snow off his boots. Thick tobacco smoke from the cheap cigars of earlier guests was still lingering under the low wooden ceiling. At a first glance, the simple, sparsely decorated dining room seemed empty.

"Anywhere you like," the waitress had said welcoming him. Across the room, at a table in the corner, Tom spotted a lone patron. A barrage of thoughts shot through his mind. Was this the one he was told about? Would the man accept his proposal? And above all, could he be trusted? Tom finally decided to approach the old man.

"Are you Johann?"

Annoyed by the interruption, the man with the leathery, weathered face looked up. "Who wants to know?"

"I need you to guide me up the mountain tonight. You come highly recommended."

Johann looked the stranger up and down and then scoffed. "No one goes out in this weather, and certainly not up the mountain," he responded in his rugged voice, and then turned his attention back to the nearly empty plate in front of him. "I'm sure people told you I was crazy enough to do it, but I can assure you I am not." He gestured for the waitress to bring him a coffee while wiping his thick, gray beard with the napkin. "Come back tomorrow morning. We will see how the weather is then."

"It has to be tonight," Tom insisted. "We have to leave as soon as humanly possible!"

The old man looked at him as if he was out of his mind.

"I understand insanity has its price," Tom rebutted, holding up a bundle of cash.

The more-than-generous compensation sure tempted the old man. "Maybe I am crazy after all," he quietly responded.

+ + +

"We are close now, about to enter the military restricted zone, but don't worry, it is rarely guarded," the old man shouted back, also breathing heavily. "It is going to be even steeper from here on, and a bit further up we will have to traverse a cliff. You got to be extra careful there. A fall would be fatal."

After the steep climb amongst towering walls of rock, a frozen creek marking their way, they carefully walked the narrow path along the top of the bluff. Right after, they finally reached the secluded, small platform that was their destination: the entrance to the cave. Tom collapsed onto its floor, trying to catch his breath. Now shielded from the unforgiving winds, he at last started to warm up a bit.

"It's perfect, isn't it?" the old man asked Tom, sitting down on one of the many artillery ammunition crates. "It's secluded, protected from the elements, and best of all, off-limits to civilians."

Tom lifted his lantern to get a better look. The interior was bigger than the entrance had suggested, the ceiling surprisingly tall, its walls nothing but rugged rock, yet the floor a thick layer of flattened dirt.

"It sure is," he agreed, happy with the location. "How do you know about this place?"

"I helped build the mountain railroad up here a long time ago. This cave was used to store explosives when the tunnels were blasted out of the mountain. It sure takes me back," the old man explained while unpacking a pick and a small shovel. "But no time for nostalgia. The storm is only going to get worse."

Without wasting anymore words, the two started to dig. After the hole reached a satisfactory depth, Tom carefully placed his small wooden box inside.

"What's in it?" Johann asked.

"None of your business," Tom snapped. "And you better not tell anyone about any of this! Or have you already forgotten our deal?" He gave the old man a stern look.

Johann nodded, but quickly curiosity got the better of him again. "C'mon, you can tell me. I won't tell a soul."

Tom just shook his head. "It is nothing of use to you. So forget about us ever having been up here. As a matter of fact, you will have to forget you ever met me. Is that clear?"

"Since it is nothing of use to me, you can tell me."

Tom glared at Johann in disbelief.

"Okay, okay, I get it," the old man responded grumpily.

"Do you?" Tom doubted it.

"Yes, I get it."

Tom followed up with another stern look, but despite the old man's assurances, a feeling of doubt lingered in his gut. They started to push the excavated dirt back into the hole, intermittently stomping on the loose soil.

"Can you at least give me a hint?" Johann probed further. Tom did not bother to answer anymore. His first impression had been that the old man could be trusted, but now, Tom saw something in the old man's eyes, a curiosity, letting him know that was a mistake. How long till he would start talking about their trip up here? How long till the old man came back himself to unearth the box? Tom's heart sank into a deep abyss. With the hiding spot filled in, the two lifted one of the heavy crates on top of the mound. It soon looked like they had never been there.

"This should do," the old man said, proud of a job well done. "Now let's head back."

Tom stared at the shovel on the ground, conflicted, again faced with a decision he did not want to make. He felt sorry for the old man, but there was no way he could take the risk, not after everything he had just gone through, not after so many had paid with their lives. With great sorrow, he reached for the wooden handle of the dirt-covered shovel and, with shaking hands, swung it around with as much power he could summon. The moment the metal hit the back of his head, Johann collapsed to the ground, unconscious.

"WHY, for god's sake? Why did you make me do this? WHY COULD YOU NOT LET THIS GO?" he screamed at him. Tom took a few seconds to compose himself, and then he went through the old man's pockets, looking for the money he had paid him. He found it on the inside of his jacket, safely placed next to another small treasure: a golden pocket watch.

"You won't need either of these anymore," he muttered and

pocketed both, and then grabbed the man by his jacket and dragged him out of the cave, through the snow, to the edge of the cliff. With deep dejection, he looked at the old man again. "WHY?" he screamed into the night. "FOR HEAVENS SAKE, WHY?" With the heaviest of hearts, he pushed him over the cliff and watched the body fall into the darkness. Riddled with guilt, he fell on his knees and, while staring into the abyss, reflected on the last fateful forty-eight hours, on every single person who had paid the ultimate price—all those innocent lives, all gone because of him. When the freezing winds ripped him out of his thoughts, he walked back to the cave and put on his backpack. He decided to give the watch another look, marveling at the golden treasure reflecting the lantern's yellow light. He pushed the small button on its side, causing the cover to snap open. The watch was old yet in perfect condition, its hands just passing the midnight hour. Intrigued by an engraving, he inched the lantern even closer.

To my precious son Johann Melchior …

Tom did not need to read the rest. Like what he just had hidden inside the cave, he could not have such implicating evidence on him. Ready to dive back into the storm, he stepped out of the cave to start his descent, but not before throwing the watch into the snow-covered bushes, grudgingly letting go of the small treasure.

Part I

Water Deeper Than Expected

1

It was a pleasant late-summer day when Susan Sobchak parked her car in front of her grandparents' beachfront mansion on Long Island. The sun was low, blinding her on the drive up. A welcome ocean breeze, fresh and cool, entered through the open windows. She had left numerous voice and text messages for her grandparents, now in their late eighties, but none had been returned. Concerned, she had decided to pay them a visit to make sure they were okay. She locked her car, more out of habit than necessity in the exclusive neighborhood, walked up to the house, and pushed the door handle. Unsurprisingly, the door was locked. She cursed herself for not bringing the spare set of keys and rang the doorbell. Nobody answered. She took the phone from her purse and dialed her grandfather's number. Just a few seconds later, she heard his phone ring inside the house. Nobody answered. She did it again, this time dialing her grandmother's, and again, a phone rang on the inside.

Alarmed, Susan made her way to the side of the house, removed her high heels, and climbed over the tall fence. She struggled but somehow managed to scale the barrier. Against expectations, her tight designer suit survived, all but a short seam at the bottom of her skirt. She made her way through the side garden, jumping from stone to stone, then reached the front terrace—her favorite area of the property—overlooking the dunes, the beach, and, beyond, the Atlantic Ocean. She remembered the many good times she had spent on the lounge chair there, breathing in the salty, fresh air, sipping sweet lemonade, taken in by an engaging novel, and enjoying the colorful sunsets. The spectacular surroundings were reflected in the floor-to-ceiling glass front, obstructing the view inside. The big glass doors were ajar, just wide enough for Susan to peek her head inside. She shouted a loud "Hello, it's me, Susan," which echoed through the large, open space. Again, there was no answer. She opened the door and entered through the kitchen into the living room, where she froze in her tracks. Right in front of her was her grandfather, in a chair, slumped over the glass table, next to him her grandmother on the polished marble floor—both in a puddle of their own blood, both heads severed by a clean cut.

Susan sank to the floor in complete shock, her eyes welling up, tears running down her face, her body shaking uncontrollably, unable to move. She tried to make sense of what she saw but was unable at first to grasp what was happening. She managed to dial 911 and waited for the authorities to arrive. When at last she took her eyes off her grandparents, her gaze met the red Paul Klee painting just behind the long dining room table. It was one of the many invaluable art pieces in her grandfather's collection and the center of many dinner conversations, especially when guests were entertained. The painting was her grandfather's favorite, and now he was gone. They both were.

One month earlier

2

July 28, 2017—12:45 PM (PDT)
Westside Towers, Offices of The New York Times, Los Angeles

Patrick Rooper was sitting in his office, close to finalizing his latest article, an investigative piece into the lack of criminal investigations by the SEC of top Wall Street players committing serious breaches of financial laws. Nobody seemed to have learned the lessons from the crash back in 2008, and even now such crimes never seemed to reach the radar of government prosecutors. It was time to rattle the cage again.

Undecided about some of the exact wording of the article's final edit, he leaned back, stretched his arms, and rested his eyes. It was amazing what a few minutes away from the screen could do for the creativity of a tired writer. His eyes drifted to his Ivy League diploma and the many plaques and awards surrounding it, recognition for his work over the years. His humble character had never allowed him to be comfortable showcasing the lot, and he would have preferred the exhibits boxed up, as he often questioned the value of the neatly framed pieces of paper. Sure, the diploma opened a few doors, but over the years he had met great journalists with community college degrees whose talents allowed them to write great articles—much better ones, in fact, than his mostly overcompensated classmates who would never have been accepted into an Ivy League university if not for the generous donations of their influential parents. It was his assistant, Eva, who insisted on keeping the accolades on the shelves, whenever necessary reminding him that not many graduate from schools of such caliber, much less with the honor of cum laude, even fewer at top of the class, and even rarer are those awarded the national Mark of Excellence in the newspaper category.

Of greater importance to him were the two pictures on his desk. The first showed him in uniform, taken the day he graduated from the Navy SEAL program, an accomplishment that still filled his chest with pride. Now in his mid-thirties, the youthful look in his cheeks had since disappeared, and so had the buzz-cut, his dark hair now styled into a classic, undercut, yet modern slicked-back look. He was still as handsome as back then, his easy smile still prominent, along with his hazel-colored eyes; his shoulders were still as wide and his body lean and muscular as ever, the entire six feet one inch of it, as he strictly kept up with his navy training routines. His days in active duty taught him more about human nature than he could have learned though any other experience. But it was not only what he learned about others; it was mostly what he learned about himself. Nothing brings out one's true character more than being under constant fire with seemingly no way out.

The other frame hosted a picture of his fiancée, Sarah, taken during a vacation abroad, a three-quarter shot from behind, her head turned toward the camera, her long blond hair flowing in the wind, her bright blue eyes piercing the lens as if in competition with the beauty of the setting sun behind her. With a smile as irresistible as one has ever seen, it reminded Patrick daily how lucky of a guy he was. She was different—good different. Meeting her a bit over a year ago was a true blessing. Patrick soon after knew she was the one, and for the first time in his life he truly was in love. After a year of dating, he finally deemed the time right to tie the knot, and it was not long ago when he went down on his knee, opened the small box with a spectacular diamond ring inside, and asked Sarah to share the rest of her life with him. She needed a second to compose herself but eventually managed to utter a "yes" while crying tears of joy, officially ending his status as eternal bachelor.

Patrick had been looking forward to a planned lunch with Sarah on Santa Monica's Third Street Promenade. Unfortunately, she had to cancel. He was disappointed, yet part of him did not mind. The workload on his desk was stacking up, and he needed time to catch up. Instead of the romantic lunch, he wolfed down a quick bite at a fast-food place around the corner. Now back at his desk, with his stomach rumbling from digesting, he had decided to first go through his stack of mail. He was in the midst of doing so, when his assistant Eva opened the door and entered.

"I just wanted to remind you of your 3:30 appointment in the big office. Don't forget. And here is your coffee."

"I have not forgotten; thank you. And thank you for the brew. Do you know what he wants?" Patrick asked without looking up, still sorting out the advertisements.

"You're welcome, and no, I don't," she replied, setting the cup down next to him, then closed the door behind her. It was the moment an envelope caught Patrick's attention. Between credit card applications and real estate mailers, there it was: an envelope, with his address written by hand with no return address, and only a stamp from a New York City post office. Patrick tossed the pile of junk mail into the recycling bin, lay back in his chair, and held the envelope against the light, curious what this could be about. At first glance, it looked suspicious. Patrick carefully opened the envelope, peeked inside, and, not seeing anything malicious, took out the letter.

Dear Mr. Rooper,

I am a faithful follower of your articles. Your insights are second to none, and I commend you for your honesty and ethics. You are an excellent journalist, probably the best in the US, if not the world, and I am sure you are well on your way to win the prestigious Pulitzer Prize one day.

I am writing this letter in need of your help. Now in the twilight years of my life, I need to right a terrible wrong that has plagued my conscience for a long time now, and I dread the thought of leaving this earth without it being resolved. But, as age has taken its toll, I am unable to act on my own and am in need of someone blessed with your unique qualities.

There are people who, given the knowledge, would do anything to prevent what I am about to do, so please forgive the secrecy about my identity—a necessary precaution, at this time, to protect me and my husband.

I want to give you a few days to think about this brief introduction and then, hopefully, once provided with more information, accept my commission. I understand your services do not come for free. At a later point, you will be given the opportunity to name your price.

I thank you in advance, with deep gratitude, and will be in touch again soon.

There was no signature. Patrick had no patience for such nonsense. He shook his head while crumpling the letter and, with a swift motion, threw it in the recycling bin next to his desk.

13:45 PM

Eva opened the door to his office once again and gave him the thirty-minute warning to his deadline. Patrick thanked her. She was about to close the door when he called her back in.

"Eva, wait a second. Have a look at what was in the mail today. Another one of these 'can you help me with whatever' letters. How many this year? Five or six?" Patrick took the paper out of the bin, flattened it as well as he could, and handed it to her. He observed her eyes following line after line. Once done, she folded the letter.

"You have unique qualities?" Eva could not help herself but chuckle. "I have to say, this one is better written than the others.

May be this time there is something to it." Patrick scoffed, shaking his head. But Eva had a feeling about the letter.

"At least keep your mind open. She mentioned she will be in touch. We will know more then." But Patrick was in no mood to waste time.

"It's just another nutcase who wants to send me on a wild goose chase. She needs a private eye, not me." Patrick gestured for her to toss the letter back into the recycling bin. Eva just shrugged.

"You are probably right. Then again, I'd be excited to hear more—but hey, that's me. More importantly, you have twenty-five minutes till your deadline." Eva turned and closed the door behind her.

10:50 AM (THAT)
Bora Bora, Tahiti

After a few years in the corporate world of high finance, Susan Sobchak desperately needed a change from the fast-paced environment of investment banking and craved something more tangible than financial data on computer screens. Her job had paid well, but she was already aware there is more to life than money. For a while, she felt increasingly frustrated, aware of a growing void inside her, till her desire for change overpowered the comforts of her employment. That was the moment she walked into her boss's office, quit without having plans for what to do next, and walked straight into the travel agency across the street, where she booked a trip to an exotic, off-grid location, not really caring where to as long as it was far away and offered a sandy beach, a tropical climate, and beautiful sunsets. She was on a plane the very next day.

For days, she could not be bothered even to look at her cell phone. She just did not care about the world outside the solitude of the resort. But after a few quiet days, she contemplated checking her messages, if just to make sure there were no emergencies. Comfortable in the hammock above the warm, turquoise water, her left foot dangling, her slender body tanning in the sun, her long, dark-brown hair pulled through the ponytail hole of her baseball cap, she finally nudged herself to switch it on. She was immediately tempted to turn if off again as the beeps interrupted her serenity, alerting her to the many voice and text messages. It took her a second or two before she decided against it, mainly to just put her mind at ease. She took off her designer sunglasses to get a better look of the screen. The first few messages were from her boss, pleading for her return with offers of increasing pay raises. She deleted one after the other. Then there was a voice mail from her granddad. Susan got up from her hammock, baffled, as he had never called when knowing she was out of town.

Susan, my sweetheart. I hope you are doing great and that you are enjoying your vacation. We sure miss you. I just wanted to let you know we love you and that you will be in our hearts always. Bye.

The message was very unlike him. His personality was more the cold and calculating one, never showing any type of emotion. She had certainly never heard him say "I love you" before. They were close, but it was unlike him to vocalize it, and certainly not with such a sentimental undertone. Concerned, she called him.

A few years back, Susan's parents had died in a hit-and-run car accident. The intoxicated driver was caught and received a lengthy prison sentence, while Susan received a hefty insurance payout. She welcomed the comfortable lifestyle the money provided, but she would have given it all just to have a bit more time with her beloved mother and father. Unfortunately, life does not offer such a choice. After her parents' untimely passing, Susan's grandparents were all the family she had left. They grew closer, supporting each other through the tough times. Susan kept up with daily phone calls and frequent visits, and she greatly valued their company, advice, and support. Now with her grandparents well into their twilight years, she felt responsible for their care and well-being.

"Oh, Susan, don't worry, everything is fine!" her grandfather responded confidently, quickly changing the topic of conversation to her vacation. Susan sensed something in his voice but knew better than to inquire further. He obviously had decided not to tell her whatever was going on, and so, she knew from experience, he never would. Unsettled by the call, Susan tried to keep herself active to distract her mind. She participated in an early afternoon hike and late-afternoon yoga on the beach, and she joined the other guests on the sunset boat ride out to one of the nearby atoll islands where a lavish dinner was served. The distractions did not work; her thoughts kept coming back to her grandfather.

August 2, 2017—9:15 AM (PDT)
Offices of *The New York Times*

As he did every Monday morning, Patrick was leafing through the weekend papers when the phone rang. It was his assistant on an internal line. Eva knew better than to disturb him during his press reviews. Somewhat annoyed, he picked up the phone. "What?"

"Patrick, there is a woman here to see you."

"Does she have an appointment?"

"No, she does not."

"Then tell her to make one." Not a minute later, Eva knocked on the door and opened it just wide enough to peek through.

"Sorry, Patrick, I know you are busy, but I think you should at least hear what she has to say. She is such a sweet old lady. Apparently, she came all the way from Long Island."

"What is her name?"

"She doesn't say, but listen to this. She is the author of the mysterious letter you received a few days ago. Please, please, please see her. I am so curious."

"Tell me you are not serious," Patrick said as he rolled his eyes.

"You know, you still owe me a favor for finding that incredible Valentine's Day gift for Sarah," Eva tried to charm her boss.

He just looked at her.

"C'mon, Patrick, I am dying to find out what is going on here. Pleeeeeeeease?"

Patrick was ever so slightly shaking his head, surprised that he was about to give in.

"Just for five minutes and we are even, okay?" Eva enticed him further.

"I did not know we were not even," he responded with a disapproving sigh. He got up from his desk, and while passing Eva, pointed his finger in her face. "Now you owe me."

With a big smile, she reminded him not to be so grumpy. Patrick followed Eva out to meet the visitor.

"Hi, Mr. Rooper. I am so glad to meet you in person."

Patrick was quite taken by his first impression. In front of him stood a woman, aged very gracefully, with well-applied, understated makeup, wearing an elegant haute couture outfit that fit perfectly. Even more striking, her charisma could have filled a ballroom. With a slightly surprised undertone, he asked her to call him Patrick.

"What can I do for you, Mrs. ...?"

"Can we speak somewhere private?"

"Sure. Please, this way." Patrick gestured toward the conference room. He then asked Eva for two coffees and, behind the old woman's back, indicated that she was to get him out in a few minutes with a made-up excuse. Patrick opened the door for his guest, who sat on one of the many chairs and looked around the room. He was about to get the conversation started but his visitor held up her hand, gesturing for him to wait. After the coffees were served and the door was closed, she turned to Patrick.

"I need to ask you a question."

9:20 AM

Olympic Boulevard, Los Angeles

Uncomfortable in his impeccable business suit, his dark hair well-groomed and his rather square face cleanly shaven, Hironori Matsubara was standing on the curb opposite the lobby of the Westside Towers, keeping his eye on the entrance to the office building while pressing the satellite phone against his ear. It was past midnight back home, but as expected his boss answered the call right away.

"She just went inside. What do you want me to do?" Hironori asked. There was a long pause.

The stocky man had been sent to New York two days ago, the very moment he had returned to Tokyo, leaving hardly any time to repack his small suitcase with a new set of clothes. As requested, he followed the old lady all the way to Los Angeles. He was used to life on the go, traveling often, trusted by his boss to take care of the organization's most important "complications," wherever they may flare up.

"Nothing yet. Keep an eye on her."

"I can take care of this right here, right now, as soon as she exits the building." There was another pause.

"We first need confirmation of the rumors. Just stay on her tail and find out what you can."

9:25 AM

Offices of *The New York Times*

Patrick told his visitor to go ahead, already knowing how the next five minutes would pass. He would patiently listen to her blabber, Eva would get him out in a few, and he would be back at his desk in no time.

"You grew up in Southern California—in Orange County, to be more precise. Is that correct?" she asked. Patrick nodded.

"Before you transitioned into the world of journalism, you were in the Navy, trained as a SEAL, correct?"

"Yes, I was," he nodded again.

"You were a part of the prestigious SEAL Team Six, specialized as an MSO, advanced special operations. Your nickname was 'The Retriever,' and you participated in delicate undercover missions to gather intelligence essential to US interests, correct?"

"It's not something on my resume, but yes," Patrick responded, surprised, wondering how she knew. "Can you please get to the point?" But the old woman was not yet ready to do so.

"Your parents were born in Lucerne, Switzerland, correct?"

"Is this some kind of interview?" Patrick responded impatiently, wondering where all this was going. "Please tell me what I can do for you."

She again ignored his objection. "Do you still have a close connection to the area?"

Patrick chuckled. Hesitantly, he decided to play along, if only to get this over with. "I spent quite a bit of time in Lucerne when I was younger. My parents sent me there during my summer vacations."

"Are you still visiting regularly?"

"Yes, I try to go there at least once a year."

"And you are still familiar with the area?"

"Listen, Mrs.—I don't even know your name."

"Please answer my question," the old woman insisted.

Patrick scoffed. "Please just tell me how I can help you."

She once again ignored him. "Mr. Rooper, are you still familiar with the area?"

Somewhat annoyed, Patrick nodded.

"And from what I hear, you do speak Swiss German, and therefore, I am assuming, German?"

"Fluently."

"Koennen sie mir bitte den Zucker reichen?" the old woman asked in German.

Patrick handed her one of the small sugar packages. "You are a lefty, too, like my fiancée," he noted.

"More out of necessity than anything else. I suffered a shoulder injury during the war, and it is still bothering me today." With a smile on her face, she poured the sugar in her coffee, stirred it, and then took a sip. Patiently, Patrick waited for her to put the cup back down, checking his watch in the hope that Eva would extricate him soon.

"Good, then. Mr. Rooper—"

"Please, call me Patrick."

Once again, she ignored him. "Mr. Rooper, I know you did extensive research into the inner workings of the various European resistance organizations during the Second World War. It is something of such importance to you that you made it the subject of your doctoral dissertation. I am assuming your interest was awoken by your early childhood friend whose grandparents used to be active in such an organization and, after a bitter betrayal, ended up in a concentration camp. It was only by a miracle that their young children, your friend's parents, survived, saved from certain death mere seconds before the Nazis could get to them. You strongly feel you must do your part so the world never forgets. Your thesis reached the highest recognition, yet, for you, it was only a starting point; your end goal was to publish a book about true heroism by examining and analyzing the changes in, and effects of, mindset in environments of disproportional power. But after investing many hours into your research, and after initial success, you hit nothing but dead ends. You could not find much beyond the content of your dissertation, and therefore, you have never managed to turn the work into a book, and your dream of publishing such a piece crumbled."

Patrick sat in pure astonishment. The old woman was spot on, with everything. She triumphantly noticed his surprise.

"Are you still interested in pursuing this dream?" she continued.

"Wait, wait, wait," he intervened. "How do you know all this?"

She smiled. "Mr. Rooper, how I know is irrelevant. What is relevant is that I *do* know. So again, are you interested in picking up where you left off?"

Patrick could not believe what he was hearing. "I think I have exhausted all avenues. If there is more information out there, I would have found it."

"What if I can give you what you need?" She strategically threw her bait right in front of him. The conference room door opened, and Eva was ready with her excuse to get Patrick out of the meeting.

"Sorry to interrupt, but Jeff is calling about the article. Apparently, you had promised to get it to him by yesterday at 6 p.m."

"Oh, thank you, Eva, but tell Jeff he will have to wait. He really does not need it till tomorrow." Eva nodded with a telling smirk and closed the door behind her.

"I got your attention, Mr. Rooper." The old women smiled triumphantly.

"I would not bet on it," Patrick responded, equally determined to avoid appearing too eager. But he had to admit, this woman was quite something.

"I personally would bet on it." His visitor smiled and took another sip from her coffee.

Well played, Patrick thought.

"Mr. Rooper, give me some credit. I may be old, but I am not stupid." The look on her face reminded him of his mother—her expression when, as a kid, he had done something he was not supposed to, yet with such charm she could not resist a smile.

"Seriously, please, call me Patrick," he asked once again while taking a notepad from one of the drawers.

"Is this necessary?" The old woman seemed uncomfortable with the idea of him writing things down.

"Well, if we go any further, you will have to trust me. But let me assure you that I never reveal my sources or any sensitive information, at least not without their consent. Now let's start with your full name."

The woman hesitated for a moment but knew he was right.

"Very well. My name is Rachel Sobchak. But since you keep insisting on calling you by your first name, please call me Rachel."

Rachel Sobchak. He had never heard the name before.

"Please, Rachel, I am all ears. Tell me why you are here."

"I am here because—well, it is complicated. But mainly, as mentioned in my letter, there is something that weighs on my conscience, and I have ignored it for too long. Now it is high time to do something about it. Who knows how much longer I have?"

"Okay, Rachel, you got my full attention. Tell me what this is all about."

"To be honest, I'm not sure where to begin."

"Well, it is always a good idea to start at the beginning."

"Right. Here we go. On January 27, 1945, very early in the morning, a small airplane, escaping the war in Poland, landed at the military airport in Alpnach in central Switzerland. On board were a pilot and a passenger: my husband Tom and me."

3

August 25, 2017—12:30 PM (CEST)
Lake Lucerne, Central Switzerland

Patrick checked once again to see if anyone was following him after stepping off the ship in Alpnachstad, a small village at the base of Mount Pilatus, close to the runway where Rachel and her husband had landed over sixty years ago. During the last few days he had felt uneasy, but he was not able to pinpoint exactly why. For some reason, he had an eerie feeling he was being watched—that someone was observing his every move.

The scenic cruise from Lucerne to the village of Alpnachstad had taken less than an hour. Despite some low-hanging clouds, the boat ride made him realize once again how truly breathtaking Switzerland was. The ship was mostly empty, hosting only a handful of tourists on the famous round trip to the top of Mount Pilatus, as well as an older man, his tanned face covered with deep wrinkles, with solid hiking boots on his feet, two hiking poles in his hands, and a backpack next to him on a bench. He struck Patrick as a local mountain farmer on his way home, not particularly enjoying the boat ride, maybe even seasick despite the rather calm waters.

Patrick was tempted to check the crossed-off location on his map once again but decided against, as he did not want to draw unnecessary attention. He already knew the X on the map was in a remote, rugged, and steep area, and that it would be a major challenge to locate the small cave. It was somewhere just after the 3.5-kilometer railway marker, about 80 percent of the way up to the summit.

Once the ship docked, Patrick walked the short distance to the base station of the Pilatus mountain railroad. The passengers from the boat transitioned to the train, looking forward to a steep ride up the mountain. With a big screech, the cogwheels engaged with the track to provide the necessary grip, rattling the entire train. With surprisingly agile steps, and just in time as the doors were closing, the old man from the boat jumped onto the slow-moving train.

1:15 PM
Mount Pilatus Railroad

Everyone was enjoying the impressive ride as the scenery grew increasingly picturesque. The trees became scarce, and the remote landscape turned rockier as the low-hanging clouds shrouded the train. Soon, through a few cracked open windows, one could hear the distinct, rather romantic sound of bells strapped around the necks of the grazing cows. As the train approached the approximate area of the cave, Patrick wondered if he was underequipped. However, turning around was not an option. Time was of the essence, and he knew he needed to find whatever secret it was holding.

A few minutes later, the train came to a full stop, and a chilled breeze welcomed the travelers. The train conductor's booming voice announced their arrival at the summit and the eventual departure of the last train at 5 p.m. Patrick zipped up his jacket and stepped out to the viewing platform. He remembered that on a clear day, one could enjoy panoramic views as far as southern Germany. Even more spectacular was Lake Lucerne, winding between the mountains. However, on this day, the weather did not allow for such vistas as the summit was covered in a cloud, the cool air even turning into a slight drizzle. Patrick could hardly see the old hotel located just a few hundred feet away. Up here, though rare, a summer storm could cover the summit in a blanket of snow, and the temperature was not too far off to allow it. For a good hour, he sat down on one of the many benches, keeping an eye on everybody. Most of the tourists quickly disappeared into the restaurant and gift shop. As for the old man, he was already gone, seemingly in a hurry to get home.

2:30 PM
Summit, Mount Pilatus

Eventually, the entire area emptied as the tourists started to leave, taking the cable-cabin on the north side of the mountain, having snapped enough pictures of their huddled-up friends in heavy jackets for their social media posts. Now all alone, Patrick started his descent on foot down the switchbacks, soon disappearing into the thickening fog. After a little over twenty minutes, he reached a stone fountain providing fresh, ice-cold spring water to hikers and cows alike. He started to worry about the worsening weather conditions when a retired couple appeared through the fog, headed in the opposite direction to him. After an initial greeting they reached into their backpacks for energy bars—protein and sugar for their last leg on their way to the summit—and sat down next to Patrick.

3:00 PM
South Side, Mount Pilatus

Patrick minded his own business, but, as was customary on these trails, the couple started a friendly conversation. They were locals surely familiar with the mountain. Patrick took the opportunity to inquire about the cave.

"Oh, no," the man replied while shaking his head, "there is no cave. Not anymore. There used to be, till after the Second World War."

"What happened to it? Caves don't just disappear," Patrick observed. The couple chuckled.

"This one did," the wife chimed in. "There used to be a secret artillery station up there, and the military used the cave for ammunition storage. One day after the war, it all blew up." Her husband nodded in agreement and continued the story.

"It was obliterated. It caused the entire side of the hill to collapse. I remember it vividly. We were only in the second grade back then, playing in the schoolyard just down the mountain. We all heard the explosion, then the rumbling of falling rocks. With the war still fresh in our minds, we thought bombers were on the attack."

"Do you know where the cave used to be?" Patrick wanted to confirm the information he had.

"From what I recall, it was somewhere near the lower entrance of the first tunnel up there, on the other side of the tracks, on the hill facing southeast." He took a bite of his energy bar. "Why do you want to know?" he asked, chewing his snack.

"No reason, really," Patrick played down his interest. "I am just fascinated with caves, and I heard about one on this mountain. Even if it is gone, I'd love to go check it out."

"Well, the area is off limits, so you did not hear this from us, but if you really want to have a look, you will have to walk up the tracks. Trains do not run that often; you can make it unnoticed between two runs. However, it is steep and slippery, especially in this weather. And there are stiff penalties for trespassing. I am not sure it is worth the risk, especially since the cave is now nothing but a part of history."

The two just confirmed what Rachel Sobchak had already told him. Yet she had not given up hope that the box buried there decades ago might still be around somewhere. Patrick had to do his due diligence. After all, he was being paid handsomely to do it. Patrick thanked the couple as they got up to continue their ascent and soon after disappeared in the lingering fog.

Patrick left the official hiking path and headed straight across the rugged field for the railroad tracks. Multiple cows chewing on fresh mountain grass kept a careful eye on him, thankfully not minding him too much. His cell phone struggled to connect to a network, but he just about managed to check the train's timetable. The next set was scheduled to pass in about twenty minutes, and then nothing for a full hour. It was a window of opportunity with plenty of time to reach the cave unnoticed.

Patrick hid himself behind a bush and awaited the passing of the trains. After the last wagon, he jumped onto the tracks and started climbing, ignoring the various signs warning away trespassers. As cautioned, the railway ties were partially mossy and wet. Just minutes later the weather changed; the fog started to lift, and sunlight pushed through the clouds. He would have preferred to continue his ascent in the cover of the fog, but, on the upside, the wooden blocks started to dry, making a slip less likely. The clouds had fully lifted by the time he got off the tracks and hiked toward the little creek that would lead him up to the cave. Around him, the Swiss Alps presented themselves in a stunning silhouette against the deep blue sky.

The terrain up the creek was steep, rocky, and rugged, as expected, but not as threatening as the narrow path traversing the cliff further up. He soldiered on, being extra careful, trying not to look down, and wondering if his compensation, though generous, was worth the risk. He checked his GPS device; his position was now close to the spot his client had marked on the map. But the path abruptly ended at a rockslide area filled with boulders giant to small and, here and there, pieces of debris rotting and rusting away, year after year, the elements taking their unforgiving toll. Though mostly washed away, black burn marks lingered, a silent witness to the forces that were at play during the explosion. The cave was gone, as he was informed; nothing was left but a few scattered remnants. Patrick regarded the massive gap in the terrain with awe, struggling to imagine the sheer force that caused the thousands of pounds of rock to violently rip from the mountainside. No wonder people heard, even felt, the event miles away. If there ever had been a cave, it was long gone. And so was whatever he was sent to retrieve, either buried deep under the rocks, most likely obliterated in the explosion, or fallen victim to the harsh weather.

Patrick sat down and rested against one of the boulders. He had started this journey with high hopes to further his research. Now, he felt defeated once again. He looked around, taking solace in the breathtaking view overlooking the lake, the valley, and the south side of Mount Pilatus. He even spotted the fountain where he had spoken to the couple. The sun was moving slowly toward its setting point, when suddenly, and just for a split second, a blinding ray of light reflected into Patrick's eye. There it was—a piece of metal stuck between two boulders.

Pushing his back against one of them and his legs against the other, he started to wiggle the smaller one backward and forward, eventually causing it to thunder down the mountain, freeing the shiny piece. Patrick picked up the intriguing object and sat down again. In his hand, he held an old, golden pocket watch, chain still attached. Curious, he opened the slightly ajar, heavily dented cover plate, then wiped the dirt off, uncovering an engraving:

To my precious son Johann Melchior. May this watch protect you always.
Love, Mom—1889.

Patrick was overcome with a feeling of nostalgia, trying to imagine the moment the precious item was gifted with all the love and care only a mother can give. Suddenly, out of nowhere, a loud bang echoed through the mountains and small pieces of rock flew upward, one hitting him in his neck. Patrick immediately felt a sharp sting. He knew the sound too well—the sound of a bullet fired by a high-powered rifle. Before he could react, another loud bang followed. With his ears ringing and his neck in pain, he immediately reached for the wound, feeling wet blood. Where were the shots coming from? It did not matter. Chances were the next would not miss its target. Patrick immediately rolled to his side and then jumped forward, desperate for cover. But the terrain was too steep for him to stop his momentum. He was tumbling down the slope, hitting rocks and debris alike. He could not tell what was up or down anymore, sliding faster and faster until a few small trees finally broke his fall.

Patrick did not know how long he had been unconscious, but when he awoke, he felt like he had been hit by a truck. Dazed and confused, he noticed blood dripping from his head. His left arm, left torso, right leg, and back were severely bruised, his ears were ringing, and an unexpectedly big goose egg had already formed on his forehead. But the most pain he felt was in his left knee. He could hardly move his leg, which made him believe it was fractured. Patrick slowly started to remember what had happened. Alerted by smaller rocks rolling down the hill, he looked up and saw, much to his disbelief, the old man from the ship standing in the middle of the rockslide area, rifle in hand, looking for him. The assignment at first had seemed innocent enough, but as warned by Rachel, someone was willing to do whatever was necessary to stop it.

Patrick was in no shape to fight or run, so the only option left was to hide. He carefully crawled a bit deeper into the trees, then laid on his back, as flat as he could, and covered himself with fallen branches. He was fairly confident about his camouflage, but one could never be sure, only hope. Now in the midst of small trees, Patrick lost sight of the old man, but telling from the sound of his steps, he was coming closer.

"Hmm … blood … he must be close," the old man muttered. Patrick could now see him through the branches only yards away. He seemed incredibly fit and agile, surprising for his age, his breathing elevated but still slow for walking in such a steep area. Patrick wondered if his fragile demeanor on the boat had been mere theatrics. If so, it had certainly fooled him. Patrick calmed himself, taking slow, shallow but regular breaths, and stayed as still as possible. Seconds passed, then the man took a few steps toward him, pulling branches out of the way to look behind. He stopped just inches from Patrick's head and looked around, carefully scanning everything, eventually looking straight down at him. It was all over now. The barrel surely would be pointed at him next, and the trigger pulled. But after a few agonizing seconds, the man turned and started to walk away, making his way further down the hill.

Patrick lost his visual on him once again and guessed he was gone. He weighed his options for a way out, but they were slim to none. His first thought was to wait for darkness, only to dismiss the idea immediately as he could not, with his injuries, get down the mountain on his own. Very careful not to make any noise, he pulled his phone out of his pocket. It was damaged but thankfully operational. He dialed the number of the emergency services. They quickly picked up the call, but when he was about to ask for help, he again heard footsteps nearby. Patrick ended the call immediately. He moved his head ever so slightly and spotted the old man again. Patrick mentally prepared for a fight, one with the odds stacked against him. All he had was the element of surprise, and he knew he needed to use it wisely even as he doubted it was enough, considering his injuries. The attacker started walking toward him again. Twenty yards, ten yards, five … Patrick calculated the exact moment to attack. Too soon and his advantage would be gone; too late and he would not have enough time to get up from the ground. Three yards, two yards … Patrick readied himself. Then the man stopped, opened his backpack, took out his phone, and dialed.

"Yes. I followed him up the mountain and kept a close eye on him …. I am not sure. I believe he found something, but I don't think it's the document …. I stand corrected, the notebook. However, I cannot be certain …. No, I don't think so. I believe he is injured …. I would have hit him if not for the unpredictable winds up here …. No, no visual on him right now. But don't worry. If not up here, he will be taken care of in the city …. Yes, he'll be dead by tonight."

The man put the phone back, and then leaned against a boulder, once again scanning the area. Patrick hoped he would soon leave, but he just sat there while the minutes passed by. The idea of taking him out at that moment was increasingly appealing to Patrick. He was getting ready to grab a fist-sized rock lying next to him, jump up, and hit the guy over the head when, in the far distance, the noise of a helicopter emerged. It grew increasingly louder. As the low-flying red rescue chopper approached, his attacker took his backpack and fled down the treacherous hill.

The helicopter circled above the rockslide area, its crew trying to locate Patrick, who pointed his small flashlight at the cockpit. The pilot maneuvered the aircraft above the small trees, while a medic was lowered, touching down next to him. After an initial assessment, Patrick was strapped into a harness and then hooked to the hoist wire rope. As soon as they were off the ground the pilot started the ascent, jolting up the helicopter, with the two still dangling below, slowly being pulled into the cabin. Flying through the air, one of the belts pressed against the old watch, which pushed against Patrick's bruised body. It hurt, but his main concern was for the old object, hoping it would not be further damaged after all this time on the mountain. Patrick decided right then and there that, to give his trip at least some worth, he would try to reunite the small treasure with its rightful heir.

10:12 PM

County Hospital, Lucerne

"You're in luck; nothing is broken. Quite surprising considering the swelling. You did twist your knee pretty badly, but nothing that cannot be taken care of with ice. Your ribs are bruised, too, but I suppose you knew that already. Here is a prescription for pain meds. You are going to need them. Otherwise, you are good to go."

The doctor's words were like music to Patrick's ears. After a five-hour wait in the emergency room, he was relieved by the update. The next challenge was to get out of the hospital unnoticed; he had a feeling someone was already waiting for him outside.

Patrick signed the discharge papers, got dressed, and then peeked from behind the curtain to check the activity board on the wall. The evening was categorized by the staff as calm; accordingly, the list of admissions was short. There were two victims of a car accident, a guy with a cut in his hand in need of stitches, a middle-aged man who might have had a heart attack, an old woman whose condition he could not decipher, and an ambulance driver who had injured his back picking up the gurney with—from what he had overheard—a rather heavy-set woman.

Patrick started to make his round. The two car accident victims were both heavily sedated. Their clothes were on the chair next to their beds, cut into pieces. He nicked a baseball cap from the small table next to one of the beds. It was badly wrinkled, but it would do. In the next stall, the old woman with the mystery condition was sitting up in her bed praying. He passed right by her. Next was the stall with the injured ambulance driver. It was empty, the man probably taken for a scan. His work uniform was on the bed, neatly folded. Jackpot! Patrick snuck in, closed the curtain, and changed. As he put on the uniform, to his excitement, a key fob fell out of one of the pockets. He picked it up. With his own clothes under his arms and much confidence, he walked out of the stall, only to run straight into a nurse.

"You must be here to check on your colleague," she said catching Patrick off guard.

"Ah … yes, I am."

"They are just finishing up the scan. From what I hear, he is going to be okay. If you want, you can wait for him here. He'll be back shortly."

Patrick put a fake smile of relief on his face. "Thank God, I was really worried about him."

"Sorry; got to go deliver some discharge papers," she returned his smile and left. He put the baseball cap on his head and, trying hard not to limp, walked toward the exit.

The outside was somewhat busy with people coming and going, but after a quick scan of the area, Patrick spotted the man from the mountain staring at him suspiciously. He stayed calm, playing his role, clicked the button on the fob, and walked to the ambulance that lit its blinkers in response. The disguise was working; the man turned his attention away from him. Patrick started the engine and took off but parked the vehicle just around the corner. He switched back into his own clothes, placed the uniform and keys on the front seat, and then called the hospital and "complained" about a parked ambulance blocking a driveway.

After the call, he crossed the street and, while waiting for the bus, opened his browser to book a local short-term rental, any place other than his hotel room. He had just finalized the booking and switched off his phone to prevent getting tracked when someone in a medic uniform climbed into the ambulance across the street. Another few minutes later, Patrick was riding the bus to the city center where, from an ATM, he withdrew enough cash to last him a few days, got his pain medication from a twenty-four-hour pharmacy, and organized a prepaid phone from the electronics store in the underpass. Pleased with his purchases, he boarded the first local train to one of the suburbs, exited at the second station, and walked the rest of the way to his overnight accommodation. It was dark and late, and he was, more or less, the only person out and about. Patrick considered changing his booking the moment he saw the run-down house, wondering where all the good reviews had come from, but then decided to ring the doorbell anyway. An overweight woman in a food-stained muumuu and curlers in her hair opened the door and, with a rough voice, asked why he was booking a room this late. She had her suspicions, but after a good look up and down, she welcomed Patrick in.

4

August 26, 2017—3:40 PM (MDT)
Navajo National Monument, Arizona

Susan was puzzled by the invitation to accompany the director of the archaeology department to one of his digs. She did not expect it to be a part of her duties and wanted to consult her boss before responding.

"Believe it or not, it was my idea. I know it is not in your job description, but soon I will be counting on your budgetary recommendations. I need you to be familiar with all our activities," he informed her. The very next day, Susan was sitting on an airplane next to Jack Darcy, doctor of archaeology specializing in early human settlements in North America, and a distinguished member on the museum's board of trustees. In his field, Jack was *the* authority, his many findings taught all over the world and his books on bestseller lists for years.

After the vacation she'd taken upon leaving the world of high finance, Susan's friend Jill had told her about the job opening at the museum. She had doubts regarding her qualifications for such a position, but she went to the interview anyway, more to appease her friend than to land the job. She managed to impress and felt right at ease with her new boss. It was refreshing to see him more interested in her qualifications than her stunningly good looks, as so often it was the other way around. Since her early teenage years, Susan was aware of the effect she had on men. She often wondered about the reason, as she herself was ignorant to the seductive powers of her physical attributes: her perfectly proportioned face, dark hazel eyes, full-bodied hair, luscious lips, and sensual, statuesque body. Even more captivating was the refined grace in her appearance, a physical manifestation of her inner beauty that turned heads from men and women alike wherever she went. It was the reason she never felt at ease around members of the opposite gender, especially in the workplace. She had grown a thick skin and learned how to laugh off sexist comments, put a stop to unwanted advances, and, above all, never let her guard down. Maybe this had something to do with her dating rarely and still being unattached at the age of thirty-two.

After a six-hour flight from Newark and a four-and-a-half-hour car ride from Phoenix, Susan and Jack turned off the 564 and parked at the historic ranger station of the Navajo National Monument in northern Arizona. They were meeting Russ, the on-site lead of the cave dwelling. Both were equally excited to get to the new findings. Photos emailed the previous day promised new insight into the early life of the local Navajo tribe. Jack had to be on the first available flight to see it for himself.

The ascent to the remote dig was strenuous. The sun was blazing, and temperatures soared above 110 degrees Fahrenheit. Susan was relieved to see the site was in the shade, just underneath a big rock overhanging the settlement. Once out of the sun, they were welcomed by a surprisingly cool breeze. Avoiding any marked-off areas where excavations were in progress, they made their way toward the newly discovered area that, as the finding suggested, was once used for spiritual ceremonies.

7:10 PM (EDT)
Long Island, New York

A classic Baltensweiler lamp dimly illuminated the oversize living room. Everything was quiet except the sound of the breaking ocean waves nearby. Outside, a sliver of sunlight on the distant horizon brightened the low, scattered clouds, and the first stars started to make an appearance. The low light suited Hironori just fine. He did not want to be seen through the floor-to-ceiling windows and doors. Luckily, the beach was mostly deserted except for a lone beach walker strolling with her dog along the shore.

"What have you done?" Hironori demanded in his heavy Japanese accent, standing on the other side of the long but slender glass table. People who knew Hironori rightfully feared him. He was a master of many martial art forms but most effective with his weapon of choice—the katana, his handmade sword. The crime world of the Eastern Hemisphere knew him as "the Last Samurai," a deserving nickname reflecting his exceptional skills with the blade.

Tom avoided looking at the Japanese assassin. He gazed around the living room, his eyes moving along the priceless artwork he had treasured all his life. Now it was all meaningless. He wished he could go back in time and relive the moment he had first laid eyes on the red Klee now gracing the dark-gray concrete wall behind the Japanese assassin, elegantly illuminated by a single spotlight. Tom looked down at his wife of sixty-four years lying next to the table, her head severed, and her blood still spreading along the grout lines of the tiled floor.

"I hid the notebook because it contains important information," he tried to explain.

"Why would you ever need this information? I just don't get it."

"The list proves legitimacy."

"It also proved origin, which, as you very well know, is a problem."

"I guess it does," Tom halfheartedly agreed.

"You have never alerted us to the existence of this notebook," Hironori probed him further. "Why?"

"Because there was an explosion right where I buried it. It's long gone."

"Have you ever told anyone about it?"

Tom shook his head. "No, nobody."

"What about your wife?"

"She was with me back then but did not know anything about

it. Even if she did, and I am not saying it was so, she would never tell. I know my wife. She is … was trustworthy."

"How long have you been married? Over sixty years?" Hironori asked cynically. "One should know his wife after such a long time. Yet you seem to not know her at all."

Not understanding what he was getting at, Tom finally looked up at the Japanese man.

"Did you know she contacted a journalist?" Hironori noticed the surprise in Tom's eyes.

"What?!" Tom shouted, surprised, then gave himself a moment to calm down. "Even if that was true, I am telling you again: the notebook is long gone."

"Let's hope you are right." There was long pause. Hironori looked out the glass front, taking in a deep breath of the fresh ocean air, looking at the distant lights of the few ships out in the ocean.

"You can imagine my boss is, let's just say, disappointed. You know what happens when he is disappointed?" Tom nodded, looking at the lifeless body of his wife.

"And now you are wondering if you are next." Hironori turned around to look at the Klee again. "Interesting painting. What is it of?"

Tom did not answer.

"I like the colors. So vibrant, so red, the color of our life-giving blood," Hironori continued.

Tom had never looked at it this way.

"Your granddaughter—is she the only family left?"

A terrified shiver ran down Tom's spine.

"What is her name? Susan?"

Tom's biggest fear had just been realized. Hironori obviously had done his research. And knowing his thoroughness, all loose ends would be taken care of, even ones that are not loose but might become so. It was as clear as day: Tom's granddaughter was the next target on the assassins list. He could not let anything happen to her, not to his beloved granddaughter. Terrified to his core, he took in a deep breath, then let out a big, resigned sigh.

"She knows nothing. Go ahead and kill me! But I am begging you; leave her out of this." He had to protect her—to do something, warn her somehow. While keeping a close eye on the Japanese man, who was still looking at the Klee, Tom carefully pulled out his phone, unlocked it with his thumb, and pushed the green button on the recent call screen. He then slid the phone into his sleeve and covered it with his hand.

5:15 PM (MDT)
Navajo National Monument

The local crew was in the midst of presenting the latest findings when Susan's phone started to buzz, alerting her to an incoming call. Despite being in the remotest of areas, the phone managed to connect to a network. On the screen, she saw the picture of her grandad. The call was puzzling as he knew she was out of town. Somewhat worried, Susan wondered what was going on.

"Susan!" Jack noticed her absentmindedness. "Susan …. Are you with us?" She snapped out of her thoughts and replied with a confident "Of course!" and let the call go to voice mail.

7:16 PM (EDT)
Long Island

"You have killed my wife for a long-gone notebook. I'm sorry; it does not make any sense. If I am going to die, can you least tell me why?" Tom requested.

Hironori grabbed his bloody sword and slowly walked along the glass table toward him. "You know it is not about the book. We know it is long gone. Your wife is dead because she contacted a journalist. You know the rules."

Silence filled the room once again. Looking at the lifeless body of his wife, Tom's thoughts took him back to their wedding day in 1952. Since then, they'd shared times of pure joy and happiness and a few times of despair, yet his love had never faltered. On the contrary, it grew stronger every year. Now, with their lives ending like this, he wondered if the wealth, luxury, and prestige were worth it all.

"I am happy to tell you why you are going to die," Hironori let the words sink in.

"Because of what my wife did?" Tom thought he already knew.

Hironori shook his head. "No."

"Because I did not tell you about that little book I hid seventy years ago? The one that does not even exist anymore?"

"Are you really sure it is gone?"

"It is gone," Tom nodded.

"Have you witnessed its destruction?"

"No," Tom was shaking his head. "But the explosion—"

"Then you cannot be certain," Hironori interrupted him. "This journalist, he is tenacious, very thorough, and he is on the mountain right now, looking for it. What if, despite what you are saying …?"

"So, I am going to die for the notebook," Tom replied.

Hironori shook his head. "No. Not because of the book."

"Then you will have to tell me, because I really do not know," Tom responded somberly.

Hironori chuckled and shook his head in disbelief. "Tom, Tom, Tom. You know. You just don't know we do too."

Tom turned his hand ever so slightly, just enough not to show the phone. "Hironori Matsubara, executioner of Matsua Yamaguchi, I do not. Let me know why I am going to die. It's the least you can do."

Hironori walked over to him, then bent down and put his face right in front of Tom's, staring deeply into his eyes.

"Your book on the mountain, the list inside, is only half the problem. The smaller half, I might add. You are going to die because of the *other* one. You know… the second list!"

Another shiver ran through Tom as he sat there in total disbelief.

"We did not know you had anything to do with that one, but now we do. Just imagine if this one surfaced. Even worse, if both did." Hironori shook his head. "Tom, you know better." Their eyes met in another long stare.

"Why on earth?" The assassin kept shaking his head. Tom

needed a moment to digest what he just had heard. Lowering his head, he finally replied.

"Insurance."

"Insurance? For her?"

"Insurance," Tom repeated. "Your boss—well, you know. It holds everything in check. Insurance!"

"Yamaguchi does not like to be held in check. And now, with Klaus dying ...." Hironori nodded his head toward the body on the floor. "There was a time you used to fight her kind. Why would you risk your life this way?" Hironori kept staring at the old man. Suddenly, the assassin chuckled. "How ironic!"

"Ironic?" Tom repeated.

"Yes, ironic," Hironori said in his usual low and calm voice.

"I am sorry; I cannot see any irony in this,"

"Your 'insurance' has turned into a liability. I call this ironic."

Tom stared at the glass table, confused. Hironori adjusted his stance, slightly spreading his feet apart, and slowly raised his sword. Tom looked up one more time, eying the blade above him. He knew he could not talk himself out of this one.

"Tom Sobchak, you are being executed on the order of boss Yamaguchi for endangering him and his organization, for creating the second list." With an elegant but swift motion, Hironori swung the katana. With blood splattering out of the old man's neck, Tom's head, like his wife's just minutes before, rolled across the dining room. His lifeless arm dropped to the side, causing the phone to slide out of the sleeve. Hironori calmly picked it up, stared at the picture of Susan, and then hit the red button to end the call.

5:27 PM (MDT)
Navajo National Monument

Susan's phone vibrated, alerting her to the newly arrived voice message. She was tempted to step aside and listen to it but knew better than to turn her focus away from the presentation again. Messages from her grandparents were rarely urgent but more along the line of chit-chat, pleasantries, and assurances confirming everything was okay. However, as before, Susan could not help but wonder why her grandad would call knowing she was out of town.

7:28 PM (EDT)
Long Island

"Susan," Hironori said to himself. On the outside calm as one could be, he was inwardly furious about Tom's stunt. He, a true professional, as good as they come, had been tricked. Now there was a recording. In his anger, Hironori recalled Tom's curious choice of words.

"Hironori Matsubara, executioner of Matsua Yamaguchi ...."

It was a cunning move. He took a deep breath to keep his cool, fighting his growing temper. He could not let his emotions interfere, especially now. They cloud the mind, causing mistakes, and he certainly could not afford to make another one. Before exiting the same way he had entered, he looked back at the two dead bodies.

Now let's go find this Susan.

5

Patrick woke up several times throughout the night, his aching body preventing a good night's rest. Each time he turned, the pain in his knee flared up despite the medications he had taken. Finally, with no intention to sleep in, he got out of bed and readied himself to tackle the day ahead.

First, he placed a strategic call to his soon-to-be-wife Sarah in the hope his phone was being compromised. After the initial pleasantries, he told her about his trip, leaving out any part that would make her worry unnecessarily but emphasizing that he did not find the notebook and that it seemed to be lost forever. He further informed her about his scheduled arrival back home. She, in turn, updated him on the planning of their wedding.

"It is all coming together nicely," she told him. Patrick could feel her excitement and thanked her for all the effort she put in to make their day extra special. They ended the call with a heartfelt "I love you!" In the hope the message about the lost notebook would reach his pursuers, he powered off his phone.

Patrick considered taking an earlier flight home but decided against it. Excited about the self-given challenge to find the rightful owner of the watch, he wondered where to start his search. With his prepaid phone, he dialed the number of the Alpnach city administration and asked the receptionist for help.

"Let me see what I can do," she responded kindly and put him on hold. Just about when he thought she had forgotten all about him, she returned and referred him to the Pilatus Railway Society, a volunteer organization preserving the historical artefacts of the mountain railway. The society was fittingly headquartered at the Swiss Transport Museum, which was located in the city of Lucerne.

"Talk to one of the museum curators, Robert Stadler. I know him personally. If there is anyone that can help you, he is your guy."

Patrick got dressed, packed, and thanked the host, who stood in the doorway of the kitchen, still in her stained muumuu, still with the rollers in her hair, and a cigarette between her lips, its ash perilously close to falling on to the ground.

"C'mon, have some breakfast with me. I won't bite," she invited him in her low voice, eyeing him up and down, unveiling her yellow teeth with a smile that would have scared away even a cat. Patrick, somewhat amused, politely turned the invitation down.

"What a shame," she responded, still eyeing him. "We could have had quite the morning."

Patrick said goodbye and took the next train back to the city center.

9:35 AM
Old Town, Lucerne

Patrick walked out of the railway station, passed the main post office, fought through the crowds of tourists on the world-famous Chapel Bridge, passed the chapel of St. Peter and the Swan Plaza, then walked a few minutes along the lake before boarding the bus to the Swiss Transport Museum, which he could have more conveniently taken right at the railway station. The diversion, however, had allowed him to determine whether he was being tailed.

"Isn't she a beauty?" the tall, thin man approaching him spoke enthusiastically as Patrick looked at the decommissioned steam engine in front of him. "This cogwheel locomotive was on duty on the now-lost railway line of Song-Pha in Vietnam. It is one of seven Hoa Xa engines, made in Switzerland, in service down there for decades. It was decommissioned and then bought back by a Swiss company and restored to its former glory. Believe it or not, this one is fully operational once again. A true marvel. Hi, I am Robert, curator here at the museum. I have been expecting you." *He expected me?* His friend at the local government must have announced his arrival. He introduced himself as he shook the curator's hand.

"I heard you found an antique pocket watch on the mountain. I can't wait to see it."

Patrick produced the piece and handed it over. Robert put on his white gloves and handled the object deserving of a valuable treasure.

"I would like to reunite it with its rightful owner. Do you think you can help?"

"What a marvelous piece, if I may say so. Where exactly did you find this?"

"I would like to think it found me. Sunlight was reflecting off it, shining right into my eye." Patrick deemed it better not to unveil the exact location of the find, unsure how the curator would react to his trespassing.

"Well, then, let's see what we can find out," Robert gestured for him to follow. They passed a few doors, a couple of narrow corridors, and after a surprising number of turns, finally reached the archives—a big room with rows of shelves stacked with boxes big and small.

"You'll have to excuse the mess in this area. We do this *pro bono*, so we are a little behind archiving everything given to us over the years," Robert explained, somewhat embarrassed. "If there is anything to be found, it is right here in this section." Robert went from shelf to shelf, checking each label. "Come on, it must be here somewhere … I just know it; it must be …. Wait! Yes!" He pulled out one of the boxes and carried it to a nearby desk. "These are the employment records from the time the railroad was built. Let's see if we can find your Johann Melchior." Patrick was asked to put on white gloves, which he gladly did. They started to go through the papers and, eventually, found an entry with the name.

"Well, this is all I can help you with. Now that you have an address, you should be able to find his descendants, if there are any, in the local city archives. They keep impeccable records."

Patrick thanked Robert profusely for his time.

"My pleasure," he responded. "Please let me know whatever you can find out. And should there not be any heirs, just so you know, I'd be interested in adding the watch to our Pilatus Railroad exhibit here in the museum."

"You have an exhibit about the railroad here? I thought you were just storing their stuff."

"At the beginning, yes, but the collection hosts such great objects, just begging to be showcased. Well, don't expect too much. It is just one case. I'd be happy to show it to you." Patrick would have preferred to go back to the hotel, take some additional pain meds, and sleep for the rest of the day, but how could he say no to such a friendly man? He gave Robert an approving nod and, with steps too big for his injured knee, followed him through the turns back to the halls. The small exhibit was placed in an inconspicuous corner. The curator pointed out various objects, from a model of the original cogwheel system with explanations of its workings, to a conductor uniform and tickets used during earlier times, original engineering plans, and tools used to build the tracks and tunnels, but something at the very bottom caught Patrick's eye.

12:37 AM (MST)
Sky Harbor International Airport, Phoenix, AZ

After much delay, the airplane was finally pushed back when the pilot announced takeoff in seven minutes. The passengers were asked to switch off all phones, but Susan had to listen to her grandad's message one more time, as all her efforts to return his call were unsuccessful. The voice mail she had received was puzzling, and despite desperately trying, she could not understand one word of it—the sounds were too muffled. The flight attendant made her last walk through the cabin and, with a stern look, told Susan to switch off her phone now.

10:30 AM (CEST)
Swiss Transport Museum, Lucerne

In the bottom corner of the exhibit was a somewhat small, sturdy wooden case, its surface heavily scratched and badly burned. Patrick could not help but ask about it.

"Ah, this is a bit of a mystery," Robert replied. "We have been trying to find out what it actually is. It was found near the upper tunnels somewhere back in the early fifties. We first thought it to be an army relic from the Second World War. But according to the Swiss military department, it is not one of their issued items. We equally failed to connect it to the railroad, be it construction, operation, or maintenance. The box must have been the personal property of one of the soldiers stationed up there. We still hope one day someone can identify what it actually is."

"Was anything inside?" Patrick asked.

"Well, it gets even more puzzling here. Do you see the little book on the acrylic stand next to it? One of our museum visitors recognized it as an old Nazi military notebook. We contacted the German authorities, who confirmed the book's origin, but they were equally puzzled about the box."

Patrick bent down to peer at the open book on the stand. Robert unlocked the case and handed it to him for a closer look.

"As you can see, only the first three pages have something written on them. The rest are blank. There are names, addresses, dates, and some kind of ... titles. It must be an inventory list of some kind. I once started to investigate it, but as the addresses listed are spread all over Eastern Europe, I did not get very far. Someone needs to hit those various archives. I just don't have the time or the resources ...."

Patrick had already stopped listening. Everything around him started to fade like tunnel vision, disappearing from his senses. Could this really be what he had been searching for? Patrick could not believe what he was holding in his hands. Was this the notebook? The one he was sent to retrieve—the very artifact that had nearly gotten him killed? The book that someone desperately did not want to be found? Here it was, publicly on display since who knows when. It was in a bad shape, suffering from tears, burn marks, and water damage, pointing to its exposure to the elements. But while most of the writing was faint, it was still legible.

"You might not believe me, but I may know something about this," Patrick interrupted the curator. "Both the box and the book, as a matter of fact. I came across something similar once. But I would have to do some research to see if there really is a connection. Do you think you can copy these pages for me?"

Robert's eyes started to glow with excitement. "Well, tell me; what do you think it is?"

"It's too early to tell. And don't get your hopes up just yet. But I will let you know as soon as I find out, I promise."

"Can you at least tell me what you think it is?"

Patrick shook his head. "I am sorry. It is nothing more than a hunch at this point."

Robert could not hide his disappointment. "To be honest, I prefer not to run these pages through a Xerox machine. You are welcome to take pictures though."

However, Patrick's prepaid phone didn't have a camera.

"Any chance you can give me actual copies? I prefer something tangible."

Robert offered to take the pictures with his phone and send them to the printer. Once back in the archives, he handed Patrick the copies. Patrick in turn thanked him with the promise to be in touch and soon was on his way. He could not believe what just had happened. Feeling like he had hit the jackpot, he exited the museum.

3:40 AM (MST)
Somewhere over Texas

Susan's plan to sleep on the red-eye had failed, as her granddad's message was plaguing her mind.

"What is wrong?" Jack, sensing her tension, finally asked, concerned.

"What are you talking about?"

"We don't really know each other, of course. But I can see something is bothering you." Susan never mixed family with business and was hesitant to do so this time.

"I am sorry, Jack, I am just a bit worried about my grandparents." She would have preferred not to bother him with matters of her private life, but he insisted, and she continued. "I got a puzzling message from my granddad yesterday. Actually, not a message. It was a recording of two people talking."

Jack laughed. "And this is what you are worried about? Sounds like a classic case of butt-dialing to me."

Susan knew it was a possibility. "Maybe. But it was not a conversation between my grandparents. Both voices were male."

Jack again tried to calm her. "So he had a visitor, big deal."

But she was not convinced. "Well, when I called him back last night, he did not pick up. Nor did my grandmother."

"Listen, Susan, I am sure there is a perfectly logical and innocent explanation for all this."

Susan tried to put on a brave face, mainly to end the conversation. "I am sure you are right, Jack. I will feel better once I go see them later today."

"You will see you are worrying for nothing," he reassured her.

Susan nodded, hoping her colleague was right.

11:15 AM (CEST)
City Center, Lucerne

The pain medication was losing its effect, and Patrick's knee started to hurt again. It had been a few hours since his strategically placed call, and he hoped going back to the hotel was now safe. While approaching the building, he kept a close eye on his surroundings. When he did not notice anything out of the ordinary, he entered through one of the back entrances, walked through a storage room, past the freezer, and limped through the restaurant kitchen into the reception area.

"Has anyone asked about me?"

"No. Are you expecting someone?" the receptionist asked.

Patrick shook his head. "Have you noticed anything ... unusual?"

"What do you mean by 'unusual'?"

"Never mind," Patrick smiled at her, assuming she would've known if she had. He could not wait to lie down and looked forward to a long nap. No sooner had the door of his room fallen back into its lock behind him than he felt something cold and hard pressed against the back of his head.

"Don't move, asshole!" Patrick recognized the voice immediately. It was of the man from the mountain, now standing behind him and pressing a silencer into his neck. Instinctively, Patrick dropped his bag and raised his hands.

"A sunny day, picturesque city, nice hotel room, and on top of that my boss said to make it quick. This is your lucky day!"

Patrick did not react. He had been in such a situation only once before, back in his active-duty days in Afghanistan, while infiltrating a residence in a rebel stronghold to retrieve a laptop packed with sensitive information. Someone had leaked the mission. He never dared to think what would have happened if his support team had not come to his rescue. This time, he was on his own.

"Please tell me what you want!" Patrick of course knew; the notebook, copies of which were in the bag right next to him.

"Sit down, slowly," the man ordered in his deep voice. Patrick had only a small window of opportunity. Once in the chair, he would be at a disadvantage. As fast as he could, hoping to catch his assailant off guard, Patrick turned and aimed a precise karate chop at his opponent's wrist. Anyone else would have screamed out in pain and dropped the gun immediately. But the man's reflexes were even faster. He withdrew his arm and counterattacked with a precise punch to the stomach. Patrick fell on his knees, the air knocked out of his lungs. As he gasped for air, pain from his injured leg shot up his spine. *What just happened?*

"You fooled me on the mountain. But not this time, asshole. Now do what you are told."

Patrick struggled to get up and then, as instructed, took the chair from under the table and sat down. The assassin handcuffed his wrists behind his back, taped his ankles to the legs of the chair, then sat down on the bed, pointing the gun at Patrick's head.

"Let's play a little game I love to play. You have two choices. Behind curtain number one is you telling me everything you know about the notebook. Then I will kill you, fast, with only one bullet. Behind curtain number two is you not telling me, and I will shoot you in your knee first, which already seems to be in pain, then in the other, then in your elbow, and so on. You will die, just with a lot of pain. I personally prefer curtain number two, but it really is your choice unless you want me to make that decision for you."

Do they know about the notebook? Or the copies? How could they know already? Patrick's brain was quickly flipping through the various scenarios, trying to decide how best to play this.

"Time's up, buddy."

Patrick chose to lie, confident he could come up with a good story. It was his only chance. He took a deep breath and started to dish one out, including the all-important "you need me to find what you are looking for and if I do not check in every four hours the authorities will be notified" routine. But the assassin just laughed in Patrick's face.

"Seriously?" he scolded him. "You got to do better than this. Curtain number two it is, then." The man leaned forward and with remarkable strength, pulled the chair with Patrick on it closer to him; then he pressed the barrel of the gun onto the injured knee. Patrick's face contorted in agony, only answered by the assassin's ecstatic grin. Patrick jerked his leg, but the silencer kept pressing into the injury. The killer slowly started to apply pressure to the trigger. Soon, the slug would shoot into the knee and shatter the joint into dozens of pieces.

Suddenly, the man's phone rang, interrupting the morbid ritual.

He cursed, took his finger off the trigger, signaled Patrick to be quiet, and answered the call. He seemed to be listening intently, eventually answering with "Hmmm!" and then with an "Okay." A few additional agonizing seconds passed with the silencer still pressing into Patrick's knee. Without a word, but disappointment written all over his face, the man lifted the gun, unscrewed the silencer, put both back into their holsters, stood, and walked over to the door. He turned halfway.

"I have to say; this was one of the nicer hotels I have worked in!" He then walked out of the room.

Patrick took a deep breath, and then let out a sigh of relief, not yet believing the man was really gone. He leaned forward to put his weight on one foot and, as well as he could, tilted the chair, and crashed it onto the floor. The process needed repeating, but after a few tries it shattered, and Patrick was able to free himself. He chuckled. Not only because he was still alive, but because his trick with the message about the notebook had worked. If only they knew!

6

August 28, 2017—6:30 AM (EDT)
Long Island, New York

The murder of her grandparents weighed heavily on Susan. Now that the house was an active crime scene, she could not stay there even if she wanted to, so she booked a room in a nearby hotel. But after a sleepless night, Susan felt the urge to return. She asked herself again and again who would do something like this to the old couple, but she came up empty every single time. Her grandparents were sweet and generous, known for their philanthropic activities, donating millions every year to people in need. Be it freshwater projects in Africa, conservation efforts in Asia, grants to various schools throughout the Americas, or the most important cause to them—supporting victims of wars—her grandparents used their status and significant wealth to selflessly help others all around the world.

The driveway to the property had been taped off and all entry points secured with official crime scene seals. Susan ignored the "Do Not Enter" sticker and went inside. She had to say her goodbyes and needed to do it in a place she felt closest to her deceased family. She walked into the dining room and stared at the body-shaped outlines on the floor. The terrible images of the previous day flashed back into her mind, and tears filled her eyes once more. In total silence, Susan stood and reflected on all the good times they had together. Suddenly, a faint buzzing of a cell phone ripped her out of her trance. Weren't the couple's phones evidence, and hence with the police? Curious, she followed the sound into her grandmother's study. It stopped before she could locate the source of the buzzing. She checked the desk, the drawers, the shelves, and then more obscure places like the space behind the desk, inside books, and even the trash bin. Still no luck. She looked around the room, wondering where the noise had been coming from. The only place she had not searched was the oversize painting on the wall—a portrait of her grandparents who now seemed to stare at her. She stretched as much as she could on her tiptoes and slid her hand along the top of the frame. There was nothing but dust. She gently pulled the bottom of the frame from the wall, just enough to peek behind, and a small cell phone dropped to the floor. Susan picked it up. Baffled by her find, she checked the call log. Only three calls were ever received, all from a restricted number. Puzzled, she tried to make sense of it all when the phone buzzed again. She jumped. Not sure what to do, she waited, contemplating, staring at the little green icon on the call button. This may have something to do with her grandparents' death, but if so, did she really want to know? She did not, but she took a deep breath anyway, and pressed the answer button. There was silence as each waited for the other to say something.

"Hello?" It was a man's voice, and Susan did not recognize it.

"Yes?" she responded.

"Rachel?"

"No."

"Who is this?"

Susan once again contemplated, not sure how much she should reveal. "This is Susan, her granddaughter."

"How did you get this phone?"

Susan deemed it better not to respond.

"I need to talk to Rachel. It's urgent."

"I am sorry; it's not possible."

"I'll call back later."

"Wait … don't hang up. I need to know what you are calling

about."

"It's a private matter. I need to talk to her."

"She is gone," Susan replied, holding back tears.

"When do you expect her back?"

"No, she is gone. Dead."

For a few seconds, nobody said anything.

"What happened?"

"Someone killed her." The line went dead. Susan cursed. With the phone in hand, she went back into the dining room and sat down, still astounded, desperate to know what was going on. Then, the phone buzzed again. Susan immediately answered. "Listen, I need to know what is—"

"Where are you?"

"In my grandparents' house."

"Listen to me. You are not safe. Get out of there, *now*. Do you understand? Get out! As fast as you can. Take yourself off the grid and go to a secure place, somewhere where no one knows you, where you cannot be found."

Susan was terrified.

"Wait! What is going on?"

"I need to talk to you. But we do not have time right now. Keep this phone on. Leave now, or you will be next."

Then the line went dead again.

Susan immediately grabbed her purse and ran out the door. She stepped outside and got startled by a man in the driveway. Her heartbeat calmed after she recognized the detective assigned to the case. He was not happy to see her walk out of his sealed-off crime scene.

"I do not expect you to understand, but I had to say my goodbyes," she tried to explain. "It looks like you have already processed everything, so I thought …" She could not care less about being reprimanded. "I had to do something. I hoped it would give me some closure. I'm sorry."

"Did it?" the detective asked. It was hardly noticeable, but Susan ever so slightly shook her head. The detective nodded, and then asked to keep herself available for further questioning. She agreed, got into her car, and drove off.

Across the street, standing behind a tall tree, Hironori had observed the arrival of the police. *What fools*, he thought, certain the case would never be solved. He was just too good at his job. In a few months, the files would be moved into the archives and end up as just another box amongst the thousands of unsolved homicides. But he was not out of the woods just yet. There still was the message on Susan's phone, the reason he was there. With the arrival of the detective, his window of opportunity had closed, but he knew another would present itself soon. It did not escape his sharp eyes that Susan was leaving in a panic. He wondered what had gotten her so spooked.

August 29, 2017—7:30 AM
A small town in Vermont

After leaving Long Island, Susan drove north, checking her mirrors every few seconds to see if she was being followed. She drove for several hours, past Hartford, but it was not till after Springfield when her nerves finally calmed down a bit. Eventually, not really knowing where she was, she exited I-91 and entered a small town. Usually, she would have opted for a higher-end bed-and-breakfast, but checking into a cheap motel felt like a safer option. Surely, nobody would look for her in a place like this. Emotionally drained, Susan entered the shabby motel room. It could do with a renovation, but she did not care. As long as there was a bed with clean sheets, she could live with the stained, brown shag carpet, the '70s wooden panels on the walls, the yellowing popcorn ceiling, and the dusty old lamp hanging in the middle of the room. After taking a few pills, she slept all through the day and the following night, not waking up till early the next morning.

When she finally opened her eyes and rolled out of bed, she first made herself a coffee. She watched the hot brew trickle down into the pot, already knowing it would taste awful. But again, she did not care. With the cup in hand, she sat down on the bed, trying to absorb the last forty-eight hours. All the same questions popped in her mind again. Why her grandparents were killed, who killed them, who the person on the phone was, was she herself in danger—all questions with no answers. Feeling overwhelmed, she did not know what to do, caught in the middle of something but with no clue what it was. All she could do was wait for the stranger's call, hoping he would shed some light on the situation. After staring into nothingness for a while, she was hit by another wave of grief. She lay down on the bed, took one of the pillows, and pressed it tightly against her abdomen as tears ran down her cheeks once again.

7:40 AM

"She checked into a motel room," Hironori informed his boss.

"Don't bother me with details," Yamaguchi scolded his faithful employee with his usual few words.

"It took me a while to find her, but I am just about to wrap things up. I will be back soon."

"Do you have a visual?" Yamaguchi probed his subordinate.

"Not yet. But I know she is there, and I am only two minutes out."

"Good. You know what is at stake," Yamaguchi reminded him. Hironori confirmed with a yes, then put his phone back into the inner pocket of his jacket, getting himself ready.

+ + +

Susan sobbed so hard she hardly heard the faint knock on her door. Taken off guard, she froze. *Who was at the door? Was this the killer knocking? Was she followed after all?* She stayed quiet and, overwhelmed by the unexpected event, did not dare to make even the slightest of sounds. Then there was another knock. Susan, terrified, did not respond. She hoped whoever it was would just go away.

"Susan?"

She panicked. Nobody knew she was here in this village, in this room. Nobody! She was about to get up and lock herself into the bathroom.

"Susan, I was the one calling your grandma's phone. We spoke two days ago."

She was relieved, but was he really the person he said he was? Even if so, could he be trusted?

"What did you tell me on the phone?" she asked through the door.

"I told you to leave as fast as you could. Listen, you must be really scared. I understand, but I need to talk to you. It is important. My life is in danger too."

Susan opened the door as far as the security chain would allow, enough to peek through the gap.

"I do not think we have a lot of time. May I come in?" Susan disengaged the security chain, opened the door, and gestured for him to enter.

"My name is Patrick Rooper. I am a journalist working for *The New York Times*." He locked the door behind him, then produced his press credentials. "I am also a client of your grandmother."

"She hired you? For what?"

"First things first," Patrick said urgently. "Where is your phone?"

"It is over there on the table. I switched it off as you told me to."

"Good. What about your grandma's phone, the one I told you to keep on?" Susan pointed to the side table.

"I was waiting for your call."

"Good. It has served its purpose. Let's switch it off also. More importantly, were you followed?"

"I don't know. I don't think so. Not that I can tell."

"Have you used any credit cards on your way up here?"

Susan contemplated for a second, and then shook her head.

"How did you pay for this room?"

"You told me to go off grid, so I paid with cash."

"Good. Have you gone online and logged into any of your

accounts? Email? Social media? Bank?"

She shook her head.

"Take your items; we have to go."

"Nobody knows I am here except you."

"We will find out soon enough."

Susan threw the few scattered clothes and her toiletries into her bag. Two minutes later, they exited her room, walked along the upper balcony, turned the corner, and entered another room across from hers. The heavy curtains were already drawn.

"We should be safe here, at least for a while," Patrick said, hoping to calm her, and stopping Susan just in time from switching on the lights.

7:47 AM

Susan had many questions, yet she was simply sitting on the bed, staring into eternity, when Patrick called her to the window.

"You probably want to see this," he whispered, waving her over. She asked what was going on. "Just come here," he urged her.

Through a tiny gap between the curtains, Susan saw a tall, well-built Japanese man with nicely groomed, thick, dark hair standing across the balcony in front of her room.

"This is what I was worried about," Patrick said. She noticed the man was well dressed, wearing stylish blue jeans, a dark blue shirt, a brown leather belt and matching Italian designer shoes. Evidently, he paid attention to his appearance. The man looked to his left, then to his right, his dark eyes carefully scanning the area.

"Is this the guy who killed my grandparents?" Susan whispered, her voice slightly shaking.

"Chances are …."

The Japanese man pulled a card out of his pocket and put it into the key reader, then connected its small cable to his cell phone. Two seconds later, a small green light flashed and the door unlocked. Susan was stunned by the speed of the hack. Once again, the man checked his surroundings, and then pulled his wakizashi—

the little brother of his treasured samurai sword—from under his shirt. Susan gasped as soon as her eyes met the blade. The man entered the room quietly and closed the door behind him. Susan did not dare to imagine what would be happening right now if she were still in her room.

Pale as a sheet, she sat back down on the bed.

"Looks like you have been followed," Patrick said to Susan, relieved he had made it just in time. She, in turn, struggled with what she had just witnessed.

"For the love of God, how did this guy find me? How did *you* find me?" she asked, her voice shaking.

"I have a 'guy who knows a guy who knows a guy,' to quote Saul Goodman. I asked him to ping the location of your grandmother's phone. Now you know why I asked you to leave it on. However, I don't know how he found you. Maybe the same way."

"But how would he have known about the phone?"

"No idea, but it's time to get rid of it." He powered the phone down, crashed it with his foot, then threw the debris out of the bathroom window, into the bushes behind the motel. Susan's eyes started to tear up again, this time not out of grief but utter disbelief, overwhelmed by what had just happened. Patrick tried to calm her, assuring her she was safe now, but it did not help. Susan was shaking all over.

"I do not know why my grandparents are dead. I do not know why this man is after me." Susan pointed in the direction of her room. "I don't know what is going on." She looked at Patrick with eyes pleading for answers. All he could do was to give her some time.

8:25 AM

"Let's be objective and try to narrow down why this man wants you dead."

Susan nodded, hoping the exercise would provide some answers.

"Certainly it has something to do with your grandparents, so we can safely eliminate any of the reactive reasons like the classic love, lust, loathing, and loot categories, as well as revenge or provocation."

Susan agreed.

"We can also eliminate mental illness, self-defense, honor, and accident."

Susan nodded again.

"You do not have any prior knowledge about this man, nor were you involved in any way, shape, or form in your grandparents' death, correct?"

"No, I was not."

"Are you sure?" Susan was slightly offended and gave Patrick a disapproving look.

"Then, I can say with some certainty this man is here out of necessity. The events in the last few days somehow turned you into a threat. You must have something he wants, needs, or does not want you to have—something he has to get rid of."

Susan shook her head. "I don't have or know anything. Really."

"We are going to figure it out, I promise," Patrick said in his most calming voice.

"And how are we going to do that?" Susan asked, still shaken.

"Let's look at the recent events starting from today and work our way backward. What did you do in the last twenty-four hours?"

Susan told him about the drive up to Vermont, checking into the motel, and then going straight to bed.

"And the day before. Was it you who discovered your grandparents?"

Susan nodded.

"Did you see anything unusual—observe anything out of the ordinary?"

"Two dead bodies in the living room," Susan responded with grief, not realizing the cynical nature of her response.

"Apart from that," Patrick gave her a minute to think. "Susan, I know this is hard, but if we can find out what this man is after, we may be able to get rid of him. Try to remember. Anything unusual, anything out of the ordinary, anything that struck you as weird, out of the norm. Anything."

She shook her head. "There is nothing. Really. I wish there was, but there isn't."

Patrick nodded, understanding her frustration. "Okay. Let me ask you this. When was the last time you were in touch with your grandparents?"

"About three days ago."

"What did you talk about?"

"Just the usual pleasantries," Susan said, desperate to come up with something, her increasing desperation fueled by her failure to do so. Patrick wondered if he should probe any further. He decided to give her a break.

"Coffee?" he asked as he pointed at the old brewer.

"Then I got a call from my granddad two days ago, but I was unable to answer. It was unusual because he knew I was out of town and he never called when I am away. But it turned out to be an accidental call."

"What makes you think that?" Patrick asked while switching on the coffee maker.

"There was no message, only people talking—too faint to understand. You know, the typical stuff when someone butt-dials you."

"When was that?"

"In the late afternoon. I was in Phoenix, so I guess it was evening in New York."

Patrick raised his right eyebrow.

"Do you still have the message?"

"No, I deleted it. It was just incoherent babbling," Susan responded with a dismissing gesture.

"Well, he died that very evening," Patrick was thinking out loud, opened his laptop, connected to his private VPN, opened the Tor browser, and accessed a website on the dark web. "What is your phone number?"

Susan told him, then asked what he needed it for.

"I am getting help, but that is all I can tell you."

"All you can tell me? Seriously?"

"I am contacting this guy I already told you about. You know, the one who knows a guy who knows a guy. Even I don't want to know." Patrick finished typing his message and hit the send button, then folded his laptop. "Now we wait!"

August 30, 2017—2:30 PM
A small town in Vermont

It had been a while since Hironori had checked in with his boss. He was expected to give regular updates and should have done so, but he did not, and now his boss was ringing him. As Susan was not in her room, he had no news yet for his impatient employer.

"Are you on your way back?" Hironori wished he could give him good news, but he had to deal with complications that proved more time consuming than anticipated. Susan was either extremely lucky, smart, or receiving help from someone, or a combination of the three.

"I just need another day. The main objective is accomplished."

"Not if there are problems."

"It is nothing more than a small cleanup, a precaution really. Just to make sure," Hironori tried to downplay his misfortunes. Both knew it was an excuse, but Hironori could not admit it to his boss, even less to himself.

"This is not like you," his boss reminded him. Hironori was greatly respected within the organization, even more so by his boss, but in his line of work one was only as good as his latest success, regardless of the years of faithful service. Hironori needed a favorable result, and fast.

"I'll be back soon," he again tried to assure his boss.

"Make sure you are," Yamaguchi responded, and ended the call.

2:45 PM

Susan was on the bed, sitting up against the many pillows behind her back. The TV had been on all day, mainly as a distraction, but there was nothing else to do to pass the time. She was not the type to watch TV and was accordingly bored. Patrick was sitting at the small table, answering a few work-related emails. He also called his fiancée and informed her of his delayed return. She was expectedly disappointed.

"Tell me; how long is this going to take?" Susan wondered.

Patrick shrugged. There was no way of knowing.

"If I have to see one more TV show ..." Susan expressed her dismay at just sitting around.

"Could be a minute, could be a week. For now, we have no choice but to stay out of sight and be patient," Patrick answered, not attempting to sugarcoat the situation.

August 31, 2017—11:30 AM

Hironori had lived out of his rental car for a few days now. It was his effort to stay under the radar as a Japanese man in rural America. He was desperate for a shower, a non-fast-food meal, and a bed. It did not even need to be a comfortable one. He had parked his car a bit more than 150 yards from the motel in a spot overlooking the facility. Through his high-power binoculars he regularly checked for any new developments. There were none except the usual bunch of travelers coming and going, and the cleaning crew making their way from room to room. Susan's car was still in the same spot, and no one was going in or out of her room. She had to be around somewhere; he just did not know where. Then something caught his eye. It was not an activity but the opposite—a non-event, and one that was telling. Upstairs, room 237 was suspiciously quiet. The "Do Not Disturb" sign was hanging on the door all night and day. Nobody had gone in or out since he took up his observation post, and the curtains were drawn the entire time. The room was certainly occupied. But by whom? Secret lovers? Undercover cops? Unlikely. There was only one possibility: Susan. And judging by the man he had observed receiving the food deliveries, she had company. It all made sense now.

Susan ran out of ways to keep herself entertained. She had already showered twice just to pass the time. With every faint ding from Patrick's laptop announcing the arrival of an email, Susan got excited, but it was never the email they were waiting for, and after a while she could not be bothered anymore.

"Can I ask you something?" She had contemplated for a while about asking Patrick about her grandmother's assignment. She kept changing her mind, unsure if she really wanted to know. She finally decided to do so. "My grandmother hiring you. What was that all about?"

"She sent me to find a document. Well, a notebook."

"A notebook? What notebook?"

"To be honest, I am not sure myself. It contains some kind of a list."

"A list of what?"

Patrick hesitated, and Susan noticed.

"What in the world is going on here? Tell me, and please be honest."

"I wish I could, but your guess is as good as mine. All I know is she came to my office and said something about feeling guilty and putting a wrong right. Something seemed to plague her conscience, and she wanted to have it resolved."

"Hmm … putting something right …. Did you find the list?"

Again, Patrick hesitated. "Listen, Susan, I think it's better if you do not know, for your own safety."

"I already have a hitman after me, so I don't think it can get much worse."

"Maybe. But before we go any further, I must tell you the matter seems to be sensitive. Someone out there does not want this document to surface and will stop at nothing to make sure it doesn't. Are you really willing and ready to get involved?" Susan had to admit she was neither willing nor ready. But did she have a choice?

"Can I ask another question?" Susan continued. Patrick nodded.

"Why are you here? I mean, if I were you, I would have gone home to my fiancée. After all, this has nothing to do with you."

The question took Patrick by surprise.

"I had not thought about that, but I guess there are multiple reasons. First, there was an attempt on my life too. I think I dodged the bullet, but I have to find out for sure. Second, I believe you are in danger and need help. Third, I am an investigative journalist, and there is a story here. I don't yet know what it is, but I can tell it is something newsworthy. And last, I love my fiancée very much, and the day I am going to marry her will be the happiest of my life. But ... she is in the middle of organizing the wedding, and it really isn't my thing. I guess not going back just yet is one way to keep my sanity for a little bit longer." Patrick grinned.

His laptop dinged again.

11:45 AM

Hironori approached the motel's receptionist with the friendliest of smiles. The young woman behind the desk welcomed him warmly. He put on a heavier than usual accent, acting out the struggles of a helpless foreigner.

"Good morning. I need help. I go meet the man in room 237. I forgot name. In my culture, very bad. I so embarrassed. Please, tell me name of man." He bowed several times, as customary back home. The receptionist politely declined, informing him about their company policy. Hironori again bowed.

"Understand." He took a moment, just for effect. "Please, do you have business center? I can print something?"

"Unfortunately, we do not. I am so sorry. There is a Kinkos about five miles from here."

"Can you print for me, please? One page only. I pay." The receptionist felt sorry for the polite man and, though hesitantly, agreed to print the page.

"As long as it is just one page," she smiled. Hironori handed her a USB stick.

"*Arigato.* Only one file on it. Please." She pushed the USB stick into her terminal, opened the document and hit the print button, then handed the stick back to him. He thanked her, bowing his head again and again. He was a master at talking people into doing things, and sometimes it was just too easy. With the virus uploaded, Hironori sat on one of the slightly stained sofas in the small lounge. He pulled his phone from the inside pocket of his jacket, opened an app, and within a few seconds was connected to the motel's registration system to retrieve the reservation of Room 237.

Small world, he thought. *In Switzerland just a few days ago, now here in a motel in Vermont.*

11:50 AM

Patrick clicked on the link in the email to download the file. To Susan's agony, the motel's Internet connection was painfully slow, the file loading only little by little.

"It's a big file. They must have found something," she speculated. Patrick nodded. Then the connection got even slower. Susan rolled her eyes.

"How long is this going to take?"

"Patience, woman. It is what it is," he tried to calm her. After it finally downloaded, the file, to test Susan's patience even further, had to be unzipped.

"How long is *that* going to take now?" she asked while rolling her eyes again.

The folder contained several hundred pdfs as well as the sound file of Susan's voice mail, its quality improved. Patrick put the plugs of his headphones in his ears and clicked on the file. It was riddled with noise, and some parts were still too faint to understand, but others were now audible. He listened intently, taking notes, rewinding the message several times to decipher parts that were hard to understand. After he was done, he took the headphones out of his ears.

"Who is Matsua Yamaguchi?" Susan shrugged. It was a name

she had never heard before. Patrick did a quick Internet search.

"Look at that. He is the head of a Japanese crime syndicate."

"Are you serious?" Susan asked, somewhat shocked. "What do my grandparents have to do with a Japanese crime syndicate?"

"You tell me," Patrick shrugged. "Maybe something in the documents will shed some light on it."

Over the years, Patrick had become proficient in browsing through files, quickly ferreting out the useful and finding needles in haystacks. The information about Susan's grandparents was plentiful but looked mostly trivial; he had hoped for better quality. He started to wonder if there was anything helpful at all. But a few minutes into the search, he found something.

"Look at this newspaper article from 1971. It is about a journalist who got killed while investigating underground trades of valuable goods. It mentions a possible connection between a Nazi organization, headed by a Klaus Heydrich, and the Japanese Yamaguchi Crime Syndicate. Guess how the journalist was killed?"

"With a samurai sword, decapitated in one swift, clean cut," Susan guessed. Patrick nodded.

"But what does this have to do with my grandparents?" Susan asked, certain it was unrelated.

"The article also implicates a prominent New York City businessman, although no one specific is named. However, a Klaus was mentioned in your phone message. Do you think your granddad ...." Both Susan and Patrick sat back in their chairs.

"My granddad?" Susan shook her head. "I don't think so ... my granddad? There is no way ... I mean, I don't even ...." Susan was lost for words.

"Let's do a quick recap of what we know," Patrick suggested. "Your grandmother told me she has information about the resistance during the Second World War. She commissioned an assignment to right a wrong, to get a notebook from back then. There are Japanese names on your voice message, connected to a crime syndicate. Your grandparents were killed the same way this journalist was while he was investigating a story involving Nazis, the Japanese mafia, and some New York businessman. I can tell when something is a coincidence and when it is not. These are all connected. We just don't know how."

Susan was quite taken aback by the revelation. "But there is no way the man outside my hotel room, who most likely killed my grandparents, decapitated this journalist. He must have been a kid back then."

"You are right, but don't focus on the person. Look at the methodology. We cannot ignore the similarities." Susan had to admit the facts did not leave much room for doubt. Slightly panicked, her eyes became misty again.

"I don't know about you, Patrick, but this is way above my head. I don't want to know any more. I just want to go home and live my life—my boring, routine life." Her grandparents' death, the killer, the new information—it was all too much.

The room was quiet for some time. Susan was scared and did not know what to think, while Patrick was figuring out their options.

"We have to face it. Someone wants us dead and will not stop till we are," he reiterated what they already knew.

Susan nodded. "Are you saying this is it?"

"No. I am saying we need to find a way out of this mess. But we can only do that if we know what this is all about."

"A way out?"

"Yes, a way out. We need to be proactive; uncover this mystery we are caught in."

"We have a killer on our heels, and you want to investigate? Are you crazy? It looks to me this is exactly what this journalist did back in the seventies, and we know how he ended up!" Susan was becoming hysterical.

"Listen for a minute," he urged, hoping to calm her down. "What do you think the alternatives are? We can run, but if we do, we need to do so forever. And with such powerful organizations and killers of this caliber"—Patrick pointed out the door—"something tells me forever may not be long."

Susan just looked at him in utter disbelief.

"It's our only option, Susan. They are after us. We need to find out why." Deep down, Susan knew he was right. She was just too scared to admit it.

"We cannot hide forever. Moving against them is our only shot," he summarized.

"Moving against them?" Susan's body was shaking again. Patrick did not know what else to say.

"But ...."

"There is no *but*, Susan," he interrupted her.

"But ...."

Patrick just looked at her. A few more minutes of panic passed, and then Susan got up, walked over to the coffee machine, filled the cups with yesterday's brew, and returned to the table, handing one of them to Patrick.

"In that case, the sooner we get to work, the better. What else does the article say?" It was like someone had flipped a switch inside her, waking up her inner phoenix from the ashes. She now projected a surprising determination, a confidence Patrick did not think she had in her, at least not in such a desperate situation as this.

"Nothing else, really. But we have a whole lot more documents to go through."

Susan looked at Patrick, who was thinking. "What?" she asked.

"Klaus Heydrich ... the name rings a bell." Encouraged by Susan's transformation, Patrick's adrenalin kicked in, feeling the thrill that came with a good story. It was his drug, the rush, reminding him once again why he became a journalist in the first place.

In only took a quick Internet search to refresh Patrick's memory. Klaus Heydrich used to be a high-ranking SS officer, one of Hitler's most loyal followers and a hard-core believer in the Nazi doctrine. He was also known for his heinous war crimes. Stationed in Warsaw, he was personally responsible for the execution of more than 300 Polish citizens. Unfortunately, he managed to escape after the war.

"The article mentions that Heydrich slipped through enemy lines with a fake Red Cross passport, and with help from the Vatican, he ended up in San Carlos de Bariloche."

Before Susan could ask, Patrick had already located it on an online map.

"Argentina, of course," Susan nodded.

Patrick logged in to one of the resource databases for journalists. "Look at that. He has a son, Dieter. The family still lives down there."

"Is this Klaus still alive? He must be really old by now," Susan wondered.

"We know from your voicemail, he is dying."

12:05 PM

Hironori now had a different set of problems. Dealing with a scared woman was one thing, but a Navy SEAL, top-of-the-line journalist was another. He was a real threat. A person like him could do a lot of damage, even from the solitude of a motel room. The situation had turned more pressing; time was now of the essence to make sure things would not snowball out of control. Hironori parked his car strategically in an inconspicuous space between an old VW bug and a newer Escalade. Despite the urgency, he had to wait for the right moment to make sure his assault would go down without a hitch. There could be no mistakes, no witnesses, and no more loose ends.

12:07 PM

Due to a poor connection, Patrick had a hard time hearing the person on the other end.

"Hello … Hello … Dieter?" Patrick thought he had lost him and was about to hang up.

"Who is this?" the person on the other end asked in a German accent. Susan pressed her ear against Patrick's phone, trying to listen in.

"My name is Patrick Rooper. I was commissioned to track down an heir to a substantial unclaimed inheritance. I need your help." It was a good cover story that usually worked.

"How did you get this number?" Patrick knew better than to tell.

"I know your dad was doing business with someone from New York. I need to find this person, so I can notify him about the inheritance." The line went dead.

"Great news!" Patrick smiled.

Susan was of a different opinion. "What are you talking about? He hung up!"

"He knows something, or he would not have done so." Patrick redialed the number. This time his call went straight to voice mail. He tried again. No answer. By the third time, the number was no longer in service.

"Oh, yes, he knows something."

Susan could hardly believe what she was about to say. "Looks like we are going to Argentina."

12:25 PM

Hironori was just about to doze off in his car when his boss rang again. *What now?*

"Yes?"

"People are inquiring," the boss informed him. Hironori had a feeling the unexpected call would not be pleasant.

"Inquiring?"

"Someone called our friends down south." The line went dead. Hironori cursed again. His fears had just been realized. He eyed the door of Room 237.

"You damn fools! You have no idea what you are getting yourselves into," he mumbled out loud.

3:15 PM

Patrick was in need of a set of clean, warm clothes. But other than that, he was ready for the trip down south. Susan asked a friend to pack her a suitcase and bring it to JFK along with her passport. The plane was not scheduled to take off before 2:20 p.m. the next day.

They decided to stay one more night in the safety of their room, then drive down to New York in the morning. For now, keeping out of sight seemed the safest option.

Patrick decided to take advantage of their downtime.

"Susan, tell me everything you know about your grandparents."

She did not know what was relevant. "Well, to be honest, it now looks like I know very little."

"Just tell me what you do know. It will help me develop a picture."

"My grandfather was born in Russia. As soon as he was old enough, he joined the army to fight in the Second World War, and then somehow ended up in the US working for the government. I heard rumors he provided Russian military information to US intelligence and was rewarded with citizenship and a position as a translator in the foreign office. He always had a passion for modern art, so eventually he opened his own gallery in New York City. His eye for talent, for spotting the next big star, was exceptional, and he made his fortune by buying low early, selling high later."

"So, he was from Russia?"

"Yes. But this is all I really know. He was always very tight-lipped about his past. And his work. As a matter of fact, I never knew where his travels took him. It was all quite mysterious. So mysterious that as a kid, I often fantasized about him being the US James Bond, a spy on dangerous missions flying to exotic locations. But as a grown up, I can see he was nothing more than a businessman with a packed schedule."

11:55 PM

Hironori had been waiting for hours. Once the sun had set, he changed into a traditional *shinobi shozoku*, his tactical uniform of choice. The motel's parking lot had been busier than anticipated, with people coming and going all evening long, even late into the night. It tested his patience to the limit. But now, just before midnight, things seemed finally to have calmed down. About thirty minutes before, the "No Vacancy" indication on the motel's neon sign had lit up, no new arrivals were expected, and all the guests seemed to be settled in.

With the katana on his back, neatly hidden under his uniform, he got out of the car and made his way toward the stairs. Everything was quiet except for the faint noise of passing cars on the freeway and crickets chirping the night away. Without making a sound, he climbed the stairs and walked along the upper balcony toward Room 237. He unscrewed every lightbulb on his way, just enough to disconnect them from the power. Three doors before Room 237, as he worked on one of the bulbs, the door opened and a little boy in his Toy Story pajamas looked at him.

"What are you doing?" the little night owl asked.

"What are *you* doing?" Hironori whispered.

"I can't sleep." The boy's eyes lit up at the Japanese attire. "Are you a ninja?"

"Sure, I am a ninja," Hironori replied, not sure if it was the best way to get him back into the room. "Where are your parents?"

"They are asleep."

Hironori had no time for this. "Listen, if you ever want to be a ninja, you need to go back to bed so you can grow big and strong. It is too late for you to be out here. Go inside and close the door, okay?"

The boy reluctantly obliged, and Hironori continued his way toward Patrick and Susan's room. As quietly as he could, he once again took advantage of his wired access card and unlocked the door, carefully cut the security chain with a pair of pliers, and entered, all within a few seconds and virtually no sound. The curtains inside the room were still drawn, though a sliver of colorful neon light penetrated the room through a small gap between them. He closed the door behind him softly, and then waited to make sure the two occupants were deep asleep. Once his eyes adjusted to the darkness, he walked between the two beds. The strikes were going to be swift, each with one elegant motion. Both would be dead without even knowing what hit them. Hironori positioned himself into his attacking pose and lifted the katana above Patrick's head. Susan, in her sleep, turned, the neon light falling on her face. Seeing her up close, Hironori was quite struck by her. *What a shame*, he thought, but he did not really care. With his feet apart, he tightened his grip, ready to strike.

Part II

The Unexpected Opportunity

7

January 24, 1945—2:35 PM
Administration Offices, Room 210, Russian Military
Headquarters, Warsaw, Poland

Tom was sitting at his desk on the second floor of the bitterly cold Russian military headquarters, stirred with emotion. The war was progressing well, and Poland had just been liberated from the Germans, only to be occupied by the Russians. The dapper young man, in his late teens and with an average build, was looking forward to the upcoming end of the conflict, which was now within reach. Contrary to his many comrades, however, he dreaded the thought of going back home.

The city was covered with a blanket of snow a few feet deep, and temperatures were well into the negatives. Thankfully, it was slightly warmer inside the building, heated just enough for the water pipes not to freeze. Tom could not find comfort in the fact that everybody was suffering alike, from the guards downstairs to the general on the top floor. Somehow, everybody managed. He stared at the oven in the corner of his office, wondering when his shipment from Moscow would arrive. He desperately needed to get his hands on a few things. Firewood was one of them.

Tom had been born on a small farm in a remote village in the heart of Siberia. He was only seven years old when he was given the opportunity to accompany his dad to Novosibirsk to take care of some government business. His memories of the trip would stay vague, but he remembered going to a picture show that left a lasting impression. Staring at the big screen, his innocent eyes were captivated by the featured news reels shown before the main attraction. It was entirely communist propaganda, showcasing the country's miraculous achievements since the revolution. He was too young to understand politics but was fascinated by the glimpse into life in a big city. The pictures of Moscow's tall buildings and wide boulevards impressed him greatly. It was the very moment he realized life on a farm in the middle of nowhere was not for him, that he was destined for more. One day he would go and discover the world beyond.

Tom's desire to do so never withered. His parents hoped and prayed the war would end before he was drafted, but as soon as he turned sixteen, he volunteered despite their many pleas. They weren't as surprised as they were heartbroken. His mom was tough, as one had to be to survive in southern Siberia, but her red eyes could not hide her crying all night, every night. She had been born and raised in Poland and understood Tom's desire to venture beyond the borders of the village, as she had felt similarly in her youth. But she could not bear the thought of losing him, and who would take over the farm and look after them during their sunset years if something happened to him? Tom was aware of the dangers, but for him, it was the opportunity of a lifetime, his ticket out of Siberia. Surely no such chance would ever present itself again. He loved his parents dearly, but he was not one to follow tradition, not one to sacrifice for others. He had his own life to live and a desire to find his own place in the world. Nevertheless conflicted, he had hugged his parents one more time before boarding the train to Moscow. His mother held him tightly; she did not want to let go. Waving goodbye as the train pulled out of the station, his tearful parents wondered if they would ever see him again. He, in turn, felt excitement about what lay ahead.

Already during his short military training, Tom had proven resourceful. While his peers preferred to get drunk on their beloved Vodka, he was making friends in important places. Being a fast learner, he quickly familiarized himself with the inner workings of Moscow's black market. If caught, such dealings were punishable by death, but nobody ever asked questions. Too many enjoyed the stream of heavily rationed goods and did not want to live without them, especially the higher-ranked military personnel in charge. With anything from sausages to cigarettes, he quickly established himself as the go-to guy. Tom made a small fortune. His trade also kept him away from the front, as the officers strategically kept him in administrative positions. Exposed to the relentless cold, wet weather, bad food, and uncomfortable beds, even a cube of sugar in the morning coffee made all the difference.

As the Russian military advanced further west, Tom was looking forward to the collapse of Germany's last stronghold in the upcoming months. He was excited about being a part of history, being among his comrades when Berlin would finally fall and the end of the war declared. But when Warsaw was taken, his direct superior, Colonel General Ivan Evanoff, was reassigned to stay in the capital, and on his explicit request Tom was reassigned with him. It came as no surprise. Tom knew how much the Colonel General appreciated his cigars.

+ + +

Tom was sitting at his desk typing a report when an MP entered his office with a prisoner.

"Not another one," Tom complained, keeping his jade-green eyes on the typewriter. "Go to Alexei. I am really busy here. I have not even had lunch yet."

"Alexei does not speak Polish. You do," the soldier snubbed him, and without waiting for a reply, he slapped the arrest record on the desk. Tom cursed without looking up, still typing away. "Have a seat then," he commanded the prisoner coldly.

After Tom was done with his form, he pulled the paper out of the typewriter and laid it onto the stack in the "out" box. He finally looked up. In front of him was a skinny, shivering female with nothing more than torn fabrics wrapped around her. Under her greasy and uncombed brown hair was a pretty face no older than fifteen or sixteen. Without saying a word, he got up, went down to the canteen, and traded his lunch voucher for a hot soup and a piece of bread, then returned and put the meal in front of her. She immediately began to wolf it down. Tom watched her, pleased with his good deed. He took another form, put it into the typewriter, and after stroking his hand through his grown-out, caramel-colored hair, was ready to start the formalities.

"Name?"

"Rachel Horowitz," she answered while chewing on the bread, avoiding eye contact.

"Address?

"I don't have one."

"Family?"

"None. They are all gone," she responded somberly. Tears started to fill her eyes.

Tom looked at the arrest record. "It says here you are charged with stealing. What happened?"

She did not answer.

"Listen, I need you to cooperate so I can fill out these forms. I don't like it either, but it keeps me away from the front, and I do not have time for games. Please answer or I have to write down that you did not, and the judge will not like that. Nor will the guards down in the prison block, and I don't want them to treat you badly. Understood?" Tom tried a stern look, but Rachel was still looking down, eating, avoiding eye contact.

"I don't know what I can tell you," she said in a very quiet voice. "I am cold. I am starving. For the last three months, I had no choice but to steal food. Today I was caught. Now I am here."

"You know the sentence under martial law for stealing food?"

"I'll be dead if I starve, too."

She had a point. By now, Tom had seen all the hardships of war during a brutal winter. One prisoner after another passed through his office, each with a story as heartbreaking as the next.

After a short trial, most were executed out in the courtyard. Only occasionally, an actual crook would be sitting across from him, a guy scheming poor people out of the little they had, but most were just trying to survive. He understood her predicament, and if he'd had the authority, he would have let her go. But he did not.

"What's next?" she asked.

"Tell me, what happened to you?"

"You do not want to know," she replied without showing any emotion. Tom was surprised; most prisoners were eager to share their story. Not her, apparently.

"You do not have to if you do not want to," he replied.

"Well, if you really want to know …" Rachel scraped up the last bit of soup, put the bowl on Tom's desk, and wiped her mouth with her arm. For the first time in months, her hands were not shivering.

"Soon after the Germans occupied Warsaw, my family was relocated to the Ghetto like all the other Jews. Then, one group after another was transported to the concentration camps. It was only a matter of time till it was our turn. We were desperate. The owner of the apartment we used to live in was a family friend. With the entire building now empty, he offered to hide us in the basement." Rachel started to tear up. "Now he is dead and so is my entire family. All because of me."

A loud knock on the door interrupted the conversation.

"There are three women here from the Polish resistance. They demand the release of this prisoner."

It was not Tom's call to make. "Send them up to Evanoff. He is in charge."

"They insist on seeing the prisoner."

Tom again referred them to his superior, and then gestured for Rachel to go on.

"Everything went well till about three months ago. My dad's friend had been supplying us with as much food and water as he could get his hands on. Often, all he had was his own dismal ration, which he gladly shared. When it was safe, we would leave our hideout to stretch our legs or use one of the upstairs bathrooms instead of the bucket in the corner. The change of scenery was priceless, because you eventually go crazy being cooped up in a room. This particular day, after the air raid sirens went off and everybody was running for cover, I snuck upstairs to go into our old apartment. I looked out my bedroom window through the broken glass, and I swear I could hear the sounds of happier times—kids playing, women mingling, when the courtyard was buzzing with life. Now it is all empty, deathly quiet. At first, I did not pay attention to the room across from my window. I should have. I was careless, caught up in my memories. Now my entire family is gone."

3:05 PM
Officers Wing, Room 474

"I am sorry, Colonel General, but they are not going away. May I suggest you hear them out? I am sure it will not take long."

Evanoff was sitting in a chair too small for his Herculean build. His wide shoulders rising dominant above the desk, his fingers moving irritably over his graying mustache, he reluctantly yielded to his assistant Alyona, telling her grumpily to usher in the representatives from the Polish resistance. Evanoff was a poster child for what one called a stickler: everything was done by the book, no exceptions, and he was sure his visitors were about to ask for exactly that.

"Thank you for seeing us right away, Colonel General."

The three women were gestured to sit down.

"We need you to release Rachel Horowitz right away, sir."

"I am informed she is a homeless Jewish girl who got arrested for breaking the law, is that right?" he asked, wondering what interest the Polish resistance had in her.

"That may be so, but she is one of ours, and she has been fighting the Germans heroically, so please release her right away."

Evanoff did not like the demanding tone. "On what grounds?" he inquired.

"She was just trying to survive, sir, as we all are. We, the Polish resistance, condemn any imprisonment and unnecessary suffering of our citizens, especially the ones with accolades as her. She deserves better. Please release her right away."

Evanoff shook his head. "Everyone is suffering, everyone is trying to survive. The law is the law, and laws are in place to protect the greater good, not the individual. If I let her go, we will soon have anarchy. We need to show the people of Poland we are here to protect everyone to the best of our ability." He then hit the buzzer to call back his assistant.

"Are you absolutely certain about your decision, sir? Your mission here needs our support, and the support of all the locals; otherwise, it will fail. And you know it."

"I'll see what I can do, but don't get your hopes up," Evanoff replied, mainly just to get rid of them, then asked Alyona to show the women out. The group exited under protest. Every now and then he had to deal with the resistance, and it was never more than an annoyance and a waste of time. In this case, knowing the judge, chances were the charges were going to be dismissed, but he, a man of his rank, could not allow such sympathies. Ivan leaned back into his chair, aching to light one of his cigars, but he was down to his last two and, not knowing when Tom's next shipment was coming in, decided to save them for a more suitable occasion.

3:10 PM

Administration Offices, Room 210

"They all died because of me," Rachel sobbed. "How can I ever forgive myself?"

Tom offered his handkerchief and waited for her to calm down. "Your family died because of you?"

Rachel tried hard to compose herself. Staring blankly ahead, she continued. "There were several soldiers in the room across, all in black uniforms, each one more decorated than the last. Five or six, at least. I jumped back as soon as I saw them. Thankfully, they had not yet noticed me. I was wondering what they were up to, so I peeked. I should not have. With them, against her will, was a frightened young girl; she couldn't have been more than thirteen or fourteen.

The officers had circled her and repeatedly slapped and punched her. She cried, begging them to stop. They just laughed, taking pleasure in their sadistic torture. Soon, the inevitable happened. They gradually ripped off her clothes and raped her, one after the other. I had to help. I had to do *something*. But what could I do? Against my better judgment, I did the only thing I could. I screamed as loud as I could. '*STOP IT! STOP! LEAVE HER ALONE!*' They turned their heads and looked at me. Even from all the way across I could see the evil in their eyes." Rachel wiped the tears from her eyes. "They sent two soldiers after me, probably thinking they had just gotten another prey. My intervention was of no use as they continued having their way with that poor girl. I ran back to our hideout, and sure enough we heard the heavy footsteps of soldiers above us shortly after. My two little brothers were so scared. As always, they cuddled up, holding me tightly. Thankfully, like so many times before, they did not find us. The next morning, despite knowing the risks, I had to go check on the girl. I found her. Naked. Dead, of course—she had bled to death. I was putting a blanket over her naked body when I heard the faint sound of truck engines. They quickly got louder and louder, and then an entire convoy entered the courtyard."

Rachel needed another moment to compose herself. She then straightened her back and continued. "I went over to the window and carefully peeked. My worst fears were confirmed. It was an SS search troop, its leading officer one of the men from the day before. He shouted something at his men I did not understand, so loud, so full of anger, his words echoed through the courtyard. Fearing for my life but even more for my family, I went down on my knees, closed my eyes, and started pleading with God. I prayed and prayed and prayed. The SS searched the entire building over and over, without success. Despite knowing they would not give up I grew a bit more hopeful with every passing minute. After coming up empty, they dragged our friend, the owner, into the courtyard and started interrogating him. Yet the good man would not tell them anything, at least not at first. But eventually, when he just could not take the brutal beating anymore, the inevitable happened. I knew the moment I heard the screams. The soldiers were kicking my family into the courtyard, shouting profanities, and hitting them with the butt of their guns. My two younger brothers were terrified, crying uncontrollably, while my parents tried to stay calm for them. But when my mother saw their friend covered in blood, his face barely recognizable, she lost it too."

Rachel shifted uncomfortably in her chair. "They were all lined up. The officer, with his intimidating stature in the all-black uniform, looked at them in such disgust as if they were cockroaches. 'Where is the girl?' he asked in a calm voice. 'What girl?' my dad dared to ask, only to be slapped in the face. Hard. The officer shook his head, pulled his gun from the holster and shot our landlord in the forehead. My brothers were so shocked, they immediately turned silent, too scared to even cry anymore. The officer then put his gun on the forehead of my grandfather. 'Where is she?' I could not fully understand what he said, but it was something along the lines of 'Please shoot and release me from this evil world.' Again, the officer asked about my whereabouts. When nobody answered, he again pulled the trigger. My grandfather fell forward onto the officer, who angrily kicked his body away and, with a handkerchief, cleaned the blood off his boots. Next in line was my dad. When I saw the barrel held against his forehead, I just could not bear to see them suffer any longer. The SS wanted me, and I know it was foolish, but I thought maybe, just maybe, giving myself up would save them all. I stepped onto the windowsill, ready to jump, hoping the impact would kill me and end the senseless killings. Nobody saw me but my mother. She looked at me, and ever so slightly shook her head, then smiled. And with that, she saved my life. The officer pulled the trigger, but to his dismay, the gun jammed. His demeanor stayed calm, but I could tell he was fuming. For some reason, probably embarrassed from the misfiring or fed up from standing out in the cold, he ordered my family to be loaded onto the trucks, to be brought back to the Gestapo headquarters. I knew right then I would never see them again."

Rachel was now inconsolable. Even Tom had a hard time controlling his emotions. She finally lifted her eyes—her unusual piercing, sapphire-blue eyes that seemed to penetrate all the way into his very soul.

"What is going to happen to me now?" she asked, looking exhausted, hopeless. Tom first needed to clear his throat.

"You will be presented to a judge. It is up to him." He again felt for her. She was a victim, not a perpetrator. However, there was nothing he could do but offer a few words of kindness.

"Listen, I know times are hard. I will try to put in a good word for you. But it really is up to the judge, not me." Tom finalized the paperwork. To his dismay, he had to change the typewriter's ribbon before doing so, wondering what else could go wrong to make this day even worse. He called in the guard to have Rachel transferred to the prison block, and then tossed the old ribbon into the trash bin. Every now and then he was confronted with a situation so tragic he second-guessed his decision to go to war. This was one of them.

8

January 25, 1945—6:45 AM
Administration Offices, Room 210

Tom was in his office at 6:30 am sharp. For once, he was on time despite the heavy snowfall. He was happy to see his shipment had finally arrived. He opened one box after another, locked up the valuable items in the cabinet behind his desk; then he chopped up the empty crates, put some of the pieces into the oven, and started the fire. He was just about to get warm for the first time in nearly a month when the phone rang.

"Hi, Tom, this is Alyona. Colonel General Evanoff wants to see you right away."

"Now?" Tom asked, annoyed.

"Right now!"

He sprinted up the two flights of stairs through the beautiful, spacious hall, dashed down the corridor of the leadership wing, and passed Alyona, who gestured for him to go right in.

"Have my cigars come in yet?" Evanoff grumpily asked. "I am down to my last two!"

+ + +

Colonel General Ivan Evanoff was not just an ordinary member of the armed forces. He was a true institution. His heroism during World War I was legendary, deservingly represented by the countless badges and medals on his uniform. If there ever was a man who had proven his bravery and commitment to the motherland, it would be him. One of his oft-told stories took place in 1914 at the Battle of Tannenberg. At the age of only sixteen, with three bullets in his lungs and shrapnel from a grenade in the side of his head, he had held off more than 300 Germans with nothing more than a machine gun while his colleagues were evacuated behind him. After everyone made it to safety, he himself ran back to his unit, through an open field, as fast as his injured lung would allow, while the Germans released a barrage of bullets at him. Miraculously, he was hit only one more time, the shot going straight through his right arm. When he finally collapsed, two Russian soldiers managed to drag him off the field, onto a truck, and straight to the field hospital. The medical staff did not think he had a chance and just left him to die on the gurney. The many pleas from his unit did not sway the medics. Only when the lieutenant pulled his gun and held it to the temple of one of the doctors, in an act of pure desperation, were Evanoff's wounds attended to.

+ + +

"Comrade Evanoff, your cigars *did* come in this morning. Do you have the money?"

"It's still Colonel General Evanoff to you, and I will bring you the goddamn money first thing tomorrow, I promise. Just go get me those damn cigars." But Tom managed his business by strict rules, no exceptions, and with good reason. He had been burnt too many times.

"Then, I will have the cigars for you tomorrow," he bluntly replied. His boss was not amused, but grudgingly turned his focus to the issue at hand.

"Okay, Timofei, I have an assignment for you."

"It's still Private Sobchak, Sir," Tom mouthed off, immediately regretting his cockiness, and rightfully so, as Evanoff got off his seat and unleashed a wave of curse words onto him. "Tom, then, Sir," he allowed. "Nobody calls me Timofei, as mentioned many times before."

But Colonel General Evanoff again ignored the request as he preferred to call people by their legal names in matters of importance. "What I am going to tell you is top secret," the Colonel General cautioned.

Tom nodded.

"While retreating, the Germans got a train stuck behind our lines. The Nazi Abwehr sent a Brandenburgers special ops team to parachute into our territory with orders to get it back at all cost. But our troops at the front intercepted the train. Intelligence is suspecting the cargo to be of great importance. Something sensitive, maybe even top secret, and High Command wants to be briefed on it as soon as possible."

Tom had a feeling what was coming next and did not like it one bit.

"The train is at our cargo hub outside Lodz. I need you to go there right away and find out what this is all about. You will report to me directly, and only to me. Is that understood?"

Tom was right. Just when his office was finally warming up, he had to trade it for a lengthy ride through the snow in an uncomfortable car with no heater. He had to get out of it.

"But, sir, such situations are not handled by us," Tom protested.

Evanoff ignored his objection. "As I said, this is top secret, do you understand? Grab a driver; time is of the essence. Alyona has the necessary paperwork. Again, you report only to me directly. No one else. Call me as soon you have any information on the matter."

Tom had to try harder. "Sir, do you really want me to drive to Lodz in this weather? Can't you send someone else? What about Boris? He does nothing but sit around all day."

The Colonel General was just about fed up with his subordinate. How dare he? "Boris? Why not? So here is the deal. You either go to Lodz, or Boris will, while you are going straight to a Siberian labor camp, despite cigars and all, do you understand?"

Tom knew he had pushed as far as he could. "Okay, sir, but this

will take a day or two. I guess your cigars will have to wait, then."
He dared to smirk at his superior. Evanoff decided to bite his tongue
on this one.

"As I said, Alyona has your paperwork."

9

4:55 PM
Train Cargo Hub, Lodz

"Papers!" the guard requested in his authoritative tone. Without saying anything, Tom handed over his ID and necessary documents. As an indispensable hub for frontline supplies, the train station was well guarded, its security protocols extra tight.

"You are to meet with Captain Michael Stanislaus. Proceed to Office 23 in Zone 9. Follow the signs."

Tom replied with a friendly "Thank you, comrade!" and then told his driver to step on it. Eventually, he arrived at his destination.

"Captain Stanislaus, I am Private Timofei Sobchak. I was sent from Warsaw headquarters to investigate the German train." Tom saluted the man in front of him.

"Finally. What took you so long?" The rather short, overweight Captain with a surprisingly intimidating voice replied grumpily, obviously not happy with what was going on. Before Tom could reply, he continued his rant. "Not sure why they sent someone all this way from headquarters, especially in this weather. There is nothing we cannot do ourselves down here." Tom could not have agreed more with the captain's bruised ego but stayed quiet. "This train is holding up my operation. I need it off my tracks, the sooner the better."

"Understood, sir. I will start right away," Tom nodded, already looking forward to getting back to his warm office.

"The Track 5 siding, over there." He pointed at the train. "There'd better be something in there or I am going to be really pissed."

"I could not agree more. I sure hope I did not drive down here for nothing," Tom replied. His effort to spur sympathy backfired.

"I am worried about supplying our troops with essential goods, and you worry about a drive in a car? Do you have even the slightest idea what our comrades at the front are going through?"

"You are right. I am sorry, sir," Tom apologized.

The captain just shook his head. "Just so you know, despite orders not to touch the train, we kept the burner going so we can move the damn thing as soon as possible."

"Smart!" Tom saluted and, with his driver, walked over to Track 5. So far, he could not have cared less about what was on that train. But now, standing in front of the wagons, he was overcome with a sense of excitement.

Officer's Wing, Room 474

Alyona informed Evanoff that the women from the resistance were back, demanding a meeting. This time, they brought reinforcements—a group of more than ten were outside his office. But he was done for the day and looking forward to an evening of poker and vodka with his fellow officers, so he told his assistant to get rid of them. Alyona politely told the group their efforts were noted but the Colonel General had prior engagements. They, in turn, informed Alyona that they would be back in the morning and would not leave till a meeting could be arranged.

Their insistence told Evanoff one thing. Rachel was a person of importance, most likely with information useful to him. He was eager to learn this information but knew, strategically, it was better to wait. The chances of her talking were better once convicted. The prospect of a lesser punishment was always a great motivator, every single time without exception. Ivan pushed the button on his intercom.

"Alyona, connect me with the judge's chamber, and get me the full story on prisoner Rachel Horowitz, will you?" Alyona complied right away.

"Comrade Judge Isakov? Colonel General Evanoff here. I need to ask you for a favor."

5:15 PM
Train Cargo Hub

The first three wagons were marked for a factory near Frankfurt, its cargo nothing but empty ammunition crates ready to be restocked. The fourth wagon contained boxes filled with bandages, gauze, sutures, syringes, morphine, surgical instruments, cots—a fully operational field hospital. Tom wondered if all this was about the morphine—desperately needed and always in short supply. The next two wagons were marked for the Anhalter Railway Station in Berlin with instructions to hold the cargo at the station. The doors were latched with sturdy locks.

Maybe it's not about the morphine, Tom thought.

He had to find a way to open the wagons. He contemplated on whether to pry or shoot the locks. But chances were, considering what was suspected about the cargo, they would need to be relocked after he was done. Hoping the keys to be somewhere on the train, he walked toward the front and climbed into the cabin of the locomotive. The comrade responsible for keeping the burner heated greeted him. Having never been inside the cockpit of a steam engine, he was stunned by the many handles and gauges, wondering what they were all for. He looked around and was quickly drawn to a locked file compartment. Tom guessed it was for logbooks, but neither he nor the private next to him knew for sure. He instructed his driver to fetch a crowbar. While waiting, Tom stretched out his hands toward the burner to warm them. It reminded him of the oven in his office, and he once again cursed Evanoff for sending him on this godforsaken trip.

"Here you go. Got your crowbar," his driver triumphantly announced. Tom quickly managed to break the lock. Inside was a small black notebook and two keys. Bingo! He peeked inside the notebook in hopes of finding clues about the wagon's contents. There was a ledger of some sort, all in German. Tom could not make sense of it. Nevertheless, he put it inside one of his pockets. With keys in hand, he exited the cockpit and walked back toward the locked wagons, his driver close on his tail.

To Tom's relief, the key fit and the lock sprung open. With the help of his traveling companion, he managed to open the frozen cargo door. Behind was a big, heavy crate blocking the entire entrance with no chance for access. Tom noticed the "Top Secret" mark branded on its side. The two tried to move the crate, but it was much too heavy even to budge. They closed up the wagon and made their way to the other one. It was equally packed, but all the way on top was a gap just big enough for Tom to squeeze through. He looked around the dark interior, barely able to see anything. The remaining sunlight shone through a small window in the corner, its light just enough to make out the sheer volume of crates. The entire wagon was packed to the fullest. Tom needed a light and once again sent his driver to fetch one.

"Sorry, this is all they had."

His companion climbed on top of the wagon and handed him an old-fashioned petroleum lamp. The crates were of various sizes, and from what he could see, every one of them was marked "Top Secret." Tom ripped off one of the labels and held it under the light. Amongst the standard information, his eyes caught the section for special instructions: "Property of Josef Goebbels." He asked for the crowbar, which was again handed to him, and for several minutes attempted to open one of the crates. The cover would not give, as leveraging the right force in the tight space was virtually impossible.

"Are you okay?" his driver asked after Tom's barrage of curse words.

"Yes. This damn box just won't open." Additional swear words followed. After a few more attempts and a lot of elbow grease, the wood finally cracked and Tom managed to remove the top, careful not to get scratched by one of the many nails sticking out. Whatever was inside, it was packed with great care, as could be expected from the Germans. He removed the layer of wool, lifted the wrapped object, barely managed to get it out of the crate in the confined space, and ripped its wrapping. He was stunned by what he saw. It all made sense now—all the fuss about the train, all the secrecy. He knew he was holding something so important, so essential to the German war effort, that nobody could know about this. And he meant absolutely nobody.

Tom put the object back into its crate, exited the wagon, put the lock in its place, and walked back to the captain's barrack.

"So, what is in this goddamn train, Comrade?"

"I actually don't know," he confidently lied. "The crates are impossible to open. I need to call my superior for further instructions."

"Whatever it takes to get that train out of here," the captain barked as he pointed to the phone on his desk. Tom asked the operator to connect him with the headquarters in Warsaw. It took a while before he was prompted to go ahead.

"Russian Headquarters Warsaw," a friendly voice answered the call.

"Tanya, it's me, Tom. How are those nylon stockings working out for you? Great … Listen, I need to speak to Colonel Yuri right away." Tanya was taken off guard.

"Yuri? There is no Yuri here," she responded, puzzled.

"Great, thank you very much," Tom replied. She had no idea what was going on.

"Tom, are you okay? Do you need help?"

"Colonel Yuri, listen, I inspected the train. There were two wagons filled with crates. But they are heavy duty. Impossible for me to open them here."

Tanya was now worried. "Tom, please talk to me. Are you in trouble?"

He did not respond to her question.

"Okay … okay … sure … right away, sir!" He continued his charade, then hung up.

Tom could not believe the hand he got dealt, asking himself more than once if he was dreaming. But after the initial excitement, he was suddenly overcome with doubts. To remedy his increasing nervousness, he took a deep breath and decided to listen to his inner voice. The next twenty-four hours would be decisive, and if he did not end up in front of an execution squad, well, then …. He smiled. But first things first.

Other than sitting in one and enjoying the ride, he had never had to deal with anything related to trains. He did not know much about coal, water, steam, and pressure, even less about the many handles, valves, and gauges he was confused by earlier.

"You know, we can help you open the crates," Captain Stanislaus offered.

"Thank you; that will not be necessary," Tom politely declined. "I have strict orders to get them back to Warsaw right away. But I need an engineer, one that can operate this German engine. The sooner the better."

"Now you are talking, son! For heaven's sake, it is about time!" The captain once again expressed his frustration. Tom took his driver to the side and, in a low voice, asked him to return to Warsaw.

"Do you know the harbor by the Zeranski Canal? There is a coal depository behind one of the piers. You cannot miss it. It has a train depot right next to it. Meet me there as soon as you can. If I am not there already, wait for us. Do not leave without me, and do not tell anyone. This is still top secret. No one! Understood?"

"Top secret!" The driver nodded while Tom handed him the necessary travel passes. Half an hour later, with the driver already on his way and the tender pressurized and ready for departure, the signal ahead turned green.

"Let's go!" Tom shouted enthusiastically through the loud puffing of the engine. The heavy wheels started to move under clouds of steam. Captain Stanislaus watched the train move out of his station, relieved, yet wondering what all the fuss was about.

10

Railroad Tracks between Lodz and Warsaw

Tom was huddled up in the corner of the cabin, ice-cold wind howling around him.

"Coffee, sir?" the engineer asked, holding a steaming cup in front of Tom. "It will warm you up." Tom had never been so happy to see a hot beverage. He took the cup, holding it close to his face while the engineer put the kettle back onto the engine's burner.

"I know. It is one big coffee maker, isn't it? And it does other things too, like pulling a train through the countryside." The engineer tried to bring a bit of amusement into the otherwise miserable ride. Tom smiled out of courtesy, his mind too distracted for jokes.

"Do you know the coal depot next to the Zeranski Canal harbor?" Tom asked.

"Sure, the one next to the pier."

"Do you know how to get there?" To Tom's relief, the engineer nodded.

They passed two checkpoints which just waved them through. So far, everything was going as smoothly as he had hoped for. Soon, they crossed the city borders of Warsaw, and the engineer slowed the train.

"Time to get off this track and take the one going north," the driver informed Tom as he halted the train with great precision in front of a switch. Tom jumped off, grabbed the handle to switch the track, and pushed as hard as he could. It was frozen solid. He kept kicking, yanking, pulling, and pushing. It would not budge. He cursed and stopped to catch his breath. Looking around, standing in the illuminated snowflakes blowing around him, some getting lost in the vapor of his own breath, it hit him. This was the point of no return. Was he really going to do this? Until now, he was repeatedly plagued with doubt. With the odds so highly stacked against him, his mind had raced backward and forward between thoughts of success and fears of failure. Now in the train's headlight, in the serene surroundings of the deep, untouched snow, the world beyond faded into darkness, doubt finally gave way to the seductive powers of his lifelong dream. He vowed to see this through—all the way. "No matter what!" He looked up into the night sky, his eyes following the peacefully falling snow, enjoying the brief moment of solitude. "No matter what! No matter what!"

With newfound motivation, Tom grabbed the lever once again. This time, he put his entire body against it and pushed, pushed, and pushed. Little by little, he could hear the ice crack till suddenly the lever finally gave way and, as Tom lost his footing and was knocked to the ground, the rails moved into position. He got up, patted the snow off his coat, and laughed at himself. *Maybe this was a good sign*, he tried to convince himself. The engineer maneuvered the train past him at a snail's pace. Tom triumphantly watched wagon after wagon go by. In the red light of the train's rear lantern, Tom switched the handle back into its original position, this time with ease. *One step closer*, he told himself. *One step closer*. But he knew things would get a bit more complicated from here on.

11

10:55 PM
Railroad Tracks, Warsaw

The train passed one neighborhood after another. From the cabin of the locomotive, the city in all its luster looked peaceful, the scars from the ongoing war covered in snow. Tom could hardly believe how deceptively serene it all looked. They were about to cross the Vistula Bridge, Tom was informed by the engineer. From there, it was only a few more minutes to the depot. Pleased with their progress and his worries pushed out of his mind, Tom allowed himself to enjoy the ride. He was imagining a time after the war, finally free—free from the shackles of his heritage, and free from life in the Red Army. His heart once again ached for places far away— America his desired destination, the land of opportunity, New York the place to be. He already saw himself in the busy crowd of lower Manhattan, strolling in the lights of the marquees around Times Square, marveling at the engineering of the Brooklyn Bridge, and enjoying a spectacular sunset from the top of the Empire State Building. In many ways, it was as far from the small farm in southern Siberia as he could imagine, and it suited him just right. Tom was too caught up in his thoughts to notice the red lantern ahead of them. It was another checkpoint, and this time they were asked to stop. Not knowing how best to play this, he was rather violently ripped out of his daydream. He had to get the train through and did not dare to think of the alternative.

After the train came to a halt, Tom climbed off the tender, saluted the two soldiers, and handed over his papers. Both checkpoint guards were young, most likely just recently drafted, barely trained, and prematurely rushed to war. As inexperienced as they come, they were still wearing their uniform with pride, committed to follow protocol to the teeth, intimidated by their superiors. Tom hoped his first impression was wrong.

"Cold, huh, comrades! Are you guys staying warm?" Tom asked, doing his best to charm the guards. He was being ignored. "I hope your shift is over soon. I, for one, cannot wait to be back at the headquarters. It sure is warmer indoors." The two still did not respond. "Do you guys have an oven here? If you need firewood, I can have some delivered." Tom continued his charm offense. He nearly managed to engage the shorter one in conversation, but when his taller colleague gave him a disapproving look, he did not dare to reply anymore. "Are you new here?" Tom shouted over the engine's noise in an attempt to entice him further. Again, the soldier did not say anything, just smiled back awkwardly.

The taller guard stretched out his arm to return the documents. "We cannot let you pass. You are off route, heading in the wrong direction. You need to go back!" he shouted, pointing toward where they had come from. Tom took the papers and nodded.

"I know what it says, but we got diverted as the main station is at capacity. I should not even tell you this, but they are preparing for a major offensive against the Germans and are running trains for the front, nonstop. We were ordered to get out of the way by none other than Colonel General Ivan Evanoff personally, instructed to go to the Warszawa Praga Depot and wait for further instructions." Tom confidently looked into the soldier's eyes.

"I have to call this in. Headquarters will have to confirm this."

Tom was in trouble. "Colonel General Evanoff is off duty. He will not be in the office till tomorrow."

The soldier was not swayed by Tom's excuses. On the contrary, his insistence raised suspicion. "I cannot let you pass without authorization. Someone at headquarters will have to confirm your new route or you will have to turn back. Understood?"

Tom was impatiently shaking his head, just for theatrics. "The Colonel General will not be happy, and he will ask me who interfered with his orders. Do you really want to be personally responsible for the delay of much-needed supplies for the front? To go against direct orders from him? There is a court-martial waiting for you if you do that."

The smaller one got nervous, but to Tom's dismay the taller kept his cool, not intimidated by the threat. "Orders are orders!" he shouted back and angrily ripped the paperwork from Tom's hands. Before he disappeared into the barrack, he gestured for his colleague to keep an eye on the travelers. Tom's adventure had just started, and he was in trouble already, caused by nothing but the stubbornness of these two greenhorns. This time, if caught, the charges would be more severe than trading sausages.

The young soldier and Tom stood in the deep new layer of snow, intermittently clouded in the locomotive's steam, its noise still somewhat deafening. Tom was desperate to come up with another way to stop the call when the soldier next to him lit a cigarette.

"My comrade, may I have one too?" Tom made a smoking gesture. When the soldier turned sideways to reach into his satchel, Tom served an uppercut right onto the unsuspecting youngster's chin. He was thrown onto his back. Tom leaped on top and pressed his elbow into his trachea, hoping he would soon pass out. But the guard kicked and clawed as hard as he could. Then, with unexpected force, he swung his body around. Tom was thrown off. His grip on the choke loosened, and the rookie managed to free himself and, even worse, reverse the positions. Now with the young man's hands firmly on Tom's throat, Tom kicked, turned his hips to the left then to the right, but his young opponent was unexpectedly strong. He tried everything to free himself without success. His face was turning blue, and the veins on his forehead started to pop out as he fought for air. The young soldier's glaring eyes were staring at him with intense rage, his face deep red, grimacing from a mix of muscular contraction and anger. Despite strenuous efforts, Tom could not reach the knife that was wrapped around his ankle. His thinking slowed, his vision blurred, and his strength gradually drained out of him. He knew he was about to pass out, yet he kept moving and kicking, not giving up. He suddenly remembered the standard-issue knife on a soldier's belt. With his last bit of strength, Tom reached for his opponent's side, managed to unbutton the small leather strap, slide the blade out of its sheath, and with an equally quick motion pushed it sideways into the youngster's throat. The soldier had not seen it coming. The rage in his face gave way first to surprise, then to eyes glazed over with fear. The hands on Tom's throat lost their grip, and without as much as a scream, he dropped sideways into the snow. With one hand on his trachea, Tom tried to catch his breath. After a few seconds of recovery, he looked at the dying teenager next to him, coughing up blood and gargling for air.

"Oh no ... oh no ... OH NO!" Tom muttered over and over again. "What did you just do? WHAT DID YOU JUST DO?" Tom screamed, but his cry of disbelief was swallowed up by the engine's noise. Distressed, he looked around for the other soldier. He was still inside the barrack, and the train engineer was out of sight too, busy feeding the burner with coal. Tom looked back at the young soldier, the snow underneath his head turning red from bleeding out.

"What the hell did you just do, Tom?" he said quietly, resigned. With a heavy heart, and scared to his core, he quickly covered the soldier's body with fresh snow. The scene of the brutal tragedy turned back into a tranquil scene, as if nothing had happened. "Oh no ..." Tom said once more, dreading what he had to do next.

As quietly as he could, he opened the door of the barrack, hoping it was well oiled. It was not. The soldier was already on the phone, too distracted to pay attention to its squeak or to the creaking of the wooden floorboards. Tom, like a cat stalking its prey, moved furtively toward the man. He could not understand what was being said, but intense yelling was audible from the phone's receiver. The tall soldier nodded.

"Yes, understood. I will make sure ... *Da!* Yes, this is an order ... *Da* ... *Da*; I will go with them ... Right away, sir!" He shook his head. "Someone is in big trouble," the soldier mumbled to himself while putting the receiver down. The last thing he felt was a hard knock on his head before everything went black. He collapsed onto the makeshift table, which caved under him. Maps, papers, phone—everything fell on the floor. Shaking badly, his breath heavy and heart pounding up to his throat, Tom made sure the man was out. He tied his hands and feet, put a piece of cloth in his mouth, and secured the gag with a rope. Tom knew better than to leave behind a witness, but with his conscience already in such turmoil, he just could not end another man's life.

Tom stuck his hands into the snow and wiped the blood off, then climbed back up the ladder into the tender's cabin.

"We are cleared!" Tom declared and urged the engineer to get moving. With the tender's usual steam release, the big wheels started to move again, slowly pushing the train forward over the Vistula Bridge. The engineer sensed the change in Tom's mood.

"Are you okay?" he asked. Tom quietly nodded. With a dead and an unconscious soldier left behind, the door of turning back was now not only shut but locked, nailed, and barricaded for good.

11:35 PM

The engineer secured the heavy wooden doors of the depot. The train was now safely hidden away. It had conquered its last stretch at a snail's pace over the badly damaged rails. The various bombing raids had their effect on the harbor, leaving the tracks in bad shape, barely good enough to keep the train from derailing. The depot itself had suffered an equal amount of damage. Parts of its roof had collapsed and most of the windows were shattered, allowing cold wind and plenty of snow to blow through the structure.

"What now?" the engineer asked.

"Now we go back to headquarters and celebrate." Tom had to find a way to get rid of him, too.

12

January 26, 1945—3:55 AM
Kanal Zeranski, Warsaw

The rendezvous point with the driver was just around the corner from the train depot, an area dimly illuminated by a single small lamp. Both Tom and the engineer stood in silence in the falling snow, hoping the driver would show up soon, not sure how much longer they could tolerate the cold winds. After a few more minutes, the light of the head beams and the sound of an engine announced the approaching car.

"What took you so long?" the engineer complained.

"I am sorry, but do you see the condition of the roads? I came as fast as I could," the driver responded, not happy with his task either.

"Back to headquarters, and make it as quick as you can." That was all Tom was interested in.

5:06 AM
Administration Offices, Room 210

The three made the best progress that the treacherous conditions allowed and reached the Russian headquarters within the expected time frame. They had less than one hour before people would start to flock into the building. The driver parked the car, and through the big front doors, the three entered the massive stone building. Tom greeted the guards, who knew him well. After all, he had sold them the warm gloves on their hands. The trio walked up the stairs and entered Tom's office. To his dismay, most of the wood from the chopped-up crates was gone. It came as no surprise. Any item not locked up was not safe. He lit the oven with pieces from the small stack that was left, and his two guests immediately huddled around to warm up. Tom had no time to do so. He made his way up the stairs to the Colonel General's office and down the deserted hallway. With the help of a paperclip he picked the lock, entered, and closed the heavy wooden door behind him.

Tom nicked the documents he needed from the drawers behind Alyona's desk, then dashed back to his office where he typed them up, added the necessary stamps, and forged Evanoff's signature as well as he could. For what it was worth, anyone could have signed the forms. There was no way to verify them out in the field; it only had to look official. Tom asked his driver and the engineer over to his desk. They reluctantly left the warm oven.

"Listen carefully. I need you two to go to Moscow right away and deliver this envelope to General Dascov at the People's Commissariat for State Security. I cannot stress this enough—this is for his eyes only. Understood?"

"Does this have anything to do with the train?" the driver asked, curious about the sealed envelope.

"This is top secret. The less you know the better. But since you have proven trustworthy, yes, this has to do with the train. But this is all I can tell you and all you two know is that this envelope needs to get to State Security right away. Is that clear?" Both answered with a resounding "*DA!*" Tom handed them the needed checkpoint passes, fuel vouchers, and the sealed envelope.

"Off you go, you two. Safe travels!"

"Wow, Moscow. I have never been," the driver told the engineer on their way out, obviously excited.

"I've never been on a secret assignment," the engineer responded, equally thrilled. Tom was pleased. Maybe he would be able to pull this off after all.

Next, Tom made his way over to the prison block. The soldier on guard was in his chair, snoring the morning away. *Sleeping on duty. No wonder it took the Russians years to turn this war around.* He was annoyed with the incompetence but knew this could work to his advantage.

"WAKE UP!" Tom screamed loudly. The soldier shot up from his chair like a launching rocket, nervously stuttering an apology.

"Sleeping on duty!" Tom shook his head. "Now get me to prisoner 240168 right away." Without asking questions, the intimidated guard took his keys and showed Tom the way.

"What do you want from me?" Rachel asked Tom, sitting on her cot, seemingly in a daze. Unable to sleep, she was exhausted, her eyes puffed up from prolonged weeping.

Tom looked out the little opening in the door to make sure no one was eavesdropping, then walked over to her. "Listen, I need something, and I need it quick." Tom immediately regretted his choice of words, knowing better than to give away leverage by expressing urgency. "You have not had your trial yet, but I know how these things work. You will be convicted and then executed. Maybe even as early as tomorrow." He strategically paused, looking down at her. "We can help each other."

"There is nothing I can give you. I have nothing."

"Well, that's not entirely true. There is something you can help me with."

"Don't ask me anything about the resistance. I'd rather die than tell you Russians," she declared loyally.

"That's not it. Let's just say, for the lack of a better word, I am here on a private matter."

"Private? Yeah, you wish. There is no way I am going to do that with you. You can forget about that." Rachel was outraged.

Tom was shaking his head, somewhat amused. "No, no, no. That's not it. Just shut up and listen for a minute, will you?"

"Why should I? You Russians put me in prison for stealing bread while you neglect to feed the civilians. And now you want my help? Get lost! I do not want to be saved."

"Come on, Rachel. Life in prison is still better than being

executed. And with the war over soon, who knows what will happen then?" Tom was confident about his offer. A little bit of information in return for her life—surely, she could not refuse?

"I am not afraid of dying. I've come to peace with it and am looking forward to reuniting with my family now," she responded solemnly.

"I'd be willing to put in a good word with the judge," Tom pressed further.

"You already promised me that."

"Not this kind of a good word. He owes me. As a matter of fact, he owes me big."

"Is that so? Why does he owe you?"

"That's not important," Tom snapped at her impatiently.

"As my life seems to depend on it, I beg to differ." Rachel looked up at him. Tom nervously checked his watch. She noted it.

"He is a diabetic. And without my black-market insulin, he'd probably be dead by now. So, as you can see, he owes me big." Rachel decided to let Tom stand in suspense, at least for short while. He again nervously checked his watch. "I can have you tortured; do you know that?"

"Go ahead, torture me if you must. I doubt it will be worse than what I am already going through. Like you said, all will be over soon—maybe even tomorrow. Do with me what you want. I really could not care less."

There truly was no point bargaining with someone who had nothing to lose. Tom again checked his watch, nervous about the minutes ticking away. He sat down next to her and gently took her hand in his. "What if I get you out of here?"

He sounded so desperate Rachel started to feel a bit sorry for him. "Chances are I would get rearrested and be back in here with additional charges. Let's not delay the inevitable. I just want to get this over with."

Tom was out of ideas. With nothing else to offer, he dropped his head into his hands as a desperate sigh crossed his lips. "Listen, I really need your help. Please. I know you have nothing to lose, but I do. Maybe you'll find it in your heart to do one more good deed before judgment day."

Rachel did not show it, but on the inside, she was triumphant. She knew the moment Tom had entered her cell he was in desperate need of something, and if she played it right, she could hustle a ticket out of there. The odds were now in her favor; she just had to play her role a little longer.

"Well, maybe there is a solution that works for the both of us," Rachel proposed, looking at him with her pleading blue eyes. "I am willing to give you what you want, if you give me what I need."

"I am listening," Tom replied with a glimmer of hope inside him.

"If you get me out of here, and you take care of me till this war is over, which, as you said, should not be much longer, I will give you whatever you need."

Not in a million years, shot through his mind. With her in tow, his chances of getting away were close to zero. Yet, he needed her. Desperately!

"Well … I don't know …" He hesitated. "Okay, fine!"

The two sealed the deal with a solid handshake. "I will call you up to my office in a few minutes with some excuse about your reports. Be ready."

5:53 AM

Tom dashed back to his office and, as luck would have it, ran straight into Evanoff. *What was he doing here so early?*

"Good, Timofei, you are back. I have your money, so bring my cigars, for heaven's sake. Also, I need your briefing on the train. Come to my office in … uh … let's say thirty minutes." Tom desperately tried to buy himself more time.

"Well, sir, I have to—"

"Thirty minutes, understood? And should you not be on time or dare to show up without my cigars, I'll have you shot! God knows I have been waiting long enough." The Colonel General was obviously in a bad mood. Not wanting to worsen it even more, Tom saluted.

"Aye, sir!" He doubted thirty minutes was enough, but it was all he had. From his office, he called the front desk of the prison and requested Rachel to be brought to his office. The guard on duty was not amused.

"You were just in her cell, for Christ's sake! Why do I have to bring her up now?" Tom reminded him of his little indiscretion and the punishments for such an infringement. It promptly ended the objection.

As he waited for Rachel, Tom prepared the paperwork he was going to need. The minutes passed, and Tom got worried. Rachel was still not in his office. He anxiously looked at the clock on the wall.

"Come on, come on, come on …." Impatiently, he picked up the phone to give the prison guard a piece of his mind when the door opened, and the guard entered with Rachel in tow.

"Thank you; that will be all. I will call you when I am done," Tom said as he dismissed the guard. As soon as they were alone, he took off her cuffs and handed her a uniform.

"Hurry. Put this on!"

6:17 AM
Officers Wing, Room 474

First, Evanoff had found his office unlocked, and now this.

"What do you mean the train is not there anymore?" Ivan raised his eyebrow. It was war; equipment disappeared, from screwdrivers to entire tanks. But never a train, nothing of such importance, and certainly not on *his* watch. It just could not be. Colonel General Evanoff was ecstatic when High Command had called and entrusted him with the situation at hand. It was an honor to serve the leadership directly. Now with the train missing, gone like the wind, he looked like a total, incompetent fool. How could this even happen?

"It must be there somewhere!" he bellowed into the receiver. "With what authority was the train moved? … Who moved it? …

No, I have not yet been briefed, but I am expecting him in my office shortly … I guess we will know more then …. Meanwhile, do your part and find this damn train, will you?" Ivan furiously slammed the receiver down, picked it up again, and asked the operator to connect him with room 210.

6:18 AM
Administration Offices, Room 210

"How do I look?" Rachel asked. The uniform did not fit her. It was a few sizes too big, but it would have to do. She adjusted her attire as well as she could. "How do you wear this all day long? It itches."

Tom was familiar with the discomfort of the uniforms. They were supposed to camouflage, keep men warm, and make moving around easy, but they failed to do any of that. It was obvious the main objective was to produce as many of them as possible, as cheaply as possible, and in the shortest amount of time, yet they were still an improvement over the uniforms issued at the beginning of the war, which were the brainchild of a tsarist general from around the turn of the century. Just then the phone started to ring. Tom did not pick it up, as he had a good idea who was calling. Instead, he checked the time again. His scheduled briefing was only minutes away.

"You do not look like a prisoner or a woman, and that is all that matters. But you need to put your hair under your cap—all of it. Walk with confidence, heads up, shoulders back, and legs a little apart. Put the collar up to cover your face," Tom instructed Rachel. He had to admit, cleaned up, and charmingly drowning in her oversized uniform, she looked quite nice.

"Time to go."

"I vividly remember Alyona locking up my office when we left last night, as she always does." Evanoff was in the middle of reporting the lock incident to the MPs when his door opened. "It is about bloody time you show, Timofei. What is going on with that train?"

"I am sorry, Colonel General Evanoff. It is me, Alyona," she chuckled.

"Ah, apologies, I was expecting Tom. He is supposed to be here by now. Can this guy never follow an order?"

"Colonel General, I was just notified of an incident at the Traugutta checkpoint last night. I thought you ought to know right away. First, a call was logged from the unit on duty there about a train that was off route. When they then did not respond to the 4 a.m. radio check, MPs were sent to investigate. Unfortunately, they found a grisly scene with one fatality and one other victim, who was tied up, with a big bump on his head."

"Isn't that the railway checkpoint by the Vistula River?" Ivan asked.

"Affirmative. Why do you ask?"

"No reason," Ivan lied. *Oh Tom, what are you up to? The train, the lock on my door, the checkpoint—please tell me you have nothing to do with any of this.* Evanoff hoped for an innocent explanation, but his instincts told him differently, and he was rarely deceived by them. "Please, Alyona, call Tom's office again. If he picks up, tell him to stay put. Since he is too good to come to me, I will go to him."

She placed the call right away, and a fuming Evanoff exited his office, making his way down the stairs. Ivan had to maneuver the stream of the incoming crowd and rudely pushed people out of his way. As for Tom, a reprimand would be needed, one that would finally get through to him. One that would make him understand that enough is enough; that thirty minutes meant thirty minutes. Not thirty-one, not thirty-two, nothing else but thirty, not even twenty-nine. Ivan was preparing a rant so unpleasant Tom would finally understand an order was an order.

Administration Offices, Room 210

Tom filled his satchel with the most valuable black-market items from his cabinet. Priority was given to small size, high value, high desirability—things he could easily liquidate. Regardless of the outcome, this was the last time he would be in this office, so he took what he could. From his window, he caught one last glimpse of the wooden execution pole and wondered how many prisoners had been tied up there, eyes covered, and then shot. It was a part of war that Tom had never gotten used to. Although he heard the commands and knew the exact moment it was going to happen, he jumped every time a salvo was fired. Rachel saw Tom staring at the pole. She could imagine what was going through his mind.

"Have some faith; it will be okay," she tried to calm him. He appreciated her effort and jokingly returned her smile with a salute.

"Understood, my lady!" The phone on his desk started to ring again.

"We need to go, NOW!" Tom grabbed Rachel by the arm and pushed her out the door. They were just outside his office when he saw Evanoff charging around the big column by the stairs.

Entry Hall

Before Rachel could react, Tom grabbed her, turned her around, and pressed his lips firmly on hers, pushing her against the hallway railing. From the corner of his eyes, he saw Evanoff rush by and disappear into his office. The phone was still ringing.

"How dare you!" Rachel started to protest as soon as Tom let go. He ignored her objection, took her by the arm, and pulled her somewhat roughly toward the stairs.

"Sorry, we really need to get out of here!" Like Evanoff before, the two had to fight the incoming crowd. Thankfully, nobody noticed Rachel in her disguise. Tom pushed her through the exit door and then turned the corner toward the vehicle park.

6:30 AM

Administration Offices, Room 210

With his head on the line, Evanoff was now desperate. He had always liked Tom despite the liberties he took. The young man had charisma, an infectious positive attitude, and a sense of humor that brightened everyone's day. With him around, life certainly was more pleasant. These were the only reasons Evanoff tolerated Tom's indiscretions but he now wondered if that was a mistake.

While waiting, the Colonel General warmed himself by the oven, looking around Tom's office. He started to walk around, opening and closing the various drawers, snooping around to pass the time. Then something caught his eye. The cabinet behind Tom's desk was unlocked, its padlock on the desk. Tom was always tight-lipped about his "shipments," so Ivan was curious. He took a peek and was stunned the second he opened the cabinet. Neatly stacked inside was Russian caviar, vodka, sugar, salt, tinned vegetables, tinned beef, biscuits, Swiss chocolate, and, of course, cigars. Not the mediocre ones he was overpaying for. No, these were Cubans of the highest quality, Romeo y Julieta cigars, stored inside an exclusive humidor, preferred and smoked by no other than Winston Churchill himself. How could he keep these from him? Romeo y Julietas, for heaven's sake! Ivan was furious, his pulse racing, his blood now boiling. And why was this office so much warmer than his? How dare he? This was going to stop, right here, right now.

6:42 AM

Vehicle Park

Tom presented the forged papers and was handed the keys to a ZIS-5 truck, the workhorse of the Russian army. It was old, beaten up, and dirty, but it had a full tank of gas. Rachel swung herself into the cabin with the grace of a woman. It was obvious she was not a soldier, but thankfully no one seemed to notice or care. The engine started right away, but the gearbox did not want to cooperate. It screeched more than once. When Tom finally managed to put the truck into gear, it jumped forward and started to roll toward the exit. The guard opened the gate without hesitation and waved them through. After a few more turns they disappeared into the city.

Tom was fighting the gearbox so much Rachel was worried he was about to destroy it. It made horrible noises every time he shifted, protesting the rough treatment.

"Where are we going?" Rachel was curious.

"America."

"America!" Rachel repeated, nodding. "Interesting. Not sure if I want to go there, though."

"Well, first Switzerland, then America. You can always stay here if you want. I don't care one way or another. But after today, America will be the safest place for me, so that's where I am going." A few hours ago, she was on death row. Now she was on her way halfway across the world.

"America it is."

"You don't sound too excited," Tom noticed.

"I don't really care. All I want is to get out of this godforsaken warzone. But what I really meant was where are we going *now* with the truck?"

"We have a rendezvous with a train. Now that I lived up to my part of the deal, it will soon be time for you to live up to yours."

Rachel still did not know what that was.

Administration Offices, Room 210

Ivan grabbed the humidor with the Cubans—all except one that was about to end up between his lips. He ceremonially cut the flag leaf at the closed end, careful not to damage the cigar's structure. Warming up the other end over his match, he patiently waited for the glowing ring to make its appearance, then enjoyed his first puff. It was the same moment the prison guard entered, taken off guard by Evanoff's presence. He immediately saluted. The Colonel General told him to be at ease.

"Where is Private Sobchak?" the guard asked.

"I wish I knew. I am looking for him too. As a matter of fact, the moment I see him, I'll send him straight down to you guys. A few days in a cell will set him straight." The guard did not know how to respond, too intimidated by his angry, high-ranked superior.

"What do you need him for?" Evanoff asked.

"Well, he had prisoner Horowitz brought up. Apparently, Tom needed to make some corrections to her report. This was over thirty minutes ago. I came by to check on her."

The cigar nearly fell out of Ivan's mouth. "What are you saying? Are you missing a prisoner?"

"Well, I am not sure. But they are supposed to be here. So yes, for now I have to say we are missing a prisoner."

"And a private, and a train," Evanoff mumbled. His day had just gone from bad to worse.

The guard did not understand what he was getting at. "Excuse me?" he asked, in order not to seem ignorant.

Evanoff just shook his head. "Oh … nothing." He then exited Tom's office and strode up one floor, straight to the offices of the military police.

"We have an escaped prisoner. Initiate an APB right away."

The MP shot up from his chair, saluting the Colonel General. "Of course, sir, who are you looking for?"

"Timofei Sobchak and Rachel Horowitz."

"Yeah right … Tom," the soldier chuckled.

"Wipe that smirk off your face, boy. The two are missing, and I need them in my office immediately. Do your job, or else."

The soldier's cheeks paled. "Right away, sir. I am sorry, sir! On it, sir!"

"And tell Colonel Vasiliev to come to my office right away. We have a serious emergency on our hands."

Part III

The Lion's Den

13

August 31, 2017—11:59 PM (EDT)
Motel Room 237, A small town in Vermont

Hironori was focused, ready to strike, when from the corner of his eye he noticed the door handle turn. He immediately adjusted his position to the new threat. The door slowly opened, and in its frame stood the little boy from before, innocently watching him.

"What are you doing?" he asked in his tender voice.

Hironori loosened his grip on the sword and put his index finger on his lips. "Shhh!"

The boy ignored his gesture. "What are you doing?" he asked again.

Hironori looked over to Patrick, who was turning in his bed.

"When I grow up, I want to be a ninja too," the boy continued. Patrick moved some more.

Hironori's thoughts raced. Any other day, he would have done what needed to be done, no questions asked. He had always killed without hesitation, and he would have done so even to a child. But not this time. There was something in the boy's eyes—those curious, innocent eyes. He just could not do it. Not anymore.

"Why won't you answer me?" the little boy asked. Hironori put his finger on his lips again. Patrick now opened his eyes, wondering what woke him. In his daze, for the briefest of moments, he thought he saw a black figure dash out the room. He looked at the open door, then saw the silhouette of the boy.

"What are you doing here?" Patrick asked him.

Susan was also awoken by the commotion and wondered what was going on.

"Did you see him?" the boy responded with excitement in his voice. "When I grow up, I want to be a ninja too!"

Patrick immediately shot up and ran out of the hotel room, carelessly shoving the boy out of his way. He kept a close eye on his surroundings and soon observed a car with no lights on rush out of the parking lot.

"Susan, pack your things. We have to leave," he said urgently.

Susan, eyes still half closed, asked what was going on. Patrick grabbed his small suitcase, threw it onto his bed, and urged Susan to put her few items on top of his. Startled, she complied. Patrick carried the piece of luggage down to the car and threw it into the trunk, with her following closely behind him. As inconspicuously as he could, he drove out of the parking lot and turned toward the freeway. The little boy remained in the doorway, watching them drive off, asking himself why everybody was running away.

Just about the time Patrick exited the parking lot, Hironori arrived back in his previous observation spot overlooking the motel. He wondered if he had been spotted, even more if the boy would talk about him. The lights in Room 237 were still on. Looking at the scene through his binoculars, he saw the boy's worried mom in her pajamas standing in the doorway, the dad on the walkway, carrying his son back to their room. People were opening their doors, one after another, checking out the commotion. Hironori cursed. The recent events back home seemed to affect him more than he had expected, and it had just turned into a problem—one he could not afford.

September 1, 2017—12:15 AM
91 Freeway South

Patrick sped down the freeway, trying to put as much distance as he could between them and the motel. Traffic was light, as expected in the middle of the night. A few headlights passed every so often on the northbound side; even fewer cars went their way.

"What was that all about?" Susan still did not know what had happened.

"We had a visitor."

"I know, but it was only a little boy."

Patrick shook his head. "I am not talking about the boy."

"Don't tell me ..." Susan could not believe she had just cheated death a second time.

"Listen, it is just past midnight, and we have a long day head of us. It is probably best if you try to get some rest."

"Rest? Are you kidding me?" She stared blankly out the window, too shaken up for sleep.

5:43 AM
A small town in Vermont

Soon after the initial commotion, things had calmed quickly. Everyone went back to sleep and one room after another turned dark again—all except Room 237, which could be expected. Hironori stayed up all night keeping his eyes on the door, but there were no further developments. In the early morning light, the sun not yet over the horizon, he peered again through his binoculars, as he had done at regular intervals throughout the night. The early birds were already making their way to the breakfast buffet. Others were lifting their suitcases into their trunks, and to the side of the building, the cleaning crew was stocking their carts. Scanning the parking lot, Hironori spotted the classic, horsepower-rich gas guzzler from the early seventies that had caught his attention the evening before. But something was different. He vividly remembered a car parked in the spot next to it, and that car was now gone.

11:05 AM

South of Newark Airport

Susan's friend had come through. At the airport, she handed Susan a fully packed carry-on, her passport, and some cash.

"Thank you; I owe you big time," Susan assured her friend. When Susan asked if she had noticed anything unusual, her friend started to worry. Susan told her not to and dismissed her own question, playing it off as paranoia, blaming it on the death of her grandparents.

"What is going on?" her friend asked, not convinced by Susan's excuse. "Are you okay?"

Susan nodded, again assuring her everything was fine. Patrick, in the meanwhile, from a nowadays-rare pay phone, notified his fiancée about the unexpected trip. She was not enthused, but she wished him safe travels, knowing he must have a good reason not to return just yet. Patrick uttered a heartfelt "I love you" with a promise to make it up to her upon his return.

Once the airplane had lifted off, Susan looked out the window toward the city of New York, gradually disappearing beneath some low-hanging clouds. Patrick was staring at the "fasten seatbelts" light, hoping it would soon turn off. He should probably catch up on sleep first, but he was anxious to get the laptop from his bag and start preparing for their upcoming challenge.

11:17 AM

A small town in Vermont

The motel's parking lot had all but emptied; there were only a few cars left. Hironori was still keeping an eye on Room 237, hoping for any sign of the two. His worry deepened when a cleaning crew entered the room, and his fears were confirmed when, shortly after, an older couple struggling with heavy suitcases took occupancy. Patrick and Susan were gone. Worse, they now had an eleven-hour head start. In his mind, Hironori replayed the events of the previous night. Did the two really manage to slip out in the short time it took him to drive up here? It seemed unlikely, but there was no other explanation for their sudden disappearance.

2:37 PM (CST)
Somewhere over the Caribbean Sea

Lunch had been served over thirty minutes ago, but Susan had not yet touched her tray.

"Eat something," Patrick encouraged her.

"I probably should," she nodded, but first she had some red wine in the hope that it would calm her nerves. Without much of an appetite, she started to chew on her salmon canape appetizer, reflecting on the last few days.

"Are we doing the right thing?" she wondered out loud.

"I asked myself the very same question," Patrick responded, done with his desert, wiping crumbs from the cobbler off his mouth. "But I cannot think of any alternative."

"Well, we could just disappear for a while," Susan proposed.

"As I said, that will only work if you plan to never come back and are willing to look over your shoulder for the rest of your life."

"Do you believe we even have a chance here?" Susan asked without even wanting to know the answer.

"Let's not sell ourselves short. We may yet have some arrows in our quiver." Patrick's confidence was assuring, but not very convincing.

"You will need to tell me what those are because I sure cannot see any."

"For a start, I am a journalist and am trained as a SEAL. I have a vast network of resources and connections that could turn out to be useful. And I am certain you have qualities that will come in handy too."

"Not for something like this," Susan responded, lifting her glass of wine to wash down the appetizer.

"Keep in mind it is not always power and force that wins. Let me quote Edward Bulwer-Lytton here: The pen is mightier than the sword." Susan nearly spit out her wine. She managed not to, but in the process the liquid went down the wrong pipe, causing a cough attack.

"Are you okay?" Patrick asked.

Susan kept coughing but managed to squeeze out a few words. "The pen is mightier than the sword? Really? So the next time I am staring at a sword, I'll just hold up a piece of paper with 'Don't' written on it. Please tell me you are kidding," she said, laughing.

"I am not," Patrick looked at her a bit offended. "The written word has proven to bring down governments, armies, organizations—you name it. Do not underestimate it."

"Well, I sure hope you are right." She was still in disbelief about Patrick's quote. "At least you have some experience in this." She coughed some more, clearing her throat.

"Experience?" Patrick frowned.

"You are an investigative journalist and considering your military background …."

"Journalist, yes. Military background, yes. Being hunted by a ruthless killer, no. I have ruffled my fair share of feathers in the past and gotten out of a few dicey situations as a SEAL, but I have never been on someone's hit list. This is a first for me too."

Susan refilled her glass and took another gulp, her biggest one yet. When the flight attendant offered to bring another bottle, Patrick deemed it better to end the alcohol intake and secretly gestured her not to.

"We will figure this out somehow," he said, trying to calm Susan.

She resumed her attempt to come up with possible alternatives. There were none. "You are right. We need to figure this out somehow."

"And we will," Patrick responded confidently.

"Somehow!" Susan said, with less certainty in her voice. She had never chewed a fingernail in her life but now caught herself doing so. She immediately clenched her hand into a fist. Patrick gestured to the flight attendant to bring more wine. Maybe it was not the worst idea after all.

1:45 AM (EDT)
91 Freeway South

Hironori had stopped to eat his first decent meal in days. American cuisine was not his thing, but restaurants clustered around freeway exits always served big portions quickly. He was on his way to New York City, heading straight to Susan's apartment, determined to pick up her trail. She had to show up eventually. With his stomach full, it was time to provide his boss with an update. With one hand on the steering wheel, he pushed the call button with the other.

"Tell me the good news," his boss requested without a greeting. It was not easy for Hironori to summon his lie.

"Everything is done."

"I will see you tomorrow, then."

"I would like to take some time off." It was a request he did not pose lightly, especially after his questionable performance. Hironori got no answer. "I have not had a vacation in years." His boss did not respond right away.

"Everything okay?" he finally asked.

"Yes; why would it not be?" Hironori tried to ease his suspicions.

"All right, then." And with that, the line went dead.

Hironori was not the type to get nervous, but now his pulse was elevated, and his hands were covered with cold sweat. Had he just lied to his boss? He'd be dead the minute Yamaguchi found out. It was a desperate move, but a necessary one, as he had just bought himself some time.

14

September 2, 2017—2:00 PM (ART)
Hotel by the Lake, San Carlos de Bariloche, Argentina

After the long flight and an overnight stay in Buenos Aires, Susan and Patrick arrived at their destination San Carlos de Bariloche just before lunch. After checking into their lakefront hotel, Susan went straight to bed. Now, in the privacy of her own room, she allowed herself to grieve about her grandparents' death again. Everything she had bottled up seemed to hit her at once. She pulled the blanket over her head and sobbed till she finally fell asleep. Patrick was in the next room, rubbing his tired eyes. After lunch, he went back to work, looking deeper into the files received from his contact, continuing the work he had begun on the plane. There were documents, newspaper clippings, pictures from microfilms, tax returns, even scans of World War II documents. Just about everything that was ever digitized about Susan's grandparents. Most things were of no importance, but he had to keep reading, making sure nothing essential was missed. So far, the files uncovered nothing but a few trivial facts.

2:30 PM (EST)
38th Street, New York City

Hironori kept his eyes on the entrance of the midtown luxury apartment building from his hotel room across. He had waited all night and morning, but Susan did not show. The tracer software on his laptop was equally quiet. Something would eventually come up— a credit card transaction, a login to a social media account— something that would pinpoint to the location of the two. The only question was when. He lay down on the bed, pushing the pillow into shape when his boss called him.

"Your vacation, make it short."

Before Hironori could respond, the call was terminated. He put the phone back onto the side table and laid his head down on the pillow. A few days were all he had.

8:00 PM (ART)
Hotel by the Lake

Patrick heard Susan walking around in her room.

"Come in," she responded to his knock on the connecting door. She was on the balcony overlooking the lake, taking solace in the mountains of the snow-covered Andes looming in the distance.

"Isn't this beautiful?" she enthusiastically praised the scenery.

"It sure is," he responded without showing much interest. "But have a look at this." Patrick sat down and put his laptop on the coffee table. "I discovered a few things. Do you know how your grandparents met?"

Susan shook her head. "I do not really know anything about their past."

"It looks like your grandmother was Jewish."

"That much I know," Susan responded.

"Well, did you know she got arrested during the war?"

"Arrested! Really?" Susan could not imagine her grandmother ever breaking the law.

"Here is the record. The Russian military police charged her with stealing food."

Susan looked at the document on the screen. "Stealing food? Poor thing, she must have been starving. She would never do anything like that otherwise."

"See anything else interesting?" Patrick asked, curious if she saw what he did.

Susan scanned the document. "Oh my God, look, this is my grandfather's signature. Is this how they met?"

"Chances are. Now, as you told me, he was Russian, and I can tell you he was born in a small village in Siberia. In early 1945, he was stationed in Warsaw, just after Poland got liberated from the Germans."

"My grandmother was Polish?"

"It looks like it, but we cannot be certain."

"I had no idea." Susan was quite puzzled.

"According to the arrest record, she lost her entire family in the Holocaust."

"Oh my God! Are you serious? She had never spoken about any of this." Susan shook her head. Maybe her grandmother had tried to forget; maybe the experiences from back then were too painful to recall.

"Listen to this. She was charged and was awaiting trial for her crime, punishable by death under martial law. However, your grandfather busted her out of prison. Somehow, they managed to get themselves to Switzerland, and from there, to the US,"

"So, my granddad risked his life to save my grandmother? What a hero!" she said proudly. This was the grandfather she knew.

"I am really curious about what exactly happened. Unfortunately, this is all the information we have," Patrick said as he wrapped up the briefing.

"So, there's nothing in all these files that can help us?"

"Actually, it sheds some light on things. Remember your grandmother had sent me on an assignment?"

Susan nodded. "To find some kind of document," she said.

"A notebook, to be exact. Guess where she sent me to?"

"Switzerland!" Susan was confident in her guess. Patrick

nodded.

"So, they hid something in Switzerland after they fled the war?" Susan connected the dots.

"Buried in the ground, in a remote location in the Swiss Alps," Patrick confirmed. "And now your grandma is dead, and some people want us dead, too, all because of this notebook."

"Must be one heck of a notebook. Did you find it?"

Patrick hesitated.

"Did you?"

Again, Patrick hesitated.

"Oh my God … you did! You found it! Show it to me," Susan said so enthusiastically, that Patrick had to ask her to lower her voice.

"Okay, okay," he said. "I only have copies."

"Copies or not, what's the deal?"

"To be honest, I don't know. It's a ledger of some sort."

"Show me!" Susan requested again, excited to see it.

But Patrick stalled again, his protective instincts kicking in. "Listen, Susan, I am asking you once more. Do you really want to do this? Your grandparents are dead, I survived an attempt on my life, twice, so did you, and a killer is on our heels—all because of this notebook."

"I cannot believe you are asking me again. This is exactly why I need to see it. You said to move forward, so let's move forward."

Patrick could not disagree. After all, he had pushed the idea. He retrieved the copies from his room and was about to hand them over. "Are you really sure?" he asked her one more time.

Without giving an answer, Susan took the papers out of Patrick's hands and tried to make sense of them. "It certainly is a list of some type. On page one, names and addresses, on page two, multiplications. Or measurements? Inches, centimeters, meters? Who can tell? On page three, more numbers, and more names. You are right. This is all very confusing."

"It sure is, but we have to figure it out. I am certain the solution to everything lies in here."

Patrick was already enjoying fresh eggs, croissants, and a cup of coffee when Susan entered the restaurant.

"How did you sleep?" he asked as he welcomed her to the table.

"Could have been better," she solemnly responded.

Patrick noticed her swollen eyes. "Your grandparents?"

Susan nodded. "I still cannot believe they are gone. Whatever they were involved in, they did not deserve to die like this."

The situation made Patrick quite uncomfortable. He never knew how to comfort a grieving person. "Listen, I know all this came as a shock. But it is going to get better, I promise. Just give it some time. Time heals all wounds. For now, eat something; it will help."

Susan took a croissant and started to tear off small pieces, then one by one put them in her mouth. "So, what's the plan?" she asked, somewhat distracted.

"Well, we are here to pay this Dieter Heydrich a visit. I'd say the sooner the better," Patrick replied.

"He definitely did not want to talk to us on the phone, so I expect he will be equally welcoming when we show up on his doorstep unannounced. Do we even know where he lives?"

"Not yet. The Heydrichs are not listed in any phone books, nor are they registered anywhere else. No one in this family shows up in any internet searches except in old articles from the war. Neither of them has a digital footprint. Now it gets even better. I inquired with the staff at the reception desk. As soon as I dropped the name Heydrich, they all looked at each other nervously, uncertain what to do. It was quite the uncomfortable silence."

"And?"

Patrick made a dismissive gesture. "Let's just say they did not want to admit knowing anything."

"That is not a promising start," Susan noted, worried.

"It sure is not. We might have to be a bit more creative than anticipated."

"Which means … start at the public library?"

"Good idea. I also want to check the Civic Center. After all these years, the Heydrich name must be on a document somewhere. The information is out there. It always is."

2:30 PM
Civic Center, San Carlos de Bariloche

Susan and Patrick were sitting on a bench, patiently waiting for their number to be called, surprised the office was even open on a Saturday. They had already visited the local newspaper and post office, only to be turned away the moment the name Heydrich was mentioned. Avoiding this name at the library, they managed to get their hands on archival microfilms of local publications, all the way back to 1945. As the data was not yet digitized, they had to go through them manually, role by role. Patrick soon noticed that the records were incomplete, pages missing here and there. As they somewhat expected, no information on the Heydrichs was to be found. No announcements, no articles, no reports. Not even a mention. Nothing.

"What if this is a dead end too?" Susan was worried.

"There are less obvious avenues we can explore. Like finding people willing to talk. I am sure not everyone is a friend of this family."

"What if your contact was wrong? What if the Heydrichs do not even live here?"

"The area code of Dieter's phone number matches the one for this area. They are here."

"Number 218, please proceed to Counter 5," an emotionless voice echoed through the long, empty corridor. A friendly young man greeted them at the counter. Patrick asked if he spoke English, and he responded with a friendly "How can I help you?"

Patrick came straight to the point. "We are here in an official capacity to find the heir of an inheritance. We need to speak to someone called Dieter Heydrich."

The clerk's demeanor immediately changed; anxiety was written all over his face. He seemed not to know what to do and excused himself. After another short wait an older gentleman walked up to the counter. He was tall and thin, mostly bald but with some thinning gray hair around his head, deep naso-labial folds, dressed in dull clothes, and wearing round glasses—his appearance as stuffy as they come.

"How may I help you?" he asked coldly.

"We are trying to locate the Heydrich family. To be more precise, Dieter Heydrich."

The man lifted his left eyebrow. "I see. And what is this regarding?"

"An inheritance. We are working for the executor of a will this Dieter is mentioned in."

"What is your name, sir?"

"Rooper. Patrick Rooper." Patrick forced a friendly smile.

Without saying another word, the man disappeared from the counter. A few minutes later, he returned.

"Well, Mr. Rooper, you must be mistaken. We checked our files. There are no records with such a name. If there was, we would certainly know." Then, without even giving Patrick a chance to respond, the man abruptly closed the counter and drew the curtain behind the glass.

"Strike three," Susan said sarcastically. "I have to agree with you now. The Heydrichs are here, with tentacles reaching far into this society."

"And by now, I am sure they know we are here, which means our Japanese friend will soon be on our heels again."

"What now?" Susan wondered.

"I could do with a coffee. We need to reassess."

15

3:15 PM (ART)
The Eyebrew Coffee Shop, San Carlos de Bariloche

The two entered a charming coffee shop not far from the Civic Center and sat at a table in a corner. The waitress, not burdened with much to do, immediately walked over to take their order. She was dressed in a black shirt, a red mini skirt, black stockings, combat boots, and braids curled into Minnie Mouse buns. Her bright red lipstick completed the ensemble. She perfectly fit the establishment, its décor industrial modern yet with plenty of charm, its brick walls a platform for local artists to showcase their work.

"Any ideas?" Susan asked Patrick, exhausted from the day's efforts and ready for a dose of caffeine.

"It is obvious people fear this family, and probably with good reason."

"We have to find someone who is willing to talk."

Patrick nodded. "That is one way to go. I have already started another. At the hotel, I checked out online maps, trying to narrow the area where this family may live. First, I limited the search to a seventy-mile radius up and down National Route 40. Second, considering the historical context under which they came here, it is unlikely they settled anywhere populated. Third, they arrived here with plenty of funds, so we are looking for a sizable property. Based on these, I have identified a few dozen haciendas that fit the profile."

"Estancias."

"Estancias?"

"Yes, here they call them estancias, I believe, not haciendas."

"Ah … okay then. I tried to narrow the results further by checking satellite images and street views for anything telling like security gates, walls, fences, and so on."

"Smart."

"Unfortunately, street views are mostly unavailable for these remote areas. And the satellite images are too blurry to make out any details."

"So, no help there to find this Dieter," said Susan, sounding disappointed.

"Well, what I am saying is, if everything else fails, we have the option to hit the roads and check them one by one. I only worry it will take time, time we probably don't have," Patrick explained.

The waitress returned, and balancing her tray on her left hand, served them their orders.

"I could not help but overhear. Are you looking for Dieter?" she asked in a near whisper.

Both Susan and Patrick, frazzled by the unexpected question, responded in an equally low voice. "Yes!"

"What do you want from him?"

"We are here on an inheritance matter. But nobody seems to be willing to talk to us."

The charming smile disappeared off the waitress's face, followed by a disapproving, even somewhat angry look. "Bullshit!" She turned and walked away.

"Wait a second," Susan tried to stop her. The waitress turned, visibly annoyed, still holding up the now empty tray with her left hand, the right on her hip.

"What?" she asked.

"We are sorry," Susan apologized in an effort to regain her sympathy.

The smile returned. "Just tell me what you are really here for.

And who knows, I may even be able to help." She underlined her statement with a wink.

Susan glanced at Patrick and nodded her head toward the waitress, encouraging him to start talking.

"You are right; this was a lie. I am truly sorry," Patrick said, hoping to remedy the situation. "It's just … we cannot disclose why we are here. And we are getting the weirdest responses as soon as his name is mentioned."

The waitress just kept standing there with no reaction, waiting for what she really wanted to hear.

"Okay. Here is the deal. We are investigating something that happened during the Second World War."

Patrick now got her attention. She carefully looked around the coffee shop, checking on the only other customers—two middle-aged women enjoying a lively chat over a cup of tea and a chocolate croissant, thankfully all the way across the room.

"Nobody wants to talk to us, and we really need to find him," Susan admitted. The waitress walked back to the table and leaned over with one hand, still balancing the tray on the other. "What do you want to know?" she whispered.

"Where we can find Dieter," Patrick responded, hopeful to finally get some answers. The waitress straightened herself back up and shook her head.

"I am sorry. I can't help you with that."

"Of course," Susan replied cynically, her hopes crushed. She turned back to Patrick, purposefully ignoring the waitress. "So, how many estancias are we looking at here?"

But the waitress was not leaving, she was still standing there. Patrick also turned away from her.

"Thirty or forty, maybe—"

"But I know someone who can," the waitress interrupted Patrick, grimacing.

"Who?" Susan shouted out.

"Please, keep your voice down," the waitress cautioned her. Again, she scanned the room before answering. "Go up to the cathedral and ask for the bishop, Alejandro Casillas. He has been here for years, and it is rumored he is well connected to this family.

Well, it's more than a rumor; it's an open secret. He will deny it, but they are close, and if you play your cards right ...."

Patrick shook his head. "If the bishop is 'connected,' for sure he will not want to tell us anything."

"Of course he won't. But our bishop ... well ... let's just say he is not an angel. Tell him you know about Cecilia. That should make him talk."

"Cecilia? Who is she?"

"A friend, but you don't need to know. Just drop the name. It will do its job."

"You have no idea how grateful we are," Susan whispered. "Thank you so much."

"No need to thank me." The waitress shook her head. "My great-grandparents were Germans. And Jewish. They did not survive. You do the math." Without saying another word, she walked away.

"Do you think what she is saying ...?" Susan was cautiously optimistic.

"We have nothing to lose," Patrick responded, knowing well it was their one and only lead.

"But messing with a bishop?"

"As she hinted, he may not be such an angel."

"Let's not get our hopes up just yet," Susan cautioned. "The Nazis came here with the help of the Catholic Church. This bishop will make every effort not to have himself embarrassed."

"I am counting on it. It is exactly what is going to make him talk, whoever this Cecilia is."

"Maybe we will not even have to mention her. If we offer to let him to talk off the record and appeal to his humanity, who knows? After all, isn't he someone who has devoted his entire life to doing good?"

"One would think so." But Patrick knew better. Things often are very different behind the scenes, even in the church. "Let's go find this bishop and see how much of a Christian he really is."

From behind the bar, the waitress watched the two leave. She quietly wished them good luck, hoping for a little bit of justice to be brought into this world.

4:05 PM

Cathedral of San Carlos de Bariloche

Patrick parked their rental in one of the vacant spots while Susan eyed the neo-gothic building. She could tell it was not as old as the ones she had visited in Europe, but she quite liked its architecture. They walked through the small park surrounding the church, passing through the well-groomed rose garden with its spectacular views of the lake, and entered the building through two heavy wooden doors. Inside, Susan was surprised by the modern décor. She had to admit, the cathedral was small but more intriguing than she had first anticipated.

They slowly made their way down the nave into the crossing, then to the side through the transept and into the ambulatory. They marveled at the colorful stained-glass windows when a priest walked by.

"Your cathedral is so beautiful. We were wondering when it was built," Susan engaged him. He stopped his brisk walk, happy about the couple's interest in the building.

"Oh, it was built between 1942 and 1944, and all from local materials, mind you. Some people joke it looks like a ski lodge in here, but I disagree. I personally prefer the rugged stone walls compared to the soft, sanded surfaces of the European cathedrals. It contrasts nicely with the weight-bearing columns, which, you can see here, are of a smoother texture. The glass windows were not added till 1947. Aren't they fantastic?"

Susan nodded. "They sure are. By the way, may I ask you a question?"

"I'd be happy to help. What can I do for you?" the priest asked in his heavy Spanish accent.

"Where can we find the bishop? We need to talk to him."

"I am sorry; he is at his residence and will not grant audiences till Monday. You can go to our offices across the street and request one. If you are lucky, he might still have an opening."

"Unfortunately, we need to see him as soon as possible," Susan stressed.

"Oh, I see. Unfortunately, as I said, he is not available till Monday. He will hold mass here tomorrow morning at 10:30 AM, but he never grants audiences on Sundays. Is there anything I can help you with?"

Patrick knew he was about to take a risk. A big one, in fact, but he figured the priest may know something.

"We are looking for Dieter Heydrich." Like all the others before him, the priest's facial expression unmistakably changed. Patrick immediately redirected to soften the flared-up tension. "We have something of great importance for him. Can you help us find him?"

No sooner had Patrick mentioned Dieter than the provincial stepped out from seemingly nowhere. The priest nervously looked at his superior, then turned back to Patrick and Susan. "I wish I could, but unfortunately, I do not know anyone with this name."

Susan was not willing to give up so easily. "We heard the bishop may be able to help. How can we get in touch with him before he grants audiences?"

The provincial stepped forward. "Brother, padre Pio is looking for you. Please go see him at once." Without hesitation, the priest followed the order and made his way out of the cathedral.

"You have to excuse my interruption," the provincial said to Patrick. "Who are you looking for?"

Patrick decided to play along. "Dieter Heydrich," he repeated himself.

"Hmm … Dieter Heydrich. I have never heard of him, and being the bishop's right hand, I certainly would know if he did. But I can ask around for you. Just tell me where you are staying so I can get in touch with you."

"We are staying—"

"Well, we have just arrived and have not yet organized accommodations," Patrick quickly interrupted Susan. "We can come back later and meet you here."

"I am not sure how quickly I can get this information for you. I really need to be able to get in touch with you," the priest pressed the two.

"As I said, we have not yet sorted our accommodations. To be honest, we do not even know if we are staying for the night," Patrick continued the bilateral charade.

"I am sorry; then there is nothing I, well … we can do for you," the priest said, uttering the already expected answer. He was on his way out of the church when he turned around one more time.

"By the way, the bishop is leaving town tonight and will be unable to grant an audience for at least two weeks," he lied with a triumphant arrogance Susan could not stand. She had no intention to let him get away with it.

"Doesn't the bishop hold mass here tomorrow? It says so on the announcement board at the entrance." She watched the provincial's reaction closely.

"Does it? The board must not have been updated then," he continued his charade.

"Someone had just placed it there when we walked in. Maybe you are not up to date with your own schedule?"

The provincial's face faded to red from anger. How dare this woman question his authority? "Thank you for dropping by. I wish you a pleasant stay, however short it may be," he countered. Patrick and Susan noted the obvious threat.

"Thank you very much," Patrick responded, "and give our regards to the bishop. From the both of us. And from our friend Cecilia." Patrick's provocation hit a bulls-eye. The provincial's eyes opened wide, and, clearly startled, he turned and steamrolled into the sacristy.

"How telling," Patrick whispered.

"What now?" Susan wondered, out of ideas.

"We definitely need to get to the bishop. Let's go back to the coffee shop. May be the waitress can tell us a bit more. And it would not surprise me if we are going to hear from the bishop soon."

5:15 PM

The Eyebrew Coffee Shop

"The usual?" the waitress joked. Patrick nodded. Susan was okay with it too.

"One Earl Grey tea, one latte," she confirmed the order.

"And your phone so I can send a quick message?" Patrick held up a twenty-dollar bill.

"Who is the lucky girl?" the waitress asked, giving Patrick a flirtatious look. "Is she cuter than me?"

Patrick, a bit embarrassed, did not know how to answer.

"I am just kidding, my friend. But you are not calling China, are you?"

"The lucky girl is my fiancée, and no, she is in Los Angeles. The message will not cost you a cent, and as for your question about cuteness, let me just say neither of you are as cute as me."

The waitress could not help but laugh. So did Susan. The waitress dug her phone from her pocket and handed it to Patrick while taking the bill with the other hand. Patrick started typing: *Thank you for your letter. Glad you are doing well.* Sarah would know what it meant. A few minutes later, the waitress returned with their beverages, and Patrick returned the phone.

"Thank you very much. I truly appreciate it," Patrick said as he handed her another twenty.

"You know, I thought you may be back," the waitress mentioned.

"You did?" Susan was bemused. So was Patrick.

"Yes, I just had this feeling our paths would cross again, as I was certain you would need more help with your homework. I'd love to be your tutor, but unfortunately, I am not very proficient in the subject either."

"We do not expect you to teach us," Patrick responded, "but we were hoping you could point us to the library that carries the book with the right subject."

"As I said, get to the bishop, then—"

No sooner had she started talking than a priest walked into the coffee shop, right up to the counter. The waitress immediately dashed back to take his order. Susan kicked Patrick under the table and, with her head, indicated the direction of the counter.

"That's the guy we just talked to," she whispered.

"The provincial?"

"No, the priest, the one that was called away from us."

Patrick inconspicuously turned his head. Susan was right. There he was, standing right by the cash register of the coffee shop. Patrick discreetly turned his head back from the direction of the priest.

"What is he doing here?" Susan was in suspense.

"Probably just a coincidence," he answered, disinterested, not reading anything into the situation.

"No, this is not a coincidence. He was following us."

Patrick did not buy it. "Why would he follow us? He can get a coffee like anyone else. Nothing wrong with that."

"Sure, he can. But don't they have a coffee machine up there?" Susan kept her eyes on the clergyman.

"I am sure they do, but maybe it does not make the quality beverage one can get here."

Susan could not just believe this was a coincidence. "What if he was sent to follow us?"

"If he were, he would not be so obvious, would he?"

Susan was not convinced. "Something is going on."

The priest paid for his coffee and after a short exchange of pleasantries with the waitress, left with coffee in hand.

"See? What did I tell you?" Patrick smiled.

"Come on, you have to admit this was strange."

Patrick had to agree. "Yes, it was a bit unusual."

The waitress walked over to their table with a second round of beverages. "Here are your refills, one EG and a caf-lat."

"I am sorry, you are serving refills here?" Susan was surprised.

"Normally not, but these are courtesy of the Diocese of Bariloche. By the way, don't be late."

"Late for what?" Patrick wondered, and so did Susan.

The waitress smirked. "Just don't be late," she repeated herself and walked away, leaving the two looking at each other, baffled, trying to make sense of it all.

"Late for what?" Patrick asked again.

"The diocese? You see, I knew he was following us," Susan triumphantly beamed at Patrick. "But why is the diocese treating us to drinks?"

"What's next? The bishop walking in and telling us he is Dieter

Heydrich?" Patrick chuffed while rolling his eyes, about to drink from the freshly served, unusually big cup, while Susan tried hard not to spit out her tea from laughing. She had just about recovered when she noticed the small paper stuck to the bottom of Patrick's cup. She reached out to pull it off and put it back onto the coaster when she noticed a handwritten note on it. It first made her chuckle, but on second thought it made her even more confused.

"Are you ready to confess your sins?" she asked Patrick, handing him the paper.

"Confess my sins? Why would I go confess my sins?"

"Because it looks like it'll be time to unburden ourselves at 9 a.m. tomorrow. I think you are right. It looks like the bishop is reaching out after all. Thank you, Cecilia."

"We are definitely not going to be late," Patrick gave the waitress a thankful nod across the room.

7:36 PM

Hotel Restaurant

Susan had ordered a local fish specialty, and she did not regret her choice. It was delicious. Patrick felt less adventurous and ordered the rib eye, his favorite cut. After all, they were in Argentina, the land of meat, and it did not disappoint either.

"I told you it wasn't a coincidence that the priest was there," Susan gloated again.

"Looks like we did not hit a dead end after all," Patrick responded, placing a piece of steak between his teeth while feeling hopeful about the upcoming meeting. He knew better than to keep talking with his mouth full, so he waited till he was finished chewing. "I really hope this time we are going to get something useful out of it."

"What if it is not what we think it is?"

"What do you mean?" Patrick asked, ready to put the next piece of steak in his mouth.

"Well, what if they want to lure us into the church to... oh, I don't know… get rid of us? We provoked them pretty heavily."

Patrick complemented the taste of the meat with some red wine.

"Get rid of us?" he replied. "First, I don't think all the parties have connected the dots just yet, and second, a house of God is not the right place to do such a thing. I am quite certain they want to talk. I would not even be surprised if the confession was with his Excellency himself—you know, Cecilia and all."

"And what if you are wrong, like you were in the coffee shop? Aren't you worried about what they might do?"

"Who? The church? Or the Heydrichs?"

"The Heydrichs."

"As I said, I don't think they know why we are here yet."

"Does it matter? Isn't anyone asking questions posing a threat?"

"I am not saying we do not have to be careful. But for now, we should be fine."

"It's quite astonishing how this family strikes fear into the locals. How is this still possible nowadays?" Susan had a hard time understanding.

"People definitely have quite the reaction when they hear the name. You know, there is a whole new generation of Nazi sympathizers working tirelessly for the resurrection of their ideology. They are well organized, with chapters around the world, taking advantage of all the latest communication channels to spread their propaganda. And even more worrisome, they have been enjoying quite the growth rate."

Susan was shaking her head when the waiter dropped by to refill their wine glasses. She waited till he was gone again before speaking. "So, are you still confident about our appointment tomorrow morning?"

"We must go. Somehow, we have to slalom our way through all this and hope for the best, because if we don't, well, you already know …"

It was already late when Sarah unlocked the door and entered her condominium. As always, she was welcomed by the cool ocean breeze blowing through the open balcony doors. Tired and looking forward to a hot shower and a good night's sleep, she removed her heels, put her jacket in the entryway closet, switched the kitchen's undercabinet lights on, opened the fridge, and poured herself a chilled glass of rosé. She'd already had plenty to drink, but wine always helped her wind down from an eventful day.

+ + +

As Sarah had narrowed her choices to three final contenders, the day to choose the gown she would walk down the aisle in had finally arrived. Despite having a slight favorite, she was counting on her friends' opinion to nudge her in the right direction. They unanimously approved her choice. After a long search, trying on dress after dress, she had finally found the one, the prefect gown to get married in: skin-tight, hugging every curve, with a long, slender skirt, long sleeves, and intricate beading, just enough to give it some texture without interfering with its extraordinary elegance celebrating every inch of her silhouette. All agreed—she looked stunning.

Right after leaving the bridal shop, the four enjoyed each other's company at a fancy dinner with good food, wine, and talk of nothing but the upcoming nuptials. Sarah was treating the small group as a thank-you for their help. After she settled the bill, her friends were ready to hit the town and celebrate. She would have preferred to go home and sleep, but her posse would not allow her. Before she knew it, Sarah was sitting on a plushy seat in a fancy nightclub, watching her friends on the dance floor enticing the male audience with their provocative moves. Till recently she had enjoyed the atmosphere, with its loud music and flashing lights, but now being engaged, she found it more an annoyance, as was the constant flow of drinks offered by random guys. Since meeting Patrick, she was drawn less and less to this kind of lifestyle, her increasing lack of interest an indication her days of partying were coming to an end. In the group, she was the first to get hitched, happy to kiss the dating scene, with all its awkwardness, goodbye. Her friends still could not believe she was getting married, as nobody had ever seemed good enough for her. After dating for years with little success, all the while being lectured by her inner circle to be less picky or end up a spinster, she was happy to finally have proven them wrong. Yet, she was worried the wedding would change the dynamics of her friendships.

+ + +

Sipping on the beverage, Sarah read Patrick's message one more time. It made her smile. She missed him but decided not to let his absence dampen her mood. After all, she finally had her gown, a big task she could check off her list now. Nevertheless, tonight was one of those nights she longed to be in his arms. His job was demanding, as she'd known from the beginning, and she certainly did not want to complain because in every other way Patrick was perfect. Still looking at his picture, taken on their last skiing vacation up north and immediately chosen as the background on her phone, a warm, intense wave of longing came over her. She wondered what he was up to at this very moment.

It was so quiet one could hear only the ocean waves breaking at the beach. Sarah leaned against the white marble countertop, which elegantly complemented the all-white cabinets and stainless-steel appliances. She wished Patrick would be home sooner rather than later. Maybe he could even take a few days off upon his return. She was still staring at his picture on her phone when something caught her eye. She looked toward a dark corner in her living room. At first, she was not certain, but as she took a closer look, the light next to her sofa switched on. She jumped backward, her heart skipping a beat, the wine glass slipping out of her hand and shattering on the floor. Her eyes had not deceived her—someone was sitting there.

"Please, have a seat."

Sarah was petrified. How did this man get in? What did he want from her? She hesitantly followed his request and sat down, at the very far side of the sofa.

"Just answer me truthfully and nothing is going to happen to you." The man's words, spoken in a Japanese accent, sounded surprisingly calm. Sarah strained her eyes to look at him without turning her head. After the initial shock, she summed up enough courage to ask who he was.

"Please forgive me for not having introduced myself. How can I be so rude? My name is Hironori Matsubara, and I am here to protect the interests of my boss, who shall stay anonymous."

Only now did she notice his sword leaning against the chair. A hot flash shot through her abdomen, tying the knot in her stomach even tighter.

"And what do you want from me?" she asked with a shaky voice.

"Good question." Hironori kept his cynical smile. "All I need is one answer. One. As you see, I will be out of your hair in no time." The statement did not calm Sarah. In her panic, she tried to think of anything she might have of interest to him but came up empty.

"What do you want to know?"

Hironori leaned forward toward Sarah. "Look at me!" he requested.

Sarah hesitantly turned her head.

"Where is Patrick?" Hironori's eyes tightened.

Was he in trouble? Or worse, in danger?

"Why do you want to know?" she asked, surprised she had the courage to do so.

"The why does not concern you," Hironori answered with growing impatience.

"I wish I could tell you, but I do not know. I really don't. Please—"

"Has he contacted you in the last few days?" Should she tell him about the message she had received earlier? Sarah was too scared even to think, but her instincts told her not to. She shook her head ever so slightly.

"HAS HE CONTACTED YOU?" Hironori screamed at her.

Sarah jumped, a jolt of fright trembling her body. Without time to even consider a change of heart, she immediately shook her head vehemently. Hironori lowered his voice again but kept his intimidating stare.

"Has he told you where he was going?"

Sarah, pushing her body against the end of the couch, legs together, nervously pressing her hands into her lap, again shook her head.

"I find that hard to believe," Hironori said and paused. It did not miss its effect. Sarah's hands started to shake. It was the reaction Hironori was looking for.

"I am asking you one more time, and one time only. Where is he?"

"I don't know. I really don't ..." Sarah started to sob. Hironori got up, walked over to the kitchen to fetch her phone from the countertop.

"Unlock it," he demanded. She entered her passcode and handed the phone back. The Japanese assassin sat back down and started to scan the logs. There were no recent calls from Patrick, which came as no surprise. He knew better. Then Hironori opened the text messages. The last one caught his eye, especially the country code it was sent from. Susan and the journalist had traveled south.

"So, he has not contacted you?" Hironori asked while taking a mental note of the phone number. Sarah again shook her head.

"Written any letters recently?" Hironori kept a close eye on her for any reaction. She ignored the question while drops of cold sweat started to run down her forehead.

"You see, I told you this was going to be easy," Hironori switched back to his overly friendly voice. Sarah forced a smile.

"I am sorry I frightened you, but in my line of work ... I am sure you understand." Hironori, ready to leave, reached for the katana.

16

September 4, 2017—8:55 AM (ART)
Cathedral of San Carlos de Bariloche

No one else seemed to be in the cathedral except one person unburdening in the confession booth, as indicated by the small red light above the door. Susan and Patrick had to wait. Other than them, the church was empty and quiet—so quiet, even whispers seemed to echo. They waited over ten minutes in silence until the door of the stand finally opened and an old, frail woman walked out. She struggled to move her arthritis-riddled body toward the front benches, where, to their surprise, she kneeled and started to pray the rosary. Patrick had offered to lend her a hand, but she politely declined. Susan wondered what she had to confess at this age. Then again, who knew what pressed the heart of an old woman? Whatever it was, Susan was impressed by her dedication to her faith.

Both Patrick and Susan squeezed into the confession chamber, and as soon as Patrick closed the door behind them, a panel moved to the side, unveiling a small opening covered by a wooden grid. Despite the dim light, they recognized the priest from the day before. He was waiting for the usual "Bless me, Father, for I have sinned …."

Instead, Patrick initiated the conversation with "We got your message."

"I am glad you came," the priest responded. His uneasy shifting in his chair indicated otherwise.

Susan came straight to the point. "Padre, we hope you can help us."

"I have called you here for this very reason. I want to help you. From what I understand, you are looking for … Dieter Heydrich." The name did not pass the priest's lips easily.

"Padre, before we go any further, let me introduce ourselves. My name is Patrick—"

"Names are inconsequential. I prefer not to know. But before I say what I have to say, tell me about your business with the Heydrichs."

"It is somewhat of a long story. My companion Susan and I got drawn into a situation, and we are looking for a way out." Patrick was careful not to unveil too much. After all, they did not yet know if the clergyman was on their side.

"I understand your hesitation to tell me, but understand I swore a holy oath on the sacrament of penance. Even if subpoenaed, I cannot disclose anything said in here. Your words are safe. It is the very reason why we are in here in the first place."

"Be that as it may … we must talk to Dieter, as he has information essential to our cause." Patrick again kept things vague.

"You are still cautious. Good, you will have to be. But also understand the risk I am taking here. You are not bound by the same sacrament. You may disclose our conversation to anyone you like. So please, be open and honest."

Susan did not wait for Patrick to answer. "We understand, Padre. Please be assured that we are promising you the same level of secrecy. As my colleague already mentioned, it is somewhat of a long story, but let me tell you this. My grandparents were executed just a couple of days ago. We do not know why, and now, their killer is after us. Dieter is our only hope to tell us what is going on. We need to resolve this somehow before this criminal catches up to us."

"So how is this killer connected to the Heydrich family?" the priest asked in a more ominous tone.

"We do not know. We just know that they are," Patrick

responded.

"If this killer is connected to the Heydrichs, you should run from them, not seek them out."

"We understand the delicacy of the situation, but it is the only way. Please, padre, please. We need your help," Susan pleaded.

"You are quite in a predicament. Damned if you do, damned if you don't." The priest brought everything to the point. He nervously shifted in his chair once again.

"Please tell us what you know," Patrick pressed the matter.

"Please tell us where we can find this Dieter," Susan doubled up.

"It is not that hard once you know what name to look for," the priest said without giving it much thought.

Of course! How could he be so shortsighted? The Heydrichs live under an assumed name. Patrick could scarcely believe such a possibility had slipped his mind.

"But be careful. The Heydrichs are well connected, and their reach goes deep into our society, today more than ever," the priest advised.

"We got a taste of that," Patrick responded, still a bit angry at himself.

"And with good reason," the priest raised his finger in caution. "Be aware they will do anything and everything necessary to protect themselves."

"And nobody is doing anything about them?" Susan objected. "The Mossad was hunting down Eichmann back in the sixties; they kidnapped him and brought him to Israel to stand trial. Why not the Heydrichs?"

"And Priebke, one of Heydrich's best friends, was caught right here in Bariloche in 1994," the priest added. "The Israeli secret service tried to get Heydrich, but after their first successful Nazi captures, Klaus made sure he was not going to be next. He fortified their home, added security surveillance, hired guards, organized a kennel of aggressive guard dogs, and called on Nazi sympathizers from all over the world to come and protect him. With great success, I might add. They quite literally flocked to his home. Even more effective, he got connected to every powerful person in the area.

Politicians, business owners, even law enforcement … you name it."

"We heard as much," Patrick responded.

"It pains me to say their long arms even reach into our church."

"How did they manage that?" Susan asked.

"Exactly the same as always. Money. Yesterday, you enjoyed our beautiful stained-glass windows. Guess who paid for them?"

"And the church accepted the gift?" Susan was outraged.

"Without hesitation. Not our finest hour, but I am quite alone in my opinion," the priest explained. "The Heydrichs have supported our diocese ever since. So much that we cannot exist anymore without their influx of cash. But not just us. They own so many local businesses; they are the biggest employer in the area. If they withdrew, our entire local economy would collapse. Everybody depends on them, directly or indirectly."

"And now we know why nobody is willing to talk," Patrick added. He had expected as much, but Susan was stunned.

"The Nazi reign may have ended in 1945, but do not underestimate this family. They are as ruthless today as they had been during the war," the priest continued his caution.

"Let me tell you; we take your advice to heart," Patrick reaffirmed. "To be honest, I … we expected as much."

The priest shook his head, somewhat consternated. "I don't think you do."

"Padre, we do, at least we do now," Susan tried to assure him.

"No, you don't! Or you would not be here. And this brings me to why I wanted to talk to you."

Patrick immediately knew what the priest was going to say next. "You are not going to tell us where Dieter is."

"I called you here to urge you to stop your search. Go back to your hotel, pack your bags, and get out of here because whatever your business with the Heydrichs is, it is not going to end well for you."

Susan, kneeling in the booth, was crushed, stunned in disbelief about what she was hearing. Was this just another dead end? It could not be. It just could not. Patrick, frustrated to his limit, was about to respond to the unexpected turn when Susan cut him off. "We already made it clear that this is not an option. We need to talk to Dieter, and we are not leaving until we do so. No matter the consequences because it is our only way out. There is no way we are going to let this go. And should you decide against helping and this killer catches up to us, our blood is on your hands." Susan surprised herself uttering the threat.

The priest let out a big sigh, took off his glasses, and started cleaning the lenses with his handkerchief. "I do not know what your business really is about, but I do know what the Heydrichs do with inquiring strangers. They will kill you for sure. If I do tell you where to find them, your blood would definitely be on my hands. I cannot let that happen."

The priest had a point. Patrick, not blindly trusting the clergyman, wondered if this was all just a stunt to throw them off track. "Padre, why are we here?"

"Because I want to save your lives."

"So you say, but why are you really sticking your head out for us? You don't even know us."

The priest put his glasses back on, adjusted his position once again while clearing his throat. "I see. You think I am one of them. You think I am doing this to protect the Heydrichs."

"Are you?" Susan pressed the clergyman.

"I understand why you may think that. But you are wrong. God be my witness; I swore my oath to better this world. It's my true and only calling as I see the injustices, hypocrisies, sufferings …" He again moved uncomfortably in his seat. "When I was young, I expected life would eventually allow me to understand people, how they think, and more importantly, why they act as they do. I thought that one day I would find an all-encompassing logic. How naive I was! The older I get, the more common sense seems to be nothing but a myth. All I see are humans preaching peace but waging wars, showing off their generosity yet endlessly trying to empty everyone's pockets, and declaring themselves trustworthy yet stabbing each other in the back. It pains me to say my faith in humanity is all but gone. Yet I keep fighting despite how senseless it often seems."

"You lost your faith in humanity? Doesn't this conflict with your duties as a representative of the church?" Susan interrupted.

"On the contrary. You see, in my role as a priest I discovered

Jesus Christ, the real Jesus, a most humble man, yet the greatest one ever. What makes him so extraordinary are not the overly celebrated miracles but his simple common sense, his unquestionable compassion for humanity, his exhaustive passion for the welfare of others, a fact that could not be more clearly reflected in the way he lived and, even more so, died. And this really is all he ever needs to be. The Jesus you know is a holy man, sent from God, conceived by a virgin, performing miracles, even rising from the dead. But it never made sense to me how a man like him, a man of such humility, could be portrayed as this seemingly out-of-this-world, greater-than-human being. Once you start to isolate his parables from the widely depicted glory of how he is portrayed, you begin to see a very different kind of leader. One that did not need to be conceived by a virgin, turn water into wine, walk on water, heal incurable ailments, nor even be resurrected. You start to see a man not sent by God but one who discovered God, inside him, making him wise and compassionate, and so much bigger and more powerful than he is currently presented. This, my friend, is the real Jesus, the one for me, the one who can teach life's true lessons to enter the kingdom of heaven, the one that I believe truly existed. And mark my words; this is the Jesus people are now gradually discovering. Our religion truly is sacred—a positive force—but the current teachings from our podiums are contradictory, and people are catching on. Why do you think our church is experiencing such a mass exodus worldwide?"

The priest shook his head, his inner struggle reflecting his deep conflict with the very organization he was a part of. He needed to calm himself somewhat before continuing. "Don't get me wrong, I know of many good people in our church, people who fight tirelessly every day for the well-being of others. I applaud them as the true leaders. My loss of faith in humanity is not a capitulation but the very fuel of my fight, right here, at the very front, to give our followers the support they so desperately need. It is nothing more than a strong indication that I am truly needed, that so much more work needs to be done."

Both Susan and Patrick were taken by the priest's convictions. Before them was a broken man, but one who had not yet given up on doing the right thing.

The priest tightened his grip on the handkerchief in his hand. "At the time of Jesus, there was no bigger outcast than a prostitute. Yet he extended his helping hand. And what are we doing today? We discriminate against everyone who is different and turn away people in need. Many curse the poor, pointing fingers, saying it is their own fault. People with better fortunes still revel in the perverted belief that they were chosen by God to have a better life. What fools! They were not blessed with wealth, but with the ability to give, to share, to support the less fortunate. The teachings of Jesus could not be any clearer. *It is easier for a camel to go through the eye of a needle than for a rich man to enter the kingdom of God.* Do these people really think they can fool our father in heaven by pretending to be Christians? It's not the unconditional belief in him that really counts but your actions, and nothing but. That is where the truth lies."

The priest dried his eyes with his handkerchief. "What I am trying to say is … I fight my small fights in my small world. Now, I was given the opportunity to save you, and God forgive me if I don't. So please, I am begging you, please, pack your bags and get out of here."

9:01 AM
Private Residence of the Bishop

"I have been holding mass here every Sunday for the last fifty-three years. I am certainly not going to skip it today," the bishop shouted angrily into the phone.

"Alejandro, I understand. But it is better just to be careful," Klaus appealed to his unofficial friend. "We just need a few days to take care of things. For now, it would be better if you stayed out of sight. This journalist … well, from what I hear, he is good. He has a way of getting things out of people, things you do not want him to know. It is important we keep you away, just for a few days."

"And what am I going to tell my congregation? They expect to see me in church at 10:30 a.m. sharp. They will ask questions," the bishop responded with contempt.

"Harmless questions. There is a bigger picture here, and I need you to see it." Klaus began to cough and needed a minute to compose himself.

"I don't know what is going on, but you need to take care of this," the bishop insisted. "You promised me our friendship would never become a problem. If any of this comes back to me, God help us all."

"You worry too much, my friend. For now, stay out of sight. This is not a request, but an order."

The bishop slammed his phone onto the desk. He would not take orders from anyone but the pope himself … and this Klaus Heydrich. He had to, and it did not please him one bit.

9:03 AM
Cathedral of San Carlos de Bariloche

"Padre, your concerns are truly noted, but what you do not know is that I am trained and experienced in tactical operations. I well understand the risks of pursuing a person like Dieter, even more so without high-tech equipment and a trained support team. But these people will stop at nothing till the threat we pose is eliminated. So, we are going to do this with or without you. If you are truly interested in bettering this world, here is your chance to fight evil." Patrick did his best to convince the man behind the wooden grill. The clergyman listened, his right fist pressed against his lips, still tightly holding on to his handkerchief. His silence gave Patrick hope.

"Let me promise you one thing," Patrick pressed on. "If at any point the risks of our endeavor start to outweigh the reward, we will abort and leave right away."

The priest was taking his time, his conscience struggling for the right answer. "You truly are in quite a situation," he admitted. Another long pause followed. "I really do not know what to do."

"Padre, please, we really—" Susan urged the priest, but he immediately interrupted her.

"I will consider telling you what you came here for." His words were hesitant, he himself still full of doubt.

"Thank you so—"

Again, the priest interrupted Susan. "But not before you hear me out. You have clarified your position, now let me do mine. You can then make an informed decision because only then I can leave this booth with a clear conscience." Both Susan and Patrick agreed. The priest took another moment, the suspense gnawing on Susan's nerves.

"Back in 1960, just after the successful abduction of Eichmann, the Israeli secret service got a lead on Klaus Heydrich, many suspected from Eichmann himself. They immediately started a covert operation, top secret and all, with an entire team of agents right here in our town. But Klaus was one step ahead. As I have already told you, he learned the lessons from Eichmann's capture and put the necessary measures in place. The Mossad could not even get close to him."

"Padre, please excuse me for being straightforward. But since it was a top-secret mission, how do you know about it?" Patrick interjected. "I mean no offense, but—"

"I did not hear about this till years later, till the late eighties. I was just a teenager back then, interning at one of the local newspapers. Late one evening, while we were all working overtime on a breaking story, a messenger dropped off a package. It turned out to be from a recently fired, disgruntled Heydrich employee. For what he was fired, I do not know."

"What was in the package?" Susan jumped the question.

The priest held his hand up, signaling her to let him tell the story. "As everyone was busy with the deadline, I was told to pre-screen its contents. I was the first to see what I can never forget, what nobody that was there that night can ever forget."

The priest once again dried his eyes with the handkerchief, fighting what he had suppressed for so long.

9:07 AM
Private Residence of the Bishop

The provincial stepped forward and offered the bishop two pills and a glass of water. "Here, your Excellency, these will calm you."

Bishop Casillas was standing next to his phone, hunched over, his fists on the desk, his face blazing red in anger. He declined the pills with a dismissive gesture. It was not the bishop's first outburst. They had gotten more frequent over the years.

"Your Excellency, I have to agree with him. You need to stay out of sight. It's just for a few days."

"WHO IS HE TO TELL ME WHAT TO DO?" the bishop yelled, staring straight ahead at the window.

"You are quite right. Nevertheless, it is better not to interact with this journalist, considering—"

"And who will hold mass today?"

"I will," the provincial proposed, him being the obvious choice.

"The 10:30 is my mass. Nobody else's."

The provincial nodded. "You are quite right."

"What will you tell them?" the bishop asked, defeated.

"I will say you are a bit under the weather. Nothing to worry about but that you prefer to rest for the day."

"I don't like it, not one bit. It makes me look weak. Can a man in my position look weak?" he snubbed the provincial.

"They were here only yesterday, standing inside your own church, your Excellency. They are already too close. I even had to tell them you are out of town. If they find out this was a lie, they will draw conclusions. Something to be avoided at all cost."

"Of course," the bishop answered arrogantly. "Nevertheless, I still don't like it."

9:10 AM
Cathedral of San Carlos de Bariloche

Susan saw the clergyman struggle with the weight of his memories, and her conscience started to weigh on her for pushing this man so deep into his emotional turmoil.

"Padre, if you prefer not to tell us, we understand. We do not want to open old wounds."

Patrick could not believe what he was hearing and threw her a dismissive look. He was not sure she noticed in the dim light.

"This is kind of you, but I feel I have to," the priest responded.

"You decide, Padre," Susan said again trying to take the pressure off him. Patrick ungently shoved his elbow into her arm, again in the hope she would stop discouraging the priest. Susan elbowed him right back. Her intervention had the effect Patrick was worried about as the priest took another moment to contemplate.

"No! The story needs to finally be told," the priest decided, very much to Patrick's relief. "Do you know which is *the* most wanted Nazi memorabilia? The one so desirable, collectors would sell their soul to the devil to get their hands on it?"

"The gun Hitler killed himself with?" Patrick guessed.

"One of Hitler's uniforms?" Susan ventured her guess but really had no idea.

"Both good choices, but no. Let me give you another hint. It is the object everybody is looking for but no one knows where it is."

Neither Patrick nor Susan could come up with another guess.

"The medical suitcase of Dr. Mengele. The very tools used in the torturous medical experiments in the concentration camps, causing the agonizing death of countless prisoners, mostly children. It is the absolute holy grail of fascist collectables, worth millions. Officially, it is lost, but it is not. Klaus has it."

"How do you know?" Susan asked.

"Once the Mossad heard people were flocking in to protect the Heydrichs, they had two of their agents go undercover and join his army of volunteers. I do not know how, but the agents were compromised. You can imagine how livid Klaus was. You can also imagine what happened next. Klaus had them strapped onto torture chairs and then personally started to work on them with the medical instruments of Dr. Mengele—the very tools that had caused suffering to so many of their people already. One cannot send a stronger message."

Susan started to have her own difficulties with the story. Now aware of her grandmother's heritage, it hit too close to home.

"The two agents were tortured to death, as slowly and painfully as possible. Pulling teeth and fingernails, beatings, burnings, electro shocks, drillings ...."

The priest gave himself another moment, catching a deep breath and struggling with his own words. "But it was not the torture alone. Klaus carefully documented everything, took detailed notes, as well as pictures and movies, those old Super 8 ones, and sent them to the Mossad agents in town daily to confront them with the deteriorating condition of their colleagues. They were absolutely enraged but could do nothing but helplessly witness their colleagues' excruciating deaths. Their bodies were found days later, discarded in a riverbed nearby. The coroner confirmed they were skinned alive. It did not miss its effect. Against the desperate pleas of the agents in town, the Mossad decided to abandon the mission and withdraw the team."

By now, the priest's voice was shaking, his eyes filled with tears again. "Inside this package I was asked to open were copies of those very documents, pictures, and movies. I never knew people could be so evil." Through the wooden grid, Susan could see the priest again pressing the handkerchief against his lips, fighting back tears. "There, on one of these pictures, was Klaus standing next to his victims, the medical bag with the insignia of Dr. Mengele clearly visible."

Dead silence filled the confession stand. Nobody could get themselves to speak.

9:12 AM
Private Residence of the Bishop

"These Heydrichs ... sometimes I wish they had never come here in the first place," the bishop continued his rant. "And how dare Klaus call me by my first name? God himself, and only him, has chosen me to be the leader here, not Klaus. Nobody is exempt from calling me 'Excellency.'"

"I quite agree, but just think of all the things your friendship with Klaus has done for our church here. Without the Heydrichs, we would be a very different congregation today."

"And this is exactly the problem. We have gotten addicted to his donations, making us slowly slip into dependency. He knew exactly what he was doing, this man, and I was too blind to see it. I am in charge, and nobody else. Do you hear what I am saying? I am in charge, NOT HIM!" the bishop shouted again. "Why can't the people of our congregation donate more? After all, the poor need our prayers the most."

9:14 AM
Cathedral of San Carlos de Bariloche

It took a good minute for the priest to get himself together. "It was the most pivotal moment of my life. After seeing all this evil, I made a vow to do whatever I could to better this world, to help in any way I could. You ask me for my help. All I know is this killer chasing you cannot be any worse than the Heydrichs. I could not live with myself if you two ended up in the same riverbed. I am urging you— no, I am begging you. Forget Dieter. Leave. Get out while you can."

The priest hunched forward, drained both physically and emotionally. Recalling the story had taken its toll. But now that it was told, maybe a time of desperately needed healing was ahead of him.

Susan took a deep breath and hoped Patrick would be okay with what she was about to say. "Listen, Padre, we would like to thank you for sharing your story. I can tell it was not easy. But it has not changed our situation. If not for myself and Patrick, I owe it to my dead grandparents to see this through."

Patrick was relieved to hear Susan's insistence. He was worried the priest may have changed her mind. The clergyman once again fell into his thoughts. Susan and Patrick were waiting. Time passed, second by second.

"Please, Padre, at least let us know what name the family now lives under. You said yourself this was the key to finding Dieter."

Again, a few seconds passed.

"You are going in the right direction, but these were not my words," he corrected Patrick.

The two waited patiently in the tense silence. *Not my words? Yes, they were.* Was the priest regretting his remarks? Patrick was puzzled.

"I will pray and ask God for your protection and to help you find your salvation. But I cannot let you walk into this lion's den; you will be eaten alive. So, I am begging you to leave this town at once." Without saying another word, the priest hastily exited the booth and ran into the sacristy. Patrick kicked the wooden wall inside the booth. So close, so damn close ….

9:45 AM

The Eyebrew Coffee Shop

Susan and Patrick went straight up to the bar of the coffee shop, but there was no sign of the waitress.

"I am sorry, she is off on Sundays. Anything I can I help you with?" the new barista responded to their inquiry. Susan was about to ask where they could find her, but Patrick immediately interrupted her.

"Will she be back tomorrow?" The waitress confirmed that she was scheduled for the early shift. Again, Susan was about to ask, and again, Patrick quickly interrupted.

"We forgot to tip her yesterday and feel bad. Would you please give her this?" Patrick handed her a ten-dollar bill.

"How generous," the barista responded. As soon as they walked out the door, Susan protested. "Why did you keep interrupting me?"

"Let's not be too obvious we are looking for her. People may not be willing to talk, but they are always willing to listen. We can come back tomorrow. For now, let's go back to the hotel."

6:15 AM (PDT)
LAX Airport—Los Angeles

Hironori was in the queue in front of the airlines check-in desks. The line was long despite the early hour. Now nearly in the front, he was again cursing the wait when his phone went off. Hesitantly, Hironori pushed the green button.

"Are you vacationing in Argentina?"

Hironori turned as pale as a sheet, the full weight of the situation hitting him at once. It was as clear as crystal. His boss knew. Equally clear were the inevitable consequences. Trust, honor, and respect were above everything, and he had broken all three.

"Why would you think I am going to Argentina?"

"Because a bishop does not lie." The line went dead. The ultimate punishment for his insubordination was now awaiting him back home; nevertheless, he could not return without the mission completed. Above anything, it was a matter of honor, and Hironori hoped to salvage at least a little of his heavily tarnished reputation. An overly friendly airline employee waved him to the check-in counter.

"May I see your ticket and passport please?"

10:30 AM (ART)
Patrick's Hotel Room

Susan was sitting on the sofa, staring at her bottle of water. "Do you think the priest was right? Would it be better to solve this on the other end?"

"The end with the Japanese guys? At this moment, we know the killer is after us. Dieter is not—we are after him. We just need to let them know, somehow, that we mean no harm. Despite what this family is capable of, I'd say we are doing the right thing."

"Then we really need to know what alias they live under," Susan repeated the obvious.

"I agree, it is key. The priest made it sound like this family is hiding in plain sight."

"Do you have any idea what it could be?"

"It must be something inconspicuous; anything else would not make any sense. But this does not narrow it down. On the contrary," Patrick was thinking, asking himself what name he would adopt given the situation. "Chances are it resembles something of their heritage. Like a typical German name but translated into Spanish. But who knows? It could be anything, really."

Susan seemed resigned. "The possibilities are endless."

"Don't give up hope just yet," Patrick said, trying to lift her spirits. "Something will show up. Meanwhile, let's make the best of our time today. Why don't you study the map, come up with a few routes to check up the estancias in the area, while I start doing my homework on the bishop here. Hopefully he will soon grant us an audience. If not, we will at least be ready to start our tour right away."

Susan agreed. "You know, I was hoping we could ask around some more, but after hearing the story of those two agents ... no wonder everyone is tight-lipped. It explains why our waitress is careful, but I have feeling she knows more than she lets us believe."

"She might. It is definitely worthwhile going to see her again." Patrick shifted his focus to the map and studied at it for quite a while. "I get this nagging feeling something is staring us right in the face, and we are just not seeing it."

17

September 5, 2017—8:15 AM (ART)
The Eyebrew Coffee Shop

Susan and Patrick entered the coffee shop and were relieved to see their waitress, busy preparing an order. She was dressed in her typical style, this time in a bright green shirt, a knee-length black skirt, thick, equally bright green stockings, and her hair in a braid all the way down to her waist. She did not seem happy to see them, even ignoring them at first. Then, without a greeting, she asked for their order. It was not the expected welcome.

"Are you okay?" Susan asked, wondering what was going on.

"What can I get you?" she asked again coldly. Susan could tell she was trying to act normal but noticed an ever-so-slight tremble, not in her voice but in her hands. "What is going on?"

"What would you like?" she responded, then specifically emphasized "To go." Patrick had a feeling he knew the reason for her unusual behavior.

"Okay, if someone from the Heydrichs paid you a visit, I would like a tea. If someone from the church is threatening you, I'd like a coffee."

"Tell me what you would you like—to go!" the waitress repeated her request.

Now Patrick was puzzled. She obviously wanted them to leave, but why? Then Susan put in her order.

"If a Japanese man was here, may we have two coffees and two croissants?"

A minute later the waitress handed her two coffees, with lids on the cups, and two croissants in a to-go bag.

8:19 AM

Susan and Patrick hurried toward the car. Patrick jumped in, and so did Susan. He started the engine and quickly drove off.

"We need to get out of here!" Patrick said, somewhat out of breath.

"Wait a second. We still need to talk to Dieter."

"Remember when I said what was going to happen should the risks outweigh the benefits? I meant it."

"Yes, but we both agreed we will see this through."

"We will, but forget Dieter for now. We are no closer to him than when we arrived; on the contrary, worse, our main hope for help has now been silenced. I am just grateful she is still alive. We were wondering how much time we had down here. The clock has just run out. We need to leave and regroup, if to just keep ourselves alive."

Patrick raced the car back to the hotel where they hastily packed and settled the bill, and then sped to the airport. One hour later, they were boarding the first flight out. They did not care about its destination—only that the plane left right away.

The Embraer RJ-190 was one of the smaller planes, perfect for local flights like the one they were on. The few seats still available were toward the back of the plane, but Susan did not care. Patrick would have preferred to be nearer the entrance, just to keep an eye on the people still boarding. The official departure time had passed, and the two hoped for the doors to close, but to their dismay, they stayed open.

"What is the holdup?" Patrick asked Susan while looking at the flight attendants chatting and laughing the time away without a care in the world. Finally, to their relief, the captain announced they would be ready to push back from the gate shortly.

Susan finally started to relax. So did Patrick, now reflecting on the latest developments. A name, just a name, was all they needed. The priest said so. They were so close, but they now seemed further away than ever. His thoughts were interrupted by the flight attendant, who was making sure everyone was wearing a seatbelt and that no carry-on luggage was blocking any of the exit routes.

"What was the holdup?" Patrick asked the woman in uniform.

"We mistakenly had a suitcase on board that was supposed to be on another flight. But don't worry; it was taken off the plane. We should be off in a minute or two now." Patrick's thoughts went back to their conversation with the priest. *You are going in the right direction, but these were not my words.* Was the priest really just worried he had unveiled too much? Or did he mean something else entirely? *Not my words.*

Susan could see the airport workers on the tarmac getting ready for the plane to be pushed back. The captain was once again on the public address system apologizing for the delay, announcing the flight time to their destination and the expected weather en route, and wishing everyone a pleasant flight. The flight attendant was about to finally close the door when Patrick jumped from his seat.

"WAIT! HOLD THE DOOR. We have to get out."

Susan looked at him like he was crazy. So did everyone else.

"What are you doing? Shut up and sit down, we are about to take off," Susan said, embarrassed, but Patrick had already opened the luggage compartment above him.

"Grab your stuff. We need to get out."

"Why?" Susan asked, baffled as one could be and quite embarrassed about the commotion Patrick was causing.

"I know where to find Dieter."

Part IV

A New Truth, Yet Still a Lie

18

Officers Wing, Room 474, Russian Military Headquarters, Warsaw

Lieutenant Colonel Grisha Vasiliev was the newly appointed head of the Russian military police in Poland. He and Colonel General Ivan Evanoff had met years ago in the academy at the beginning of World War I and had been friends ever since. When Ivan was tasked with organizing the military governance in Poland after its taking, he knew there was no better candidate for the job than Grisha. The work required a sharp and analytical mind combined with the tenacity of a bulldog. Vasiliev fit the profile perfectly.

"Ivan, I was told you have a situation on your hands?"

"Grisha, please have a seat," Ivan welcomed him into his office while hastily clearing some paperwork off his desk. He then picked up his humidor and, with an open lid, held it toward his friend. "Cigar?"

"Don't mind if I do." Grisha gladly accepted the rare commodity. "Romeo y Julieta. Impressive. What is the occasion?"

Ivan did not respond. He took one for himself, despite his somber mood, and the two ceremonially lit their full-bodied roll of tobacco. Grisha leaned back in his chair, savoring the creamy, earthy taste while the room filled with a cloud of smoke. Ivan, with his elbows on his desk, started his briefing.

"A little over thirty hours ago, I was awoken by a call from the very top, Central Command in Moscow, top secret, and informed our frontline logistics unit had intercepted a train near Lodz trying to break through our lines into German territory. I was given the order to inspect its cargo, and then report back."

Grisha shook his head.

"If I had a ruble for every time I was asked to check out a train—or truck, car, plane, building, you name it. I tell you right now, and this comes from experience, it's a waste of time. The Germans are too efficient to ever leave anything of value behind," Grisha was laughing, still shaking his head. "Checking out a train … come on."

"My very first reaction also. But soon after, the matter was assigned to intelligence. You know what that means."

"Intelligence?" Grisha raised both his eyebrows in surprise.

"Yes, and they do not get involved for no reason. I also asked myself why this particular train had tried to break through our lines because under normal circumstances war equipment left behind is either blown up or just … left behind." Evanoff paused to take a puff of his cigar. "Now listen to this. The crew were all part of a German special-forces unit, parachuted in behind our lines with strict orders to get this train back home at all costs. The planning and execution of their mission were immaculate, but luck was not on their side. One of our soldiers at that particular checkpoint used to be a specialist in the People's Commissariat for Internal Affairs forgery unit. By pure coincidence, he was on duty that very evening, filling in for a sick friend. He noticed a small mistake on the otherwise high-quality copy of the transit papers." Evanoff took another puff. "As you can see, this was not just an ordinary train."

"Hmm … this is quite a story," Grisha responded in a very different mood.

"Now …" Ivan gave his friend a worried glance.

"Now what?"

"I sent one of my men to go inspect the train. Now … the train is missing. It just disappeared into thin air. My first thought was there must be an innocent explanation, but then an incident at the

Traugutta rail line checkpoint, just south of the Vistula Bridge, was reported to me. One soldier dead, the other injured."

"Yes, I heard. Did the German send in a backup team?"

"That could be a logical conclusion. But there is more."

"More?"

Ivan nervously took another puff. "Unfortunately, yes. This morning I was briefed that the train was moved by orders of the very man I had sent to inspect its cargo. As coincidence would have it, I ran into him less than two hours ago, right here in our lobby. I ordered him to come to my office and brief me right away. Not only did he not show, he is now missing, and so is one of our prisoners."

Alyona entered and served coffee.

"Yes, Timofei Sobchak," said Grisha. "Everyone seems to like him around here. Hmm … and a prisoner too?" Grisha wished there was milk and sugar, but he stirred the brew even without, out of habit.

"As you can see, this is somewhat … embarrassing. I will have to explain all this to Central Command, how we … well, how I lost this train. I cannot stress enough the importance of having this resolved before my report is due. We need to have the cargo identified, and Private Sobchak and prisoner Horowitz brought back here to headquarters. The sooner the better."

"This is quite a situation." Grisha pressed his lips together as he stirred his coffee. "Be assured my department will do whatever is necessary." Grisha's assurance did not do much to calm Ivan. "Let me ask you this," the MP leader continued. "Was this special-ops team interrogated?"

"Unfortunately, we were unable to do so. They did everything to avoid capture. All died in the shootout."

"I see. Well, let me know where you want me to start." Grisha hoped Ivan could send him in the right direction as he was still acclimating to his new position.

"I believe we can safely assume all these events are connected," Ivan stressed his concern.

Grisha agreed.

"Other than last night's event at Traugutta checkpoint, have any other unusual activities been reported? From any other checkpoints?"

Ivan shook his head.

"In that case, I am quite certain the train is somewhere between this checkpoint and the ones at the city limits."

"Unless some lazy guards did not do their job and just let the train pass," Ivan expressed his concern as he placed his coffee cup back onto his desk. "Nevertheless, I suggest you have your MPs follow the tracks, split at every switch, without exception, and hopefully we will soon find this train. With any luck, we will be one step closer to our fugitives, too."

Grisha picked up the receiver of Ivan's phone and held it up. "Do you mind?"

"Be my guest." Ivan gestured for him to go ahead.

The MP chief asked the operator for the Traugutta checkpoint. After a few rings, he spoke to the unit on scene and instructed the leader to start the search without delay. He then, once again, stirred his hot cup of coffee. It helped him think. "Ivan, why do you think Private Sobchak busted Horowitz out of prison? Why would he do something like that?"

Ivan shrugged. He had not yet asked this himself. "To be honest, I have no idea."

"Well, I am assuming he has served under you for some time now. You must know him. Is he the kind of person who would fall under the spell of a woman?"

"Aren't we all?" Ivan uncomfortably chuckled.

Grisha smiled. "I guess you are right."

"I do not know him privately, so it is hard to say. Maybe."

"Any ideological problems?" Grisha probed further. "Do you think this Tom works for the Germans?"

"Highly unlikely. I know he is a proud Russian serving our motherland with highest dedication. I have never heard him negatively comment on communism, our government, the war, or anything of the sort. Unless he is a master at deception, I can tell you for sure he hates the Nazis."

"If he is not a spy, I can think of only two possibilities. Either he is in love, or …."

"Or?"

"I am just wondering if we are looking at this the wrong way."

"What do you mean?"

"We know he busted her out. But what if, as strange as it may sound, it was him who convinced her to escape with him?"

"Interesting hypothesis," Ivan responded, blowing out more smoke. "But why would a prisoner with such a grim outlook have to be convinced to be busted out?"

"Well, 'convinced' may be the wrong word here, but you know what I am getting at."

"Tom is quite the wheeler and dealer, a shrewd businessman through and through, and he sure is up to something. Looking at a bigger picture, this could make sense. But why would he do that?"

"Because this Horowitz has something of interest to Private Sobchak, something he needs … or wants. Something important enough for him to risk his life to bust her out."

"Quite possible."

Grisha, with his hands on the chair's armrests, pushed himself up. "Well, we will find out sooner or later. Thank you for the briefing. We will get to work right away, and I will keep you updated on any developments. And please, you do the same."

Ivan agreed. Grisha grabbed his hat, placed it under his arm, sloppily saluted, and turned to exit.

"Before you leave, Grisha, I feel there is something I need to clarify. You are my friend, and I know I can trust you. I really need your help here."

"I understand." Grisha turned to give him a reassuring nod, then placed his hat neatly on his head.

"I don't think you do. I was given the order from Central Command to investigate the train."

"I understand, and you executed it. Things went a bit haywire, but we are going to fix it now."

Ivan, visibly uncomfortable, arose from his chair and walked over to his friend. "No, Grisha. I did not execute the order. I was *personally* given the order to check the train. But I am busy here, and to be honest, the trip to Lodz did not appeal to me with the inclement weather and all. So I sent Tom instead. Like you, I thought this was much ado about nothing."

"I see," Grisha responded, now realizing the true implications of the situation at hand.

"I need this train found. You can imagine what will happen to me if ...." Ivan did not dare to think of the consequences.

"Sure thing, Ivan," Grisha tried to reassure his friend again. "We will find them. Don't you worry!"

Warehouse, Kanal Zeranski

The area around the train depot was quiet; there was not a soul in sight. Tom drove through the big wooden gates and closed the doors behind him. Only the fresh tire tracks hinted at their presence, and they would soon be covered by the falling snow again.

"What are we doing here?" Rachel asked while climbing off the truck. She still had no idea what this was all about.

"Just close your eyes, will you? I will be right back. Don't peek!" Tom quickly ran to the train wagon, opened its lock, and retrieved the item from the crate he had opened in Lodz. "Remember; no peeking, okay?" he reminded her. Rachel nodded.

"Okay, open your eyes," Tom finally asked her in highest anticipation. For the first few seconds, she just stared. Tom could hardly wait for Rachel to say something. "What do you think?"

She at first did not know what to say. She simply stood with her mouth wide open, with no words forming.

"Oh my God!" She finally expressed her surprise, not knowing what else to say. "Is this ... is this a portrait of a child?" she wondered. In front of her was the most beautiful thing she had ever seen in her life—a striking painting, all in red tones, composed in a variety of shapes. She had seen landscapes, still life, and classical portraits, but never anything like this.

"Maybe!" Tom had no idea. "I believe it is what they call an abstract. I have seen similar pieces in an article about the State Heritage Museum collection in Leningrad." Tom turned the frame so he could have another look. For him, it was not just a painting. It was a representation of the future he had always dreamed of, the start of something new, the juncture in his life where he said goodbye to Tom the farmer and welcomed whatever the future had in store for him.

Officers Wing, Room 474

An MP entered Evanoff's office and interrupted the conversation. "I was looking for you, sir," he addressed to his direct superior. "There is something you need to know right away."

"What is it, comrade?" Grisha told his soldier to be at ease.

"Sir, the APB we have triggered for the two fugitives—it is useless."

"And why is that?"

"They are not traveling under their real names, sir. They are posing as a husband-and-wife couple under the names Stanislaus and Dimitra Montonov, with all the necessary paperwork to get through all the checkpoints throughout Russian-controlled territory."

Grisha furrowed his eyebrows. "Where is this information coming from? Is the source reliable?"

"As reliable as it gets," the MP replied. "On a hunch, we got hold of Tom's typewriter ribbon and reconstructed the imprinted letters. The impressions are miniscule, but enough to decipher. We managed to match the sequence of the words to our forms and have identified the ones that fit."

Grisha and Ivan glanced at each other, both impressed. "Excellent work, comrade. Keep it up. I'll be right over. You are dismissed."

"Sir, there is more."

"More?" Grisha gestured for the MP to continue his impromptu briefing.

"Tom also issued paperwork for two people to go to Moscow, to the People's Commissariat for State Security. One is a driver, the other a train engineer. Everything is ready to put out an APB for them also; we just need your signature."

Grisha now had more questions than answers. Why would Tom send people to Moscow? What made him involve State Security? Did it have anything to do with the train?

Ivan was in no mood to laugh but nevertheless had to chuckle. How bold of Tom. "There is no mission," he said, surprising both his friend and the MP.

"What are you talking about?" Grisha asked.

"Forget the trip to Moscow. It is a fake."

"A fake, sir? How do you know?" the MP inquired.

"Think about it. Tom could never have pulled this off on his own. These two—the driver and the train engineer—know the location of the train. He sent them away from us, as far as possible."

"We need to question them. The sooner the better. Go put all checkpoints on high alert. I'll be right down to sign the paperwork," Grisha commanded the private. The MP left at once.

Ivan, still in disbelief, was increasingly angry at himself. How could he have been so shortsighted? How could he send someone like Tom, an opportunist through and through, a top-class hustler, on such a delicate mission? Would one send an addicted gambler to a casino or an alcoholic to the liquor store? No. Certainly, there was no excuse for Tom's actions, but Ivan could not help but blame himself. Now, in hindsight, it struck him as all too obvious. He leaned back in his chair and rubbed his hands over his face from top to bottom.

"At least we know one thing for sure. This definitely is not a story about love," Grisha mentioned to his friend.

"Tom never struck me as a hopeless romantic," Ivan responded.

"It's a promising lead, these two, but Tom could be long gone before they turn up. We need to find out why Rachel is with him. Then we might manage to get a step ahead of them." Grisha put his cigar out in the ashtray on Ivan's desk. "I am going to sign that APB, then get a few of my men and meet you down in Tom's office. Let's turn everything upside down. Maybe we will find something."

7:46 AM

Administration Offices, Room 210

Ivan was already going through Tom's file cabinets when Grisha and his crew entered.

"Okay, comrades. Each one of you take a few folders and check them thoroughly. We need to find everything we can on prisoner Horowitz. Also pay attention to anything else you come across that strikes you as unusual."

Grisha watched his soldiers go to work. "I cannot believe how warm it is in here," he whispered to Ivan.

"Don't ask!" he replied, giving Grisha a disapproving look.

"Hmm … Rachel … Rachel … She had no money, no resources. It must be something intangible. Does she have connections?"

Ivan liked Grisha's line of thought. "Well, she was—*is*—a part of the Polish resistance."

"So, maybe Tom is hoping to tap into their resources to escape?"

"Possible, but unlikely. The resistance would not risk their relationship with us for an unknown fugitive. They have too much to lose."

"If it is not a 'who,' maybe it is a 'where'?"

"Where? What do you mean, *where*?"

"Well, if not a person, maybe it is a place?"

"Why would Tom need a pl—" Ivan stopped mid-sentence. "My God! Of course, a place. Rachel and her family were hiding from the Germans. Whatever is on that train, Tom would not be able to get it out of here, at least not now. He is going to stash it."

"You know, Ivan, you might be on to something," Grisha concurred.

"When it fits, it just fits, doesn't it?"

"Listen, soldiers. Hurry up! Look in every drawer as well as behind, under, to the left, and right. Turn over furniture if you must. The Horowitz file is in here somewhere. Find it!" With the MPs hard at work, Grisha once again turned to Ivan. He put his hand inside his jacket to reach his cigarettes, and then offered one to Ivan. Ivan politely declined.

"How can you smoke these?" Ivan asked his friend. "They taste like sandpaper."

"One can get used to anything, especially during a war," Grisha smiled as he put one between his lips. "But let me ask you, are you at all concerned about her?"

"Rachel? Why should I be concerned?"

"Well, if Tom was willing enough to kill a soldier at the checkpoint, what do you think will happen to her once she has fulfilled her purpose? He has no choice but to get rid of her. Or is Tom the kind of guy who would compromise his getaway?"

Grisha had a point, a good one.

"I am sorry, we looked everywhere. The file is not here," one of the MPs reported. To Ivan, it came as no surprise. The Tom he knew was thorough. The file was surely in the office, but probably inside the oven, now nothing more than ash. They had no choice but to wait for the driver and the engineer on their way to Moscow, even as their chance of catching the fugitive diminished with every passing minute.

But Grisha was not the type to wait around. "Isn't Tom the one who fills out the arrest reports we are looking for?"

"It is one of his duties," Ivan acknowledged.

"Well then, the typewriter ribbon may have more secrets to reveal."

7:51 AM

Warszawa Praga Depot, North of Vistula Bridge, Warsaw

The eyes of the two railroad workers met in a stare, each looking for a tell in the eyes of the other.

"Your hand is not that good. I call."

The man on the other side of the table threw his cards, swearing loudly. "How in the world did you know? Every day … every single day you win. That's it for me. No more playing cards with you."

"Better luck tomorrow," his comrade tried to entice him.

Still swearing and quite angry, the station attendant walked across the room and looked out the windows of the train switch track tower. Only one cigarette was left in his pack; all the others had been gambled away. He was contemplating keeping it for later but lit it anyway. He closed his eyes, took in a deep breath to enjoy the aroma, and while stretching out his arms, exhaled. When he opened his eyes again, he noticed some unusual activity on the tracks below. He took another deep breath, blew the warm air onto the glass, and with his sleeve wiped the frosty layer off the window.

"Hmm … look at that, comrade. MPs are walking the tracks. I wonder what is going on. Have you heard anything?"

"What should I know about anything? Leave me alone. Just don't forget to wake me up before the next trains are due."

"I am wondering if this has to do with the soldier at the checkpoint. Did you hear about that?" With his last cigarette burning in the corner of his mouth, he watched the soldiers check every single wagon at the station.

Warehouse

Rachel could not take her eyes off the painting. It was astonishing, its poetic beauty triggering emotional warmth she had not experienced since the start of this terrible war. Forms, colors, lines, textures, patterns all worked together to create what seemed to be a child's face. Many questions shot through her mind: Who was this person portrayed? Where was it painted? Who did it belong to? But most important of all, who painted it? She lifted the frame to find the signature at the bottom corner: *KLEE 1923*. A name she had never heard before. It was of an artist privileged with a truly divine talent.

Rachel was so deeply engulfed, she hesitated to let go when Tom took the painting from her hands. More questions entered her mind.

"Is the entire train filled with paintings?" she wondered.

"I do not know. It seems to be."

"And what do you have to do with all this?"

"That is a long story. But if you want to hear the short version, I kind of diverted it all."

"YOU STOLE THE TRAIN?!" She could not believe what she was hearing.

"Yes."

"And what are you going to do with it?"

"I am going to load as many crates as possible onto our truck here, and you are going to show me where I can hide them."

She was as flabbergasted as one could be.

"But for now, I need you to go over to that window and keep your eyes open. They must be looking for us by now. Let me know as soon as you see anything out of the ordinary, okay?"

She continued to stare at him in utter disbelief.

"Rachel, I really need you to …."

Still lost in her thoughts, she finally obliged. Tom tied one end of a rope around the big, heavy crate blocking the entrance of the first wagon, the other around the hitch of the truck, and pulled forward, inch by inch, till it finally crashed onto the ground with a thunderous noise. Tom kept pulling until it was well clear of the train, then parked the truck parallel to the wagon. One after the other, he moved the crates onto the flatbed. It gradually filled up. Curious, he wished he could peek inside every single one but knew there was not time to do so.

8:15 AM

Warszawa Praga Depot

"This is unit MP1027. We are done with the trains in this location. All findings negative. Heading out further north now. Next check-in in three zero," the search unit reported to headquarters.

"Affirmative. Have you heard from the guys going southeast?"

"Negative. I will let you know as soon as we do. MP1027 out."

The MP switched off the radio to preserve its battery, as the cold temperatures were always a challenge for the equipment. The search team soon reached another switch and once again split.

"Don't forget to launch your flares if you find anything," the commander reminded the two privates. "If not, return and catch up with us."

The pair separated from their unit and moved forward step by step, wading through the fresh snow, breaking often to catch their breath. Then, in in the distance, they could finally see the warehouse at end of the track.

9:05 AM
Warehouse

Rachel squinted her eyes.

"Tom, I see … looks like soldiers, but I am not sure."

Tom rushed over to the window to have a look.

"We are out of time. Keep your eyes on these men; let me know once they are closer, like one hundred feet away." He hurried back to the wagon and hastily loaded a few more crates onto the flatbed, as many as he could.

"They are coming closer. One hundred fifty feet. We'd better leave."

"Two more minutes."

"I don't think we have two more minutes," Rachel warned.

Tom was finally covering the crates with a tarp when Rachel started to open the big wooden gate. He stopped her just in time.

"No! Don't open the doors. Lock them! Then get into the truck. Hurry!" There were no keys to the locks but a mechanism with two big locking beams. It reminded her of the gates in old castles. Rachel rotated them into the locking position. No sooner did she finish than the door's handles were pushed down.

"Tom! Let's go! They are here," she whispered as loudly as she could while hurrying back to the truck. "How are we going to get out of here now, with the doors locked and all?" Tom got behind the steering wheel, happy with his bounty. With the flatbed fully loaded, Tom started the truck and, after struggling with the gear box one more time, stepped on the accelerator. With a roaring engine, the truck headed straight toward the doors, faster and faster. Thirty feet ... twenty feet ... ten feet ... Rachel realized what was about to happen.

"TOM! NO!" she screamed.

+ + +

The two soldiers tried to open the heavy doors, but no matter how much they pushed, the doors did not budge. They pressed their ears against the wood.

"I can hear something."

"Me too. What do you think is going on?"

"Hard to say. We need to get inside and check it out." There was only one other way to get the doors opened—by force. They stacked two hand grenades together and taped them to the door, pulled the pin, and bolted behind the stack of neatly packed railroad planks nearby. They both counted down. Four ... three ... two ... one ....

+ + +

Five feet ... two feet ... With a big, deafening noise, the doors splintered into thousands of pieces, big and small, flying through the air. The truck's windshield cracked and the fenders ripped off, along with the front bumper, grill, and headlights. Rachel screamed as both were thrown around the truck's cabin. Tom tried to regain control of the vehicle, struggling to get a good grip on the violently turning steering wheel. The truck hit the stack of planks with full force. Rachel, still screaming, watched the two soldiers scramble to get out of the way to save their lives. The heavy wooden beams flew through the air with such velocity they destroyed anything in their path. She looked on in horror, certain the soldiers had been hit, if not by the truck then by one of the planks. Tom finally regained control of the steering wheel without ever having taken his foot of the accelerator, forcing the truck to go full-speed ahead. Rachel, hoping for the best but fearing the worst, desperately tried to catch a glimpse of the two soldiers left behind. Were they injured? Were they dead? The broken side mirror was vibrating too strongly for her to make out anything. She turned to get a better look but could not see either of them. She did, however, see flares being launched into the sky.

"They really are looking for us, aren't they?" she asked nervously.

Tom nodded. "They sure are. And if you believe in God, any God, this is the perfect time to start praying. We are going to need it."

Once again, they disappeared into the city.

9:15 AM

Officers Wing, Room 474

Alyona stormed into Ivan's office. He was on the phone, but she did not care.

"They found the train. They found the train," she announced triumphantly, interrupting his conversation.

Ivan terminated the call right away. "Where?"

"The radio unit reported flares being launched by one of their patrol units by the harbor northwest of the Warszawa Praga Depot. They found it."

"Tell them to secure the area right away and let us know the second they have a positive ID on this train. Does Grisha know already?" Alyona nodded. Ivan thanked his assistant and requested a connection to the MP offices to check for any other progress. There was none. Worse, they'd had a setback. As it turned out, Tom had just recently changed the ribbon of his typewriter.

"We are currently going through all the trash containers hoping for the best," Grisha reported.

"And I am assuming no update on our two friends on their way to Moscow?"

"I wish I had better news, but no, not yet."

19

10:05 AM

The Hideout, Ursynow District, Warsaw

It seemed to take forever to cover the fourteen miles to the hideout. The snow was throwing the city traffic into chaos. Tom was irritated by their slow progress, but eventually, the two entered the Ursynow District, and Rachel directed Tom into a courtyard surrounded by a cluster of buildings. The descent into the basement was narrow and dark. The electricity was still out, the supply lines bombed and not yet restored, and the windows of the cellar were still covered from the now-lifted blackout. Tom removed the taped-on cardboard first, letting light penetrate the room through the narrow band of glass near the ceiling.

"Here it is," Rachel announced.

Tom looked around but could not make out anything that resembled a door or a hatch.

"Let's see if you can find it," she challenged him. For the first time he noticed a slight smile on her face. He paced around the room, checking every corner, every wall, every inch of the floor, but he failed to find the entrance. Then Rachel grabbed a small metal handle from behind one of the beams, put it inside a tiny gap between two floor bricks, hooked it, and pulled.

"Help me! It has a spring mechanism, but it is still heavy."

Tom was truly astonished. "I could have been in here for years and still not found it," he confessed. In his defense, it was impossible to spot. The floor was covered by bricks in various shades and colors, laid in a busy pattern, confusing the eye every which way.

10:15 AM
Officers Wing, Room 474

When Alyona entered Ivan's office again, he had been fiddling with the papers on his desk, but despite repeated reads he was too distracted to absorb the information.

"My dear, you'd better have some good news for me," he said as he glanced at her.

She could not hide her excitement. "Our unit reached the depot and positively identified the train."

Ivan let out a sigh of relief. This was a victory, but one too early to celebrate. Nevertheless, satisfied, he leaned back in his chair, hands behind his head and a confident look on his face. "You know, Alyona, my luck is finally turning around. I can feel it." He took a minute to enjoy the moment, then called his friend Vasiliev. "Do you have someone you can trust? I mean, really trust?"

"What do you need?"

"I need to go inspect the train, but with everything going on here …"

"Really? You should go yourself this time," Grisha advised his friend.

"I know I should. This is why I ask for someone that can really be trusted."

"I wish I could help, but I am new here. Seriously, you go. I will watch the fortress here."

"No offense, Grisha, but no, I cannot leave. I just can't." Ivan hung up. Alyona was standing in front of his desk, waiting to be dismissed. He stared at her, his fingers tapping on the desk, the wheels in his head turning.

"What?!" she asked, now feeling somewhat uncomfortable with the silent gazing.

"Alyona, I need you to do something for me."

10:20 AM
The Hideout

Tom was ecstatic. He did not expect the place to be so well concealed. He stuck his head through the unexpectedly big opening down into the room, pointing his flashlight in every direction. "You did good, Rachel. You did really good." However, there were still a few items in the room, no doubt belongings of her family. Tom was concerned about how being back in this place would affect Rachel. Unexpectedly, she seemed quite okay. He had seen traumatic events like this before, how the subconscious subdues, even hides, distressing memories, suppressing emotions as an act of self-preservation. All the items in the room were of a practical nature, except one. Caught in the beam of his flashlight, on top of a mattress, a small stuffed bear was smiling at him, undoubtedly a comforting toy to one of her younger brothers.

"Listen, I understand if you want to wait for me in the truck," he said, hoping to spare her whatever the toy may have triggered inside her.

"We do not have time for sentimentalities right now," she responded rather coldly, and without hesitation, she descended the ladder and started moving everything to the side.

11:15 AM
Officers Wing, Room 474

Finding the train was a huge win. Thanks to the good news, Ivan finally made some headway with his paperwork, only to be interrupted by another call. Vasiliev had an update.

"The MPs have found several ribbons, which is not surprising considering all the typewriters in this building. According to the logs, trash has not been collected since Horowitz was arrested, so we definitely have it. We just need to find the right one."

"Let me know when you do." Ivan once again stressed the urgency of the matter. He was now even more confident that everything would be resolved before his report to Central Command the next morning.

12:05 PM
The Hideout

Despite the cold temperatures, sweat was dripping from Tom's forehead from the heavy lifting. He had not slept in over thirty hours and not eaten since the day before. However, despite being tired and hungry, he had to keep going. Thankfully, Rachel was of great help, surprising Tom with the strength and stamina of her slender body. It would have been impossible to get the heavy items from the truck down the stairs and into the hideout all by himself. She truly came through, and soon they had the unloading down to a routine, each knowing what to do to expedite the process.

"Do you need a break?" Rachel asked Tom.

A woman two-thirds his weight and stature doing the same heavy lifting had just asked him if he needed a rest.

"Do you need one?" Tom countered, his ego slightly bruised.

All Rachel returned was a telling smirk, and they both continued with the task at hand. Tom would not admit it, but he sure could have used one, if only for a minute to catch his breath.

2:15 PM
MP Offices, Room 325

"Lieutenant Colonel Vasiliev, the prison guard from last night's shift is finally here," the MP informed Grisha. He was asked to enter and sit down. The soldier was clearly uncomfortable in his own skin, not knowing what this meeting was all about. He wondered if Tom had reported his indiscretion.

"Cigarette?" Vasiliev opened his silver case. The soldier politely declined, too timid to accept.

"Listen, I know this is a long shot. I have already asked your colleagues, and nobody was able to help. So, I hope you can. Have you, by any chance, ever talked to prisoner Horowitz?"

"We are not allowed to talk to prisoners, sir," the guard fearfully responded.

"I know the rules, comrade, but I also understand the rules are, well, let's just say not always followed. Believe me, this time I truly wish you had spoken to her. And let me assure you, you are not in trouble here."

The guard began to relax, asking the Lieutenant Colonel what kind of information he was interested in.

"I need to know where she and her family were hiding from the Germans," Vasiliev asked while laying his piercing eyes onto the intimidated man.

"Well ... I talked to her a little bit ..." The guard did not dare to look at Vasiliev. "But just a little!" he was quick to add. "To be honest, there was something about her ... I don't know how to describe it ..."

"Yes, from what I have heard, she is quite the temptation. Now, what did she tell you?"

"Well, nothing really ..."

Vasiliev walked over to the soldier. "Did she or did she not?"

"Well, she told me it was somewhere in the Ursynow District. But that is all."

"Nothing else?"

"No, I swear."

"Are you one hundred percent sure?"

The soldier nodded.

"Great, thank you. You've been of great help."

The soldier was visibly relieved. "Maybe I'll take that cigarette after all," he even dared to ask.

With large steps, the Lieutenant Colonel walked back behind his desk, sat down, pushed the intercom button, and summoned an

MP. Not two seconds later the door opened.

"Take the private downstairs and put him in a cell." The guard immediately looked from Vasiliev to the MP and back, dumbfounded, wondering what was going on.

"But you said …"

"I know what I said, Private. Rules are rules, and they are in place for a reason. I will see you in court." While the MP took the shaken guard into custody, Lieutenant Colonel Vasiliev called his deputy.

"Seal off the Ursynow District right away."

2:45 PM

Pole Mekotowskie Park, Warsaw

The numerous birds surrounding the two old men sitting on the park bench were begging for more food, but the friends had already dropped all the breadcrumbs they had. Food was rationed, yet they happily shared their sparse leftovers—here and there a few small pieces of bread, but mostly just crumbs—with the hungry birds. It provided a little bit of happiness in this otherwise bleak world, something to look forward to a few days a week. It also gave the two men a chance to reminisce about the good old times and their hope for a better future. Their chat was suddenly interrupted by several vehicles racing by. A few minutes later, the ground started to tremble, and their conversation was overpowered by tremendously loud engine noises. At once, all the birds flew to the sky, rattled by the commotion. A lengthy convoy passed them, truck after truck with tanks between, all fully loaded either with personnel or equipment. The two kept a close eye on the spectacle.

"This is like the day the Germans moved in," one shouted to the other, remembering the fateful day.

"What in the world is going on now?"

"It looks like something big."

3:15 PM

The Hideout

At first glimpse, Tom had wished the hideout was bigger. Nevertheless, they had managed, just barely, to get all the crates inside. He lowered the heavy door into its place, then exchanged a satisfied look with Rachel who was resting, sitting down.

"We did it," she said with relief.

"We sure did," Tom replied. "I could not have done it without you." He reached out his hand as a gesture of thanks.

Rachel did not reciprocate. "You can thank me once we are safely out of here."

Tom withdrew his hand.

"What are you going to do with all this?" Rachel pointed with her head toward the hatch.

"I don't know yet. Except the one, I don't even know what is inside these crates. I hope something of value."

"After all this, it better be!" Rachel chuckled.

"Whatever it is, it will have to wait till after the war." Tom again extended his arm to help her up, and this time she took advantage of the kind offer. They made sure the place looked like they had never been there.

"Thank you, Rachel. Thank you very much. I really mean it."

"No need. I owe you as much as you do me. Now let's get out of here." Rachel put the metal handle into the inner pocket of her uniform. "This should come with us."

3:43 PM

Section 8 Roadblock, Ursynow District

Lieutenant Kuznetsov was satisfied with the progress. His unit, like a dozen others in the area, had set up the roadblock in record time, which was not easy in this kind of weather. The entire operation seemed to go like clockwork, as it had in exhaustive trainings many times before. His asked his subordinate to line up his men, and then addressed them in his usual serious tone.

"As you probably have already heard, we are looking for two fugitives. One is a Russian soldier, a deserter, and the second a charged criminal, a girl in her teens. They are somewhere in this district. Listen carefully, and I cannot stress this enough. Keep your eyes and ears open. Follow up on anything and everything that looks out of the ordinary. Report back regularly. Now we are going to organize seven patrols of two men each. The rest will stay here with me, manning the roadblock. Just to be clear, nobody sleeps till they are in custody, do you understand?" A few minutes later, the patrol units spread out, as did other search parties all over the district, each eager to become the hero of the day.

The Courtyard

A few hundred feet away, Tom and Rachel both stared at the truck. They'd known it had taken a hit but had not yet noticed how badly damaged it really was.

"Do you think this banged-up thing can get us out of here?" Rachel wondered. It did look like something ready for the junkyard.

Tom shrugged. "It got us this far; hopefully, it will get us a bit farther. I am more worried about how much we are going to stand out with this thing. People will notice, and with everybody looking for us now ..."

"Well, we cannot just walk out of here."

"The truck it is then. I'll get it started. You go see if the street is clear."

Just a few seconds later, Rachel came in running back. "Quick, go park the truck over there, on the other side of the courtyard," she shouted at Tom.

"What is going on?"

"I'll explain later. Hurry!"

Tom complied, and then ran back to her.

"We need to get out of here," she said as he protested. "There is a roadblock just up the street, and a patrol is coming toward us right now. We only have seconds. We need to go."

"Go? I just moved the truck...."

"Come on, now!" Rachel shouted at him.

Tom was flabbergasted. "We need the truck. Without it—" Their eyes locked. For the first time, Rachel could see fear in Tom's eyes.

20

Russian Headquarters, MP Offices

It had been hours since the last update, and Ivan could not just sit in his office any longer. He decided to go down to the MP offices to check on the progress first hand.

"Things are moving nicely. The roadblocks are set up, and patrols are now combing the neighborhood." Grisha saw Ivan check his watch. Less than sixteen hours till his report to Central Command. "Calm down, my friend. We are close now. Just try to enjoy the hunt."

But Ivan could not. His excitement about the initial successes had faded, and with the clock ticking away, he was worried once again. He was taking in the busy scene inside the MP's operation room when one of the radios received a call. It was Alyona, reporting from the train depot.

"You would not believe what is on the train," she shouted into the microphone.

"Tell us already," Ivan responded impatiently.

"I expected some experimental, top-secret weapon or something like that. But no. It's artwork."

"Artwork?!" Ivan first thought he did not hear right. Grisha, next to Ivan, was equally struck.

"Yes, mostly paintings; I believe a few statues, enough for an entire museum. Well, not anymore. Except for some bulkier items, most of it is gone. But it is all very puzzling. It is destined for Berlin for no other than Joseph Goebbels, yet the artwork is the modern kind—you know… the kind the Nazis despise."

"You know, my friend, it all makes perfect sense now," Ivan scoffed in disbelief.

"You must be joking. Artwork?" Grisha still could not believe it. "How does this make sense?"

"You don't know?" Ivan was surprised. "This is how the Germans fund their war. They loot whatever they can, then sell the valuable items to fill their war chest. Rumors have it they are out of money, probably the very reason they are so desperate to get their hands on this train. They need these millions to keep the war going. And therefore, as you can imagine, High Command is equally desperate to prevent them from getting it."

"… because with no funds, it will handicap their war machinery, shorten the war, probably by months, and save countless lives."

Ivan nodded.

3:50 PM
The Courtyard

"Follow me," Rachel instructed Tom and disappeared into the building. *Great idea; back to the hideout,* Tom thought and ran after her. But instead of heading for the basement, she started to climb the stairs, passing one floor after another all the way to the top, and then up a pull-down ladder into the attic. She opened a skylight and climbed onto the roof, then further up the steep slope onto the ridge.

"I hope you are not afraid of heights," she warned Tom. Rachel's "just don't look down" did not help as the roof tiles were too slippery not to cause worry. While she moved comfortably along the ridge with the agility of a cat, balancing herself with her arms out by her sides, Tom had a very different kind of experience. His knees increasingly softened and eventually started to tremble. He got down on all fours, crawling forward inch by inch, scared to death, and quite embarrassed.

"We do not have all day," Rachel urged him along. She could not help but chuckle. This was a guy who had the nerve to steal a train carrying millions of dollars' worth of artwork, yet he could not handle heights. A few yards over, Rachel opened another skylight and climbed in. A minute later, Tom followed.

"You are full of surprises, aren't you?" Tom was relieved to be off the roof.

"I guess I am," Rachel responded.

"Please tell me there is another way out of here," he pleaded.

Rachel shook her head. "Not unless you want to burst through the wall. This room is completely separated from any other space in the building, and with good reason." She lit a few candles, then shut the blacked-out skylight.

4:05 PM
Section 8 Roadblock

Kuznetsov was sitting inside the small temporary guard hut, a structure designed for protection from the ice-cold winds. He opened his wallet and gazed at the picture of his fiancée. How he missed her; how he longed to hold her in his arms and whisper sweet words into her ear. He gently glided his finger over her long hair and took comfort in how proud she was of him, serving Mother Russia as the dedicated lieutenant he was. In reality, he cursed the war and could not wait for it to be over. He wanted nothing more than to go home. Yet, if his unit could arrest the fugitives, it would without a doubt impress Lieutenant Colonel Vasiliev, maybe enough to finally get his long overdue promotion. How exciting it would be to share such news with his dearest. He was still staring at the photo, his mind deep in the memories of past times, when the radio suddenly received a transmission. As always, the reception was terrible—only fragmented bits and pieces were intelligible—but he heard enough for him to jump to his feet.

4:12 PM
Hidden Attic

The room was small, dusty, and cold, like any typical under-the-roof space. Nothing was insulated; the roof tiles were their only cover from the weather outside. An old carpet covered most of the floor, and the walls were overlaid with egg cartons, both acting as rather crude soundproofing. Rachel removed the old linen sheet covering whatever was on the table. To Tom's surprise, a long-range radio appeared.

"Go to the generator and put your muscles to work. This thing needs power," Rachel whispered, instructing Tom to operate the crank, its mechanism feeding the battery pack. She put the headphones over her ears and pushed the radio's power button. The unit lit up. She positioned the frequency wheel and started to push the Morse code transmitter in a specific sequence. A minute later she repeated it, trying once more. With no response, she turned the radio off again.

"I am off the usual rendezvous time. We will have to try again later," she said, explaining the failure to make contact.

"Keep going. They must hear you eventually."

Rachel shook her head. "Bad idea. You do not want to give the Russians the opportunity to ping our location."

Quite exhausted, the two sat on the floor, each leaning against one of the massive wooden columns supporting the roof. Rachel's eyes were closed when the distinct sound of shouting soldiers interrupted the silence. Tom looked at his companion. She glanced right back. They both knew what it meant: The truck. They had found the truck.

4:30 PM

The Courtyard

Kuznetsov stood in front of the badly damaged vehicle, in disbelief it could still run. His unit reported there was no cargo on it, as expected, but that the engine was still warm. With a pounding heart, he asked his unit to line up once again, and from the flatbed of the truck ordered them to start searching the buildings.

"Comrades, you know what the truck here means. The fugitives, as the artwork, are right here in our section, and we are going to find both. I cannot stress this enough—look everywhere; do not stop till they are found, and report anything that strikes you as unusual, no matter how minute or unimportant it may seem! Now go find them."

As his unit disbursed, Kuznetsov walked over to the communications soldier and personally informed headquarters of the latest developments.

4:55 PM

MP Offices, Room 325

Under normal circumstances, Grisha would leave the office around five o'clock and head back to his quarters, put up his feet, and enjoy a shot of vodka, but for now, tea would have to do. The latest update was promising, yet he was happy not to be in Ivan's shoes. On the other hand, as chief of the MP division, in charge of catching the renegades, his head was on the line too. It was time to pull an ace out of his sleeve—the newly integrated search-and-rescue specialists. They had arrived only recently with their sensitive listening technology to triangulate the source of the minutest soundwave traveling through objects. Working with trained rescue dogs, the groundbreaking equipment had proven highly effective in locating comrades trapped under collapsed structures. They were equally efficient in finding hiding fugitives. Grisha looked down into the vehicle park and watched the unit get ready to move out.

"All this for two people. Good God! Why can't this Tom just do all of us a favor and give himself up?" He was shaking his head.

"Wishful thinking, Grisha, wishful thinking," Ivan replied.

"The district is locked down. The specialists are on their way. He is done."

"Or so you might think. Knowing Tom ..." Ivan cautioned.

5:25 PM

The Attic

The commotion in the courtyard was still going on. The risks of breaking radio silence were high, but Rachel had to get her message out. She went back to the radio and pushed the sequence of clicks, then pressed the headphones against her ears. She kept repeating her call until; finally, she got an answer. Relieved, she took the microphone.

"This is Gray Mustache ... Gray Mustache." Her call sign was acknowledged with two clicks.

"3–2–2. 7–4–5. 1–2–8. 1–5–2. 4–4–5."

It did not make any sense to Tom. But whoever received the message repeated the numbers, and Rachel confirmed with a double click, just before she powered the radio off.

"What now?" Tom asked.

"Now we wait."

"... and pray we are not found."

5:30 PM

MP Offices, Room 325

"Lieutenant Colonel Vasiliev, we have just tracked unauthorized radio activity out of the Ursynow district. I thought you ought to know," the private reported.

"It's not one of ours?"

"Sir, it was an unusually strong signal. We do not have such powerful equipment anywhere near there."

"It must be one of the resistance's then," Evanoff noted.

"I would agree, but they ceased radio communications the day the Germans were pushed out of here."

"But Horowitz, being a member of the resistance, would have access to such equipment," Grisha speculated.

"Yes, sir, she would," the private responded.

"Were you able to ping the position?"

"Only the direction from our station. The transmission ended before our other units could locate the signal."

"Does the direction correspond with Kuznetsov's search area?" Grisha wanted to know.

The solider took the rolled-up map from under his arm and put it on the desk. "The red line here is the direction of the transmission. As you can see, it goes straight through the courtyard where the truck was found."

"So, we are on the right track?" Ivan asked for confirmation.

"Yes and no. This is the courtyard here." The soldier outlined the area, then marked an X inside. "And this is the corner where the truck was found. Kuznetsov's unit is currently searching these buildings, right next to the truck." The soldier added a few more Xs to the map. "However, when you look at the direction of the transmission, it is shown to have originated from the other side of the courtyard," he added.

"What is the margin of error?"

"If the transmission was indeed from our fugitives, I can tell you with certainty we are currently searching the wrong place, sir."

Grisha kept his eye on the map, contemplating what to do.

"What was communicated?" Ivan wanted to know.

"First only a few clicks, which is standard handshake protocol. Then a fifteen-digit number, five sets of three. The voice was that of a young female, the responding one of a male."

"Horowitz!" Ivan blurted out. "It has to be her."

"There is one more thing that struck me as unusual, sir," the soldier continued.

The Lieutenant Colonel looked up from the map. "Yes?"

"While the signal was strong, the sender's voice was, well, low.

Whoever sent the message was whispering."

"Whispering!" Grisha knew what it meant.

So did Ivan. "They can hear our units on the ground," he chimed in.

"Horowitz and Sobchak are there, and we are close," Grisha responded.

"Very close," Ivan added.

"Send whatever was transmitted to the cryptography unit in Moscow. Highest priority. Hopefully they can make sense of it," Grisha commanded the MP to hurry.

"I don't need specialists to know they issued a distress call," Ivan responded. "By the time our comrades in the capital have figured out the code, our mission here is over."

Grisha agreed. "Nevertheless, Moscow may surprise us. And who knows, the message may still unveil vital information."

The soldier saluted and was about to leave.

"Wait," Evanoff reminded him that he was not yet dismissed. "Your line here." He pointed to the map. "Is it really this accurate?"

The soldier nodded. So did Grisha.

"So accurate you would bet your life on it?"

"Absolutely," the soldier responded without hesitation.

"Then inform Kuznetsov. Dismissed."

5:46 PM
The Attic

"Let's get some sleep while we can. You must be exhausted," Rachel proposed, but Tom knew he would not be able to rest. Rachel was not yet tired but lay down on the dusty mattress anyway. After all, she did not know when the next opportunity to do so would present itself. Tom lay next to her but, as expected, was unable to fall asleep. He could have done with a few hours, but with the soldiers closing in …. Rachel's call for help did not calm him either. They were surrounded, the intersections blocked off, and the streets crawling with MPs. They were trapped and had to stick it out to the point where the Russians would call off the search. It could be days, and with no food or water, the outlook was grim. In his head, he was running through alternative getaways, trying to think of one with acceptable odds. Maybe if he was on his own, he could somehow slip through. But together, there just was no way.

His thoughts began to race, plaguing him with repeating what-ifs. What if they were found? What if the artwork was discovered? What if they had to stay here for days on end? What if the resistance got them out but wanted to get their hands on his treasure? He did not dare to think of the consequences of any of these scenarios yet could not steer his thoughts clear. His mind grew increasingly restless, stirred up by the soldiers in the courtyard, each more eager than the next to find them, and with every passing minute getting closer. It surely was just a matter of time now. He had to do something. But what? He could just get out and leave Rachel behind. But what if she got caught? She would most certainly bargain the hideout for her life. And what if she managed to escape, against all odds? She would try to get the collection for herself, if only to get back at him. With her connections, it would be a snap to relocate the lot out of his reach. There simply was no feasible way out. His mind paused. *Unless…*

5:51 PM
MP Offices, Room 325

More good news was reaching the Russian headquarters. The two soldiers on their way to Moscow were finally halted. Vasiliev immediately requested a line and within minutes spoke to the driver.

"I am not at liberty to disclose anything to anyone," the driver told Grisha, who had to suppress a laugh.

"Great job, soldiers, you are following your directives. However, I am part of this operation and circumstances have changed."

"As this may be, we have our strict orders, sir. I cannot disclose anything," the driver insisted.

"You don't have to. I already know every detail about your

mission. First, the train you were sent to investigate in Lodz is now inside the harbor depot by the Zeranski Canal. Second, you are to deliver documents of great importance to the People's Commissariat for State Security in Moscow."

"That is correct," the driver hesitantly confirmed.

"These documents have to do with the very train Private Sobchak was investigating."

"From what I know, yes." The driver was still hesitant to respond.

"If I can tell you what is inside the envelope, will that prove that I have clearance for this mission and you can talk to me?" The driver, uncertain what to do, consulted with his traveling companion. This was over their heads, but after a short discussion, they agreed.

"If you know what is in these documents, then yes," the driver acknowledged.

"Great, open the envelope."

"We are not supposed to do that," the driver objected. Grisha was rolling his eyes.

"I give you permission to open the envelope and look at the first page only. It is just a cover page. Nothing secret on it."

"But sir, we—"

"Just do it, for the love of God," Vasiliev shouted at them impatiently. A few seconds later, he heard the sound of tearing paper.

"The first page is blank, is it not?" he asked.

"Yes, sir," the baffled driver responded.

"So is the second, and third. As a matter of fact, you have nothing but blank papers in your hands." Grisha gave them a moment to check.

"Sir, I don't understand," the driver responded.

"It is a long story," Grisha responded with an excuse. "But I need both of you to now pay attention."

The driver gestured for the engineer to listen in on the call, and both pressed their heads against the receiver.

"As I said before, we had a bit of a development. Private Sobchak is missing. We think he is in danger and are looking for him. Has he, by any chance, said anything to you? Anything that could help us find him?"

"I am not sure if this will help," the engineer chimed in, "but he told me he was about to leave for Norway. Apparently, he has family near a city called Hondem, or something like that. I deemed it strange, Norway being German-occupied and all, but this is what he told me."

"Hondem? Do you mean Trondheim by any chance?"

"Yes, that's it! Trondheim."

5:55 PM
The Attic

Tom nervously looked at Rachel lying next to him on her side, facing him. How could she fall asleep, and so quickly? How could she even close her eyes? How could she be so at peace with the search troops closing in? Slowly, he pulled up his right pant leg, opened the leg strap sheath, and silently slid out the knife inside. Wasn't Rachel about to be convicted anyway, to be executed? Didn't she want nothing more than be united with her family? Those were her very own words. Why should he risk his life for someone like her? Tom silently raised the blade above her. But then the face of the young soldier from the checkpoint popped into his mind. Tom closed his eyes, pressing his eyelids together, trying to get the haunting image out of his head. *No matter what! No matter what!* Tom reminded himself, cursing God to test him so dearly for what he had vowed. *No matter what!* He knew one day he would have to deal with the fallout of all this. If not with the authorities, then with himself, with his own conscience. Yet, it was better than facing a firing squad. He forced his thoughts back to the switch, the moment he swore to see this through. *No matter what! No matter what!* Then, his mind drifted to the terrible events at the checkpoint once again, only for Tom to redirect it to the satisfying memory of closing the hatch of the hideout. Defying his efforts not to, it jumped again to the red snow below the dying solider; the excitement he felt when the train was steaming out of Lodz; the blood gushing out of the young guard's neck, the fear of dying in his eyes; the executions in the headquarters' courtyard; him opening the crate and looking at the red painting; Rachel inside her moldy prison cell; the modern cities in the newsreels; the godforsaken farm of his parents in the middle of nowhere. On top, the shouting soldiers in the courtyard: STOP!

"No matter what! No matter what!" Tom whispered, breathing heavily, his pulse beating up to his neck, a hot flash shooting through his body. He raised his hand, tightening his grip on the knife, ready for the lethal strike. He gazed at Rachel's innocent, youthful face once again. *No matter what!* Tom thrust the knife.

21

5:57 PM
MP Offices, Room 325

"Trondheim, why Trondheim?" Grisha Vasiliev wondered.

"Trondheim has a major port. Maybe he plans to catch a ship from there? Or a submarine?" Ivan speculated.

But Grisha disagreed. "We are missing something. Why would Tom go to German-occupied territory?"

"Just think about what this cargo means to them. Tom has enough leverage to negotiate safe passage to anywhere in the world plus a hefty finder's fee in return for the artwork's location. Goebbels will agree to anything to get his hands on these crates."

Grisha was not quite convinced.

"It's quite smart; I'd probably do the same," Ivan underlined his point.

"Maybe. Maybe not," Grisha respectfully disagreed.

But Ivan urged him to act. "Let's notify the MP stations north of here as well as the Vistula River and Baltic sea harbor authorities."

Confidently, Grisha shook his head. "That won't be necessary, my friend. There is no way the two will get out of the city. Let's not make this a bigger deal than it already is."

5:58 PM

The Attic

Rachel landed a precise punch on Tom's incoming hand. The knife went deep into the mattress, missing her throat by only a fraction of an inch. She immediately kicked him in his groin, knocking all the air out of him. Tom winced. With her left hand, she grabbed him by the collar and tossed him onto the floor, face down, forcing herself on his back, her knees pinning his wrists, all while she took the knife out of the mattress with the other. She grabbed his hair, pulled back his head, and pressed the blade onto his exposed throat. Tom could not catch his breath, hurting so much he felt like throwing up.

"Ah … I think you broke my wrist," he complained.

"Don't worry, I did not. But I would have if I wanted to."

What just happened? How could he have missed?

"WHAT A COWARDLY LITTLE WEASEL YOU ARE!" Rachel shouted in anger, then immediately lowered her voice. "I knew you would try to get rid of me, you son of a bitch." She withdrew the knife and got off him. Tom rolled over, coughing.

"Go ahead!" Rachel pointed to the skylight. "Leave! Your little secret is safe. But mark my words—without me, you will soon be staring into the barrels of an execution squad." She flipped the knife elegantly and, holding on to the blade, shooting a look that could kill, offered it back to him. "Try pulling this little stunt again and you are a dead man."

Tom nodded, took the knife, and placed it back into the leather sheath while Rachel sat down to catch her breath.

"Okay. What is going on?" Tom whispered.

"I don't know what you mean," she snapped at him.

"You are not the innocent girl you are portraying here. The Polish resistance coming to my office asking for your release, the hidden rooms, the radio, your trained reflexes … I think I have a right to know."

"A *right* to know?" Rachel scoffed. "I think I have the right to put this knife between your ribs, you two-faced—whatever."

Tom wished Rachel would lower her voice. "I got you out of

prison. I saved you from being executed. What game are you playing, Rachel Horowitz?"

She did not respond.

"If you really feel I deserve this knife between my ribs, then please, be my guest. At least I can kill you with a clear conscience, in self-defense," he whispered, equally angry.

Did this guy really not just learn his lesson? "Don't bet on it, Russian boy," she responded coldly. "Don't bet on it!"

6:15 PM
The Courtyard

One of the search groups had returned to the truck and lined up to brief Kuznetsov on their progress.

"Nothing, sir, absolutely nothing," the group leader reported.

The lieutenant was less than pleased. "Headquarters has just informed me they have intel on the fugitives. And guess what! They are here, right under our noses. As a matter of fact, we are so close they can hear us. And you are telling me you cannot find them? Not a dusty footprint? An unusual sound? Nothing?"

"Nothing, sir. We looked everywhere. We really did our best."

"Obviously, your best is not good enough," Kuznetsov reproached the group leader. He turned and walked down the line of the intimidated soldiers, his hands behind his back, looking closely into each face. He could not really tell why one of the soldiers stood out to him. Maybe he sensed his nervousness; maybe he just did not like his face. Whatever it was, he stopped in front of him.

"Really nothing?" He gave this private a good stare. "Nothing unusual, suspicious, out of the ordinary?" Kuznetsov kept staring. The soldier looked anxiously at his group leader, but he did not dare to interfere.

"I am not sure, sir ..."

"You are not sure about what?"

"Well, I thought I heard a rumble above us. But it was so faint I cannot even tell you if I heard anything at all."

The group leader immediately stepped forward, shouting angrily at his team member.

"And why did you not tell me—"

But Kuznetsov lifted his hand, gesturing for him to stop. "Tell me, where did you hear this rumbling?"

The soldier pointed with his finger. "In the building over there. All the way up in the attic."

"You really think it is nothing?" Kuznetsov unholstered his gun, put the barrel on the soldier's forehead, and cocked the gun.

"Please, sir, please! I really did not hear anything. I am sure now." The soldier pleaded for his life, staring at the gun. Alerted by the commotion, everybody in the courtyard stopped in their tracks.

"Please, sir. Please … I have a wife, and a young child. Please!" The soldier begged.

"Did I not say to report anything, no matter how insignificant it may seem?"

The soldier quickly nodded.

"So, tell me, my friend, why in the world DO I HAVE TO DRAG IT OUT OF YOU THEN?" Kuznetsov screamed at the intimidated youngster, and then looked around the courtyard. "Let this be a lesson for each one of you," he said loudly, his words echoing from the facade.

"Please!" the soldier pleaded again. Kuznetsov looked down at the growing urine stain wetting the soldier's pants. He laughed, shook his head, and pulled the trigger.

Without showing the slightest emotion, gun still in hand, Kuznetsov stepped back onto the flatbed of the truck and addressed his unit once again. "What you are tasked to do is not complicated. Report anything suspicious, no matter how inconsequential you deem it to be. Now go and find these fugitives, for heaven's sake."

The soldiers in the courtyard scrambled, each now scared for his own life. Despite their newfound motivation, even the intensified search did not produce the desired results. Kuznetsov started to have doubts. *May be the soldier was right… maybe what he heard was nothing.* Then again, everything pointed toward the fugitives to be there, behind panels, inside a wall, up a chimney—somewhere.

"Lieutenant Kuznetsov," a man behind him requested his attention. Kuznetsov turned and returned the salute. "Lieutenant Antonov," the man reported. "I am heading the search-and-rescue team."

Kuznetsov stared him down. "We have been waiting for you. What took you so long?"

"We came as fast as we could."

"Well, to be honest, your timing could not be better. It looks like we have about exhausted what we can do here," Kuznetsov dejectedly had to admit.

"No worries. If they are in there, we will find them."

6:35 PM
The Attic

Rachel stayed calm while Tom looked nervously at the skylight.

"Maybe you are right. Maybe I do owe you an explanation," Rachel broke the silence. "You already know I am a part of the Polish resistance. During German occupation, one of my jobs was to communicate with British intelligence. We supplied them with top-secret information—anything on the Germans the resistance could put their hands on. They, in turn, provided lists of targets to coordinate our efforts with their overall strategies."

Rachel stopped abruptly when they heard footsteps on the other side of the wall. She waited till they were gone again. "Communication interruptions, supply line sabotages, even killing strategic command targets—you name it, we did it all. Our job was to make their lives as miserable as humanly possible. We succeeded, not only because we are well organized but also because we always have each other's backs. My radio message has activated an emergency rescue protocol. All I ask you to do is trust they will get us out of here."

Tom listened, but it was not in his nature to just sit around and wait. He had learned early in his military days that he could depend only on himself, never on others. Despite Rachel's assurances, he was still shaken by the gunshot that had startled them mere minutes earlier, his brain restless again, desperate to come up with another way out.

Rachel could sense his nervousness and rolled her eyes. "Stop panicking; sit back and be happy you are still alive. Any other day that knife of yours would be stuck in your throat right now."

The two exchanged angry looks. Rachel decided to be quiet and let Tom pout for a while.

6:52 PM

The soldiers with the dogs had already made it to the attic. The trained animals had quickly picked up a scent but soon lost the trail again. The other part of the search-and-rescue team was hauling the heavy equipment up the stairs. Maneuvering it around the damaged staircase took longer than expected. But after a good forty-five minutes, the gear was finally set up; the sensitive microphones attached to the building's structure, ready to triangulate the origin of any sound, even ones too faint for the human ear. For the first fifteen minutes there was silence. Then, suddenly, the operator picked up a conversation. It was loud and clear, but not what he had expected.

7:35 PM

Rachel and Tom sat in silence. Everything had gotten quiet on the other side of the brick wall; even the shouting in the courtyard had stopped. It did not calm Tom's nerves, though. They got worse when he heard footsteps on the roof, right above them. Tom looked up, worry written all over his face, and so did Rachel, but she stayed surprisingly calm. Suddenly, the glass of the skylight shattered, and three Russian soldiers jumped into the room, all within a split second. By the time Tom realized what was happening, he had a rifle pointed at his head.

"GET DOWN!" They were screamed at. The two fugitives were handcuffed and pulled off the floor.

"Sorry it took so long," one of the soldiers apologized to Rachel. Tom was in utter disbelief. She had not called for help; she had called the Russians.

"You BITCH!" He spat in her face. "You think you will save yourself by ratting me out? I know them better than you do, and I can tell you with certainty you are dead, woman, DEAD!"

The two were pulled out of the hidden room and ushered over the rooftop back through the other skylight into the attic. Tom desperately attempted to find a way to escape. He even considered, if only for a split second, jumping off the roof and hoping for the best, but looking down, he quickly changed his mind. The barking German Shepherds with their bared teeth were equally intimidating. There was just no way. The fugitives were escorted down the stairs into the courtyard and presented to Kuznetsov. He was ecstatic. What a success this was! Even better, his promotion was now nothing more than a logical conclusion. But something did not seem quite right. Not only did he not recognize the arresting soldiers, but curiously enough, their uniform had patches of a different unit.

"You're from the 9th," Kuznetsov said, surprised. "What are you doing in my sector?"

"Lieutenant Kuznetsov, you are right. We are from the 9th."

The fugitives found on his turf by another unit? How dare they? It was like a punch in the gut.

"We got a tip from a local about a hidden room up here. We were, however, not sure if the lead could be trusted. When our lieutenant heard about the truck being over here, and the ping matching the location, he thought it best to at least check it out. Not wanting to waste your resources, he sent us. When we did find the fugitives, we deemed it best to make the arrest without delay, with them having reached out for help and all."

"I see," Kuznetsov replied, still not happy with the interference.

"We have strict orders to hand over the prisoners to you. Officially, we have never been here. This is your accomplishment, sir. We are just happy we could assist, and that it is all over now."

"Thank you. We were actually just about to find them

ourselves," Kuznetsov tried to recover his somewhat battered ego. "But you are right. The sooner this is wrapped up, the better. Well done. And may I commend you for this prime example of how the Russians should always work together, as one united team. Duty before glory. Excellent work, comrades!" Kuznetsov's chest was filled with pride, and not without gratitude. For years, he had been bending over backward, always going the extra step, impressing his superiors with extraordinary accomplishments, only for them to take the credit. For once, it was the other way around.

Kuznetsov walked over to the radio and personally took the microphone to talk to no other than Lieutenant Colonel Vasiliev himself.

"Well done, my friend. Well done," Vasiliev praised his lieutenant. Kuznetsov could not be more ecstatic. The leader of the MP division had just called him his "friend."

"A prison transporter is on its way. Come to my office once you are packed up. We have to celebrate."

"Sir, we still have to locate the artwork."

"No need to waste time on that. With the fugitives in custody, we will soon know where it is."

Ivan was as relieved as he had ever been in his life. "Kuznetsov! That son of a bitch; he did it!"

8:05 PM
The Courtyard

The mood among Kuznetsov's men was less celebratory. What weighed on their minds was not their success, but the loss of their colleague. To some, he was even a friend. The shooting was senseless. The much-liked fellow did not need to die, yet no one dared to speak up. Some members of the unit were in the midst of grudgingly packing up the roadblock, and the rest were busy in the courtyard when the prison transporter entered. The smallest of trucks halted right in front of Kuznetsov.

"Finally, someone is on time," the lieutenant acknowledged

their arrival. The crew of three got out of the vehicle. The leader introduced himself to Kuznetsov while another took custody of the fugitives, and the third unlocked the heavy door in the back. The prisoner compartment was nothing more than a metal box welded onto the pickup's chassis, with walls thick enough to withstand a small projectile. Tom and Rachel were loaded and their handcuffs secured to the metal benches. All three of the crew congratulated Kuznetsov for his success, then saluted him goodbye, got back into the vehicle, and drove out of the courtyard.

"How proud you are going to be of me, my dearest," Kuznetsov said quietly, again thinking of his fiancée.

22

Streets of Warsaw

The transporter, like most military vehicles, was not equipped with a heater. The freezing cold metal was radiating the outside temperatures into its interior. On top, snow was drifting through the two small, barred windows. Tom, in the dim light of a small light bulb, glared at Rachel with a hatred she had never seen in anyone's eyes before. Given the opportunity, he would have killed her right there. It was not for the lack of trying. He attempted to free himself, angrily pulling on the restraints, but they did not give.

"I swear to God almighty if the Russians won't kill you, I will. From this moment on, consider yourself a hunted woman. Never ever let your guard down because, mark my words, I will find you, wherever you are hiding. And I will kill you."

She did not waste a thought on his threat and just told him to shut it.

The Courtyard

Kuznetsov was glancing at the picture of his woman again. He was deep in thought when the driver asked him what destination to drive to.

"To the 9th checkpoint, and make it fast." Credit needed to be given where credit was due, and the 9th truly came through for him tonight, more than anyone ever had before. He needed to personally thank his counterpart and express his gratitude—something that, in his opinion, was too often neglected.

While the vehicle was making its way through the streets, he closed his eyes. After all the excitement of the day, he enjoyed the little bit of peace and quiet. He reflected on the arrest and could not help but be impressed. Not only did the 9th find the fugitives, but also their professionalism was something to strive for. If the tip had been fake, they would have been in and out without him even knowing. No harm done. But it was not, and they made the arrest swiftly and handed over the prisoners without any claim for glory. What impressed him even more was that they, the foot soldiers, knew his name. He had always strived for such a level of performance but never managed to get it of his men. They needed to do better. *He* needed to do better. And not just better: from today onward he would do whatever was necessary to drill his unit to the very top. Things were about to change.

Officers Wing, Room 474

With the fugitives on their way to headquarters, Ivan went back to his office and retrieved the finest bottle of champagne he could find. The irony at hand did not escape him. He was about to celebrate the arrest with one of Tom's finest. *How satisfying!* he thought and laughed. It would make it taste even sweeter. He could not wait to look Timofei in the eye and tell him how he had betrayed his trust, how he had betrayed the war effort, how he had betrayed Mother Russia. Knowing Tom, he would come up with some kind of excuse, an explanation that even sounded plausible. Ivan knew better than to be fooled again. This time, Tom was done for good. Finally! With the bottle in hand, he made his way down to the prison block, to be right there when the fugitives were brought in.

8:32 PM

Streets of Warsaw

Tom leaned toward the small opening connecting the cabin with the prisoner's compartment, trying to listen in on the MPs conversation.

"Don't even try," Rachel tried to discourage him. "There is no way you are going to talk your way out of this one."

He shushed Rachel and listened intently. But with the sound of the engine overpowering the voices, he could not make out what was being said, not even during the briefest of moments during a gear shift. And before he could grasp anything, the conversation ceased, the transporter slowed and came to halt. It was now time to face the music. Tom, curious about what was going on, tried to look out the window. As it was high up, he could see nothing but the snow falling from the night sky. He began to mentally prepare himself for endless interrogations, torture, and the inevitable end, his execution.

"Seriously, what have they offered you? A limited sentence? Full immunity?" It was his last chance to get answers. But Rachel did not say anything. "Tell me what they are giving you. It's the least you can do."

Still, she kept quiet.

"Just never forget. Because of you, and only because of you, I am going to be killed. My execution is going to weigh on your conscience for the rest of your life, which, as I know the Russians, will also be a short one."

Rachel still did not respond.

Section 9 Roadblock, Ursynow District

Kuznetsov warmly greeted his counterpart. "My friend. Thank you for your support tonight. I would like to commend you for everything. I cannot stress enough how impressed I am."

"Good to see you, my comrade. But why are you here?" the leader of the 9th asked him.

"To personally thank you and your unit now that the fugitives are in custody."

The lieutenant looked at him, puzzled. "What are you thanking me for, my friend? You are the one who got the fugitives."

"For the soldiers you sent over. The ones that followed up on the tip?"

"Soldiers? Tip? What are you talking about? We had strict orders to patrol our allocated sector. I can guarantee you, none of my men strayed."

"But what about the tip?"

"What tip?"

"The one about the room in the attic and the whereabouts of the fugitives?"

The lieutenant shook his head. "I would know if we had gotten a tip."

The Courtyard

The checkpoint was packed up and the unit ready to head back to the headquarters; they just had to wait for Kuznetsov to return. Two soldiers were working on the truck, attempting to get the engine started, when a vehicle entered the courtyard. The driver asked for the lieutenant.

"He should be back soon," his deputy informed them. "Anything I can I help you with?"

"We were sent to pick up the prisoners."

"The prisoners?" The deputy was surprised.

"Yes, the prisoners. Here is the paperwork on our orders."

"Who sent you?"

"What do you mean who sent us? Lieutenant Colonel Vasiliev, of course."

"But the fugitives were picked up earlier. They are already on their way back to the headquarters."

"That's not possible!"

"They left about half an hour ago."

"But that is not possible," the driver repeated himself.

"Why not?"

"Because we are the only unit sent from headquarters."

8:34 PM

Section 9 Roadblock

Kuznetsov was frowning, visibly embarrassed, and above all confused. Nothing made any sense whatsoever. Did he err in the section? He clearly remembered their patches, and the soldiers stating they were from the 9th, no doubt about that. If it was not the 9th, then who was it? His face turned as white as a sheet. Without losing another second, Kuznetsov ran over to the radio and ripped the microphone out of the soldier's hands.

"Lieutenant Kuznetsov from the 7th here. I have an urgent message for Lieutenant Colonel Vasiliev."

A few seconds passed before he got a reply. "Lieutenant Colonel Vasiliev here. We read you, lieutenant. Go ahead."

He was surprised to be speaking to his superior directly. "Lieutenant Colonel Vasiliev …" He started but hesitated and took his finger off the microphone again, thinking of the imminent fallout from these latest developments. Soon, everyone would know him as the idiot who let the fugitives slip through his fingers—as the antagonist in this fiasco of gargantuan proportions. Nonetheless, they could still be caught, and any delay would only make things even worse. Much worse. With a sinking heart, he issued his alert. Vasiliev was still screaming when Lieutenant Kuznetsov dropped the microphone and, without saying another word, went back into his car and gestured the driver to head back. He again took the photo of his fiancée from his wallet, and while looking at it, again stroked the image of her long, brown hair. He thought of all the things that could have been. After a last glance, he ripped it into pieces, rolled down the window to a sufficient gap, threw them out, and let the wind decide where they may fall. Nothing mattered anymore.

23

Streets of Warsaw

"You of all people should know what it means to be found and taken away by the enemy." Tom hoped the reference to Rachel's lost family would trigger a bit of sympathy. It did not. With nothing else to say, Tom lowered his head and sat there resigned, waiting for the door to open. Instead, the transporter's engine suddenly revved. The vehicle sped up as much as the underpowered engine and the tire's grip in the snow allowed. The truck started to shake, and then, with increasing speed, fiercely swayed from left to right and back, its suspension heavily tested by the road's many potholes. The car went faster … and faster … and faster. Then there was shouting nearby. Someone commanded the car to stop. Just when Tom was wondering what was going on, bullets started to fly, hitting the transporter all over. With a blaring noise, the windshield shattered, its thousands of small fragments flying everywhere. An even more deafening sound pierced their ears as the crew in the front started to return fire, their machine guns spraying whoever was shooting at them. Sharp fragments from the shattered glass had hit the driver's face, cutting deep into his flesh like shrapnel from a grenade, immediately blinding him. In his agony, he let go of the steering wheel, causing the car to veer off the road. Inside, Rachel was screaming. Both their bodies were being thrown around, the force on the restraints nearly ripping their arms out of their sockets as their heads and shoulders were violently smashed against the hard metal walls. Only seconds later, the car hit a mine, the thrust of the explosion throwing it up in the air and flipping it around its own axis. By the time the transporter crashed back onto the ground, the two had blacked out.

Prison Block, Russian Headquarters

All Colonel General Evanoff needed was a few minutes with each of the prisoners—just to get the most pertinent information, enough for the 0900 report to Moscow. There would be plenty of time to get the details the following day. Another thirty minutes and they all would finally be on their way out of here. Impatiently, he was pacing the corridors of the prison block.

"Where are they?" he asked the guard on duty again, but the private knew no more than he did.

"Sir, I am sure they will be here shortly. The snowy conditions are slowing everyone down."

"I am telling you, I cannot wait to punch that mother ... the second he walks through this door. And at his execution, I will make sure to be holding one of the rifles—" The phone interrupted Ivan's rant. The two looked at each other.

"Must be the gate. They are finally here," Ivan crowed, gesturing for the guard to pick up the call. With the receiver against his ear, the soldier listened intently, looking into the anticipating stares of the Colonel General. Evanoff sensed something did not seem quite right.

"What?" he asked the guard impatiently, who put the receiver down, then nervously looked at his superior. What he would have given to be anywhere but at his desk right now.

"I ... I ..." the guard stuttered.

"What?" Evanoff shouted at him. "Don't you dare telling me

they are not here yet!"

"Well ..."

8:43 PM
Checkpoint 0906, Southeast of Warsaw

The first thing Tom noticed was a loud ringing in his ears, then his head pounding with the most terrible headache, as well as pain from his wrists. Confused, he slowly opened his eyes. All he could make out behind a thick layer of smoke was the dim, flickering light from the fires outside shining through the small window above him. He managed to sit up in the heavily tilted compartment, then noticed Rachel next to him. She was out cold. He started to remember their capture, the shootout, the car being tossed through the air. He blankly stared, sitting there in his pain, when a strong smell of gasoline hit his nose. Immediately alerted, he pulled on his restraints, but as before they would not give.

"RACHEL! RACHEL!" He screamed at the top of his lungs. She did not respond. He kept shouting her name and kicking her legs. After a few seconds, he heard a groan.

"What? What is going on?" she asked in her daze.

"Wake up! We need to get out of here. WAKE UP! This car is going to blow ... Rachel!"

She held her hand toward her throbbing head. "Where are we?"

"RACHEL!"

When she finally opened her eyes, everything seemed to move in slow motion. She noticed Tom moving around as if stung by a bee, and his screams sounded like someone shouting through a pipe from far away.

"Rachel! Wake up! We need to get out of here! We are going to burn!"

Then everything went dark again.

Prison Block

Evanoff felt like someone had stabbed him into his very soul. With just one short phone call, absolute triumph had turned into total disaster. How could this have happened? The Colonel General slammed his fist onto the desk so hard everything on it jumped. The phone, the papers, the pens, even the bottle of champagne. It fell to its side, rolled over the edge and onto the floor, smashing into pieces, wasting the valuable brut. Evanoff did not care.

"Call them back and tell them I want the prisoners here now. NOW!" He screamed at the intimidated guard. The anger inside him was boiling over, his face now dark red, and his temples pulsating. "And if they are not captured within the hour, heads will roll, and I mean that. HEADS WILL ROLL!" Once again, he had underestimated Tom. Once again, this boy from that god forsaken farm had gotten the better of him. Once again, he himself did not see the obvious, ONCE AGAIN! It was now as clear as daylight. Even with absolutely no way out, Tom always seemed to find one.

Checkpoint 0906

"RACHEL! RACHEL!" Tom desperately tried to wake her, screaming and kicking.

She finally opened her eyes again. Still confused, in a hoarse voice, she once more asked where they were, trying to make sense of what was happening.

"Your hand! Your hand—it is free! Quick, get the keys."

It took her a few additional seconds to realize what was going on. Also jolted awake by the heavy smell of gasoline, she tried to get the attention of the people in the front.

"They are all dead," Tom assumed.

She peeked through the little opening into the driver's cabin and saw the destruction the machine guns had done. But what really caught her attention were the rising flames out of the engine compartment passing the heavily mangled hood. With urgency, she squeezed her arm through the small opening, but her reach was limited by her other, still-restrained hand.

"We need the keys!" Tom shouted.

She stretched her arm as far out as she could, tapping down the soldier's jacket, but the pockets were out of reach. She got a good grip on its collar and pulled as hard as she could. She pulled till one button after the other started to pop off, and with the fabric now loose, managed to lift the jacket and get her hand onto the key ring.

"Let's hope it is one of these," she said, barely hearing her own voice. She sorted through the many keys on the ring, trying the ones that could fit the lock of the handcuffs. The first one did not work— neither did the second or the third. Rachel struggled handling the ring with only one hand. Nervously she looked at Tom.

"Keep going!"

The fourth key did not open the lock either, but with the fifth she felt a click. With both hands out of the cuffs, she quickly freed Tom. He ripped the keys from Rachel's hands and started to work on the door, frantically trying key after key. The wait was agonizing, but one of them finally turned. Tom pushed the door. It hardly moved, only enough to let a sliver of light penetrate the compartment.

"What are you waiting for? Open the damn door!" Rachel shouted at him.

"It's stuck. Either something is blocking it from the outside, or the frame is too distorted." Inside, the nauseating smell was getting stronger, and Rachel could tell the flames in the front had gotten longer.

Underneath them, gasoline kept flowing from its ruptured line, forming a small creek beneath the rapidly melting layer of snow, inching its way toward the burning engine.

8:47 PM

MP Offices, Room 325

Ivan was sitting in Grisha's chair while the latter stood at the window, looking outside. The last ninety minutes were a rollercoaster they both could have done without. They had them in custody. They had them and now they were gone again. The line between success and failure had never been so thin, and certainly never so consequential. Ivan could think of nothing but the upcoming consequences. Like no other, he had worked himself up through the ranks, giving his all, heroically mastering every situation, every fight, and every battle, ready and willing to lay down his life for the cause. He had selflessly put himself in danger countless times to save the lives of others. Country first, everything for the good of everyone—an ethos he followed with deep conviction, guiding the actions he was so heavily decorated for. And now, so close to the end of the war, everything was about to crumble right before his eyes. It was not how he wanted to end his career. It was not how someone of his legendary status should have to end his career. What an absolute travesty this was!

He checked his watch; there was still a bit over twelve hours till his report. He had a special talent of putting positive spins on bad news, but this time, he truly needed to pull a rabbit out of a hat. He doubted it was possible. Yet, twelve hours were twelve hours. He ordered Grisha to arrest whoever they could get their hands on from the Polish resistance. They had gotten the fugitives; they surely knew where they were. With any goodwill toward them now assuredly gone, he could do whatever was necessary to get the information he so desperately needed.

Checkpoint 0906

Tom kicked against the door again and again, but it did not budge. To make matters worse, he felt increasingly drained.

"Don't give up. Keep going!" Rachel encouraged him.

"You got to help me. Kick as hard as you can on the count of three, okay?"

Rachel nodded and got herself into position.

"One, two, three." The door finally moved a fraction of an inch. Encouraged, they repeated their synchronized effort. With every kick the door gave, bit by bit, till it would not give again. Rachel did not think the opening was big enough, but she managed to squeeze herself through. Tom, on the other hand, did not fit. Rachel tried to pull the door from the outside but was not strong enough to make it move.

"The fire! Go take care of the fire," Tom shouted at her. Rachel immediately ran to the other side of the small truck. By now, the flames were raging, the area too hot for her to go anywhere near, and the snow she threw on it did not make the slightest bit of difference. The fire continued to burn the engine's oil leaking onto the hot exhaust manifold.

"It is too strong," she shouted. "I cannot put it out."

"You have to. Try harder," Tom screamed right back. But Rachel knew it was of no use. Instead, she hurried the few yards back to whatever was left of the checkpoint and picked up the longer part of the broken red-and-white painted barrier pole. It was the only thing she could find sturdy enough. She leveraged it between the door and the frame and bent the big metal panel another inch. Tom finally managed to squeeze himself into the gap. Again encouraged by the progress, he pushed harder and so did Rachel. Tom was about halfway out when, with a loud cracking sound, the pole broke and the door snapped back, squeezing Tom into the frame. It felt like an elephant had just jumped onto his chest. Struggling to breathe, he pushed again but was unable to go forward or backward. With Tom in agony, Rachel tried to find another lever, but everything was either too short or too weak. Desperate, she again tried to open the door with her bare hands again. As before, it did not work. More out of panic than anything else, she took Tom's arm, and started to pull. It became all too obvious, at least to Tom; he was stuck.

"Rachel!"

She kept pulling his arm.

"Rachel," he shouted to get her attention.

She finally stopped and looked at him.

"Rachel, I am so sorry. I should have trusted you. I know now. I am so sorry," Tom said with the gentlest of undertones.

"Forget about it. You saved my life. Now, I will save yours."

"Rachel, listen. You have to go."

"Never," she replied, determined, and without wasting a thought pulled on his arm again.

"Rachel!"

She kept pulling.

"RACHEL!"

This time, reality was finally sinking in.

"We are on borrowed time here. You have to go."

With sorrow in her eyes, she looked deep into his. "I can't just leave you here."

"You have to."

"NO!" she shouted.

Tom took as deep a breath as he could. "Go!" he told her again. "Just go. You don't need me anymore. It is all yours now."

"This can't be it. It just can't." She shook her head and kept trying to grab his arm, but Tom was fighting her.

"Listen, Rachel, you must go! NOW!" He forcefully tried to convince her. But she kept trying, and he kept fending her off. Frustrated and desperate, with all hope lost, her pulling faded into hitting. She then stopped, burying her head into his shoulder, and wept in despair.

"Go," Tom told her again, eerily calm. This time, it was more of a plea than a command. She looked up and tenderly moved the back of her hand over his cheek. No more words were needed. Her face lit by the flickering flames around them, Tom saw the gratitude in her tearful, blue eyes. Then, without looking back, she ran away.

8:52 PM

MP Offices, Room 325

"Would you like some tea?" Grisha offered Ivan his cup. He declined. "Listen; is there anything else you can tell me about Tom?"

"By now, you know as much as I do," Ivan responded.

"Do you know if he has a girlfriend, a lover, friends, an area he is familiar with he might seek refuge in?" Ivan shook his head.

"Nobody wants to help more than me here, Grisha. But I know

Tom the soldier, and only very little of Tom the person. Nevertheless, I doubt it."

"What do you think they are going to do next?"

Ivan shrugged his shoulders.

"Okay, let me ask you this. What would *you* do next?"

"Good question. What would I do ..." Ivan took a few seconds to think.

"Would you split from Horowitz, or would you stick with her? Would you try to get out of the city as fast as possible? Or would you hide and wait for things to calm down?"

"She knows the area and has the connections, so I would definitely stick with her. But I could not tell you where they might be going as what I would do may very well be different. Nevertheless, the resistance will soon tell us everything we will need to know."

"I know it does not help us, but at least it gives me hope this Rachel will survive all of this."

"Hope? Survive? Have you forgotten her role in all of this? Forget hope. If he does not kill her, I sure will."

"It may still turn out she is only a victim here."

"She is no victim. Open your eyes, my friend."

"It looks like you are right," Grisha had to admit. "But we do not have all the facts yet, so can we really be certain?"

"Damn right we can. Without her, Tom would be in custody right now, and that is all I need to know," Ivan doubled up. "Now let's cross our fingers that their luck will finally run out. It just has to." Grisha again looked out the window, drinking from his cup. For now, they could do nothing but wait for the first arrests to come in. The door suddenly slammed open, and a young soldier stormed into the office.

"Sir, we just got a report of a skirmish, shots fired, and grenades exploding. We contacted the checkpoint nearby, but they are not responding." Grisha put his tea down so hastily the saucer under the cup broke. "Send all units there. Highest priority. Go! Go! Go!" he screamed while running after the soldier into the operations room.

8:53 PM
Checkpoint 0906

Tom, stuck inside the burning truck, had come to terms with his fate. During these last, soul-searching moments of his life, the young soldier from back at the railway checkpoint entered his mind once more. Then, with his eyes drifting over the carnage around him, his thoughts shifted to the three bodies inside whatever was left of the transporter, as well as the guards that were stationed here and whoever was on the receiving end of that bullet fired back in the courtyard, all now dead. Tom was overcome with sorrow. It took a moment like this to open his eyes, to understand it was nothing but his selfish greed that had caused all this carnage, all this suffering, not only for the victims but for their mothers, fathers, brothers, sisters, lovers, and not least, friends. If he were granted a dying wish, he would go back in time and never leave his family's farm.

In his grief, Tom looked up, taking comfort in the grace of the snow-covered trees. How had he never noticed all this beauty? Even in the midst of the most brutal war zone, there was so much, yet no one ever paid the slightest attention to it. He closed his eyes, feeling the cold air brushing against one side of his face, the radiating warmth of the flames on the other, listening intently to the soothing sounds of the blowing winds and crackling fires, with an appreciation as never before. He took it all in, waiting for the inevitable to bring him to heaven, or in his case most likely to hell. But instead of a loud explosion, he heard the sound of clinking metal. He opened his eyes and saw Rachel struggling through the snow, holding a heavy machine gun, a fully stocked 250-round ammunition belt draped around her neck. Out of breath, she set the tripod in the snow, mounted the gun on top, loaded the ammunition belt, and aimed the muzzle at the upper hinge of the metal door.

"Ready?" she asked Tom. He pressed his index fingers in his ears as well as he could and nodded. Not a second later, the 7.65 caliber bullets started to fly. As if the firing was not already thunderous enough, the impact of each projectile was resonated by the big metal box so loud Tom thought the world around him was exploding. To make things worse, the violent vibrations of the door gave him a thorough shaking. Rachel did not take her finger off the trigger till the last bullet was fired. Tom at first did not dare to open his eyes. When he finally did, he saw Rachel right behind the glowing red barrel of the gun, staring intently at the door. The ammunition belt was gone, the area around her steaming from the hot casings spit into the cold snow.

At first, nothing happened. But then, gradually, Tom felt the pressure on his chest weaken, and with a dull thump, the heavy door fell into the snow. He immediately started running, grabbing Rachel by her arm, pulling her as fast as he could. She could hardly keep up, barely stumbling ahead. Ten feet, fifteen feet ... Underneath the transporter, the heat of the fire had melted the snow, allowing the leaking gasoline to spread over the growing puddle. Twenty feet ... twenty-five feet ... The flames jumped onto the flammable liquid, rapidly making their way toward the gas tank. With a violent jolt, Rachel and Tom were thrown onto the ground. The engulfing fireball rolled over them, then up into the night sky, brightly illuminating the surrounding area for a mere second or two. Stunned, both looked back, their eyes following the mangled transporter engulfed in a fiery inferno as it fell from the sky, crashing onto the ground once more. Relieved to her core, Rachel could not help herself but throw her arms around Tom.

"You are right; I did save your life, but lucky for me, you forgot I also tried to kill you," Tom smirked.

"You are not quick enough," Rachel said, smirking right back. They allowed themselves a brief moment to laugh.

"This place will be swarming with Russians soon," Rachel warned, certain the fireball did not go unnoticed.

Still startled by the close call, the two got up and patted the snow off their uniforms. Tom pointed to the transporter. "Do you know where these three were taking us?" His concern was valid.

"I believe I do."

"You don't know, do you?"

"I am more worried about getting out of here before the Russians show up," Rachel responded.

She had a point. Tom looked around. The small wooden guard

house was shattered into pieces. A heavily banged-up car, barbed wire, and two dead soldiers lay intertwined. Fires still raged all around them. Tom could scarcely believe a few machine guns and a mine could cause such carnage. In the mess, he spotted the handle of a motorcycle sticking out from a pile of debris. He cleared the few items around it, and then managed to pull it out. The IMZ Dnepr-72 bike was heavily banged up, but the engine started, and the wheels turned. Tom asked Rachel to get into the side car. She suggested otherwise.

"I'll drive! You are better with this," she pointed to the mounted machine gun. "Just in case we are going to need it."

"After everything I saw, I am not sure if I am the better shot here," Tom protested.

"And after everything I saw, I am not sure you are the better driver either," she snarked back at him. There was no time to argue, and since Rachel had already made herself comfortable on the bike, Tom got into the side car. She kicked the vehicle into gear and yanked the throttle.

A few seconds later, a three-axel BA-10 light armored vehicle fishtailed through the destroyed checkpoint at a dizzying speed. Foot by foot, the pursuers were catching up with the fugitives.

"Unit 1027 to Headquarters, unit 1027 to headquarters. We have a visual and are in pursuit. They are on a motorbike, heading southeast."

The reply came promptly. "Understood. Apprehend at any cost."

Meanwhile, the gunner had loaded and unlocked the equipped 7.62 DT machine gun. With the fugitives in his visor, he looked at the radio operator for permission.

"We are ready to fire," headquarters was informed.

Not a second later, the gunner was given an approving nod.

MP Operations Room

Every MP was communicating with multiple units on the field simultaneously. After the initial chaos, the effort was now better coordinated, and the hunt for the fugitives was on.

"Corporal, give me an update," Grisha Vasiliev requested. But the soldier was busy keeping his ear on the incoming messages.

"Corporal, an update please," Grisha repeated his command. While pressing the headphones against his ear, the corporal held up his index finger, signaling Vasiliev to hold on. In any other situation, with any other crew, Vasiliev would have dealt with such an act of defiance, but he knew better than to interfere at this very moment. Just a few seconds later, the corporal finally put his headphone down.

"Sir, one of our units is at the checkpoint. They spotted the fugitives."

"Good. How far out is the closest backup unit?"

"Several are on their way. My best guess, ten minutes tops."

Ten minutes was too long. "Tell the unit in pursuit they are on their own for now. They need to apprehend the fugitives."

"They already know. And just to confirm your order, sir. They were given permission to shoot."

"As I said. Whatever necessary."

"Whatever necessary?" Evanoff immediately objected. "He still needs to tell us where his treasure is hidden."

"Wouldn't you rather have him dead than gone?"

24

Somewhere at the Edge of Warsaw

Tom thought he heard gunfire. His ears still ringing, he hardly even noticed the bike's noisy engine next to him. A bright light shone onto them, and not a second later, lines of tracer bullets were slicing through the dark, shredding the trees ahead of them. Rachel turned the throttle to accelerate, but Tom knew they could not outrun whatever was behind them. They needed to get off the road, and fast. He grabbed the bike's handlebar and, despite Rachel's grip, yanked it around. It did not have the desired effect. The bike turned sideways but hardly changed its direction. Sliding forward on the snowy road, Rachel pushed against the turn but overcorrected, making it veer the other way, then again to the other side. She had nearly regained control just before a bend in the road when the tires hit a patch of ice. Rapidly approaching the edge of the forest, she desperately attempted to steer back on course. However, with no grip on the slippery surface, the bike slid into the trees, the wheels hitting roots, branches, and rocks—whatever was in their way. Both Tom and Rachel were thoroughly shaken, but she managed to hold on to the handlebars, desperate to keep some control. Bullets were still flying around them, now mixed with wooden shards of trees hit by the gun fire. Suddenly, Rachel felt a sharp pain in her right shoulder. Her hand immediately lost grip. The two crashed into a tree, ripping the sidecar off the bike. Missing the trunk by only a fraction of an inch, Tom was ejected while Rachel avoided collision with the other side of the trunk. He landed hard onto the frozen ground, and so did Rachel. As she was not moving, Tom, keeping low under the flying bullets, crawled over to her, grabbed her jacket by the shoulder, and pulled her to safety. When he let go of her, he noticed a wet, warm sensation on his hand. Only then did he see the dark, red bloodstain on her jacket.

"You were hit!"

She nodded.

"Are you okay?"

"It hurts like hell."

With both leaning against the sturdy trunk, Tom gently put his arms around her, shielding her from everything that was still flying through the air.

The forest was too dense for the BA-10 to follow. The gunner was looking for the two through the small hole in its armor, but all he could see was the reflector of the sidecar glowing in the light beam from his vehicle. He immediately opened fire again. Under cover of his barrage, the other three crew members jumped out and took up positions behind a fallen tree, right at the edge of the forest. A flare rocketed into the sky, illuminating the area, and the three also started firing into the forest.

"What now?" Rachel shouted over the sound of the blazing guns.

Tom did not have time to answer. He crawled to the side car, or what was left of it, and with all the strength he could summon, heaved it toward the tree, and turned the mounted machine gun toward their pursuers. He knew he had to pace himself, not blindly waste bullets, however many there were in the magazine. Soon after, in the cover of the firings, one soldier leaped over the fallen tree, entering the forest. Tom aimed quickly and pulled the trigger, and the soldier immediately dropped to the ground. *One down, three to go*. Tom again bunkered down next to Rachel. She was clutching her right shoulder, exhausted.

"This time *you* need to get us out of here," she tasked Tom. No sooner had she finished her sentence than the firing stopped. Tom hoped the unit had run out of bullets, but hope was replaced by dread the second he heard the sound of the turning turret. There was no way the tree could withstand a high-velocity anti-tank projectile. They'd be dead the moment it hit anywhere near them.

"And it is now or never," Tom replied. He took another peek and saw the anti-tank gun slowly turning. It was nearly in position. He took a quick glance at the two soldiers outside the vehicle. One was preparing a hand grenade, covered by his firing colleague. The young man had already removed the pin, now timing his throw to its detonation. Tom got him in his visor while still keeping an eye on the turret, its muzzle just about pointing toward them. It truly was now or never.

"Come on, come on, come on! Throw the damn thing already," Tom was saying to himself. He could not wait any longer. He pulled the trigger and hoped for the best. Nothing happened—nothing but the click of an empty gun.

"YOU HAVE GOT TO BE KIDDING ME!" he screamed in frustration. "One lousy bullet? ONE!" There was no time to dwell on his misfortune. He had to stop the grenade from being thrown and the gunner from firing the anti-tank shell. He pulled his knife from his leg sheath and ran toward the edge of the forest, zigzagging between the trees, dodging each of the incoming bullets. The soldier was finally about to throw the grenade. Still further away than Tom wanted to be, he propelled his knife, then dropped onto the ground for cover. It hit the soldier straight in the face, not with the blade, but with the handle. It did not cause the hoped-for injury, but it startled the soldier enough for him to drop the grenade. He frantically tapped through the snow and finally found it, but it was too late. The explosion took both him and his colleague out. Tom was showered with dirt and rocks. Nevertheless, he stood up and sprinted toward the armored vehicle. He pressed his body against the metal wall, right next to the open hatch. Inside, the radio was receiving calls from headquarters. No one replied. Tom took a quick peek inside. The last crew member was hunched over in his seat, riddled with shrapnel from the grenade, his finger on the firing button.

+ + +

"Let's hope the bike still runs, because this car sure doesn't," Rachel said as she pointed at the mangled wheels with their blown-off tires. She scavenged some water, binoculars, and a small first aid kit from the armored vehicle while Tom managed to get the bike out of the forest. The brake cables were ripped off, and so was the exhaust pipe. The headlight was in pieces, and the frame severely distorted. But to their astonishment, as before, the engine still ran, and the wheels turned. Rachel gave the small red light in the back of the bike a good kick.

"Just to make sure," she said.

The radio received another call from headquarters.

MP Operations Room

"Sir, we lost contact with the unit in pursuit."

"Try again," Vasiliev commanded. "And put it on speaker."

The radio operator did as commanded, and when there was still no answer, he looked up at his leader again.

"Try again."

"Sir, I don't think—"

"Try again," Vasiliev repeated his command in his authoritative voice. The radio started to crackle.

"Colonel General Evanoff?"

Evanoff and Vasiliev looked at each other in astonishment. They could not believe what they were hearing. Tom! Vasiliev held out his hand, stopping Ivan from answering. "What is the ETA of the closest backup unit?" he asked his corporal.

"Four minutes, sir." *Four minutes!* That was not soon enough. Vasiliev instructed Evanoff to engage Tom for as long as possible.

"Tom, Timofei, Ivan here. Come back to headquarters. I can

still turn this story in your favor. Let me make you a war hero, but you have to give yourself up."

"Listen, Colonel General, I just need you to know I never wanted this to get out of hand. I certainly never wanted anyone to die. Please tell the parents their sons died as heroes, and that I am very sorry."

"The only meaningful thing you can do for them is to give yourself up," Evanoff pressed.

"Please promise me."

"Promise you? Why should I do that?"

"As payment for the Romeo y Julieta cigars you have most definitely stolen from my office."

Vasiliev was gesturing to Ivan to keep the conversation going. "Timofei, I will promise to tell them whatever you want, but you will have to turn yourself in."

There was no answer.

"Try again," Vasiliev suggested.

"Timofei!" Again, nothing but silence. They had just lost the fugitives. Again. Vasiliev cursed Tom. He felt like he was hunting a man with more lives than a damned cat.

Somewhere Outside Warsaw

With one arm in a makeshift sling and the other tightly around Tom, Rachel held fast as the two drove off, first on the dirt path through the forest and then on the snow-covered roads between open fields. It was not long until she asked him to turn and drive up a small hill. Tom was still wondering where they were going but now knew better than to question his traveling companion. Once they arrived at the top of the hill, Rachel told him to stop and kill the noisy engine. She got off the bike and, through her binoculars, started checking their surroundings.

"There is a patrol over there." She pointed in the direction of an abandoned farm at the foot of the hill. Tom squinted his eyes. He thought he saw something move in the dark.

"Let's wait till it is gone," Rachel suggested. Two minutes later, she got back on the bike, asked Tom to put it into neutral and roll it down the road to the farm. They entered the barn and closed the big wooden door behind them.

"What are we doing here?" he asked. Rachel struggled to climb the ladder but managed to get herself up to the platform. Tom followed. She opened the upper-level door to a gap barely wide enough to see outside.

"Now we wait," she said.

"Wait?! The Russians are already patrolling the area," Tom protested. "At least tell me how long we have to wait?" he added when he got no response.

"I do not know. We will have to see."

"Are you serious? What are we waiting for?"

"Too many questions, my friend. Too many questions. Just be patient." Rachel sat down on one of the hay bales while Tom attended to her wound. With items from the first aid kit, he cleaned it as well as he could and bandaged her shoulder up tightly.

"Yup, straight through. You are one lucky girl. This bullet could have easily … well … you know."

"Yeah, I know," she responded.

"Keep it elevated, but at least rest your eyes a bit. No offense, but you look like you need it."

"Soon, we can rest all we want. We are not out of this just yet."

10:05 PM

MP Operations Room

"We have five units on scene now," the MP reported.

"What's the damage?" Vasiliev asked, without any hope for even the slightest bit of good news.

"They are gone. Their tracks clearly indicate they are still on the motorcycle, heading southwest. However, they have not been spotted by any of our patrols."

"They could not have gotten far. The bike must have some

degree of damage," Ivan speculated.

"This may very well be the case, sir. It was involved in quite the crash; a tree split the sidecar right off. We also found blood on the scene so we can say with certainty at least one of the fugitives is injured," the corporal reported further.

"Could it be from one of ours?"

"I doubt it, sir. It was on the tree bark where the fugitives must have taken cover from our fire."

Finally, a bit of good news. Their rescuers were dead, their vehicle beaten up, and now the two had an injury to deal with, Vasiliev thought.

"They must still be in the area somewhere," Grisha rightfully concluded. "Tell the unit on scene to follow their tracks."

"They already are, sir, but with the falling snow and winds, they will soon be too obscure to follow."

"What else?"

"We are looking at a destroyed checkpoint, several destroyed vehicles including the BA-10, and of course, the missing bike."

"Casualties?"

"Seven of ours, three of theirs. None wounded."

"Ten!" Vasiliev was flabbergasted. "No survivors?" The soldier shook his head. Grisha sighed heavily, then turned to Ivan. "They are not out of the woods yet, but I am realistic enough not to expect a miracle here. If we are going to find them, it probably won't happen before your report is due. If I were you, I would start preparing."

Without a word, Ivan exited the operations room, heading toward his office. Grisha immediately triggered an alarm, highest priority, mobilizing every single soldier on and off duty for the most intensive search he had ever organized. The area needed a thorough combing through, inch by inch. Less than five minutes later, the first personnel carriers were already leaving headquarters.

11:25 PM

Somewhere Outside Warsaw

Tom had noticed the increase in patrols. So far, they had kept to the road, but he knew this was to change soon. He was right. Soon after, forty to fifty lights emerged from the dark on the horizon, then spread apart in equal increments, combing through the fields.

"Rachel, how much longer?"

"Are you in a hurry?"

"Not I—*we* are," he replied, pointing into the direction of the flashlights. Just when Rachel stood up to have a look, a second row appeared not far from the first one, then a third, inside the forest. Things continued to worsen. An airplane was now circling the area.

Rachel took her satchel, and Tom helped her down the ladder.

"Follow me," she ordered Tom, and ran toward the edge of the closest field, waving her flashlight into the sky. The plane immediately went into a dive, then abruptly turned and landed right in front of them. Rachel again took off running, Tom following closely behind. By the time they reached the plane, the pilot had already gotten out of his seat and jumped off the wing. He was wearing a Russian uniform, but to Tom's surprise the plane had no markings.

"Can you fly?" the pilot asked looking at Rachel's bandaged shoulder.

"Do I have a choice?" she asked back.

"She's all yours then. Good luck!"

She thanked him with a quick hug before the pilot started running toward the barn. He would soon take advantage of the ongoing chaos and blend in with one of the search crews.

Motorcycles and armored vehicles were approaching from all directions at a worrying speed. Suddenly, a salvo of bullets shot through the body of the plane, ripping holes into the fuselage. There was not a second to lose. Tom helped Rachel onto the wing and then followed. She hurried into the pilot's seat and immediately pushed the throttle to full speed. Tom had not yet managed to get into his. The plane jolted forward, throwing him off balance. Only thanks to a strong reflex did he manage to grab the frame of the canopy, saving himself from falling off the plane. He tried to pull himself toward his seat but was not strong enough to fight the increasingly strong airstream from the propeller. On the contrary, his arms were rapidly tiring, his muscles increasingly burning, and below the plane, the frozen field was passing at an ever-increasing speed. He wondered how much longer he could hold on to the heavily rattling fuselage fighting itself through the snow. Not for long—a few more seconds, tops. He tried once more to gather his strength, but his grip weakened further. His right hand slid off, finger by finger, all the while his feet tried to get a grip on the wing's surface. He was hanging on with only his left arm, which was now tiring twice as fast. Tom tried to regain his grip with his right, but the winds were too strong. When the plane finally took off, the g-forces shifted, pressing Tom onto the wing. It did little to take pressure off his arm, and by now the airflow was so strong, Tom had a hard time breathing. Bullets were still flying all around them, tracers lighting up the sky like fireworks, one hitting the fuselage or wing every so often. Alarmed, Rachel looked back to see where the shots were being fired from. She did not expect to see Tom about to fall off the plane.

"Hold on!" she screamed from the top of her lungs and immediately pulled the stick backward, pushing Tom even harder into the wing. With the plane rising into the sky, his left hand was also about to lose its grip. Just when he could not hold on any longer, Rachel pushed the stick forward, turning the plane into a nosedive. Tom was lifted off the frame, and with his last bit of strength, he regained his hold with both hands and managed to position himself above his seat. He still struggled to get in. Dangerously close to the ground, Rachel reversed the course once again. The plane's near-vertical trajectory evened out, and after missing the ground by only a few feet, it ascended once again into the few scattered, low-hanging clouds. With the changing forces, Tom was thrown into his compartment, head on. It took another act of strength to turn himself around inside the narrow space, but he finally managed to get into his seat. He immediately closed the glass canopy around him. Now safe, he finally was able to relax. He buckled up and immediately felt something press against his leg. He opened the side pocket of his pants and pulled out the black notebook from the train. In the craziness of the events, he had forgotten all about it. He opened it, scanned the pages, chuckled, then carefully put it into the inside pocket of his jacket. It all made sense now.

Out of reach of the firing guns, the plane disappeared into the starry night sky.

25

January 27, 1945—9:15 AM
Officers Wing, Room 474

As expected, the report was not received well. Ivan did his best to stress the positives—that they knew the plane was heading toward Norway, that everyone was on high alert, the skies patrolled, radar units alerted, members of the resistance interrogated, the search on the ground close to finding the missing cargo, and that it was just a matter of time till everything would be resolved. However, the path of destruction, the death toll, and the vast resources mobilized, all under his command, were undeniable.

Tom's escape, even the loss of the artwork, as bad as they were, were not the biggest problem. At least not for the leadership in Moscow. They could easily have been categorized as another unfortunate story of war. An unusual one, yes; nevertheless, the war was full of such. The problem was that Ivan, the Colonel General, had defied a direct order. And not just any order, but one from the very top. Such an act of defiance carried dire consequences. It came as no surprise that his presence was requested at High Command the very next day, and he was already aware of what was in the mail: a court-martial, at minimum a dishonorable discharge, ending his beloved military career. All his years of faithful service, all his accomplishments, all his heroics, all out the window. Because of one mistake.

As bad as this was, one thing was even worse for the Colonel General. He and the entire organization under his command had been outsmarted by a common private, a boy from the middle of nowhere. Ivan had miserably failed as a commander, failed as a soldier, and failed as a person. The unbearable shame ate away at his very soul. He popped the cork of another one of Tom's champagnes and listened to the tiny bubbles fill his glass. He then opened his humidor, took another one of his Romeo y Julieta cigars, removed its head with the cutter, toasted the foot over his match, then pressed it between his lips. After a few puffs, he lifted the flute.

"To you, Timofei! To you! Now let's drink to whatever comes next." He emptied the glass in one go, enjoying the refreshing crispness that only comes from a bottle with a *grand cru* designation. He refilled the glass, and after one last puff, placed the cigar into the sparkling beverage.

All alone, his office as quiet as it could be, the Colonel General unholstered his pistol.

Part V

The Two Betrayals

26

September 5, 2017—10:30 AM (ART)
San Carlos de Bariloche

Patrick had caused quite the commotion, delaying the plane even more, but he did not care. He raced their new rental down Route 80, back toward the city of Bariloche, then turned onto the 40 North. Susan still had no idea what was going on. Now, in the privacy of the car, he finally let her in on his epiphany.

"As the priest said, it is all in the name. Remember when I asked him about Dieter's assumed family name? His exact response was, 'These were not my words,' and he was right."

"So, what are we looking for then?" Susan asked, somewhat distracted by how fast Patrick was driving.

"A place." Patrick still could not believe how he did not see this earlier.

"A place? Look at that. But we still don't know what name to look for."

Patrick took his eyes off the road just for a second, and with a triumphant smile turned his head toward Susan. "I do."

"How in the world do you know? And please slow down. You may kill us before you get a chance to tell me."

But Patrick didn't take his foot off the pedal. "Remember, back in the hotel, I looked over the map to see where this family may live? I learned that, around here, most of the rural properties are named after their owners, like Estancia Garcia, or after some kind of geographical quality, like Estancia La Providencia, Estancia Montana, or Estancia Alta Vista."

"Yes?" Susan was going along.

"Now, every single one I looked at had a Spanish name, except one: Estancia de Gobineau." Susan still did not see what Patrick was getting at.

"What is wrong with Gobineau?"

"De Gobineau," he corrected her, "and nothing is wrong with it. But the name caught my attention, because it is French."

"It is the home of a French family, no?"

"This is exactly what I thought at first, too. But then it dawned on me. Joseph Arthur de Gobineau was a nineteenth-century French aristocrat who wrote an essay about the inequality of races based on a supposedly scientific racist theory. He argued that civilizations decline and eventually fall when races mix, and praised the Aryans as the pinnacle of human development. You can only imagine how quick the fascists were to jump on his theories to legitimize their policy of ethnic cleansing. The entire Nazi dogma is based on his hypothesis. Who else would name their home after such a man? Nobody but someone like Klaus."

"Or a French family called Gobineau."

"De Gobineau," he corrected her again. "But tell me, what are the odds?"

Susan had to agree; Patrick was on to something. "Go figure!" she replied. "If you are right, I have to give it to this Klaus. It's really quite ingenious; a name like a beacon to Nazi sympathizers, yet like any other to the rest of us."

12:05 PM

Estancia de Gobineau, San Carlos de Bariloche

It took Susan and Patrick a little over an hour and a half on the pothole-riddled 40 North till they reached the small road turning off toward their destination. It was one of those nondescript side streets that one could easily miss. Patrick stopped the car, trying to see where the road was leading, but it soon disappeared into the thick forest.

"Look at the new asphalt. Somebody keeps it meticulously maintained."

Susan nodded. "Very German."

"It sure is," Patrick said as he turned off the 40 and drove into the forest.

"How do you want to do this?" Susan asked. "We can't just walk up to the door, ring the bell, and ask them if they are interested in a new vacuum cleaner."

"We certainly can't," Patrick chuckled. "Let's have a look first, and then we will decide." They drove for another fifteen minutes through the thickening trees until they reached a sizable opening. They could see the estancia right ahead, next to an idyllic lake and surrounded by the forest, the majestic Andes towering behind. The scenery was truly breathtaking. Patrick kept driving, passing by the tall stone walls surrounding the property, noticing the multiple cameras pointing in every possible direction.

"This place is too beautiful for such a fortress," Susan said, who thought the walls, barbed wire, and cameras to be oddly out of place.

"It is remote, and it is secure. Anything else probably does not matter to them," Patrick explained. They continued driving, passing the estancia, and soon after, turned onto a dirt road that entered the forest again, this time on the other side of the opening. Patrick parked once they were out of sight. With binoculars in hand, the two walked a few feet through the bushes to the edge of the forest, and took a good look at the property.

"You were right, Patrick. This is it, the home of someone who does not want to be bothered. Look at all this security. Now, how do we get in?" Susan asked.

"There is no way in," Patrick responded bluntly. He had already suspected as much before scouting the location.

"No way in?" Susan was startled. "How are we—"

"We wait till someone comes out."

12:25 PM

Hironori had followed Patrick and Susan to the airport and purchased a ticket for the next flight out the same route. He had some time to kill as it would not take off for another two hours. While waiting for his coffee at one of the few shops, he suddenly spotted Patrick and Susan storm by, heading straight back to the rental cars. Without showing the slightest emotion, his eyes followed the duo. He could only speculate on what had happened but had a good idea where they were heading—a remote area, in the middle of nowhere. It suited him just right. The only caveat was that he had to get to them before the Heydrichs did. The two were done for either way, but considering what was at stake for him personally, he had to be the one to finally end it all. He waited patiently for his beverage before following the two, making sure they were gone before he approached the counter.

Like Patrick and Susan a few minutes ahead of him, he drove up the 40 North and took the small road through the forest. Hironori turned off the well-paved road, just before the opening and parked his car next to the old well. It was close to the estancia, yet still out of sight. He took his sword from the trunk, put it on his back, then stalked through the trees without delay. It did not take him long to spot Patrick and Susan. He made his way toward them, along the forest's edge, behind the thick shrubs, not making the slightest of sounds.

12:45 PM

Patrick was keeping an eye on the property for any kind of movement. Susan did the same, but not without looking around here and there to take in the scenery.

"How beautiful it is up here. Look at this: sunshine, mountains, forests, lakes, fresh air, you name it …. And look, over there is even a herd of grazing deer, without a care in the world. It's all so wonderful …. What a paradise this is up here." She could not contain her effusive praise. "And did you notice how quiet it is here? All you hear is the sounds of the trees and the birds—"

Patrick shushed her as the estancia's main gate opened and a black Chevy Suburban with dark tinted windows pulled out. Despite the powerful binoculars, Patrick could not make out anyone inside but the driver and a passenger, the dark windows obscuring his view.

"Time to go," Patrick told Susan.

+ + +

Hironori had made better progress than expected. Now closing in on the two, he adjusted his pace, his feet probing the surface of the path through his soft shoes, balancing his footing to even the most minute obstacle, as the sound of even the smallest twig breaking would echo through the forest, giving away as his presence. It did slow his progress, though in his favor, the slight wind worked to his advantage, its direction carrying his scent away from the deer nearby. With their highly sensitive sense of smell, he knew how easily they could be spooked. But alerted deer were soon the least of his worries. From the corner of his eye, he saw the black Suburban exit the main gate, and straight ahead of him, Susan and Patrick walking back to their car. He had to get to the two before they took off.

+ + +

"Go already; we are going to lose them," Susan urged Patrick to catch up.

"Let's not follow too closely. We don't want to raise any suspicion"—Patrick pointed to the security cameras—"or they will alert the driver."

"We are going to lose them," Susan argued.

"Don't worry," Patrick tried to calm her; "it is a long way down."

"Seriously, go already," Susan repeated, now nagging.

"Just a few more seconds," Patrick responded calmly. "They have not even closed the gate yet."

Suddenly, out of the blue, the deer took off running. Patrick could only imagine what startled them. "You are right; time to go," he said and immediately started the engine and drove out of the forest.

+ + +

The Japanese hit man's eyes watched the car pass the estancia as inconspicuously as possible, then enter the forest on the other side. Judging by the engine's sound, the car sped up as soon as it was out of sight. Hironori stepped out of the forest. *How can these two be so stupid yet so lucky?* he asked himself, shaking his head. Susan and Patrick were now out of his reach, the two about to walk right into the arms of the Heydrichs. Dying by his sword would have been bad enough, but dying by the hands of the Heydrichs was a whole different ball game. Hironori knew very well that his fate was not far different from theirs now that it was time to go back home.

12:55 PM

Susan was not used to such high speeds, especially on narrow roads. It made her more than nervous, to say the least. Holding on as tightly as she could, she instinctively pushed herself back into the seat. Even worse, the sharp curves made her nauseous. She asked Patrick to slow down repeatedly.

"Open the window," was all he proposed. Fresh air would help, and worst-case scenario, she could hold her head out the window. The trees seemed to fly by faster and faster, and with every bend in the road, the tires screeched louder and louder. Susan was now downright scared, fearing Patrick would lose control any second. One small mistake and the car would crash into the trees and slide down the steep hill, killing them both. But her repeated pleas were only answered with a "Hang in there!"

Then out of nowhere, just behind one of the many curves, the black Suburban appeared right in front of them, stopped in the middle of the road. With both feet, Patrick hit the brake pedal, pressing as hard as he could. With screeching tires, they slid further and further toward the beefed-up SUV. Their car did not want to stop. Patrick pushed the brake even harder and harder still, frantically attempting to bring the car to a halt before impact.

"Shit!" Patrick was screaming. "Shit! Shit! Shit!" But his words were drowned by the sound of the locked-up wheels. A fraction of a second later, the rental smashed into the back of the massive SUV. With the ear-splitting noise of crashing metal, the force of the impact buried their faces deep into the deploying airbags. Patrick managed to stay calm. Susan did not. Adrenaline shooting through her body, her heart pounding in her chest, she was staring at the deflated airbag right in front of her, oblivious to the German-produced HK416 assault rifles pointing at them.

"Shit," Patrick said once more, this time rather quietly, resigned.

Susan just sat, shaking, and turned her head to look up at Patrick. "I told you to slow down. You nearly killed me," she screamed at him.

"You may wish you were dead soon enough," he solemnly responded to Susan's frantic reaction, glaring at the tactical team surrounding them. Not a second later, the side windows shattered and hands reached in to push a piece of cloth against their noses. Everything went black before they even had a chance to react.

9:57 AM (PDT)
Eva's Condominium, Westwood, CA

Eva's work schedule was more flexible whenever Patrick was out of town, so she had planned to take advantage of a late start. Celebrating a friend's birthday the evening before, she did not get home till the wee hours of the morning. She knew it was going to be a struggle to get up the next day, and not only because it was a Monday. When she was awoken by the ringing of her cell phone, she could not be bothered to even peek at the screen. She let the call go to voice mail, pulled the blanket over her head and hoped to get another half hour of sleep. Not a minute later her phone rang again. Then again and once more. She finally opened her eyes. Four missed calls from work. Without listening to the voice mails, she called back. The receptionist put her right through to the office of vice president Dave Marshall, the man in charge of the West Coast operations. His personal assistant picked up the phone.

"Eva, where are you? We have been frantically trying to get in touch with you."

"I am sorry; I overslept. What is going on?"

"Dave has a visitor, and they are looking for you. Something urgent, but that is all I know. Hold on, I am putting you through." Her call was immediately picked up, and as usual, Dave came right to the point.

"Eva, we have a situation. Where in the world are you?" Eva asked again what was going on, but Dave refused to share anything further.

"You'd better come in right away. I'll fill you in once you are here." Then, without saying goodbye, he hung up.

Eva got up, dressed, and poured herself some coffee already hot in the brewer. She hurriedly left her condominium with a full cup in hand, worried sick.

2:12 PM (ART)
Basement Community Room, Estancia de Gobineau

Where was he? What had happened? How long had he been out? Patrick was dazed and confused, further distracted by the sharp pain in his head. After a few tries, he finally managed to open one of his eyes just enough to catch a glimpse of his surroundings.

"Susan?" There was no response. "Susan?" he asked again. Still no response. But he could hear voices: "He is waking up. Go let them know."

Through the tiny gap between his eyelids, he could make out a few people, all dressed in black with red armbands, a white dot and a black swastika on each.

"Where am I?" Patrick asked.

An unfamiliar voice answered. "Don't worry; you will know soon enough."

Then a bucketful of cold water hit his face.

"Throw some on the bitch, too. She is still out," someone suggested.

It took another minute or two till Patrick could see more clearly. To his relief, Susan was right next to him, slowly waking up.

"Are you okay?" Patrick asked, desperate for an answer. She was still too muddled to respond. He managed to look around a bit more. They were in an unusually big room with no windows. He did notice, however, the many Nazi artifacts—flags, military items, uniforms. It was like a museum in there. When he turned his head, he saw an old metal autopsy table. On top was a bag, its insignia sending a shiver down his spine: Dr. Mengele.

He had witnessed death more than he ever wanted during his active-duty days. But dying slowly under unimaginable pain …. He was supposed to be trained for situations like this, but nobody and nothing could ever prepare one for torture. Even more than fear he felt guilt. Guilt for not leaving Susan on the plane, especially after the priest's dire warning. He had clearly underestimated his enemy, and now Susan too was going to pay for it.

Patrick still struggled to use his eyes. With his somewhat blurred vision, he saw the door open and someone enter the room. This someone walked over to the autopsy table with big steps, grabbed a chair, and sat down right in front of them. Now closer, Patrick could tell he was older, tall, and pale, with short but neatly styled blond hair, highly manicured fingernails, and nicely dressed in brown slacks and a khaki-colored, meticulously pressed shirt covering his bulging stomach. He was as clean cut yet as intimidating as one could expect from a German Nazi.

"Hello, Mr. Rooper. You found me. How is my inheritance coming along?" the man asked sarcastically. The guards chuckled. It was the voice Patrick had heard on the phone just a few days ago. Dieter!

"What is it that you want from me?" the German asked in his brisk manner. Patrick ignored the question.

"If I were you, I would answer," somebody said from the other side of the room in a heavy Japanese accent. Hironori walked over and leaned against the autopsy table. "We meet again, and this time you two will not get away."

The close relationship between the Heydrichs and the Japanese hitman did not come as a surprise, but it was now clear Dieter's hoped-for cooperation was nothing but a pipe dream. Patrick kept quiet, trying to think of a way out, fast, as one of the guards punched him in the face.

"He asked you a question, and when he does, you answer!"

Pain shot through Patrick's cheek, immediately followed by the taste of blood. He was still dazed, struggling to talk.

"Maybe we need to open this suitcase and take out some of the tools," one of the guards suggested. In their thirst for blood, they all laughed. It took a strenuous effort for Patrick to mumble a few words.

"Tell me about your dad Klaus, Tom Sobchak, and Yamaguchi."

Did he just hear that right? Dieter was aghast. How dare this American...! He got up and slapped Patrick across the face, causing more pain.

"It is me asking the questions and you who are going to talk, not the other way around!" Dieter screamed at him. Despite a swelling cheek and blood dripping from his mouth, Patrick managed to put on a slight smile.

"You are mistaken, my friend. *You* are going to answer my questions, or I am going to destroy you and your family."

Dieter was bewildered by Patrick's blunt defiance. He had to admit, this guy had guts.

"You would need to be quite the magician, my friend," Dieter chuckled and slapped Patrick once more. The guards laughed again. But against all expectations, Patrick's smile got even bigger.

"I, we, have the movies," Patrick told him. "You know—the ones of your dad and those agents? Back in 1960? Just imagine what would happen if they were, let's say, shown on the national news. Or internationally on CNN. What if these movies are already digitized and uploaded to a server, the link ready to be distributed, and I am the only one who can stop it?"

Visibly upset, Dieter, with his deep blue eyes, shot him a look that could kill, and with equally big steps as he entered, left the room. Maybe, just maybe, the priest who was so worried about them being killed had just saved their lives.

10:21 AM (PDT)
Offices of *The New York Times*, Los Angeles

It took Eva a while to drive to work. The proximity to her office was one of the main reasons she had decided to buy her condo in Westwood a few months earlier. She greatly enjoyed not sitting in traffic every day for over an hour each way, instead spending her freed-up time hanging out with friends, reading, and her favorite, cooking, making every meal from scratch. Only after she moved did she realize how poorly she had been eating. She did not miss the unhealthy takeout options, enjoying instead the renewed energy her freshly prepared meals provided.

But today of all days, despite the late hour, traffic was worse than usual. It only took one accident to clog up the streets and massively delay the usual commute. Finally reaching the office, Eva parked in the lot, entered the building, rode the elevator to the top floor, and entered the offices. To her surprise, the usual bustling atmosphere was strangely subdued.

"What is going on?" she asked the teary-eyed receptionist.

"I am not at liberty to tell," she responded.

"Is it Patrick?"

The receptionist, who was struggling to keep her composure, did not say another word. Now worried to her core, Eva headed straight toward the vice president's office, who indeed had a visitor, sitting in one of the chairs facing his desk.

"Ah, here you are, Eva. Please sit down." Dave gestured to the other chair.

"Is everything okay?" Eva asked, concerned.

"I am afraid not," he answered, equally troubled.

2:25 PM (ART)
Basement Community Room

Susan had fully woken and gotten over the initial shock of seeing Hironori standing right in front of her. Patrick tried to calm her, but the guards, with the help of a few additional slaps, made it clear that was not allowed. Patrick could not tell how much time had passed since Dieter's return, but it could not have been long. He noticed an executive document holder under the German's arm, which was also placed on the autopsy table.

"So, Miss Sobchak, Mr. Rooper, it is time to get started." Dieter opened the medical bag and contemplated which instrument best fit the occasion. He finally decided on a scalpel.

"So, these movies, huh?"

"Yes, these movies," Patrick replied confidently.

"All lies! You heard some bullshit story about my family, and now you are trying to use it against us. We both know those movies don't exist anymore. Nice try, though," Dieter smiled while holding the scalpel against the light. He moved his thumb gently against the blade, making sure it was as sharp as it could be. Susan was petrified. Patrick managed to keep his cool.

"Are you really willing to gamble your family's existence on it?" Patrick asked, but he did not get the response he hoped for. Dieter just chuckled as he looked down at him, his right hand performing a dismissive gesture.

"Please, don't make me laugh, Mr. Rooper." He again checked the blade against the light.

Susan shivered; cold sweat rolled down her forehead. She could not help but think of every other poor soul that had been mistreated by these very instruments, of every single person in the Auschwitz concentration camp who became victim of Dr. Mengele's cruel and inhumane experiments.

"Please, please, we'll do whatever you want. Please, don't hurt us," she pleaded.

There was nothing Patrick could do to stop her from interfering, except push on. "Dieter, your dad has organized a nice life here for you. These movies will destroy everything."

Dieter again shook his head. "I have had just about enough of this nonsense," he countered the empty threat. He then told the guards to leave the room. They obeyed. "You too, my friend," he instructed Hironori. "For work like this, I cannot have witnesses."

"I am here to make sure these two will not be a problem anymore," the assassin protested.

"Trust me, my friend, they won't. Now leave!" Hironori reluctantly followed suit.

Susan looked in horror as the thick, well-insulated door closed behind him. Dieter once again sat down, again holding up the scalpel. "Now that we are alone ..."

10:27 AM (PDT)

Offices of *The New York Times*

"Is Patrick okay?" Eva inquired worriedly.

"Yes, he is okay. At least, as far as we know."

"Then what is going on?" she asked impatiently.

"It's Patrick's fiancée, Sarah ..."

"Is she okay?"

Dave was biting down on his lower lip and ever so slightly shook his head. "No, she is not. She is dead."

"What?!" Eva could not believe what she was hearing. Tears immediately shot in her eyes. "Dead? That ... that can't be! How? When?" Dave handed her a tissue.

"We can't say too much at this point. It is an ongoing investigation," the visitor answered.

Dave offered Eva a glass of water. "Do you want something stronger? Bourbon?"

She declined and took the glass. "Just give me a minute; I'll be all right."

Dave did. After a moment, he spoke again. "Eva, this is First Lieutenant Muller from Santa Monica homicide. He wants to ask you a few questions."

"I'm not sure if I can be of any help. I hardly know her."

The detective got up from his seat. "Eva—may I call you Eva?" She nodded, and the detective continued. "We have reason to believe Sarah's death was not the result of a random robbery or home invasion. It looks like she was specifically targeted. However, we could not find anything that would explain our theory, or at least make it plausible." Eva stared at the detective in utter disbelief. "We are, of course, looking into various avenues, and one of them is her connection to Patrick."

"Patrick?" she said, shocked. "I am sure he has nothing to do with her death!"

Without turning his head, the detective looked at Dave, and then back to Eva. "We are asking ourselves if the attack on Sarah is somehow related to his work, given the nature of his profession." The detective paused a moment. "As you can imagine, we would like to ask him a few questions as soon as possible, but we understand he is out of town. Do you know, by any chance, how we can get in touch with him?"

27

2:31 PM (ART)

Basement Community Room

"I need your help."

Susan thought she had heard a bad joke. Patrick started to wonder if his bluff might be working after all. He pressed on. "All we want is to talk to you. Then, if you let us go, we will destroy the movies, and you will never see or hear from us again," he promised.

Dieter, already nervous, was getting more irritated. "Listen, Mr. Rooper, it's time to stop the shenanigans. There are no movies."

"I'd be happy to help you get rid of—"

"Just STOP with the movies, will you?" Dieter snapped, obviously irritated. The room fell silent. Patrick tried to make sense of this unexpected turn but could not, neither could Susan. Unless this was a clever ploy to encourage them to lower their guard and admit their bluff. It would be an ingenious move, yet not one good enough to fool Patrick.

"Then what are you talking about?" Patrick emphasized each word individually.

"As I said, I need your help." Dieter's cold, sarcastic tone had turned into a compassionate, even charming one. Patrick and Susan glanced at each other, each wondering if the other had any idea what was going on.

"But if this is not about the movies, we really do not know what you are talking about," Patrick asked, somewhat frustrated.

Dieter leaned into them. "No, it's not about the movies," he responded, still irritated, then disappeared behind them, scalpel in hand. Patrick prepared for the worst. Susan turned her head, eyeing the German, terrified. A second later, she felt the blade cutting through the zip tie, freeing her hands. She instinctively rubbed her wrists, trying to soothe the discomfort. Patrick, freed next, did the same. Dieter walked over to the bar, poured two glasses of water, and handed them to his captives.

"Let's talk!"

10:33 AM (PDT)
Offices of *The New York Times*

"I only know he is on a private assignment, and I have not heard from him in a few days. That's all. But it's not unusual. He goes off-grid every so often."

"Yes, the private assignment," Dave confirmed. "I told the detective all about it. At least what I know. Shouldn't he be back already?"

"Yes, he should be, but sometimes his research turns out to be more extensive than expected. You know that, Dave."

"And he always delivers," the vice president confirmed.

"This private assignment. Anything you can tell me about it?" the detective inquired.

"Not really. I know as much as Dave does."

The detective nodded. "Have you tried calling him on his cell?"

"Yes," Eva responded. "It goes straight to voice mail."

The detective was perched on Dave's desk, his right leg still on the floor, his left hanging over the edge, looking down at Patrick's assistant.

"Eva, I understand this is difficult. But I have to ask you a few more questions."

Eva nodded.

"What can you tell me about their relationship? You know—Patrick and Sarah?"

"Oh, they could not have been happier, a true match made in heaven. They were very much in love, both looking forward to their upcoming nuptial."

"No fights or major disagreements?"

Eva felt a little offended by the detective's line of questioning. "I already told you; Patrick has nothing to do with Sarah's death—I can guarantee you that. They are—were—the perfect couple."

The detective thoughts circled back to Patrick's work. "Is there nothing else you can tell me about what he is currently working on?"

Eva shook her head, her eyes still filled with tears.

"Nothing unusual, anything out of the ordinary recently? Any conflicts, threats, anything of that nature?"

Eva contemplated carefully before answering. "No conflicts, no threats, nothing really. It has all been business as usual recently."

The detective nodded once again, then got up from the desk. "Thank you, Eva, you were of great—"

"Wait. Now that I think about it, there is one thing about his private assignment that's, let's say, a little bit out of the ordinary. Not too long ago, a woman came to see Patrick. It was all very mysterious. She would not tell me what her visit was about."

"A woman?" Dave asked.

"Yes, a woman. She was older, very distinctive, and very stylish. She first wrote an anonymous letter asking Patrick for help. Then, out of the blue, she showed up here at the office, requesting a meeting. He first declined, of course. But I suggested he should at least hear her out since she had come all this way. She was such a sweet old lady, you know, and I was curious … Oh my God, is this all my fault?" Her voice broke, tears again filling her eyes.

"You have nothing to do with Sarah's passing," Dave tried to assure her.

"By any chance, do you still have this letter?" the detective pressed on.

Eva ignored the question, now weeping heavily. "If I hadn't pestered Patrick into seeing the old lady, Sarah might still be alive.

It *is* all my fault."

"We don't know that," Dave tried to calm her. "And even if Sarah's death is related to this visit, you can't blame yourself, Eva. Isn't that right, detective?"

"Listen, do you know what was in the letter? It is important," Detective Muller pressed on.

Eva shook her head ever so slightly.

"Patrick threw it in the trash the minute he opened it. You must understand, he gets letters like this ... oh, not too often, but too many to take them seriously. I only remember her mentioning something was weighing on her conscience, and that she needed his help."

"I see. Can you describe the woman to me?"

Eva closed her eyes, trying to picture her. "Well, she was about five foot seven, slender, gray hair—immaculately styled like she had just walked out of a salon—piercing blue eyes, and, as I already said, very elegantly dressed. You should have seen the ring on her finger. It was out of this world."

"You said something about her coming all this way. Did she say where she was from?"

"Yes, she told me she had flown in from the East Coast, just to see Patrick."

The detective looked up from his notepad. "Did you say East Coast?"

"Yes, the East Coast," she confirmed.

"By any chance, did she say she was from Long Island?"

"Yes, that's it." Eva was puzzled. "How do you know?"

"Oh, just a hunch. There was some water cooler talk in our office about an unusual double homicide there. I did not make the connection before, but the crimes seem eerily similar."

"Do you think they are connected?" Dave asked.

"They might be."

2:45 PM (ART)
Basement Community Room

Susan and Patrick had gulped down the water to quench their thirst. They were grateful for the unexpected refreshment and immediately felt better.

"I am sorry about all this. I have to keep up appearances when the guards are around," Dieter attempted to apologize. "Their loyalty is with my father, not me, and my father, well …."

Even now, neither Patrick nor Susan knew what to make of the sudden change in attitude. In the dark about what this was all about, they took the unexpected kindness with caution. Dieter took the chair, turned it around, and sat down, once again facing the two, his arm resting on top of the chair's back. The strong, intimidating Aryan bully was all but gone. He took a long pause, then a deep breath. "We do not have much time, so please hear me out."

10:47 AM (PDT)
Offices of *The New York Times*

Dave called his assistant and asked to get the IT guy from the New York main office on the phone.

"Listen, we have a bit of a situation here. I need a copy of the L.A. office security tapes from August 2, 9 a.m. onward." He turned to Eva for confirmation. "It was the second, correct?" She nodded. "Yes, the second. Keep your eyes out for an older lady, elegantly dressed, meeting with Patrick Rooper. We need to have her identified …. Yes, send the video and extract some frames that show her face. This is urgent, highest priority. Do you understand? Great, thank you."

"How long will this take?" the detective asked as soon as Dave finished the call.

"I'd say we'll have it within half an hour."

The detective gave Dave an approving nod. "Listen, I do not have a warrant, but may I have a look at Patrick's office?"

Dave had already expected the request. "Anything we can do to help."

"Eva, I believe this is all for now. But please keep yourself available. Chances are we are going to have a few more questions," the detective instructed her.

"Take the day off, go home, and rest," Dave proposed. "Let me know if you need anything. Otherwise, we will see you tomorrow."

2:48 PM (ART)

Basement Community Room

Dieter was aware of the consequences of what he was about to do. For the briefest of moments he second-guessed himself, but after a dose of self-encouragement he started talking.

"Back in 1949, an attractive young woman named Greta came to see my father. From what I know, she was Nazi royalty, twenty-something years old, the daughter of a German aristocrat, Earl Karl von Badenholz, and his wife, Polish Baroness Anja Brunowski. Karl was a high-ranking officer, killed somewhere on the eastern front during the early years of the war. Her mother's fate was worse. She was raped and killed in her own home by a Russian elite team during a covert raid inside Germany. As luck would have it, Greta was having a sleepover at a friend's house that very evening, sparing her the same fate. But it was she who found the body of her slaughtered mother the next morning, a memory that would haunt her for years. Not being able to come to terms with her parents' untimely demise, she dedicated her life to avenge their violent deaths. She could not have been older than fifteen when she asked to join the Gestapo, the German secret service. They immediately welcomed her. Fluent in both German and Polish and equally familiar with both cultures, she was sent to Warsaw, where she proved herself a capable operative and quickly turned into an invaluable asset. She would have preferred an assignment inside the Russian territory, but when the Germans were driven out of Poland, she volunteered to stay behind to finally get her revenge.

"One day she received an order of a special kind: to locate and retrieve two train wagons full of valuable art destined for Berlin but intercepted by the Red Army. She could not have been more ecstatic as it was a mission that could attract even the Führer's attention. She never told anyone how she managed to get her hands on the collection, but somehow she did—just not till after the war. By then, the need for war funding was gone, and so were the Nazi elite. There was no one to hand over the art to, and she did not waste a thought on giving it back to its rightful Jewish owners. As her family's wealth was gone, the valuables looted, the mansion bombed to the ground, and the bank accounts confiscated for purpose of reparations, she decided to liquidate the valuable artwork and pocket the proceeds herself. But keeping the artwork in Europe was not without risk. She barely managed to stay one step ahead of the so-called Venus Fixers or Monument Men—specialized Allied troops tasked to recover displaced art. So, one day back in forty-nine, she knocked on our door and asked my father to store it for her, here in South America, safe from prying eyes in Europe. My father hesitated at first, but as he was quite taken by her, and being the master manipulator that she was, it did not take her long to get him to agree."

Dieter got up again and pulled a sizable, flat piece of carton from one of the few cabinets. "Let me show you this," he said, not without pride, while removing its wrapping paper. "This is an original Chagall, believe it or not. One of his early ones, painted when he was in Paris. Just imagine—not speaking French, with no friends, and fifteen hundred miles away from the love of his life, Bella. He was miserable ... Anyway," Dieter continued as he put the painting back in its place, "Greta gifted it to my father as a thank-you for his help. It is worth millions, at least to anyone but him. He was not too happy about the gesture, Chagall being Jewish and all. I, on the other hand, love it. I have, ever since I saw it for the very first time, back when I was only a small child. It is the very painting that awakened my interest in the arts. Maybe another reason my father hates it so much. But I digress ...."

Dieter sat back on his chair. "While organizing the sale of the stolen artwork, Greta became a regular in our home. Over time, she and my father became good friends, and she often visited even after the entire collection was sold. Then one day in the late fifties, for reasons I do not know, she stayed longer and … became pregnant. Maybe there was some love; maybe she just wanted to say thank you again, this time in a way only a woman can. Whatever it was, the pregnancy certainly came as a surprise. Not wanting to jeopardize her marriage, she begged my father to keep it a secret. He did. She stayed right here at our estancia for the remainder of the nine months. As soon as I was born, she took off."

Despite Dieter's best effort not to, he had gotten emotional. "So, where did this all leave me? I grew up without a mother, with a father who did not want me in the first place, in a true Nazi home with zero compassion, no warmth whatsoever. For as long as I can remember, I had to live up to the Nazi stereotype, my life nothing more than a seemingly eternal military drill. To be strong, every time, all the time, if for nothing else than to make my father look good. I was exposed to nothing but Nazi ideology, documentaries about Hitler, German war successes, and propaganda about the final solution. I could watch nothing but long-winded Leni Riefenstahl movies celebrating this terrible ethos, over and over. Once, during one of these never-ending screenings, I was so bored, I dared to ask my father if I could go to my room and play with my toy soldiers instead. He hit me so hard he broke my jaw. I never dared to ask again. You cannot imagine how lost, how alone I felt, and how often I cried myself to sleep at night."

It was impossible not to sense the deep hatred Dieter carried for his own father. Susan could only imagine the dread of his childhood. Patrick made an effort to look at the story more objectively, but even he was quite taken.

"When I was old enough to be home schooled, I got a teacher who truly changed my life. After I showed her the Chagall, she tailored her curriculum around my passion for the arts and introduced me to music, poetry, and painting. For the first time, it was about me, the true me. But soon, my father found out, and despite her pleas and objections, she was literally dragged out of the compound. The new teacher was handpicked by him, a specialist of a different kind, and from then on, my days were again filled with nothing but warfare, ideology, the Aryan race, German history, the rise and reign of Hitler … you get the picture."

Dieter stopped talking. He sat with his head slightly downward, staring ahead of himself; all the while, Susan started to feel increasingly uncomfortable with the silence.

"Oh, Dieter …" she tried to show her empathy. Like coming out of a trance, the German man slightly shook his head and continued.

"One day during my early teenage years, my father decided the time had come for me to prove myself at competitive sports. Of course, I was not allowed to join a team in the city, so the guards had to fill in, all of them bigger and stronger than me. I had no chance. With the help of his belt, he would let me know his disappointment every time I, according to him, had not given my best. He found other ways to humiliate me too. It was especially bad when he entertained guests, when he needed to show off his toughness on my account. It was his idea of valuable life lessons, as this was sure to teach me to grow strong and develop the winner mentality I was lacking."

Dieter took in another deep breath. "I tried so hard to live up to his expectations, to be the son he wanted, but it just is not me. I may look and act like a typical Nazi, but inside I am not, never have been, and never will be. My life is nothing but one big lie, leaving me completely alone." Dieter adjusted himself in his seat, pained by the memories of times gone by. "As you can see, I have learned to act my role in this ridiculous play. But my true self, even after all these years, after all these decades, is still a prisoner in the very place I call home. I have never been able to go out and meet people. I have never dated. Yes, my father invited eligible girls and their families for meets-and-greets, all of them in line with his ideology. I don't need to mention I was not interested in any of them. Needless to say, after turning down girl after girl, he eventually asked if I was a homosexual. I am not, but had I told him so, he would have killed me right then and there."

Dieter tried hard not to get choked up. Already as a child he had learned to suppress his feelings, to refrain from crying, to ignore his emotions, but now, close to his father's demise, things were different. Visibly uncomfortable, he once again adjusted his position, struggling with the very words that passed his lips, yet as they did, a heavy stone seemed to gradually lift from his soul.

"I hate what my father stands for, I hate what he does, and I hate to be his son. I hate this place, I hate this house, and I hate everything in it. All this represents everything that is wrong in this world. Every day I live in pain; every day is another lie, another day wasted. And for what? For the outdated beliefs of a bitter old man clinging to a past that should never have existed in the first place. World War II may have ended back in forty-five. For me, it is still raging on."

10:57 AM (PDT)
Offices of *The New York Times*

Detective Muller entered Patrick's office and was surprised by how immaculate it was. "Either ex-military or obsessive compulsive," he guessed.

"Both, but 'neat' may be a better fit here than 'obsessive compulsive,'" Dave responded.

The detective peeked inside a few drawers, but as he found so often these days, there was nothing of importance lying around.

"Is the work of your writers being backed up on a company server?"

"It depends," Dave responded. "Often, they don't upload an article till it is ready for print. Even then, sensitive data can never end up in a cloud because the more privacy we grant our resources, the better articles our journalists can write. Officially, it is against company policy, but enforcement would be counterproductive. It's just better for the bottom line this way."

Sarah's picture on Patrick's desk caught the detective's eye. "We have to get in touch with him."

"We do. Yet I am dreading the moment," Dave said, interrupted by the buzz of his phone, alerting him to a new message. "The security video just arrived. Let's go have a look."

3:02 PM (ART)
Basement Community Room

"Why didn't you just leave?" Susan interrupted.

"I would have if I could, and a few times I was close," Dieter responded. "But as long as my father is alive, I am at risk. You mentioned these movies, so you know the story. What you probably do not know is that, back then, the Mossad eventually decided to end their mission to get my father. It was a highly unpopular move they soon began to regret, as the withdrawal of the detail in town sent shockwaves through the organization. The discontent was so strong that many of their agents quit and formed their own independent group with one goal, and one goal only: justice for their murdered colleagues. They have never forgotten, and even today, they are going strong. Among their members are many former and active agents, young and old. And don't underestimate their resources, either, as they are funded by very capable donors from all around the world. These people cannot wait to skin my father alive, even after all these years. Now imagine what they would do to me, just to get back at him. No, I can't leave. I am safe only here. For now."

Dieter looked around the room with all its Nazi memorabilia. "But things are about to change, and I can finally look forward to a life outside all this, outside our tall walls. Yes, I will soon be free because my father is dying. It is just a matter of time now—maybe a few more weeks, maybe just days, maybe even less. Who knows? Yes, soon everything will change." A feeling of excitement snuck up inside him, in his eyes a hint of the longed-for freedom.

Susan could not help but feel sorry for the burly German. He truly was a broken soul, beaten into someone he was not. She could not even come close to imagining the emotional and mental hell this man had been forced to endure, decade after decade, knowing well she would not have the strength to do so.

"Listen, Dieter," Patrick said, "I understand what you are saying. However, I am failing to see how we can help."

September 6, 2017—3:04 AM (JST)
Minato-Ku, Tokyo, Japan

Yamaguchi was the kind of person who liked to stay up late. There was something appealing about the nocturnal hours, the solitude one gets only while everybody else is asleep. However, it was unusual even for him to be up this late. He had been anxiously awaiting an update, which he had finally received.

Hironori was not merely an employee; he was a leader, and he was a friend. A most loyal one who had been with him from the very beginning, even before Yamaguchi took over from his father—an essential cog in the machinery of the vast and ever-expanding empire. Without Hironori, the organization would not be what it was today. Yet, facts were facts, and Yamaguchi could not ignore them. He thought he would never see the day when his master employee failed him. His disappointment gradually turned into anger. Not because the failure would have any direct consequences, now that the fugitives had ended up in the hands of the Heydrichs—no. Yamaguchi was angry with himself. Looking back at what he had recently learned, he should have seen it coming. His master assassin was not the man he used to be, not the rock he could count on or, more importantly, trust.

September 5, 2017—3:07 PM (ART)
Basement Community Room

"I was just getting to that part. You see, old Yamaguchi was Greta's biggest client, virtually purchasing the entire collection, which is now worth billions. When he died, his son inherited the lot. Let me tell you, the Yamaguchis love their art, the son even more than his father. It is everything to him, and he will do anything to protect it. Anything."

"I am starting to see how this Japanese crime boss and your father got acquainted. Through the collection," Patrick chimed in.

Dieter nodded. "So, old Yamaguchi considered Greta a true

friend. He trusted her. Yamaguchi's son, not so much. He is more of the paranoid kind, not seeing Greta as a friend but a threat, like everyone else with knowledge of the illegally acquired artwork. When old Yamaguchi died, she knew her life was in danger. She sent a copy of a detailed list of all the paintings in the collection, a record for every single piece she had sold to his father, to the son, threat attached, that the list would be published should anything happen to her."

"A list? What would that accomplish? People must know about the collection," Susan ventured.

"No, they don't," Dieter responded.

"Stolen artwork is a very hot item," Patrick explained. "Interpol, and many other private organizations, spend enormous efforts to locate such illegally acquired art, and they are quite successful at it. In the last twenty years, the Commission for Stolen Art alone managed to reunite over 3,500 paintings with their original owners. You can imagine what would happen to Yamaguchi's artwork if such a list were to become public. It would be the find of the century."

"And this is why Greta was perceived as such a threat to him," Dieter emphasized.

"How can one keep such a collection a secret? People must be going in and out of his house constantly," Susan wondered. "People talk."

"Only a select few have the privilege of entering his private residence," Dieter explained. "And they probably don't know the pieces on the walls were illegally acquired."

"And of those who do, nobody would ever dare cross this powerful man. Just think of the consequences," Patrick added.

"There was one person, and one person only, my mother Greta could trust the original to: my father. And it has been right here in the safe of our well-guarded estancia ever since."

"But with the list in hand, your father became a threat too, no?" Susan wondered.

"He already knew about the collection. But threat or not, Yamaguchi would not dare to make a move against him."

"Why not?" Patrick asked.

"First, he would get himself involved in a war with the

numerous Japanese Nazi sympathizers, many in his very own organization. Remember, Japan and Germany shared their ideology during World War II. They were allies, a fact with far-reaching consequences even today. And second, business between them is just too profitable for anyone to do something as stupid as jeopardize it."

"Business?" Patrick asked, surprised. "They are in business together?"

Dieter nodded while nervously looking at his watch. There was not much time left. "My father deemed it best to disclosed to Yamaguchi that he was entrusted with the list, with the assurance to safeguard it with his own life."

"He wanted to be transparent with his business partner," Patrick guessed.

"Yes, one of the reasons. You see, he still greatly cared about Greta and wanted to let Yamaguchi know the list was not just an empty threat. He was going to do his part to protect her, his close friend, the accomplished Nazi, and mother of his only child, however much of a disappointment I may be."

"So, young Yamaguchi knows the list is here, and once your father is gone ..." Patrick summarized.

"Yes, once he is gone ...."

Patrick started to understand the mechanics at play. "The family stake in the business will cease to exist, whatever it is, and he will not hesitate to come after you."

"As of now, everything is held in check by the profits. Once he has nothing to lose, yet everything to gain ...."

Susan flinched.

Dieter nodded again. "As you can see, it's quite a situation."

Then suddenly, Patrick's mind was about to explode.

3:10 PM
Well in the Forest, Estancia de Gobineau

Before leaving the estancia, Hironori had paid his respects to the dying old man with wishes of a swift recovery from his boss

Yamaguchi. In his culture, it was customary to do so. But even more importantly, Yamaguchi would want a firsthand report on the old man's health. Such knowledge was essential to his already ongoing planning for the post-Klaus Era. Hironori, after politely turning down a ride to the airport, walked the short distance from the estancia through the opening into the forest and toward the well to his car. He was about to place his sword inside the trunk but could not find the keys. He patted himself down multiple times, with no luck. They were gone. After the usual barrage of curse words, he started heading back, through the forest and the opening, toward the tall entry gate of the estancia.

3:12 PM
Basement Community Room

A rush of adrenaline shot through Patrick's body. From his travel bag, he took out the copies of the notebook he got back in Switzerland. "Dieter, tell me, on this list, have you seen words like Ruhm, Ruhe, and Rhapsodie, by any chance?" he asked.

"Glory, Calm, and Rhapsody?" Dieter repeated while opening the holder, then took one of the documents, and handed it to Patrick. It was a few pages long, authored on a typewriter, every page signed in slightly faded ink, the paper yellowed over the years like a relic from past times. Susan and Patrick scanned it over.

"Is this the list?" Susan asked. Dieter nodded.

"I mean... THE list?" she asked again. Dieter nodded again.

"Here it is—Glory. And here is Rhapsody ... and Calm," Patrick pointed out.

"How did you know?" Dieter was puzzled.

Patrick had a closer look at both documents. "Oh my God, the lists match," he repeated. "This is why your grandmother came to see me," he continued, not holding back his excitement. "For whatever reason, she needed to organize her own 'insurance,' like this Greta did years back. So she sent me to Switzerland to retrieve the notebook."

"So we know they needed this 'insurance,' but why?" asked Susan. "And why now, after all these years?"

Patrick and Susan looked to Dieter for answers.

"All I know is that the three—Yamaguchi, my father, and your granddad—are, or were, doing business together. That's all," Dieter explained.

"You have got to be kidding me. My granddad? That can't be!" Susan protested.

"Then your grandparents knew Klaus, and they knew he was dying. That might hint toward the 'why now.'"

"The second list! Remember? On my voice mail from my granddad?" Susan interrupted. "The Japanese hit man was saying my grandfather was about to die because of a second list. Was he referring to this list here?"

But Dieter had questions of his own. "Switzerland ... a notebook?"

"A few weeks back, Susan's grandmother Rachel came to see me in my office, commissioning me to retrieve a notebook. I rarely accept private assignments, but her story was intriguing. When I tried to call Rachel with an update, Susan answered the phone, informing me that her grandparents had just been murdered. Since then, we have been chased by this Japanese hit man, the one right outside this door. He is after the notebook ... and my copies."

"I would assume he is after both lists," Dieter chimed in.

"He is after everything that poses a threat to his boss," Patrick confirmed. "The efforts of reuniting stolen pieces of art with their rightful owners are often unsuccessful because the victims have the burden of proof to show it was illegally taken from them, which is rarely possible, especially after decades. The black notebook does exactly that. It proves when and, more importantly, from whom every single item in Yamaguchi's collection was misappropriated. Greta's list here—this second list—shows who it was sold to. With evidence as strong as these two combined, if they were ever leaked, Yamaguchi would lose his entire collection, and he knows it."

"That is why he is after you, and as soon as my father is gone, he will be after me." Dieter stated the obvious.

"I have to hand it to my grandmother," said Susan. "She knew this story would intrigue you, Patrick. She knew you would find out what is going on and eventually print an article about all this. She was not only getting 'insurance,' but also organizing a preemptive strike against this Japanese crime boss. How cunning!" Susan could not help but be proud.

"Wait!" Dieter interjected. "Your grandfather died because of the list here on our estancia? What did he have to do with all this?"

"We don't know," Patrick shrugged.

"It tells us he must have known Greta," Susan chimed in.

"Could it be they were talking about another list?" Dieter wondered.

"It's possible, but even more intriguing, how did your grandparents get this notebook in 1945, listing the very artwork later sold by a Nazi woman and sold to a Japanese crime lord—with whom, as it turns out, they were doing business?" Patrick continued. None of the three could even come up with a plausible theory.

"Dieter," Susan said finally, interrupted the silence, "have you thought about your mother, Greta? What will happen to her if you give up her list here?"

"To be honest, I don't know if she is even around anymore. She showed up here way back then, did her deals, gave birth to me, apparently came back years later with this list, and then nobody ever heard from her again. I pressed my father many times but never managed to get as much as one word out of him. Maybe she went into hiding, with Yamaguchi after her and all."

"She had your father's protection, didn't she?" Patrick raised a valid point.

Dieter shrugged. "Maybe she did not trust it was enough. Or maybe it just all became too much for her."

"Do you think Yamaguchi got to her?" Susan wondered.

"I would like to think my father would have intervened. But who knows? Whatever the truth is, you need to take this list, bring this man down, and save us all. And should my mother be still around, it will also save her. Who knows? She may even surface once all this is settled."

"Wait a second, everyone," Patrick intervened.

"What?" Susan asked, impatiently.

"This is all quite astonishing, but despite everything, none of this is going to solve our problems. Losing the collection will anger Yamaguchi. Infuriate him, in fact. But at the end of the day, the paintings on his walls are non-existential. He can live without them. Unless the loss will cause him to have a fatal heart attack, it will not mean the end of him."

Dieter, with a happy grin on his face, confirmed otherwise. "Oh yes, it will. It sure will."

3:18 PM
Master Bedroom, Estancia de Gobineau

A few sunbeams penetrated between the heavy curtains, illuminating the dust particles floating through the air. Still, the room was rather dark, the stuffy air somehow matching the outdated décor. The entire estancia, while true to the local architecture on the outside, was a shrine to old Germany on the inside, decorated with flags, pictures of castles, painted seals of aristocratic families, oil paintings of German leaders and heroes from World Wars I and II alike, beer steins, Bavarian cuckoo clocks, and coat of arms from the Weimar Republic, to name just a few of the many items overcrowding the rooms.

Klaus fell asleep just after Hironori's visit, taking one of his short but increasingly frequent naps. The lamp on the nightstand shone its dim light onto his creased face in a most unflattering angle, emphasizing his deep wrinkles. His heavy and somewhat irregular breathing worried the nurse. She looked down at the old man, his silver hair all but gone, his skin pale, his stubbly face fallen in—the once-proud Nazi now nothing more than a shadow of his former self.

+ + +

It was no accident that Klaus, as young as he was, had risen to such a high-profile position in the German hierarchy as Hitler had personally fast-tracked his career, making him the youngest brigadier general in the Waffen-SS. Klaus was a born leader, but the influence of his own father was undeniable, he himself being a member of Hitler's elite, a generous donor to the Nazi party and a personal friend to none other than the Führer himself. In the somewhat short span of time between his latest promotion and the end of the war, Klaus had managed to cause enough havoc to draw the attention of the international war tribunal. He was lucky enough to escape; his father, however, was less fortunate. He was captured, tried at Nuremberg, and hanged just minutes after the verdict. Despite years of investigation, what had happened to his mother remained a mystery.

+ + +

The nurse wondered about the old man, now in the very last chapter of his life—his rise and fall, about life in Germany back in the early forties, quite taken by the picture on the nightstand, right next to the lamp, of the old man and the Führer shaking hands on the terrace of the Eagle's Nest compound in Berchtesgaden. She was not sure if it had to do with the intimidating uniform, but had to admit, the old man used to be an impressively good-looking guy. The sudden buzzing of the satellite phone, also on the side table, ripped her out of her daydream, puzzling her as it had always been there, but never rung before. The guard sitting next to the bed, equally startled, looked over at her, not sure what to do. Klaus opened his eyes ever so slightly and gestured to hand him the phone.

3:19 PM
Basement Community Room

"You see, Yamaguchi is not as disciplined as his father," Dieter started to explain. "On the contrary, he is more like a spoiled child. He loves owning things, showing off expensive things. Private jets, mansions in every city all over the world, extravagant jewelry for his wife and many lovers, and so on. On top of that, there is his biggest and most money-draining habit: gambling. It got him in deep, and from what I know, he owes money to a whole bunch of dubious people. A lot. We are talking billions here. To satisfy his ever-growing losses, he had no choice but to mortgage the collection. Rumor has it every single painting is now borrowed against at two or three times its value."

"And once the collection is gone, so is the collateral. The loans would be immediately recalled," Susan concluded.

"He could never come up with all that money at once. Not even a criminal of his caliber can afford such a default. He'd be bankrupt, at the mercy of his debtors—not all friends, some even happy to see him destroyed."

"All his power, everything he owns and controls, lost in the blink of an eye," Patrick commented.

Dieter nodded. "The absolute end, not only of him and his family but his entire empire. The art collection is Yamaguchi's everything, yet, funnily enough, his Achilles' heel."

3:21 PM
Master Bedroom

The guard could tell by the old man's expression the call was important. In the last few days, Klaus had been relaxed, seemingly letting go of things. Now, suddenly, he seemed alert, even aggravated, visibly anxious to speak to whoever was on the line. As the guard handed him the phone, the old man struggled to get a good grip on it.

"It's been a while, my friend. How are you?" Klaus opened the conversation. Then, he just listened. "I understand," he whispered into the phone as well as he could. "I will take care of it." The old man handed the phone back to the guard, who pushed the button to end the call. Klaus, with his index finger, gestured for him to come closer, and in his weak voice instructed the guard to summon his son.

"Tell him it is urgent."

Basement Community Room

"Here you go," Susan said, feeling triumphant, but the deepening frown lines on Dieter's face immediately dampened her enthusiasm.

"We are not there yet," he cautioned. "Greta's list is quite old. Yamaguchi will deny the collection is still in his possession. He can easily claim he sold it."

Patrick shook his head. "It does not matter what he claims. All we have to do is to make the lenders nervous. Publishing the lists will shake the cage enough for the loans to be immediately withdrawn."

"We don't know that for sure," Susan countered.

"We cannot give time to a man like Yamaguchi. He will manage to secure the collection and thereby calm his investors," Dieter cautioned. "Remember, he is well connected. He can pull strings. We need the Japanese authorities to move in, swiftly and unexpectedly, taking him by surprise, and they are only going to do it with solid, up-to-date proof."

"I agree. Yamaguchi could stall the matter in the courts for years," Susan doubled up on Dieter's concern.

"I know how investors think, and so do you, Susan," Patrick defended his stand. "You just have to plant a seed of fear. Panic will follow and do the rest."

A loud knock on the door interrupted their conversation. The three looked at each other. Dieter opened the door, a gap just enough to peek through, his body covering the inside. "I asked not to be disturbed."

"I am sorry, it's your father. He would like to see you right away."

Dieter closed the door and, with a great sense of urgency, handed Patrick the entire document holder. "Here, take this! It contains everything you will need." He hastily walked over to one of the Bavarian-made wooden closets, opened its doors, and, to the surprise of both Susan and Patrick, slid the back panel to its side. "Go to the end of the tunnel. There is a ladder. Climb up the well.

Hironori's car will be there. Here is a flashlight, and here are the keys to his car."

"How did you get those?" Patrick asked, somewhat baffled.

"Not important. I can keep your escape secret for a little while, but not very long. Make sure you are out of Bariloche as soon as possible. I am counting on you. And with any luck, we will meet again."

He bid them goodbye. Susan and Patrick hurried into the tunnel. The secret panel closed behind them, leaving them in complete darkness.

3:35 PM
Master Bedroom

"Open a window, will you?" Dieter asked the guard, disgusted by the pungent smell that hit his nose as soon as he entered the room.

"We have instructions not to. The air is too cold for him," the guard responded.

Dieter did not care about his father's orders and opened one himself, taking a deep breath of the brisk air, but the guard immediately pushed him aside and closed it again.

"Come here, Dieter," his father requested. The cancer finally seemed to be winning the hard-fought battle, eating itself through the old man's body. After various treatments, some helpful, many not, the doctor could now do nothing but keep him comfortable. Dieter had no particular emotion toward his father's demise; he just felt sorry for the dying man, sorry for a life so shamefully wasted.

"What is going on downstairs?" Klaus asked his son in a hardly audible voice.

"We have visitors, but no one you know," Dieter downplayed the situation. His father once again closed his eyes, resting for longer than Dieter cared for, and then opened them again.

"What do they want?"

"Security picked them up. They are just lost tourists. I will make sure they find their way back."

"Why are you lying to me?" his father countered angrily.

"I have to head back now," Dieter insisted, not interested in what he had to say.

"Wait. Before you go …."

Escape Tunnel, Estancia de Gobineau

Susan did not mind the muddy floor, damp from the constant dripping of water, nor the musty smell, but the reflecting eyes of a few rats caught in the light beam of her flashlight made her shudder.

"How long is this thing? It seems endless," she complained, shining the light down the tunnel, anxious to get out.

"The longer it is, the better," Patrick responded. "We need to be out of the security cameras' range."

They walked quite a bit farther when Patrick finally noticed a patch of light ahead. It was the opening into the well. As mentioned by Dieter, a ladder was mounted on its wall.

"Do you want to go first?" he asked.

"After you," Susan politely declined.

Patrick went up the ladder and stuck his head out of the round rim. As expected, everything was quiet, and as they were told, a car was right there. Patrick headed for the driver's seat, but Susan intervened.

"Last time you nearly killed us," she complained, knowing the winding road would make her nauseous again. Patrick, holding the door, invited her to get in. She took the keys from his hands, and Patrick took his place next to her. Then, as quietly as she could, Susan steered the car up the small gravel road and turned onto the one they had raced down just hours earlier.

3:49 PM
Master Bedroom

Klaus gestured for Dieter to come closer. He reluctantly sat down on the bed. For the first time in Dieter's life, his father took his hand

and laid it in his, he even asked him to come closer. Dieter, already uncomfortable, hesitantly complied, leaning over to better understand the old man. Klaus struggled to keep his eyelids open. The eyes underneath were still as blue and clear as they could be, but his usual strong voice was gone. What passed his lips were nothing but painful whispers.

"I tried to make you stronger, to turn you into a real man, but I failed." Klaus paused to take a deep breath. "You have never been the son I wanted. Before I die, I want to let you know ... I forgive you."

Dieter was not surprised. And he certainly did not deem his father's statement worthy of a reply, nor was he interested in listening further. He straightened his back, lifting his head away from the old man.

"Listen, my son, now that my time has come, you need to know my final wish. Such must be respected, always, my son, no matter what."

"It's better if you save your energy—"

"Listen to me," his father interrupted him with his voice raised. "Do you think I don't know? All these years? I saw the lack of enthusiasm, your lack of interest. But it is not too late for you. You still have strength." Klaus paused to take the deep breath that his body was demanding. "I am giving you one last chance to make it up to me. Take it. You owe it to me." He again paused. "My legacy, it cannot die. The fight must go on. With you. It has to, or all will go to waste." With great effort, he pointed at the picture on the side table. "This is the greatest man that ever lived. Mark my words: We cannot lose. We will not lose. We will reign again. People will eventually see the truth because the truth cannot be negated. We can only survive if we respect the laws of purity. Fight the inferior races. Humankind depends on it."

Exhausted, Klaus again closed his eyes, breathing heavily, resting. Dieter tried to remove his hand, but his father, with surprising strength, clutched onto it, refusing to let go. Their eyes met in a stare, each pair looking at the other in deep disgust.

Despite his struggles, Klaus raised his voice again, and with eyes as fiery and piercing as ever, continued. "Do your part; do what you have been born to do. Promise me you will! Finally be the son I always wanted so I can die in peace."

Dieter did not show the slightest of reactions.

"Don't shame me any further. Take my gun," said Klaus, somewhat resigned but pointing at the firearm next to the picture frame. "Your guests ... they are the enemy. They must be eliminated. I am begging you; start to be a man ... for our cause!"

Without saying a word, Dieter forcefully withdrew his hand from his father's grip, stood up, and, after their eyes met once more, walked out of the room. Despite the continued struggle for air, the weakening man continued shouting after him.

"Promise me you will do it. Promise me! For our cause!" Then exhausted, Klaus sank his head back into his pillow. With deep disappointment showing on his face, he turned to the guard next to him. "My son ... what a fool! Go do what he won't."

4:05 PM
Intersection of RN41 and RN231

Thankfully, the roads were virtually deserted. Only a handful of cars had passed them since they had turned from the access road onto the 40. Susan was speeding back toward Bariloche. But at the intersection of the 231, she abruptly hit the brakes and stopped the car.

"What is going on?" Patrick asked her.

"I am thinking," Susan promptly responded. A few more seconds passed before she stepped on the accelerator. Without using the blinker, she turned.

"I guess we are going to Chile," Patrick noticed. "Not the worst idea, lady!"

Susan agreed. "By the time they realize we are not on our way back to the airport, we will be gone."

A few minutes later, an entire convoy of black Suburbans, carrying a small army of heavily armed guards, passed the intersection at dizzying speeds, racing toward Bariloche.

9:45 PM (CLST)
Airplane above Chile

Susan looked out the small window of the plane. The mountains were barely visible, but she marveled at the snow-covered Andes reflecting in the moon light. She was tired and wanted nothing more than to push her seat back and sleep. The events of the last few days had been overwhelming. Now safe, her body crashed into a state of exhaustion. Patrick was equally drained but was anxious to check out Dieter's paperwork. Inside the document holder, next to a pile of papers, he also found a generous bundle of US dollars and a satellite phone. He was already familiar with the yellowed document on top of the stack, but there was a great deal more. He rifled through business papers, mostly financial statements. But none made any sense to him.

"Why did Dieter give us all these papers?" Patrick wondered.

"Because somewhere in here lies the answer to our problems." Susan put down the little plastic cup filled with surprisingly good Chilean Pinot Noir and took the documents from his hands.

"We need someone who can go through these," Patrick was thinking out loud. "Like a forensic accountant."

Susan laughed. "Yes, someone good with numbers. I already have the right person for the job."

"You do? Excellent!" Patrick could not hide his excitement.

"Yes, I sure do."

"Who?"

"Who? Seriously? You are asking me who? Me, doofus! This is exactly my field of expertise, what I had been doing at my previous job. I've spent years investigating companies, analyzing statements, finding hidden skeletons. Quite simply, making sure companies are rock solid before issuing a stock recommendation. I know this stuff inside out."

28

September 6, 2017—8:35 AM (CLST)
Bed and Breakfast in Providencia, Santiago, Chile

It was just past midnight when a taxi took them to Casa Rosaria, a charming and upscale B&B within walking distance of the historic district. The place was highly recommended by the driver, probably because the owner happened to be his cousin. But both Patrick and Susan had to admit the place was rather nice. Only one room was still available, but it had two beds, so they were happy to take it. They checked in under false names, paid with cash, and added an extra hundred so the night porter would forget to ask for their passports. After a good night's sleep, desperately needed by both, Susan started to tackle the stack of Dieter's documents while Patrick made good use of his time by outlining an article intended to bring down an entire Japanese crime empire. They were both working all day, during which Patrick could not help himself but periodically ask Susan for updates. She was not pleased with being interrupted. He eventually stopped but looked over occasionally, watching Susan go through the papers and write down notes, page after page; she was on fire. For both lunch and dinner, she asked Patrick to order from the room service menu as she did not want to take any breaks. It was already deep into the night when he finally shut off his laptop, lay down, and fell asleep, with Susan still hard at work, papers spread all over her bed.

The next morning, Patrick entered the room with a tray filled with toast, bread, butter, jam, fruits, and a pot of fresh coffee. He thought Susan deserved a hearty start to the day and had decided to fetch breakfast as a small token of his appreciation for her hard work. To his surprise, her bed was already empty, and he could hear the running shower from the bathroom. He placed the tray on the small table on their balcony. The outside air was cool, but the early morning sun was surprisingly warming. Not knowing how long it would be till Susan was done, he poured himself a cup and sat down with his laptop to resume work on his article.

Less than ten minutes later, Susan stepped out onto the balcony dressed in nothing but a bathrobe, the soft belt tied tightly around her waist, and on her feet the provided white, fluffy slippers. Holding her head to the side, she patted her wet hair with a soft towel.

"Coffee smells good! Can you pour me some?" she asked, seemingly refreshed and ready for breakfast. "How did you sleep?"

"Very well, thank you. But maybe not as well as you," Patrick smiled while pouring the brew. He was anxious for an update. "So, what's the verdict? What did you find?"

"Well, there is a lot of information, but I believe I got what we need. There definitely is some interesting stuff in these papers." Susan put her towel over the back of her chair and sat down. To Patrick's annoyance, she began buttering a slice of toast and took in the cityscape around them.

"And?" he asked impatiently.

"Well, the documents are not very specific. Everything is coded to make it hard for an outsider like me to decipher what really is going on. Financial papers should be the exact opposite, set up according to international standards, to be as clear and descriptive as possible." She took a generous bite of her toast, too hungry not to talk with her mouth full. "Unless, of course, you are trying to hide something. The vagueness, the secrecy … they alone speak volumes. These documents are definitely hot, the secret kind, surely not intended for our eyes."

"I can see you enjoy keeping me in suspense," Patrick chuckled. "Anything solid?"

"Solid? No!"

"No?"

"Well, Dieter said these documents will bring Yamaguchi down. Now, they are all related to the business between the Japanese guy and Klaus, which was to be expected, and most will not help us here. But deep inside these papers, a specific transaction caught my eye: a loan document. I am fairly certain Klaus is one of these 'investors' in Yamaguchi's artwork—not a significant amount, but not too small either. The information is nothing solid, to use your parlance, certainly not the kind of evidence that would hold up in court, but ...."

Patrick watched her take another bite from her toast. "But?"

"Through this loan document, in connection with a few others, I managed to identify a new player, a legal counsel, most likely a go-between. This law firm is not directly implicated, but once you connect the dots, follow the money trail, and pay attention to what these papers are telling you between the lines, a clearer picture starts to unfold. If what we need really is in there, as Dieter claims it is ... this is it." Susan took another generous bite of her toast and washed it down with coffee.

"So, who is this new player?"

"It's a law firm operating out of the Cayman Islands— Hamilton & Hamilton—two brothers with an international law degree from Yale, offering offshore tax strategies for the super-rich. It is the type of firm that seems legit on the surface but, in actuality, offers more than questionable services. Tax evasion, covert transactions, you name it, mostly for multinational corporations suspected of illegal offshore dealings. Even money laundering for businesses like ... well, you know, our friends in Argentina and Japan."

"You got all that from these papers?"

"Their ties to this specific loan transaction and to the illegal drug trade of these two? Yes. The rest, no. I came across this law firm before, a few years back."

"I wonder why Dieter had not just told us all this. He could have saved you all this work."

"I can imagine his dad does not involve him too much in his business activities. He may never have heard of Hamilton & Hamilton. On top of that, I am assuming he only had a few minutes to get all this together."

"How certain are you about your interpretation of the data?"

Susan was pressing her lips together as she tilted her head from side to side. "Well, I wish I could be more specific. But what I can tell you with certainty is that this law firm is involved. To what degree? Who knows?"

"It all seems quite speculative."

"If this loan document really is connected to the money borrowed against the artwork, then this law firm, with high certainty, is the one brokering these deals. And if we can get our hands on the paperwork, we can prove that Yamaguchi is in possession of the artwork."

"Since these people are high-priced lawyers, specialized in secrecy, and even governments cannot get anything out of them, there is no way we will. We might as well try to steal a few gold bars out of Fort Knox," he said, reaching for a toothpick.

"Maybe. Nevertheless, we need to go and see what we can find out," Susan urged as she refilled her cup of coffee.

Patrick put his elbows on the table, hands interlaced, holding the toothpick between his lips, thinking. He shook his head. "Hm … It's a dead end. I am talking from experience here. There is just no way."

"What else can we do?" Susan shrugged.

"As I said before, we already have everything we need, right here." Patrick pointed to the two lists.

Susan shook her head. "Dieter is right on this one. We need to prove the artwork is hanging on Yamaguchi's walls right now, or he will find a way to weasel himself out of all this."

"I respectfully disagree," Patrick responded, confident about his position.

"Yamaguchi will get creative quickly to keep his investors happy, and, given time, he will succeed," Susan argued. Patrick contemplated her words. "Listen," she continued, "nobody will make a move against such a powerful man unless his downfall is certain. The creditors will act very cautiously, standing by, waiting to see what is going to happen. Only once Yamaguchi's end is inevitable, and only then, will the rats abandon the ship. Not a second sooner. We need to get our hands on those loan docs." She took another slice of toast and again began to cover it with jam.

Patrick took another moment to think, then removed the toothpick from his lips, pointing it at Susan. "Even if you are right, and I am not saying you are, do you really think we can just walk into this law office and ask for the documents? There is no chance in hell they will volunteer such information. We won't even make it to the reception desk. I say, let's publish the list and end it now."

Susan did not respond immediately. She placed both the knife and toast on her plate, put her elbows on the table and folded her arms. "You are right; I have no clue how to approach these lawyers. But if we do not present this case on a silver platter, it will not end, and we will be right back at square one, only worse, with our only chance to get this sorted blown."

"And if we go to the Cayman Islands, our friend with the sword will be waiting, just to see if we are stupid enough to show up. What you are proposing is not just dangerous, it is flat out impossible."

Susan's reply came equally quick. "This is pretty much what I said back in the Vermont motel room. Do you remember your response? 'It's our only chance.'" She looked at him, her head slightly tilted, strands of her wet hair partially covering her face.

Patrick once again pointed the toothpick at Susan. "But you see, once the list is published, he can't come after us. Everybody would know he'd be the one behind our murder. It would put him right in the spotlight, where he is desperate not to be."

In her frustration, Susan took a deep breath. "There are probably a thousand bodies with his name on it, and everyone knows it. He does not care. He knows he is untouchable. The information we need is inside those law offices, and we need to go get them," Susan pleaded, lowering her head as well as the volume of her voice. "You would agree if your grandparents were killed. You would want to make sure that bastard is locked up as soon as possible."

"Susan, wake up. Are we really so naïve to walk right into this? There is no chance of success here." Patrick looked deep into her dark, hazel eyes. "I understand, I really do. But revenge is a dangerous motivator. I know you are upset, and you have every right to be. But your thirst for payback is clouding your judgment. Let's not put ourselves in any more unnecessary danger. We have what we need."

Susan did not respond.

"Try to look at it from my point of view. I need to end this, go home, and get married."

Susan was not ready to give in. "First, it is not revenge, it's justice. Second, you are a journalist, an investigative journalist. I understand you do not want to do it for me or my grandparents. But do it for the story. It will make a great one, maybe your best yet."

Patrick rolled his eyes, at the brink of being annoyed. "The story? Forget the story! Don't you consider yourself lucky to be still alive after what we have been through? How many more times do you want to tempt death? Right now, for me, there is nothing more important than Sarah. I am telling you as an experienced specialist in tactical operations, as a journalist, and as a friend—it's too risky! And there is absolutely no reward. We have what we need."

Susan did not like what she was hearing.

"I need to go back to L.A., publish the article, and then turn my focus on my fiancée. She sure deserves it. I understand this is not the conclusion you had in mind, but at least we will live to see another day."

Susan did not really know what to say next, yet it was she who eventually broke the uncomfortable silence. "Tell me, what do you think the chances of success are if you just publish what we already have?"

"Pretty good. Seventy-five percent?"

"And if we get our hands on those loan papers?"

Patrick hesitantly answered, "Ninety-nine point nine-nine."

"So, do we take the easy way out that's most likely succeed, or the difficult one and risk our lives for another twenty-five percent …?" Susan was summarizing the stakes.

"Do you see my point?" Patrick responded.

"Exactly. Do you see my point?" Susan countered. Nevertheless, she felt a wave of empathy come over her. She had lost her family. He had different responsibilities, as he was about to start his. It was against what she thought was best, but maybe he was right; maybe it was time to call it quits. If Patrick decided to end this here, she had no choice but to accept.

However, Patrick was not without doubt himself; Susan had made some valid points. Would the article really be enough? If only he had a crystal ball. Patrick went back to chewing on the toothpick, still mulling over their discussion.

"Speaking of your fiancée, shouldn't you give her a call? She must be worried sick by now."

"You have no idea how much I want to, but it is still too early to switch my phone back on. I need some time to finalize the article."

"Use the satellite phone. From what I know, they are untraceable."

Without saying a word, Patrick shot up from his seat and darted into the room. Susan chuckled. She continued with her breakfast, reflecting on things, still feeling strongly about her position. Yet she had to admit that Patrick was right about one thing: the undertaking would not be without its dangers, and the risks were probably too high. Whatever they were, it did not matter anymore. The dice had fallen; she just had to have some faith now.

Patrick returned sooner than anticipated, topped off his coffee, and took the cup, all the while pressing the phone between his shoulder and ear.

"You couldn't reach her?" Susan asked.

"I got her voice mail. Now I am calling my office to give them an update." He also took a croissant off the tray and disappeared back into the room. Still eating, Susan closed her eyes and consciously felt the sun warm her face. She enjoyed the brief moment of bliss, absorbing the various sounds of the city around her. She took another deep, healing breath and slowly pressed the air out of her lungs. For the first time in quite a while she was at peace, and it felt good. Then, suddenly, Susan's meditation was interrupted by a low thump coming from inside the room. She opened her eyes.

"Patrick?" There was no answer. "Patrick, what is going on? Everything okay?" Still no answer. Alarmed, she got up and peeked inside the room. She first noticed the phone on the floor. Her eyes shifted to Patrick sitting on the couch, pale, as if he had just seen a ghost.

"Are you alright?" she asked, taking a sweeping gaze of the hotel room. Everything seemed in order. Patrick did not move at first; then he raised his head to look at her, his face stone cold.

"What is going on?" Susan pleaded, worried to her core.

"You won, Susan. Pack your bags. You won!"

"I won what?"

"Let's go get that son of a bitch."

10:45 AM (ART)
Ezeiza International Airport, Buenos Aires, Argentina

Hironori was standing in the departure terminal right in front of the gate, waiting to board the plane to take him back to Japan, his phone held tight against his ear.

"Our problem is solved, you say," Yamaguchi started the conversation.

Hironori had a terrible sense of déjà vu. "Yes. Our friends ..."

"The threat is eliminated, you say."

"Yes!" Hironori once again responded confidently.

"QUIET!" Yamaguchi screamed. After a short, uncomfortable silence, he continued in a deceptively calmer tone. "I wish this was true, but things are much worse than they seem to be."

Hironori simply stood, staring into nothingness.

"You don't know, do you?" Yamaguchi asked.

Know what? Hironori wondered. *Surely it could not be ...*

"It is your job to know," his boss scolded him.

Hironori tried to stay as calm as possible.

"If you had only made sure," Yamaguchi told him off, "as you should have done." Another few seconds of silence followed. "The German—the son—he let them go."

Hironori could not believe what he was hearing. "Rotten luck," he said, trying to divert the accusation, but he immediately regretted his response. Luck? No. His boss was right. He trusted the situation to be taken care of. He should have made sure, but he so longed to go back home.

"And, worse ..." Yamaguchi was going on.

What could possibly be worse? Hironori wondered.

"From what we hear, he has both lists. Do you know what that means?"

Hironori did not answer, could not answer. He dropped his head forward in total disbelief, aware of the possible dire consequences.

"At first, I thought you had met your match in this military man," Yamaguchi continued. "But now, I know it is something else altogether."

Hironori initially did not know what his boss was hinting at, but then—*Oh no, it can't be!* For the first time in his life, the ice-cold man's knees started to buckle, his hands shook, and his heart sank into a deep abyss.

"There is someone here who wants to talk to you," Yamaguchi announced in his usual dry manner.

10:46 PM (JST)
Yamaguchi Family Residence, Kyoto, Japan

The many rooms in the estate now looked quite different. Less than two hours ago, the walls had been covered with Yamaguchi's beloved collection. Now it was all packed up, replaced by traditional Japanese art with motifs of samurais, geishas, waves, gardens, cherry blossoms, bamboo, and pine trees. His father had acquired the selection decades ago, and now it was resurrected from storage.

In the driveway, the workers closed the hatch of the truck as his personal assistant gave instructions.

"Again, go straight to the airport. Obey all traffic rules so you won't get pulled over. You are expected at Cargo Terminal 23 no later than midnight. Take your time, but you can't be late." The truck driver nodded, started the engine, and disappeared through the gates of the estate. The truck was followed by two black SUVs with tinted windows, carrying a small but heavily armed security detail. Yuzuki, Yamaguchi's personal assistant, pulled out her phone and texted the requested update. "The package is on its way."

10:47AM (ART)
Ezeiza International Airport

Hironori clenched his fist and said a quick prayer.

"Hiro, is that you?" a frightened female voice spoke on the other end.

"Akiko!" Hironori said quietly, his head dropping further, the blood draining from his face as if a big rock had just thundered onto his soul. "Akiko, are you okay? Is little Shin okay?" But the phone had already been ripped from her tender hands.

"As you can see, I know your little secret," Yamaguchi shouted into the phone.

Hironori would never forget the first time he held his son, the first time he looked into his eyes, the first time little Shin grabbed his finger, so tightly, and would not let go. Hironori had never experienced a sweeter moment in his life. In just the blink of an eye, his world had changed. Akiko had begged him so many times to leave the organization, even before the boy was born. "Once you are in, you are in for life," he had told her repeatedly. But now, holding little Shin in his arms, the little bundle of precious life, he knew he could no longer be the person solving the unsolvable problems of his boss.

"Did you really think you could keep this from me?" Yamaguchi asked in his harsh tone. Overcome with worry, Hironori did not know how to respond anymore.

"I now know the reason for your latest ... performance," Yamaguchi continued his rant. Hironori's thoughts went back to the motel room in Vermont, to the very moment he was ready to strike, the very moment he looked into the innocent eyes of the little boy appearing in the doorway—these dark eyes that reminded him of little Shin, oh, so much. He could not force himself to do it in front of the small toddler. And he certainly could not kill—Hironori did not dare to finish the thought.

His reflections returned to little Shin, Akiko, and the future they were looking forward to. It gave him the necessary strength to finally utter the words he had been pondering for a while now.

"I'm out."

The following silence was gnawing at Hironori's nerves. Suddenly, Yamaguchi burst out in loud, cynical laughter. "NEVER!" he screamed. "Now go do what you were told to do."

"NO!" Hironori boldly countered, summoning all the courage he could.

"NO? You are telling me 'no'?" The boss laughed again.

"I can't! I can't do this anymore," Hironori insisted, again thinking of his baby boy. "And if you touch my family, even as much as a hair, you are dead."

"And if you do not finish what you were told to do, you will never see them again," Yamaguchi replied angrily. Then, in the background, Hironori heard a scream.

"AKIKO!" he shouted into his phone, but the line was already dead.

29

September 7, 2017—9:05 AM (EST)
George Town, Cayman Islands

Susan and Patrick were standing in front of the six-story office building that hosted a number of local and international banks. People wearing expensive suits were walking in and out of it just as they would any other building in the vicinity.

"So this is where it all happens. All the activities away from the prying eyes of governments," Susan said, feeling a bit intimidated.

"Yes, this is where it all happens," Patrick repeated. "Let's see how this lawyer performs under pressure. He will not be easily swayed."

"We have enough to corner him. But you are right. Let's see how tough a guy he really is."

They entered the building and were welcomed by one of the receptionists at the lobby desk. Susan immediately noticed the many security cameras and the unusual number of guards.

Patrick dished out his fullest charm. "Good morning, my dear. We are here to see Alfonso Hamilton."

"Do you have an appointment?"

"No, we do not. But we really need to see him," Patrick pressed on.

"May I see some identification?"

The two handed over their driver's licenses.

"Mr. Rooper, Ms. Sobchak, we have been expecting you. Mr. Hamilton has asked me to pass you a message. He is not able to grant you a visit, and he kindly asks you to respect his privacy." The receptionist handed back the licenses.

"Please call and let him know it is in his best interest to speak to us," Susan insisted.

The receptionist nervously looked over to the guards. "I am sorry, that is not possible. And I cannot let you go upstairs without an appointment," the young woman politely turned them down while two of the security guards approached.

"May I help you?" the taller one asked.

"I don't think so, but thank you," Susan replied in her most flirtatious voice, putting on a friendly face.

"Please call up there and tell him he really should see us, for his sake," Patrick asked the receptionist again.

The guard grabbed Patrick by the arm, but with a swift motion he freed himself from the grip. "This won't be necessary," Patrick insisted.

Two more guards approached, and with the four uniformed men in tow, Susan and Patrick were ushered out of the building.

"Well, this went exactly as expected," Susan chuckled.

"Nevertheless, it was enlightening. The good news: this Alfonso has the information we need. The bad news: they have been expecting us, and now they know we are here."

9:12 AM

Offices of Hamilton & Hamilton, George Town

It was not the first time Alfonso Hamilton had to handle a delicate situation. As a matter of fact, he was quite the master at it.

"Yes, they are here," he notified his Japanese client. Yamaguchi had expected the news. He was anything but happy, amazed how these two had gotten so far.

"You know what to do."

"Of course," Alfonso replied with a confidence that worried Yamaguchi.

"Do not underestimate the situation," he cautioned.

"Don't worry," Alfonso replied, characteristically cocky.

"Considering what is at stake …," Yamaguchi doubled down.

"You have nothing to worry about," Alfonso once more assured his client.

"It's just … this journalist … he has a way of getting people to talk."

Alfonso was struck. Never before had Yamaguchi expressed concern. "My friend, you know why you hired our law firm. Me. Everything is under control."

The assurance did not calm the Japanese crime boss. "My associate is on his way. He will take care of everything. Till then, fend them off."

Alfonso put the receiver down, happy how he handled the call, but his mind suddenly started racing. *My associate will take care of everything.* He could not help but wonder: now that these two had made contact, was he himself considered a part of the looming threat? *Will take care of everything.* Yamaguchi's caution underlined his worries, but would he go as far as eliminate him—Alfonso?

He tried hard to dismiss his thoughts as a fluke, but they kept crawling back into his head. He needed a distraction, something to take his mind off the worry. He picked up the phone and instructed his assistant to make a lunch reservation at his favorite restaurant. Whatever delicacy chef Emilio would prepare for him today was at least something to look forward to.

12:45 PM

Seashore Restaurant, George Town

Alfonso was sitting at his usual table overlooking the ocean, just having enjoyed his meal, waiting for his coffee. Despite living on a small island, he could never get enough of the seemingly endless water views. The sunny and warm climate and the tropical setting were the reasons he and his brother had never moved back to England. Their first employment, years back, was supposed to be nothing more than a short-term adventure, but once they discovered all the island had to offer, they decided to stay a bit longer, and then even longer, all the while their roots gradually took hold and their stay became permanent. This was years back. Not too long ago, Alfonso's brother suffered a heart attack during one of his morning swims in the Caribbean Sea. It came as a surprise as he was the sporty one, his physique taking after their dad's, tall and muscular, his body well built. Now he was gone, his ashes scattered at their favorite spot overlooking the turquoise bay. Neither of them had ever gotten married; the only family they ever had was each other, at least on the island. Alfonso missed his brother dearly.

He was checking his cell phone for messages when, from the corner of his eye, he noticed a man and a woman walking through the busy restaurant and approaching his table. To his surprise, they sat down next to him. The waiter sensed something was off and approached the table, but Patrick waved him away. He stopped and, after an assuring nod from Alfonso, backed off.

"Alfonso Hamilton, I am assuming. My name is—"

"Susan Sobchak, and this is your associate Patrick Rooper," Alfonso interrupted her.

"We know you have been expecting us," Susan continued, scanning the busy restaurant. Like the waiter, the patrons around them noticed the awkward situation. But as quickly as it arose, the commotion calmed, and the guests, one after the other, turned back to their meals.

"Expecting you, yes. For us to meet, no. But here we are," Alfonso replied calmly.

"Yes, here we are. So, let's have a little chat," Patrick said, forcing the conversation.

Alfonso was a man of great wealth, bearing a certain elegance one usually associates with old money. His movements, though rather slow, were filled with a confident grace. Gray roots were showing through his darkly colored hair and in his out-of-fashion Balbo-styled beard. An impeccable dark blue suit and tie, a prominent gold watch, and a shiny ring and bracelet distracting from his unusually hairy hands completed the somewhat outdated ensemble of the short, oval-shaped man.

For a split second, Alfonso considered getting up and leaving, then he quickly realized an opportunity.

"There really is nothing I can do for you," he responded in a surprisingly calm manner.

"We will see about that," Susan countered with a certainty that took even Patrick by surprise. "Before we start, let me tell you this. If we walk out of here with a feeling that you were not fully forthcoming, I will make sure this will be your last meal in a fancy restaurant."

Alfonso reacted with nothing but a chuckle. "That would be quite the achievement, my dear," he countered with a confidence that matched Susan's.

"Not with what we have uncovered," she upped the pressure.

But Alfonso shook his head. "Why don't we cut to the chase?" he proposed. "I know what you are here for."

"Good, this will save us some time," Patrick responded.

"It might. But before we get started, allow me one question," Alfonso requested.

Susan nodded. "Go ahead."

"Why are you doing this, Ms. Sobchak? Why don't you just go back to your comfortable life?"

"We can't, and you know it."

"But you can. Stop your investigation and hand over everything you have gathered, and this hitman will be off your back. My client is even willing to throw in a handsome reward for you doing so."

"If only that were the case," Patrick cautioned Susan.

"Mr. Hamilton, your offer sounds tempting, but I don't think so," she asserted her position.

"Wouldn't you like to score some major points with the big man?" Patrick added to her counter. "We know he kills people who know too much, and not just because it is cheaper than to pay them off."

"Ms. Sobchak, you have not yet answered my question. Why, of all people, are *you* doing this? I really don't understand, considering the stakes for you in the matter. I can help you."

Susan had expected such diversions. "Listen, Alfonso—"

"Mr. Hamilton," he insisted.

But Susan saw through the small power play. "Listen, Alfonso, let's stop the shenanigans and get down to business. Manifest Shipping, Overseas Consulting, Natural Resources Group, Lewis Worldwide Insurance, to name a few. All clients of yours, and all companies with offshore activities, all of them illegal. And next to me sits Mr. Rooper, a world-renowned journalist. Do you get my drift?"

"So?" Alfonso wondered.

"Look at these," Susan said and took a carefully selected stack of papers from their document holder and placed them in front of him. He disinterestedly glanced through them, handed them back, and shrugged his shoulders.

"These give a strong indication that your firm is involved in money laundering for the Heydrichs and for the Yamaguchi Empire," Susan stated firmly.

"Indication is not proof," Alfonso coldly responded.

"You are right. But money laundering is a serious crime, and these documents are enough for probable cause, which means investigations, which, in turn, means search warrants and police knocking on your clients' doors, all because of you. Just imagine the embarrassment, and more importantly, the loss of trust in you and your services."

Alfonso did not react.

"I know what you are thinking," Patrick upped the pressure. "The US Government has no jurisdiction over you here on this island. But most of your clients are US-based, and the FBI, hand in hand with the US Treasury Department, will get to them to get to you. In your line of business, it's a death warrant, and you know it," Patrick added.

Against expectations, Alfonso again did not show any kind of reaction.

Susan felt the need to double down. "I have to say, hats off to you. This is incredibly creative accounting. I have never seen so many ciphers. There is only one problem. I cracked your little code."

Alfonso seemed to be amused, turning his lips into an ever so slight, even proud, smile. "Thank you, my dear. I am glad you noticed the quality of our work. It is everything we stand for. But let me tell you this: If I had a penny for every time some overly eager journalist knocked on my door … good God! So, my advice to you is this: go ahead, contact my clients. They will laugh in your face. It is all a part of the game, and they know it. You know it too."

Alfonso's unnerving confidence began to irritate Susan. "This may be true. But this time, it is a bit different. You see, I am sure none of our predecessors had my accounting expertise, and none of them had the journalistic qualities of my friend here."

"Anyone making sense of these papers truly has a special gift. I must admit, your knack for numbers is outstanding," Alfonso replied as he looked through the papers again. "You have correctly identified companies, numbered ledgers, and secret bank accounts. And, more importantly, connected the assets to the individual owners. Bingo! Now, Mr. Rooper here can write an explosive story about international companies evading taxes. But he can also tell you the story has been told before. Granted, you uncovered some new, rather damaging information, and Mr. Rooper of course can come up with a new angle to give it a fresh spin, but even Mr. Bigshot Journalist here knows it will never make the paper."

Susan started to worry as she ran out of ammunition. On top of this man's nerves of steel, he seemed to have an answer for everything.

Alfonso leaned over to Susan and gave her a stern look. "Now it is up to me to give you a word of advice, my dear. My clients are powerful. You know what happens when powerful people are threatened?" Alfonso let the question sink in before addressing Patrick. "I read your paper, Mr. Rooper, and I have always enjoyed your articles. Very insightful. Kudos to you; you are quite the journalist. But you already know why your paper will never publish such a story. Go ahead, tell her."

"He is right," Patrick grudgingly admitted.

Susan could not believe her presentation was faltering. Every single one of her shots had missed its target, despite all the highly damaging information. Alfonso was not buckling, not even the slightest bit. On the contrary, he seemed to grow more confident with every one of her attacks. *What was happening?*

"And why would that be?" Susan asked, her confidence gradually being chiseled away.

Alfonso chuckled, gloating in his success. "Go ahead, Mr. Rooper, tell her."

"The same reason as always. Money!"

"Yes, that's the one. Money," Alfonso chuckled. "It should come to no surprise that I work with some of his newspaper's—well, let's just say, financial backers. Your paper would not survive without their influx of cash. I am not saying your organization, Mr. Rooper, knows about the dubious activities of these companies, but outing your money sources for tax evasion would be economical suicide. I am assuming this is why you sit here so quietly, Mr. Rooper?" Alfonso, without waiting for an answer, turned back to Susan. "I have to tell you again, Ms. Sobchak ... your accounting skills ... you should come work for me," he said, gesturing for the waiter to come to their table. "As I said, I am still questioning your motives, though," Alfonso repeated. "*You* of all people cannot possibly want this story uncovered." He turned to the waiter. "Three coffees, please. Cream and sugar, anyone?"

Patrick kept a close eye on the old man's demeanor. Alfonso was quick with words, blessed with a talent to make even the biggest lie believable. Nevertheless, something did not seem quite right. The information Susan had dug up was deeply harmful. It should have pushed him right to the edge, despite his counters. Yet he was sitting there as collected as one can be.

"I know what you are doing, Mr. Hamilton, but it will not work," Patrick finally spoke up.

"And what is it that I am doing?" Alfonso asked in his usual monotonous voice with his bushy left eyebrow raised.

"You are stalling for time. You are counting on the Japanese henchman to take care of us before things get out of control. Tell me, is he here already?"

Alfonso still stayed calm. "Very good, Mr. Rooper. You managed to impress me once again."

"Is he here already?" Susan nervously insisted on an answer.

"He will be soon," Alfonso replied dryly.

"Now that all cards are on the table, we are paying your office a little visit, and you are going to hand over the documents we came to collect, or—"

"I will have to kill you first," the lawyer coldly interrupted.

Patrick was done with the intimidations. "I have an offer for you, Mr. Hamilton, one too good to refuse. You hand over the Yamaguchi files, and you will keep your business—minus one client, of course. If not, my article will put you on the radar of the authorities. Now let's go get these contracts or all hell will break lose. I guarantee it."

"But before we go," Susan began, still wondering about Alfonso's prior statement, "please clarify what you mentioned earlier."

"If I can," Alfonso replied, his calm bearing now tearing on Susan's nerves.

"You said something about my stake in the matter. What were you talking about?"

Did she really not know? Alfonso was triumphant. This may work out, after all, he realized. "Don't you know that if this story ever gets uncovered, all the wealth of your grandparents—your entire inheritance—will be gone? Are you ready to give up your comfortable lifestyle? The beautiful mansion on the beach? Nobody sane would ever turn their life upside down like this willingly!"

Patrick immediately intervened. "Don't listen to him; he is trying to mess with your head."

It was working. Susan was increasingly confused. Alfonso could tell, and so could Patrick.

"We are done here. Let's go!" Patrick tried to put a stop to it.

Alfonso would not allow it. "I heard you are getting married soon. How is the planning coming along?"

Patrick's blood immediately started to boil. But after a second of rage, using all the self-control he could summon, he calmed himself, not allowing the cunning man to manipulate the situation. Patrick grabbed him by the arm rather roughly and tried to pull him up. "Let's go," he ordered Alfonso.

"Wait a second," Susan intervened.

"He is only trying to mess with you."

"I know," she replied. "Nevertheless …."

Patrick looked at Susan and then hesitantly let go of the lawyer.

"What are you talking about, Mr. Hamilton? My grandfather was an art dealer, but that is hardly illegal," she defended her grandfather.

Patrick was relieved by Susan's tough stand. The waiter walked over, tray in hand, and served the coffees. Alfonso waited patiently till he left their table again. "Oh, Ms. Sobchak—Susan—I cannot believe you do not know."

September 8, 2017—2:53 AM (JST)
Minato-Ku

The crime syndicate was one of the oldest in the country, headquartered in the heart of Kobe. For years, Yamaguchi had contemplated moving his organization to Tokyo for its strategic advantages, but his strong sensibility to tradition had kept him from ever relocating. In the late 1990s, going against a decade-old pact with the other crime syndicates, he made a move to the capital city nevertheless. Consequences were threatened, but Yamaguchi did not care. Business in Tokyo was soon booming, increasingly requiring his presence there. Tired of hotel rooms, he eventually purchased a villa in the high-end neighborhood of Minato-Ku. The mansion had all the luxuries one could imagine, yet it never felt like home.

Little Shin was sleeping peacefully in the protective arms of his mother. Akiko was awake, watching over him. They were well taken care of, but not free to leave. She was worried, well aware of the implications surrounding her situation. Akiko looked down at her baby, her lips forming into a gentle smile. The door opened quietly, and Yamaguchi walked into the room. She immediately turned her back toward him and tightened her hold on little Shin, shielding him from the evil man.

"So, how long has this been going on?" Yamaguchi asked.

Akiko did not answer. She just sat and held her baby tightly.

Yamaguchi came closer and looked at the little boy. "Obviously a while ...."

Akiko turned her head and looked at the intimidating man through teary eyes, wishing he would leave.

"You can tell me," he tried to encourage her. With no response given, he turned to exit the room. "I remember the moment my first boy was born. What a proud day it was." Yamaguchi stood in the doorway, reminiscing the moment. "In any case, we will soon know. Very soon," he said before closing the door.

Akiko, relieved he was gone, pressed little Shin to her chest and let the tears roll down her cheeks.

"You are safe, my son. I will not let him hurt you. I will not allow it. Ever!"

September 7, 2017—12:57 PM (EST)
Seashore Restaurant

"Know what?" Susan asked vehemently, visibly annoyed.

"Okay." Alfonso put some sugar and cream into his coffee. "Okay," he said again, enjoying the suspense lingering in the air. "Before I tell you, let me propose a deal, a better one. You know I cannot give you any documents. But ... I can give you other information to bring Yamaguchi down. In return, my company and I will stay out of the papers."

"No," Patrick immediately suspected another distraction. "We will not leave without these contracts. And we are going to get them *now*."

Alfonso was shaking his head. "Out of the question. However, I know a few things that will help you achieve your goal even without these loan documents. Accept my deal, and we will have an even better win–win scenario. I guarantee it."

Susan and Patrick took a moment to think. Alfonso noted their hesitation.

"You two have no idea what kind of wasp nest you are stepping into," he warned and turned to Susan. "If you do not accept my deal, you will die. Both of you. And should you survive, against all odds, you will lose everything. And I mean *everything*."

His threat did not miss its impact. Susan did not know what to think anymore. They needed these papers. On the other hand, if Alfonso could deliver what he was promising …. She looked at Patrick in need of guidance. He gestured to turn the deal down, whatever it was. Alfonso stared at her, awaiting her response.

"Okay, here it is," she finally broke the silence. "If the information really is as impactful as you state it to be, we do have a deal. But let me be very clear, it all depends on the quality. Otherwise, no deal."

Patrick, impressed, gave her an assuring nod. "This information needs to bring Yamaguchi down, understood?"

"No question about it," Alfonso responded.

"Then, yes, your name will not be in the papers. But only then," Patrick reiterated.

Alfonso straightened his posture and cleared his throat, all the while stirring his coffee. "Old Yamaguchi had always been a man with a big vision. His goal was to globalize his empire and become the world's number one."

"Number one in what? Extortion? Human trafficking? Arms smuggling?" Patrick wondered.

"Wanted man?" Susan added.

"Not a wanted man, but everything else. Above all, drugs."

"Drugs? Is that what they are up to?" Susan asked, surprised. She had never heard of Japan being a producing country.

"Yes, drugs. Any kind of drugs. Old Yamaguchi had been working aggressively on his vision for years but struggled to find the right distribution partners internationally. It was not going well, to say it mildly, and his global expansion never took off. But Yamaguchi was not the kind of man to give up easily; he was always on the lookout for a solution. Then, one day long ago, while visiting Argentina to authenticate the art collection he was about to acquire, Yamaguchi met Klaus." Alfonso took a sip from his coffee, and, with his usual slow elegance, placed the cup carefully on the table again. "They got to talking, and it soon became clear Klaus could provide what Yamaguchi had been looking for all these years: a solid, worldwide distribution network. Klaus was first hesitant to enter into the partnership, but once he was told what the funds could do for his cause, he quickly changed his mind. With one handshake, all Yamaguchi's problems were solved. Heydrich, through his international contacts in the various Nazi networks, started to distribute the goods. You would not believe the impact this one handshake had on the global drug trade. These two truly revolutionized the industry. Business was exploding."

"I have heard of the Colombians and the Mexicans in the drug trade, but never of the Japanese," Susan interjected.

"Because they were smart enough to keep out of the limelight. I know you've heard of Escobar and El Chapo, but believe me, it was these two who started it all. But I digress. In this business, you have to accept a certain amount of loss. Drugs get intercepted in customs, and so do proceeds smuggled back. Yamaguchi was unhappy about the millions lost. He needed a new, more sophisticated way than to smuggle money in suitcases. But how do you move millions of dollars safely without raising red flags with the authorities?" Alfonso unfolded the little chocolate that had come with his coffee, unwrapped it, and put it in his mouth. "Now, Yamaguchi, as you already know, was a great admirer of the arts, especially the modern era."

"So is his son," Patrick chimed in.

"His happiest day was not the day he wed, nor when his first son was born, but the day he held his own Picasso. So I have been told."

Susan was shaking her head in disbelieve.

"One evening, while relaxing on his couch with a glass of fine wine in hand, proudly looking at his favorite painting above the fireplace, he was reflecting on how its purchase had laundered him a substantial amount of money. It hit him right then and there that he was not merely looking at an exclusive work of art, but at a solution."

"How can artwork solve smuggling problems?" Susan interrupted, increasingly skeptical about the merit of Alfonso's proposal.

"More than you think," he responded. "Let's say, as an example, drugs worth five million dollars are shipped from Japan to one of

Heydrich's many destinations. Now, how does the contact at this destination pay for the drugs? He buys a painting from Yamaguchi for ten million dollars just to sell it back to him a few days later for five, all the money transferred safely through official bank accounts twice without anyone raising an eyebrow."

"Losses eliminated!" Patrick added.

"Correct," Alfonso confirmed. "The scheme works so well, it catapulted profits to new heights once again. At least till the Colombians claimed their stake in the late eighties, and the Mexican cartels a bit later, copying them. Nevertheless, their operation is quite sizable still."

"And my grandfather was brokering the art deals," Susan realized.

Alfonso nodded. "Yes, and pocketing a nice commission with each and every transaction. I have to say, the system is ingenious." Alfonso chuckled again, proud to be a part of it all. "And most astonishing, the paintings never even came off Yamaguchi's wall. The transactions are all just on paper, with no way to prove otherwise."

"I cannot believe this would not alert the authorities. Somewhere someone must have noticed," Susan intervened.

"Sending money back and forth for art between two parties over and over again would not have worked," Alfonso confirmed. "That is true. But once you are putting a few international companies in between, obfuscating the trail, it becomes impossible to ever find out what is going on."

"And you were in charge of setting up these companies," Patrick assumed.

"Yes. And funneling the money through local and international banks. But as I said earlier, I did not come into the picture till later, after old Yamaguchi had already died and his son had inherited the empire." Alfonso wiped his mouth with the napkin. "Now you will have to excuse me. It is time for me to go."

He began to rise from the table, but Patrick immediately grabbed his wrist. "Not so fast, my friend. You have not given us anything yet."

Alfonso shot him an angry look. "Let go, and never ever touch me again!"

Patrick did not.

"Do you really not see the value of what I just told you? Knowing the inner workings of an international crime syndicate is everything. It is information every police organization would be dying to know. It took the FBI years to infiltrate the Cosa Nostra, just to find out how they operate, which in turn allowed them to bring the mafia to its knees. A journalist of your caliber should be able to make good use of such information. At least, if you really are as good as they say you are."

"Then again, your information is a bit generic, nothing any police organization doesn't already suspect or even know," Patrick countered, tightening his grip.

Susan leaned forward. "Listen, don't try to send us on a wild goose chase here. What you are giving us may be of great value for someone with a few months to investigate. But it is of no use here, and you know it. If this is all you have, the deal is off. Now let's go get those documents."

Alfonso tried to free his hand, but Patrick tightened his hold again. The people at the next table again noticed the commotion. Patrick immediately moved his hand down the side of the table, pulling Alfonso down to sit back onto the cushioned bench.

"Okay, okay ... I am going to tell you more. In good faith, so you believe I really want to help you here."

"Stop the BS," Patrick responded as a warning and finally let go of his wrist.

Despite being held against his will, Alfonso was still as collected as before. Nothing seemed to shake his world. "As you can imagine, young Yamaguchi had ambitions of his own, not content with the status quo. He was always looking for new ways to generate 'clean' revenue. One day, he came up with the idea of mortgaging the collection."

"We heard he had no choice but to," Patrick interrupted.

"Be that as it may, one day he commissioned me to find investors, which was hard at first, but over the last few decades the Cayman Islands has enjoyed an ever-increasing influx of money— for obvious reasons."

"Tax evasion," Susan said.

"Let's just call it tax-free investments. Nowadays, we are sitting on billions here on the island, cash that is just sitting in bank accounts. It was just is a matter of connecting this undeclared money with the illegal artwork, and voila, a whole new investment vehicle was created. Yamaguchi Junior received his influx of clean cash, and my clients received a return on their 'parked' money."

"We heard about these investments," Susan added.

"And this is just the tip of the iceberg," Alfonso continued with a smile. "Listen to this. Young Yamaguchi goes even farther to maximize profits. He asks your grandfather Tom to hook him up with upcoming artists, then anonymously buys up their work. He lets a few months pass before auctioning off one of these paintings at a high-profile auction, but not with the intention to sell. On the contrary, he places several of his own people to bid against each other, artificially driving up the price. The value balloons out of control. Now, taking the latest auction price as a base, he mortgages the entire collection of this new artist, the face value of these loans a multiple of the actual worth."

"And this flies with the investors?" Susan was flabbergasted.

"It does because the investors don't know, and Yamaguchi makes sure no red flags are raised. He pays them a handsome return, all part of his bigger money laundering scheme, so everyone is happy."

"It's the perfect front," Patrick added. "After 9/11, the banks got heavily scrutinized. But for art, collector items, and jewelry, you can still pay with a bag of cash, no questions asked. On top of that, after drugs and prostitution, art is the third biggest unregulated market. It is one of the last safe havens for money laundering."

Susan thought she had seen it all during her years in the financial industry. Illegal write-offs, fake beneficiaries, loss diversions, every legal and illegal trick in the book of creative accounting. But this kind of offshore financing was off the charts. "Finally, we are getting somewhere. Now we need these mortgage documents," Susan insisted.

"Unfortunately," Alfonso continued—*Of course*, Susan thought—"Yamaguchi is very careful with his artwork. He only mortgaged a few of his paintings, less than—"

"Stop it right there," Susan was quick to interrupt. "We know about the gambling debts. I give you one more chance to accept our deal. Give us these loan papers or you will go down."

"And with that Japanese hit man on his way, we need to go now," Patrick pressed on.

It was finally Alfonso who got nervous. "I am not lying. As I have a fiduciary duty toward my client, I cannot simply tell you the entire truth, but I am telling you just enough," he said, trying to explain himself.

Patrick and Susan did not buy it, observing his façade finally crumble.

"Okay, you are right," Alfonso reluctantly admitted after a brief stare-down. "The entire collection is mortgaged to the max. But I still cannot hand over the documents. However, I can tell you Yamaguchi is close to the end anyway. All you have to do is wait a little bit longer."

"How so? And before you continue, let me tell you the information better be good this time, for your sake," Patrick warned, uttering a necessary threat.

"You see," Alfonso explained, "these loans nowadays are nothing more than a pyramid scheme. One would think he would have stopped bleeding money once his collection was fully mortgaged. But he never managed to adjust his lifestyle, and things started to spiral out of control. On top of that, he needed to start paying hefty, ever-growing interest fees and repay the maturing loans. He has gotten himself in deeper and deeper, mortgaging the collection all over again, defrauding investors with collateral that is already fully borrowed against, or, as I already mentioned, of no actual value. In only a few months, from my analysis, he won't be able to satisfy his obligations any longer. Once he defaults on even just one of these loans, everything will tumble like a house of cards. It's already in the mail. Now, if a journalist were to write an article about this ...."

"This is quite the anecdote," Patrick responded. "Unfortunately for you, we already have such a story—you know, one to rattle the investors' cages. We are here for solid evidence, and we will not leave without."

"I see," he coldly responded. Alfonso was aware of his talents with words, and combined with his quick thinking, he had always managed to talk himself out of any situation. Now, however, he had only one more ace up his sleeve. It was time to put it on the table.

"Susan, I have not answered your question yet," he diverted.

"Don't listen to him," Patrick cautioned her again while getting up from his seat. "Let's go get these documents."

"Hold on. I want to hear what he has to say."

"He is just trying to mess with you. Let's go." He held out his hand to help her out of her seat. For a brief moment, she was contemplating to follow Patrick's lead, but Alfonso's statement was nagging her.

"I already know he is full of crap, so why not pour a bit more on top?"

Patrick hesitantly sat back down, ready to counter whatever came out of the lawyer's mouth next.

Alfonso looked deep into Susan's dark hazel eyes. "I am truly puzzled you work so hard, even risk your life, for all this. You really must be blind toward what you are doing."

"I understand my granddad was no saint, and he participated, indirectly, in money laundering. But all he did was brokering art deals. I am no lawyer, but I just cannot imagine this could lead to the seizure of their assets," Susan replied.

"I am not talking about his brokering deals."

"Then what are you talking about?" Susan snapped at him.

Alfonso again looked at her. "You of all people should know ...."

Susan shook her head.

3:03 PM (ART)
Estancia de Gobineau

Dieter was frantically pacing up and down his room, his future now in the hands of two strangers on a quest to frame an international crime lord before his father lost the fight against his illness. He was hoping to get an update from Patrick sooner than later. There was no word yet, and he knew there might not be for a few days. Thankfully, for now, the old man was still hanging in there. Despite the uncertainty, for the first time in his life, Dieter dared to plan his own future. But all he had decided so far was not to stay on the estancia. Pondering upon where to go, he thought of the old cities of Europe, the beaches of Tahiti, the outback of Australia, the modern cities of the Middle East, the plains of Africa, but he could not make up his mind, changing the destination ever so often. Maybe he should just travel for a few years—discover what was out there before settling somewhere. After being stuck inside this golden cage his entire life, the thought of roaming around the globe was tempting, the potential adventures beyond what he could imagine. He asked himself again where he should go first. The possibilities were endless, and he was too excited to decide. He looked down at the phone again. How much longer till it would ring? Would it ever? It had to, or else ....

1:08 PM (EST)

Seashore Restaurant

"Well, then, this could get interesting," Alfonso responded with a taunting smile.

Patrick recognized an upcoming attack. He had to make sure Susan would not fall for it.

"What do you know about your grandmother?" Alfonso asked.

"What about my grandmother?" Susan returned, offended he was trying to involve her.

"Mainly her role in all of this."

Susan shrugged. "She was the wife of my grandfather, who brokered the art deals."

It was the answer Alfonso was hoping for. "Let's go back to World War II for a moment. Your grandparents, Susan, met in Poland a few months before the end of the war. From what she told me, they had quite the adventure together."

"We already know how they met," Susan snubbed the old man.

"Do you know where Yamaguchi's collection came from?"

"We know it was German war loot that ended up in the hands of a young Nazi woman who sold the collection, most of it to Yamaguchi."

"You are right," Alfonse nodded. "In early 1945, the Russians intercepted a train headed for Germany. You already know what was on the train."

"The looted artwork," Patrick had a feeling it was more than a good guess. Alfonso nodded again.

"The very artwork that now hangs on Yamaguchi's walls. Tom was the one who stole the lot, right under the Russians' noses. And with the help of your grandmother, they diverted the collection to a secret location. Once it was safely stashed, the two escaped to Switzerland."

"That can't be. Yes, my grandfather was a Russian soldier stationed in Poland, and my grandmother was a Polish resistance fighter who got herself in trouble because she was starving. My grandad felt sorry for her and helped her escape," she countered proudly.

"You are right, he did save her. But it was not as noble a gesture as you are assuming. Once Tom was in possession of the artwork, he desperately needed a hiding place, and your grandmother just happened to know a good one."

"Wait a second. Are you saying my grandparents stole the artwork and brought it out of Europe to sell it?"

"Bingo," Alfonso nodded, with a smirk back on his face.

"This is just another one of your lies," Susan protested. "We know the lot was sold by a German woman. Greta something, not my grandparents."

"Greta von Badenholz," Alfonso confirmed.

"Yes. You see? My grandmother never would have participated in such a scheme. Especially being Jewish, and considering who the artwork was stolen from. It just does not add up."

"How little you know, my dear Susan," Alfonso shook his head. "Then again, your grandmother even fooled your grandfather."

"Fooled my grandfather?"

Patrick did not like where this was going.

"Your grandmother was no Polish underground fighter; she was a German operative ordered to infiltrate the Polish resistance and relay information back to the Gestapo. She was a spy, and one of the very best. Do you want to know about her last mission?"

"To go find a train," Patrick chimed in.

"Very good, Mr. Rooper. She received orders from Mr. Goebbels personally, I might add, to retrieve the valuable artwork and somehow bring it to Berlin. It was a mission of greatest importance."

"Nice try," Susan protested. "She was not German."

"Do you know how she got the needed intelligence about the train?"

Susan shook her head.

"She got herself arrested to infiltrate the Russian headquarters."

"As a prisoner, she would not have gotten the information she needed," Patrick objected.

"She fancied her chances to pick up enough quality gossip from the guards."

"Her crime was punishable by death. Why would she take on such a risk? It does not make any sense," Patrick objected again.

"First, she got herself arrested for a low-level crime that, yes, was punishable by death but would most likely be excused with a bit of compassion. Who would not feel sorry for a poor, suffering girl in the midst of a brutal winter, having to steal food to survive? Second, she was part of the Polish resistance, having heroically fought the Germans, or so everybody thought. Third, the resistance and the Russians had a codependent relationship, supporting each other. She counted on her friends to get her released. Her chances of success were better than good."

"Quite ingenious," Patrick had to admit.

"It's not true! It can't be," Susan objected.

"Now, Tom was the guy who processed her arrest. This is how they first met," Alfonso continued. "The evening before the escape, she overheard two guards talking about him. Something about black market goods that were delayed now that he was sent to another city to inspect a train. She knew right then Tom was her target, and she could not believe her luck when, the very next morning, he walked into her cell asking for help. She knew immediately it had to do with the artwork, and she manipulated him to get her out. As soon as everything was safely stashed, she radioed Berlin, informing High Command that the collection was secured."

"But, but … we read the arrest record. It was my grandmother Rachel," Susan stuttered.

"Sure, you did. Greta, to infiltrate the Polish resistance, took on the identity of a Jewish girl—one whose family she had helped arrest, a family hiding in the very basement they then used to hide the artwork."

"She … she ratted out an entire family hiding from the Germans? No, that just can't be … What happened to them?" Susan did not trust what she was hearing.

"The ones not shot on the spot were sent to Auschwitz. Kids, parents, grandparents …" Alfonso answered.

"No!" A hot flash rushed through Susan's body, her face first turning red and then white. Her soul desperately reached for something to hold on to. Her grandmother a Nazi? NO! Her only family … everything a lie. Everything! She sat in silence, unable to process anything anymore.

"This was how she knew of the hiding place." Patrick connected the pieces. It was not the first astonishing story Patrick had heard, but even he had not seen this one coming.

"How did he …?" Susan could not even finish the sentence. "When did my grandfather …?"

"Find out? As far as I know, not till sometime in the fifties. He was devastated. Not so much about her true identity but for keeping it a secret all these years. He felt so betrayed that he told her to leave and never return."

"And I am assuming Greta"—Patrick looked over at Susan, immediately correcting himself—"Rachel found refuge in Argentina."

"Yes. It took Tom a few months to get over everything. In the end, their love for each other prevailed. She eventually returned, but not at first."

"Not before she gave birth to a baby boy," Susan noted, still in shock.

"A baby?" Alfonso asked surprised. "I don't know anything about that."

Susan sat staring, her gaze disappearing into eternity. "Greta von something," she mumbled, deep in her thoughts.

"How do you know all this?" Patrick asked Alfonso.

"During one of our business dinners, we all had a bit too much to drink, and—"

"She started to talk," Patrick finished the sentence, looking at Susan. He could only imagine how she felt.

"Greta von something," Susan repeated, still staring through the coffee cup in front of her. They all sat quietly.

"Dieter. He is my … I have an uncle in Argentina," she finally looked up.

"It looks like you still have family, after all," Patrick tried to stress the positive, but it missed the hoped-for effect.

"Now you can see what I mean. If this became public, the FBI would be all over you. And just think what it would do to your family name, its impeccable reputation—all gone." Hands shaking, she put her napkin on the table and got up.

"Please excuse me. I need to go powder my nose." Patrick's eyes followed Susan away from the table, concerned. Should he go after her or give her a moment? Alfonso, on the other hand, was glowing. One down, and ready to take on Patrick, whose eyes were still on Susan.

"I am wondering, my friend, what's in it for you? None of this really concerns you," he said in a dismissive manner.

"You already know what is in it for me." Patrick tried hard to contain the anger again rising inside him.

"Revenge," Alfonso guessed right.

"You can call it that," Patrick responded, trying hard to hold his emotions in check.

"It will not bring her back." Alfonso got back a look from Patrick that spoke volumes. It left little doubt that there was no way he could convince Patrick to just walk away. So close to achieving his goal, he had run out of steam. He now had to depend on the

Japanese hit man to do his work. Another minute or two passed in silence.

"Maybe you want to check on our friend," Alfonso finally proposed.

Patrick, lost in his thoughts about Sarah, got up, and walked around the corner and down the corridor toward the ladies' room. He knocked on the door.

"Susan?" There was no answer.

"Susan, are you okay?" Still there was no response. He opened the door, just enough to take a peek.

"Are you in there?" Still no answer. He opened the door a bit further and saw her purse on the floor, its contents scattered.

"Susan!" he shouted, pushing the door wide open. He checked every stall; the restroom was empty. Fearing the worst, he rushed out and further down the corridor, through the back door into the alley. He looked to his right and then to his left. Nothing. He turned around and hurried back into the restaurant, shoving waiters out of his way. As expected, Alfonso was gone.

Patrick ran toward the exit, startling the guests and knocking over a few chairs, then through the front door. He again scanned his surroundings. No sight of anyone.

"Ticket, please?" the frazzled valet finally asked.

"Where did they go?" Patrick screamed at him.

"Who?"

"Hamilton!"

"Ah, Mr. Hamilton. He just left, sir."

"With a woman?"

"A woman? No, with his driver," the confused youngster responded. From the corner of his eye, Patrick saw a Maybach limousine turn the corner, all the way on the other side of the Plaza. He started to run as fast as he could, jumped over the planters, then dashed straight through the parking lot and, without a care for oncoming traffic, across the street. Several cars swerved around him, missing him narrowly. One car appeared right in front of Patrick. He jumped, but it was too late. His legs were hit, and his torso was thrown onto the hood and then rolled against the windshield. The glass underneath him gave way as a sharp pain shot through his back, but he had no time to waste. He rolled off the car, jumped back onto his feet, and kept running.

30

1:21 PM (EST)

Two Blocks Away from the Restaurant

The driver waited impatiently for the light to turn green.

"Everything okay, Mr. Hamilton?" he finally asked. With his boss distracted, certainly quieter than usual, he could tell something was not quite right.

"We will see," Alfonso responded, gazing out the window, lost in his thoughts. The driver looked at him in his back mirror, wondering what was going on, when, in the far distance, a man caught his eye, running toward them. He turned around to get a better look. Alfonso was still staring out the window, contemplating the possible fallout of the situation at hand.

"Señor Hamilton, look at that!" The driver, obviously amused by the curiosity, pointed through the back window. "There is a man running in the middle of the street. I hope he does not get hit." Alfonso, immediately alarmed, turned his head. Keeping an eye on Patrick, he nervously shouted at his employee.

"Step on it! Go! Go! Go!" The driver yanked the steering wheel around and hit the gas pedal, catapulting the 621-horsepower Maybach forward, narrowly missing the car in front of him. Alfonso, pushed back into his seat, immediately tensed up, holding on as well as he could as the S650's engine accelerated the heavy car at a dizzying pace. The driver ignored the red light and shot through the intersection, swerving around traffic and narrowly missing a car or two. Just when he thought they had cleared the crossing, a truck crashed into their rear, spinning the heavy car around its own axis and catapulting it onto the sidewalk. Alfonso, not a believer in seatbelts, was violently thrown around the back seat. His body crashed into the door and then, propelled all the way across the bench, into the other, only the deploying airbags preventing serious injuries. Traffic came to a total standstill, drivers and pedestrians alike frozen in place, rattled by the severity of the crash. The scene turned eerily quiet, only the hissing steam of a ruptured coolant line inside the truck's engine compartment breaking the silence.

+ + +

Patrick saw the crash from a few hundred feet away. It was now or never. He had to get to the car before it took off again. He pushed harder, running as fast as he could. Was it enough? He dug even deeper inside him, just to find that little bit of extra energy, but his legs would not go any faster, his breathing was as labored as it could be, and his heart pounded as on the harshest of military drills. He was at his absolute limit, yet he kept pushing.

+ + +

The driver, like his boss, looked around, dizzy and disoriented. The last thing he could remember was waiting at the red light, then everything went black. Buried deep in airbags, he unbuckled, then tried to take a deep breath, but the exploding pain in his ribcage would not allow it. Through the ringing in his ears, he faintly heard his boss screaming at him.

"Go! Go now! Go!" He started to vaguely remember a man running toward them, and his boss telling him to take off. Still dizzy, the driver put the gearstick back into the drive position, wondering if the car would even run anymore.

Patrick was approaching the intersection, still forcing a faster pace, completely out of breath. Not able to take in enough oxygen, his legs were burning, his body digging deep into its reserves. Any other time, he would have given up. Not today! Not now! Susan was in danger, and he could not afford to lose Alfonso. In the middle of the intersection, Patrick vaulted himself over the cars blocking his way and then forcefully pushed aside a few onlookers surrounding the scene of the accident. He had only a few feet to go when the Maybach's backup lights briefly flashed. It told Patrick the gearbox was being engaged, and the car about to take off. He forced a few more big steps, and with a huge jump, fist in the air, flew toward the limousine.

+ + +

Trying hard to suppress his pain, the driver was about to release the break and step on the gas when the window next to him shattered. Startled to a level of paralysis, he felt a strong hand grab his uniform and pull him out the window, throwing him onto the asphalt. His already injured ribs absorbed the brunt of the impact. He tried to scream, but there was no air coming out of his lungs to even make the slightest of sound.

+ + +

Alfonso panicked. He desperately tried to get out of the now slowly moving car, but Patrick jumped over the hood, grabbed the open door, engaged the child's safety lock with a swift flick, and immediately slammed it back shut.

"DON'T DO ANYTHING STUPID IF YOU WANT TO LIVE," he screamed at the lawyer, leaving little doubt what would happen if the man did not cooperate. Patrick got into the driver's seat and, with screeching tires, sped away from the scene of the accident.

"Where are we going?" a rattled Alfonso asked nervously.

Patrick did not answer. He did not know himself.

Only a few hundred yards away, police cars with lights and sirens passed them, speeding toward the scene of the accident. Patrick could tell the bent fender in the back was rubbing against the tire, and a light but steady stream of smoke was flowing out of the engine compartment. He wondered how much farther the car would go. He kept driving—past the airport, the Halfway Pond, and farther down the main road. In a more sparsely populated area, he decided to turn onto one of the secluded dirt roads. Patrick stopped the car, exited, calmly walked to the other side, opened the back door, and pulled Alfonso out of the car. He immediately got him into a chokehold, snapping his head back.

"You are going to tell me what is going on right now or I'll break your damn neck!"

Alfonso was too scared to say anything. He just winced in pain.

"I swear to God if you do not tell me where Susan is ... TELL ME!" Patrick screamed at the older man again.

"Don't," Alfonso managed to say, weeping heavily. "Don't, please don't!" he pleaded, sobbing. "I don't know, I really don't. Please ...."

Patrick loosened his grip, and Alfonso, like a bag of potatoes, dropped onto the dirt.

"You said the Japanese guy would not be here till later," Patrick screamed at him.

"It's not him. It cannot be ...."

"Then tell me where Susan is!"

Alfonso looked up at him, the sunlight blinding his eyes. "What do you mean where Susan is?"

"Don't play dumb or I am going to kick your teeth in. Tell me right now where she is."

"I DON'T KNOW! I SWEAR! I have nothing to do with this," Alfonso said weeping. He curled up, still very much in pain.

"You had me distracted, and then had her kidnapped. This is why you took off so quickly." Patrick grabbed him again by his hair, pulled him off the dirt road and threw him on the Maybach's oversize hood. Alfonso screamed in agony, but Patrick did not care. "Tell me, or you'll die right now." Alfonso did not answer, with tears in his eyes, holding his aching shoulder. With his left hand, Patrick lifted the lawyer by the collar, ready to punch him with his right. But after looking at the man, obviously scared to death, dirt all over him, his eyes in total panic, Patrick snapped out of his fury. This man was a numbers guy—a crook, yes, but not a gangster. Patrick dropped him back onto the hood. Alfonso lay where he fell, sobbing uncontrollably. With Patrick's compassion awoken by the pitiful scene, he finally extended his arm, helping the short man back to his feet. Without wiping the dirt off his suit, Alfonso struggled to walk the few steps around the car to sit sideways on the back seat, his feet still on the dusty dirt, and wiped the tears off his face.

"If it is not the Japanese guy, and it is not you, then who in the world has her?"

Alfonso, gasping for air, shook his head. "I don't know, my friend. I really don't."

Patrick turned away from him and, angrily, kicked a small rock into the nearby bushes. In his frustration, he let out a loud yell. "DAMN IT!" he shouted into the landscape. With his hands on his hips, he stared at the horizon.

"What now?" Alfonso whimpered.

"We wait," Patrick answered somberly. "We will go to your office, and you will give me those loan contracts so I can finalize my article. Sooner or later, we will hear something."

There was nothing else that could be done.

5:30 PM

George Town/Owen Roberts Airport, Cayman Islands

Hironori was standing in line to pass immigration. Despite his inner turmoil about Akiko and little Shin, he tried to stay collected.

"What is the purpose of your visit, Mr. Matsubara?" the officer asked once he finally made it to the counter.

"I am here on vacation," he confidently answered.

"How long will you stay on the Cayman Islands?"

"Three days." It was a lie. He was hoping to be out of there on the first flight the next morning.

"Short vacation, isn't it?"

"Yes. I am officially vacationing in Miami, but I always wanted to visit the Caribbean. I got a flight and hotel for a good price. So, here I am." The immigration officer looked into Hironori's eyes. After a few seconds, he stamped his passport and waved him through. Hironori was looking forward to finishing this godforsaken mission once and for all.

5:37 PM

Abandoned Warehouse, Somewhere on the Cayman Islands

A woman had entered the restaurant's restroom and started to wash her hands at the sink next to Susan. Susan recognized her as the patron from the next table. Other than a slight sting on her neck, she could not remember what followed. Now she was tied to a chair, blindfolded, and her mouth shut with duct tape. Without a warning, the blindfold got pulled from her head, and the intense brightness immediately stung her eyes. In a reflex, she pressed her eyelids together and turned her head away from the lights. When her pupils finally adjusted, Susan saw nothing but two powerful white spots in front of her.

"Interrogation of Susan Sobchak on September 7, 2017, by team members 0013765 and 0012433. The local time is 5:42 p.m." Susan could not see who was talking but noticed a distinct accent she could not place. A man stepped forward, blocking part of the light with his burly silhouette, grabbed the edge of the duct tape, and with one swift motion, ripped it off her face. With her lips feeling like they were about to explode and her cheeks throbbing from the violent peel, she let out a scream.

"Are you Ms. Sobchak, granddaughter of the deceased Rachel Sobchak?"

Susan was too scared to even answer. Her mind was racing, unable to think clearly.

"Ms. Sobchak, I need you to talk to us." The man in front of her lowered his head, now just inches away, breathing on her face. Her scared eyes looked deep into his, nervously jumping from one eye to the other. Susan had a déjà vu of the worst kind, certain this time the interrogation would end much differently. The man gently moved his hands inside her blouse between two of the buttons, ripped it open with one violent tear, then held a combat knife right in front of her face. With a disgusting grin, he slowly slid the knife under her bra and cut its center. The undergarment snapped open, exposing her breasts. He then fastened two electrical clamps, wires connected, to her nipples. Susan looked at him terror-stricken.

"I ... I am sorry, there must be a mistake." Susan was frazzled.

"No mistake, Ms. Sobchak," responded the powerful voice from an old man behind the darkness of the lights. "Let's start again. Are you the granddaughter of Rachel Sobchak?"

The man in front of her patiently waited, chest out, shoulders back, arms crossed, and the knife still in his hand. She tried to answer but she just stuttered, paralyzed.

"Ms. Sobchak. Answer the question!" the old voice commanded.

She knew she had to say something. "Pl ... pl ... please tell me, what do you want? Who are you?" she finally managed to ask.

"Irrelevant, Ms. Sobchak!"

"Please, tell me what is going on," she pleaded.

The old man stepped into the light, struggling to walk, supporting his left side with a cane. Against the brightness, Susan first noticed the fragile physique, then his thin, white hair and his weathered face. He must have been in his late eighties, maybe even early nineties. But it was not the age that caught her attention but the intense aura of hatred emanating from him.

"Ms. Sobchak, you do not want to anger the man in front of you," he warned her, catching his breath. "I recommend cooperating now because you will sooner or later. My colleague here will make sure of that. It really is your choice."

The burly man fetched a chair for the elder, who struggled to sit down.

"Let me ask you one more time, and this will be the last. Are you the granddaughter of Rachel Sobchak?"

Susan nodded.

"You need to answer loud and clear!" The burly one demanded.

"Yes, yes, she is … was my grandmother."

"We understand she was also known under the name Greta von Badenholz. Is that correct?"

Again, Susan nodded. A powerful jolt of electricity immediately shot through the wires, jabbing Susan's torso. The room immediately filled with her terrified scream, a few seconds long, till the old man gestured to stop.

"What is it that you do not—"

"YES … YES … FROM WHAT I NOW KNOW … she was also known as Greta von Badenholz," Susan rapidly replied, breathing heavily.

"What can you tell us about Klaus Heydrich?" the old man continued the interrogation.

There it was. This name. This name Susan desperately hoped would not come up.

7:42 PM (ART)
Master Bedroom, Estancia de Gobineau

Everything was calm. Klaus lay on his bed, the medical devices around him emitting their usual sounds at regular intervals. Carlos, Klaus's uncontested number two, put down the magazine. He had read enough gossip for the day. He looked at his boss and reflected on the recent developments. Yamaguchi soon needed a new partner, and Carlos had not hesitated to throw his name into the mix. During his loyal service in the Heydrich clan for over three decades, he had learned the ins and outs of the business and, parallel with the demise of his boss, had increasingly taken over responsibilities, proving himself capable of running the operation. As the boss's right hand, he stood out as the obvious successor, but Yamaguchi took his time deciding. When he last called, Carlos had expected to hear the good news. Instead, he was asked for a personal favor. A big one.

His gaze at the old man was interrupted as his phone started to ring. Carlos checked who was calling. *Speak of the devil.* He leaned over Klaus to make sure he was asleep.

"How is he doing?"

"No change. Hanging in there," Carlos responded.

"The old man is tougher than I thought. How much longer?"

Carlos did not—could not—answer.

"Are you with him right now?"

"Yes."

There was a pause. "You know what needs to be done, once ...."

"I know!" Carlos confirmed coldly.

"Let's see if you have what it takes," Yamaguchi responded.

Carlos understood the favor as his rite of passage, a test to prove himself to the Japanese crime lord. But he did not understand why Yamaguchi wanted Dieter dead. The Dieter he knew was harmless, a man wanting nothing more than to be left alone and, soon, to be out of the picture. Nevertheless, it was not up to him to question motives.

"You can count on me," Carlos answered confidently.

5:45 PM (EST)
Offices of Hamilton & Hamilton

Patrick chauffeured the limousine back to the restaurant to pick up his bag, Alfonso then directed him to his office. The space was smaller than Patrick had expected, nevertheless impressive, elegantly modern, with unusual yet exquisite materials of the finest kinds. Expensive stones, wood, and glass complemented each other in an awe-inspiring symphony of interlacing spaces. Patrick could not tell what impressed him most. It was probably the spectacular views of the ocean, but the fountain in the reception area, the translucent color-changing light wall, and the custom-made furniture were all close contenders.

Alfonso walked out of the men's room where he had freshened up. "I need a drink. Can I offer you one?" he asked. Patrick shook his head, not wanting to compromise his thinking. Alfonso unscrewed the top of the noblest single malt whiskey in his cabinet, put some ice in a glass, and then filled it to the top. To Patrick's surprise, he downed it, then another, and then another, washing down the excitement of the day. An unexpected, not-so-noble "Ahh" followed.

"What makes you so sure we are going to hear from whoever has Susan?" Alfonso asked Patrick, trying hard to suppress the air pushing up from his stomach.

"Because they must want something. In the meantime, you are going to scan the documents for me. And I have an article to write." Patrick took his laptop from his bag. "Where can I sit?" Before he could organize himself, he heard a phone ring. Alfonso and Patrick looked at each other.

"Aren't you going to answer?" Patrick asked.

"It's not one of ours."

Patrick had forgotten all about the satellite phone. He pulled it out of his bag and answered. "Dieter?"

"Patrick, what is going on up there?"

Patrick noticed the distress in his voice. "What do you mean?"

"I just got a call from someone telling me they have Susan. Isn't she with you?"

"Who has her?" Patrick asked, hoping for any kind of information.

"So, it is true," Dieter responded somberly.

"Who has her?" Patrick asked again. "What do they want?"

31

5:47 PM (EST)
Abandoned Warehouse

"I … I have never met him. All I know is that he is a former Nazi hiding in Argentina. I just recently learned he is also involved in drug trafficking."

"And what is your relationship with him?" the old man asked.

"There is no relationship. As I said, I have never met him."

The sitting elder gestured for his colleague to again nudge Susan to cooperate.

"NO! DON'T!" she pleaded. This time the released electricity was even stronger, and again Susan screamed in absolute agony, all the while the old man shook his head.

"I have never understood why it always has to be this way. In the end, everyone talks. All this pain and suffering … for what? Nothing!"

"We know that you and your friend, the journalist, were in his home only two days ago," the burly man stated.

"Yes, we were," Susan quickly responded.

"So?"

"We needed to talk to Dieter."

"Why?"

"We needed information."

The old man shook his head. "Ms. Sobchak. This is like pulling teeth. Are you not yet sore enough?" He again gestured the young man.

"NO! I mean, I am …" she shouted, desperate to avoid another round of pain. "I am happy to … it's just … I can tell you do not want to hear what I have to say. You are not going to believe me anyway."

"All you have to do is tell us the truth."

Susan tried to get herself together. "Well, my … my grandparents were murdered by a Japanese hit man. Now he is after me and my friend. We are trying to find out what is going on, which led us to the Heydrichs, but they did not exactly roll out the red carpet for us. However, Dieter let us escape. Without him, we both would be dead."

"You were not welcomed," the burly man repeated. "Right!"

"That is quite a story you are telling us, Ms. Sobchak, but you know fairy tales are for kids and not for when one is tied to a chair. But I do have to give it to you, you have guts," the old man responded, nodding to his colleague again.

"NO!" Susan shouted. "You said you want the truth. This is the truth and nothing but the truth, no matter how much you hurt me."

The burly man produced his knife again and held it in front of Susan. Her eyes followed the blade moving down to her chest, where the man, with the knife's tip, started to caress her areola.

"They are so perfect! Such a shame!"

Susan looked at him in total disgust.

"Ms. Sobchak, you see, here is our problem with your story," the old man continued. "Your family enjoys a close friendship with the Heydrichs. They did a lot of business together. And you are telling us you were not welcomed? You even want us to believe Klaus tried to get rid of you? I am sorry, but … this just does not add up."

The burly one leaned over Susan again and brutally yanked her head back. His hand interwoven with her hair, holding on tightly, he pressed his temple against hers, getting lost in the aroma of her scent. His breathing was getting faster and heavier as he pressed the flat side of the cold blade hard onto her breast. He took another intense sniff.

"Again, all you have to do is to tell us the truth! But please don't," he said in a shaky voice.

Not sure if it was from pain, fear, or pure revulsion, tears started rolling down Susan's cheeks. "It is the truth," she protested in a resigned whisper.

"Enough!" A man she had not seen before walked out of the shadows, gesturing for his colleague to back off. He opened a new pack of cigarettes, put one between his lips, lit it, inhaled a big puff, and pressed the smoke out through his lips.

"We heard Klaus is in a rather fragile state. How bad is it?"

"He is dying," she responded.

"So we have been told. How very unfortunate."

"I don't understand," Susan responded.

"Let me tell you, my dear. It makes your story nothing more than a bunch of horse manure." The tall, fit, middle-aged man confidently stood there in his elegant black suit, white shirt, black tie, black shoes, salt-and-pepper hair, with one hand in his trousers pocket, the index and middle finger of the other holding the cigarette. "We all know the real reason you went down there."

"And what reason would that be?" Susan dared to ask.

"To pay your final respects to a close friend."

"I told you. I do not know Klaus. I have never met him in my life." Susan looked at him, her eyes begging for this to end. "Till recently, I had never even heard of him, I did not even know he existed. You've got to believe me! You've got to! It's the truth."

Without saying a word, the man took in another long winding puff from his cigarette.

She was right; it did not matter what she was saying. She lowered her head, resigned to the inevitable. "You are not interested in the truth."

Nobody responded.

"Just tell me what you want from me."

The man in the black suit looked at her long and hard, now oblivious to the cigarette slowly burning down in his hand.

"You really don't know?"

"No, I really don't!"

He looked at her again.

"Tell her," the old man requested.

"Back in 1960—"

"Your agents," Susan interrupted. "I heard what Klaus did to them."

"So, you can imagine how desperate we are to get our hands on him, or any family member of his."

"That has nothing to do with me," Susan objected.

The man in the black suit took another step forward. "After years of hunting down the long-lost Greta von Badenholz, the lover of Klaus and mother of Dieter, you can imagine our excitement when her name finally surfaced again not too long ago. We got a tip she was hiding in plain sight—that she was, in fact, Rachel Sobchak, that these two were one and the same. Yet, despite our best efforts, we could never find definitive proof. That is, till today."

The man threw his cigarette on the floor and stubbed it out with his shoe, got his phone from the inside pocket of his jacket and held it in front of Susan.

"Your grandmother was no Polish underground fighter; she was a German operative ordered to infiltrate the Polish resistance and relay information back to the Gestapo. She was a spy, and one of the very best. Do you want to know about her last mission?"

The man stopped the recording.

"The couple on the next table … the woman in the bathroom …," Susan noted.

"Yes, operatives of ours," he confirmed.

"You want Klaus. Not my grandmother and certainly not me. Seriously, I have nothing to do with him," Susan vehemently objected.

The man took his time to light another cigarette. Surrounded by smoke that glowed in the bright lights as it wafted around his torso, he shook his head and pointed the cigarette-holding hand at Susan.

"You see, while you are not directly related to Klaus, his son is your uncle, your grandmother his mother. And that, my dear, makes you family."

5:52 PM
Offices of Hamilton & Hamilton

"It's not what they want, it is *who* they want!" Dieter answered.

"Don't tell me. Your father?" Patrick guessed.

"Yes, my father."

"The Mossad?"

"Well, not the Mossad. You know ...."

"So, what is the deal here?" Patrick anxiously wanted to know.

"We have till noon tomorrow. 10 a.m. your time," Dieter responded.

"And if you do not deliver your father, Susan is going to pay for him," Patrick stated the obvious.

"So they tell me," Dieter somberly confirmed.

"Shit!" Patrick cursed. He could not believe what was happening. Everything had just gotten much more complicated. He did not dare to think what Susan was going through, even worse what they had in store for her if ....

"Tell me, Patrick, is it true?" Dieter interrupted his thoughts.

"Is what true?"

"Is Susan's grandmother really my mother?"

"It seems so," Patrick confirmed.

"I never knew! Rachel, my mother ...."

Patrick felt for Dieter, but there were more pressing issues at hand. "What does your father say about all this?"

"He does not know. Things would not end well for anyone but him if he took charge."

"He does not seem to be a guy who takes prisoners. Well played."

"I don't know how well played it is, but I cannot have Susan pay for my father's crimes. Yet, for my sake, I cannot hand him over either, as long as Yamaguchi is after me. I really do not know what to do."

"For now, just hang in there. Yamaguchi will have to deal with bigger fires once my article is published. And I am close," Patrick tried to calm his new friend.

"Hopefully close enough. For Susan's sake … and mine."

"It will be up before 10 a.m. tomorrow," Patrick again reassured him. Dieter let out a big, worried sigh.

"It's our only way out of this mess."

After the call ended, Patrick nervously glanced at his watch, watching the seconds tick by.

"Alfonso, time's up. I need those loan contracts now."

The old man shook his head.

Patrick was tired of the lawyer's delay tactics. He walked over and towered his fit body in front of him once again. "Hand over these docs NOW!"

Alfonso again shook his head. "I wish I could, but I really can't."

"What do you mean you can't?" Patrick said loudly.

"You do not seem to understand. I don't have them."

"WHAT?!" Patrick screamed.

Alfonso callously shrugged his shoulders. "Do you really think a man like Yamaguchi would leave such important documents in the care of a third party? He is smarter than that."

"You are his lawyer!"

"Nevertheless …."

Patrick sensed suppressed happiness. "You knew. You knew all this time."

"I kept telling you I am unable to give you these contracts." Alfonso walked over to the safe, fiddled with the combination lock, and opened its door. "Here, suit yourself."

Patrick did not bother. "If you don't have them, then who does?"

"Let's just say they are out of my reach," Alfonso replied in his now blasé manner.

Patrick grabbed him by the collar again, about to lift him off the floor. "WHERE ARE THEY?"

"Not here, that's all I know. Now let go of me," Alfonso

replied, this time more annoyed than intimidated.

Patrick refused. "Are you telling me they are in Japan?"

Alfonso shrugged again. "I don't know. The last time I saw these documents was when they were signed. I have never received anything executed, not even as much as a copy. To be honest, I prefer it this way."

Patrick knew better than to trust the cunning lawyer. He tightened his grip on the collar.

"Listen, Alfonso, if you don't get me these documents, people will die. And mark my words—you will be one of them. So, at this point, I'd be happy to beat it out of you because it may even save your own life." Holding him with his left, he clenched his right into a fist, his arm pulled back and ready to strike the uncooperative man.

"Do what you need to do, but I really do not have these papers," Alfonso again explained calmly.

5:54 PM
Abandoned Warehouse

"It all makes sense now. You kidnapping me, your accent ... I understand your thirst for revenge. Nevertheless, I really do not know Klaus. As a matter of fact, he wants me dead too. Go ahead, kill me. You would be doing him a favor."

"And why would he want you dead?" the man in the black suit asked.

"Why would Klaus Heydrich welcome us if his closest friend and business partner wants us dead?" she asked.

"And why would you go to the Heydrichs if you knew his best friend and business partner wants you dead?"

"And why would I pay my respects to a man who did not object to the killing of my family? We had to go there because it was our only lead, because we needed to find out what was going on. Anything else would have meant our certain deaths. Visiting the estancia at least gave us a chance. We knew we might not get out of there alive, but look, here we are."

"Yes, here we are ...."

"Enough of your stories," the old man shouted angrily, the glare in his eyes intensified by years of bottled-up hate. "Stop your lies!" Furious, he struggled to get up from his chair, lifted his arm, and released his fist toward Susan. But despite his iron will, the aged body did not cooperate. He missed, lost his balance, and nearly fell over. His younger colleague caught him just in time and helped the old man back onto the chair. Legs apart, his right hand resting on his cane, head down, he started to cry. Then, with a force that seemed to have inherited all the old man's pain, Susan was punched in the face, a hit so powerful she passed out before she could even feel the pain.

"Stop it," the smoking man scolded his younger colleague. "She will be of no use if she dies now."

The old man looked up at him, pointing his finger at Susan. "Someone ... someone has to pay. Someone must pay for it all. If not Klaus, it may as well be this one."

"What if she is telling the truth?"

"The truth? Pah! She is one of them," he dismissed the objection. "You were not there. You did not see what he did to my friends. Someone finally has to pay. SOMEONE HAS TO!" he shouted, so forceful he needed a moment to catch his breath. "All these years, all the time invested, all the money spent. This is our last chance to get some justice before this monster dies." He once again started to cry.

"I understand, my friend. We are with you. All of us. But ... what if she is telling the truth? What if killing her would actually do this Nazi a favor?"

It was not what the old man wanted to hear. Enraged and riddled with frustration, he got up, walked over to the door, as fast as his old body allowed, and slammed it shut behind him.

"Susan, can you hear me?" the man in the black suit asked her again and again. Her left eye was swollen shut, her cheek glowing red, pulsating, and her mouth was spitting out blood, but she finally nodded.

"Listen, I believe your story may have merit, but I am in the minority here. Their thirst for revenge—well, it is clouding their minds. Let me ask you this: How close are you to Dieter?"

Susan tried to lift her head. "What do you mean?"

"Unless Klaus is giving himself up … well, unless Dieter … Let's just hope he will save your life one more time."

Susan saw the small gesture with his cigarette holding hand just before she was blindfolded again.

6:15 PM
Offices of Hamilton & Hamilton

"I am sorry, Patrick, but without solid evidence …." His boss Dave was in turmoil. He was well aware of the stakes—of the dire consequences of not printing the article. It was one of those rare moments he despised his job, but he could not allow the newspaper to become a pawn in Patrick's story. "Show me evidence, and I even promise you the front page. But without … I am sorry."

All of Patrick's pleading did not sway his boss. He pressed hard, but without success.

"Send me the article. We will prep everything on our side. I promise you it will be online the minute you get me copies of these contracts."

"Trouble?" Alfonso wanted to know, the sarcastic undertone back in his voice.

"Not yet."

"I wish I could help," he responded coldly.

Patrick was thinking. "As a matter of fact, you can. You drew up these documents, so print me a copy, will you?"

"What good are they? They are not signed."

"I need to know their exact wording. It will help me finalize my article."

"They are backed up somewhere."

"Start digging then," Patrick ordered the lawyer before making his way to the restroom.

32

Offices of Hamilton & Hamilton

Alfonso was looking through the archived folders when, in the corner of his eye, he saw Patrick return from the restroom. He looked up and jumped, spooked to his core.

"Good evening!" Hironori greeted him.

Alfonso sat there aghast.

"Why so nervous, my friend?"

Hironori's timing could not have been worse. Alfonso's eyes went back to his desktop monitor with Yamaguchi's contract on its screen.

"You know why I am here," Hironori continued in his usual confident manner.

"The contracts are safe. There is nothing to worry about," Alfonso desperately tried to ensure his counterpart, but through the glass walls, he worriedly looked at Patrick's laptop and notebook on the conference room table.

"I will make sure of that," Hironori responded, approaching the desk. "For now, I only have one question. Any visitors today?"

Alfonso did not know how to answer best, yet he could not afford to hesitate. "Your boss told me to make myself unavailable," he responded as confidently as possible, all the while keeping a nervous eye on the bathroom door.

Hironori stood without saying a word, and it was tearing at Alfonso's nerves. "Good," he finally answered.

"I was just about to write a quick note for my assistant before heading out for dinner. Why don't you join me? My treat." Alfonso hoped to get the assassin out of his office before Patrick's return.

"No dinner. You are coming with me."

"I can take care of myself," Alfonso protested.

"Can you?"

6:23 PM

Patrick was about to press the flush when he heard an exchange of words. Alarmed, he switched off the lights and pressed his ear against the restroom door. Here and there he managed to understand what was being said. What he clearly noticed was the Japanese accent. Patrick cursed. Seconds later, the shadow of a man passing the bathroom showed through the narrow gap under the door. Moments later, another one. Aware of the arsenal underneath the assassin's baggy clothes, Patrick weighed his options. All he had was the element of surprise. But with Hironori's reflexes, the odds were clearly stacked against him. He needed an opening, one that would give him the upper hand, and he needed it quick.

+ + +

The two made their way toward the elevators, but just when they had passed through the heavy entry door, Hironori stopped. He turned to take another look.

"So, no visitors today?" he asked again.

Alfonso summoned all his courage to lie to the towering man again. "No visitors. Let's go!"

But Hironori walked back into the office, silently, and positioned himself in front of the restroom door, legs apart.

30 Seconds Earlier

In his head, Patrick was visualizing the two men's movements through the building, counting the advances of the phosphor-illuminated hands on his watch, giving them a head start. He pressed his ear against the door once more. *Where they gone?* Everything was quiet. He kept an eye on his watch, waiting for the second hand to pass the sixty-second mark. *They must be by the elevator now.* He put his hand on the door handle, but then hesitated. He had not yet heard the office door fall into its lock, and again he pressed his ear against the wooden panel. With a loud bang right in front of his face, the door shattered into pieces. A mere split second later, Patrick was hit by the rock-hard heel of a boot, his chin taking the brunt of the impact. His entire body was thrown into the stalls and then onto the floor, the sturdy wall panels crashing on top of him. The bathroom started to spin around him. Spitting out pieces of a broken tooth, he wondered if his jaw was still in one piece. After pushing the panels off him, Patrick saw the silhouette of a man, somewhat blurry against the light, the tip of a sword hovering right before his eyes.

"I thought so," Hironori smirked.

Then the heavy boot, with an equally hard kick, smashed across Patrick's face once more.

September 8, 2017—8:27 AM (JST)
Minato-Ku

When Hironori had finally told Akiko who he worked for, she was shocked. So shocked, she was determined to end the relationship. But he assured her it would never be a problem and vowed to keep their relationship a secret, at least till after his resignation. It took much pleading for Akiko to reluctantly change her mind. Then, early in the morning two days ago, Yamaguchi's men were knocking on her door, commanding her to pack a few things and accompany them with her son. She first refused, but being unable to stand up to the thugs, she unwillingly complied.

"You have no right to hold us," Akiko told Yamaguchi in her shaky voice, intimidated by the powerful man in front of her. "Why were we brought here?"

"It's nothing more than a precaution," Yamaguchi lied.

"Hironori … is he okay?"

"He is fine."

"Then why are we here?"

"Because I need your help," Yamaguchi said, looking at little Shin resting comfortably in Akiko's arms. Without asking, he reached for him. Akiko immediately tightened her grip, only for the crime boss to do the same. Not wanting her baby to be harmed, she reluctantly let go. To her dread, Yamaguchi held him up to take a good look. Startled by the unfamiliar face in front of him, little Shin started to cry.

"What a strong boy. How proud his dad must be," Yamaguchi smiled.

Angry, Akiko tried to take him back, but he did not let go.

"I want to leave," she demanded.

"That is not yet possible. But don't worry, Hironori will be back soon."

September 7, 2017—6:33 PM (EST)
Offices of Hamilton & Hamilton

With an overwhelming sense of trepidation, Alfonso watched Hironori emerge from the restroom. He did not dare to venture a guess about his own fate now.

"What did you do to him?"

"He got what he deserved. He won't be bothering us any longer," Hironori coldly replied. Then, with the sword in his right hand, he looked at Alfonso, who now rightfully feared for his own life.

"I have not said nor given them anything. I swear," he was quick to say.

Hironori reacted in the worst possible way—as he did not.

"I swear I did as I was told. You've got to believe—"

"You lied to me!" Hironori cut him off coldly.

Alfonso was immediately overcome with nausea. With a burning sensation in his chest, he began to hyperventilate. Hironori put his sword back into its sheath, passed the old man, and walked over to the elevator. Alfonso was unable to move. He could not stop looking inside the office, hoping Patrick would somehow emerge and come to his rescue. A few seconds later, the ding of the arriving elevator ripped Alfonso's gaze from the office. Hironori held the doors back from closing.

"Last chance if you do not want to join your friend in there."

Resigned, Alfonso got into the elevator and let the doors close behind him.

11:45 PM (ART)
Dieter's Bedroom, Estancia de Gobineau

It was late, but Dieter was restless. Only twelve more hours to go. *Ring, damn it, ring.* He was pacing up and down his room, telling himself again and again to stay calm but still too nervous to put the phone down. Various scenarios, not one with a positive outcome, kept creeping into his mind. He needed to do something, to finally take charge and not, for once, have his life depend on others. He was done with that. But what could he do? The frustration inside him intensified. With every passing second, he got more nervous, his worries stronger. He had to find a way out, somehow come up with a plan B, just in case, to make sure all this would not fall apart. Then, out of nowhere, a little lightbulb in his head switched on. The idea was not perfect, not by a long shot. On the contrary, it was a gamble. Worse, the stakes could not be higher. But maybe, just maybe, it would work. If everything else failed, it had to.

The sounds around Susan did not give her any clues about her whereabouts. The most prominent one was nothing more than water dripping on the floor at regular intervals. At some point, she thought she heard distant cars driving by; then again, she could have been mistaken. Sitting in the same position for hours had started to take its toll. In addition to her swollen eye, her entire left side was getting sore, and a tingling sensation crept up her leg. To make matters worse, the solitude inside the dark room was starting to mess with her mind—so much that when the door opened again, despite the threat of further torment, she actually felt some relief. When her blindfold was pulled, she saw the old man from before. From what she could tell, he was alone. He laid the piece of cloth on the table and then, with his shaky hands, removed the electric clamps and, with a safety pin, crudely fixed Susan's ripped blouse. The hunchbacked man struggled to sit down. Unable to straighten, he looked up at her.

"I was there when Heydrich … you know. I was there when their families were told. I was there at their funeral. But worst of all, I was there when they were found. I saw the bodies. It was not for the eyes of a young man. Those images … they burned themselves into my brain. Still today, they haunt me in my thoughts, in my nightmares. I tried so hard to forget, but no matter how much one tries, you just can't. Not something like this. Now I am the last survivor of this detail, and the burden their death is never forgotten, even more important, the way they died is on me and me alone."

He pulled a handkerchief from his pants pocket to wipe a drop off his nose. "I had given up believing the day would ever come," he said, somewhat out of breath. "I have waited for decades. But when I got the call, you cannot even imagine … And now here we are. After all these years."

Susan looked at the fragile man through her swollen eye.

"You know," he continued, "things were different back then. It wasn't all about technology like nowadays. We were hands-on, a part of an incredible group of agents, working closely together. It was about people, teams."

The old man blew his nose, then leaned to the side to put the handkerchief back in his pocket, all the while shaking his head. "You know, we were all in the academy together. And our class was quite the breed, the top graduates quickly summoned to an elite team. So often I had put my life into their hands, not with the slightest of hesitations, and they often put theirs into mine. We all had this extraordinary trust in each other, and rightfully so. It was exactly this trust that soon made us top gun, but then, in Bariloche, back in 1960, I made this terrible mistake. I did not pay attention, and in one moment, all our lives changed forever." The old man again shook his head. "We had more than enough intelligence. How could I not see it? How could I not! I sent my friends right into that trap."

The old man was out of tears, out of anger, just numb, resigned to these long-gone events. "Do you know what it means to live with this burden? Often, I could not. More than once I was tempted … but when you hold a barrel to your temple, ready to pull the trigger …." The old man paused. Susan just stared at him, not knowing what to say. "In the end, I could not become another victim of this terrible man." He again paused, sitting in silence.

"I understand," Susan said, trying to express her empathy despite her precarious situation.

"I doubt you do. You see, well, not many know what I am about to tell you. Back then, no one could. One of these two agents was more than a dear colleague. The moment we laid eyes on each other, we clicked. He made me laugh, he made me cry, but above all, he made me indescribably happy. He brought up feelings inside me I never even knew I had, making every moment together a true gift. And then I sent him …."

The old man stared ahead of himself, for a moment lost in his thoughts, then lifted his hand and pointed his finger at Susan. "This Heydrich, he took him away from me. He took him … in the worst possible way one can imagine. You have no idea what it means to have to live with this, to be haunted by this terrible memory, to be torn apart every single moment of every single day. This man must pay. He MUST! And now, after all these years, the time has finally come to bring it all to an end and honor my friend's death—their deaths."

"How lost you are, you poor old man," Susan countered. "You really think there is salvation in revenge? Torturing and killing me will not set you free from your torments. On the contrary, it will make it worse. How disappointed you are going to be."

But the old man was not interested in what she had to say.

"And I have already told you; I have nothing to do with any of this."

"Heydrich is dying. We are out of time. Someone must pay *now*."

"Whatever you are going to do to me, it will not matter to him. You will do him a favor."

But again, Susan's words bounced right off his ears.

"Now we finally have someone from his family, *and* a descendent of a notorious Nazi operative of the war. A little bit of justice at last—not only for my two colleagues, but for everyone who suffered during these terrible times."

Susan noticed the relief, the slight smile on his face. "Listen, you want Klaus, and I can help you get him. As a matter of fact, this is why we are here, to bring him down. And not just him but all his business partners, everybody. It can all be over within a day, but you will have to let me go."

The elder laughed. "I may be old, but I am not senile. Not yet, anyway."

"It is the truth," Susan protested.

"STOP YOUR LIES!" he shouted. "We know all about your family, their business, and now, after all these years, your grandmother's true identity. This old lawyer is right. If this story becomes public, you are done. So, don't tell me—"

Susan had not yet thought of the personal consequences of what they had uncovered. What if it became known that her grandmother was indeed Greta von Badenholz? That their entire legacy was built on stolen war loot and laundering drug money for a major crime organization? It would send shockwaves through the societies of the rich and famous. Alfonso was right. The fallout would be dire.

"Our time has finally come, and it could not have done so a second too early. I will personally make sure Klaus gets to see our pictures this time. An eye for an eye, my dear. An eye for an eye." Saying so, the old man got up and, without bothering to put the blindfold back on or switching off the lights, exited the room.

4:15 AM (ART)
Estancia de Gobineau

Dieter lay on his bed, unable to fall back asleep. He was too rattled by the nightmare that had awoken him. In his dream, he saw a person sitting in a poorly lit room, bound to a chair, a dim light hanging above. Three men were applying various torture instruments. The victim was screaming, the kind that rattles one to the core. Next to the chair was a little table. On it, the victim's eyeballs. Dieter had to stop whatever was going on. He tried to run toward the victim, but although his legs were moving, his body stayed put. He screamed to get the men's attention. For a moment, they looked up at each other, but then they carried on with their malicious activities, not bothered by his presence. Suddenly, another man stepped into the light, giving instructions. It was his father. Dieter pleaded with him, without success. He tried to run faster, but the faster he ran, the more he was pulled away from the eerie scene. Then, on a gesture of his father, one of the men turned the chair toward him. Dieter was catapulted forward, his head now right in the tortured face. Despite missing both eyes, he immediately recognized the victim as Susan.

"Don't worry, everything will be okay!" she whispered, then broke into a laugh more evil than anything he had ever heard before, louder and louder. Dieter held his ears and tried to run, but wherever he turned another person in another chair was blocking his way, also tied, eyes missing and face swollen. They were all around him, countless copies equally distributed deep into space. Barely alive, all these proxies were desperately crying out for help in unison, their words terribly distorted, a choir of pure terror. Blurry at first,

Dieter soon recognized their identity: himself!

It was then he awoke, soaked in his own sweat. He reached for his phone to check the time. Less than eight hours to go. He called Patrick, more than once, desperate for an update, but none of his calls were answered. He also went online to recheck *The New York Times* home page. No article yet.

33

5:31 AM (EST)
Offices of Hamilton & Hamilton

The moment Patrick regained consciousness, he knew he was dying. His feet and knees were tightly bound together; so were his hands behind his back. He could hardly move. Worse still, his neck was tied to the metal P-trap assembly under the sink so tightly it was nearly impossible for him to breathe. The leather strap around his neck was moist and getting tighter while drying off. Eventually, it would cut off the air supply to his lungs as well as the blood flow to the brain. Already struggling, breathing short, heartbeat increased, his focus was slipping away again. As one could expect, Hironori had done his job with the finesse of a true professional. The two spotlights above the mirror were bright enough to illuminate the space under the sink through the elegant, translucent glass bowl just above him.

He needed to free himself. But how? *Think Patrick, think.* He looked around, but every time he tried to turn his head, even slightly, the sturdy strap cut deeper into his throat. Patrick moved his legs, bending them as much as he could, and then, with all the energy he could summon, jolted his knees upward toward the glass bowl. The move put the entire weight of his body onto the leather band around his neck. He gagged and tried hard not to throw up. To his own surprise, he managed to hit the bowl, but the solid piece of glass did not give. His chest was tightening, heart pounding, and his throat felt like an entire truck was resting on it. *Don't give up. You can't!* He was desperately close to doing so. He let his body replenish itself with the little oxygen he could get through his tightening windpipe, letting strength flow back into his legs. With his heartbeat slowing, Patrick was ready for another try. He closed his eyes to visualize the move and jerked up his knees to strike the bowl again. The compression on the neck once again cut off air and blood supply alike. Still, the bowl did not budge. Patrick cursed his luck, or lack thereof. This time, his body needed more time to recuperate. The little air passing into his lungs was now emitting sounds of struggle. He again closed his eyes, visualized the move, and with all the force he could summon, jolted his knees upward. This time, the glass cracked a tiny bit. With new-found energy, he immediately hit it again. It cracked a bit more. Then again. Part of the bowl finally shattered.

The strap had cut so deep into his neck he was now unable to breathe. With his tied hands, he frantically felt around for a broken piece of glass. There were none nearby. He moved his body the little he could, only for the neck strap to tighten even more. Wondering how much longer he had before passing out, he started tapping around the area behind his back again, frantically feeling for a shard of glass with a sharp edge. He reached with his hands as far out as possible, all the way to his side, where he finally felt such a piece. With the tips of his fingers, he struggled to pull it closer but managed to position it behind him, right against the back wall of the cabinet. Patrick immediately started to press his ties against the shard. But they did not cut. Everything around him started to spin again. With no more air in his lungs, he pushed his entire body onto his wrists, pressing down as hard as he could. The glass was cutting into his skin, and blood started to flow down his hands. Now close to respiratory failure, desperately gasping for air, his heart racing, Patrick felt his body going into shock. In his panic, he pushed even harder. His lips were turning blue, his face pale, all the while the glass cut more and more into his wrists. With his eyes pressed shut, he started to see glowing dots flying around him. *Stay awake, don't give up!* He kept up the pressure on the ties, still pushing as hard as he could. *Why are they not—* Just then, the ties finally snapped. Patrick immediately grabbed the piece of glass and started to rub it against the leather band around his neck. Two seconds later, he was released. With no energy left to even hold himself up, he fell to his side, heaving in air as if he hadn't had a breath in years, interspersed by heavy coughing. With every second, life was flowing back into his body. Staring at the pieces of the broken door, he let his body recover.

A few minutes passed till he finally managed to get himself up. It was more difficult than he had anticipated. His knees kept giving way underneath him, yet he managed to crawl to the satellite phone on the floor just a few feet away. It looked like it also had encountered the assassin's boot as it would not switch on. Struggling to walk out of the restroom, Patrick collapsed onto the sofa in the reception area. Unable to hold it, he dropped the phone onto the floor. He closed his eyes again, blood slowly dripping from his hands.

6:05 AM

When Patrick finally opened his eyes again, he caught a glimpse of the clock on the wall nearby. With time running out, he got up, bandaged his wrists with supplies from the first aid kit he found in the breakroom, tended his throbbing head with ice from the fridge, and replenished his body with what seemed to be a full gallon of water. Still at a point of exhaustion, he walked back to the conference room. With the satellite phone gone, he took his PDA out of his bag and, for the first time in what seemed forever, switched it on. It immediately alerted him to various messages and emails, but he could not be bothered to check any of them. He did, however, see a voice mail, six days old, from Sarah. He could not get himself to listen to it; it was not the right time or place. But seeing her name rejuvenated his determination. *Time to bring you down, you son of a bitch!* Sitting behind his laptop, he organized his notes and eagerly began typing away. After a rough start, the words began to flow, though he did not yet have the required proof to back them up. Somehow, he had to convince his boss to publish the article without.

7:42 AM

Abandoned Warehouse

Susan was rattled, but eventually her body gave in, her eyelids too heavy to stay open. She was asleep when the agents came back into the room. When a slap on her face had woken her up, she wondered how much time had passed. Was it already morning? Or was it still night? It did not really matter. With her body sore from not moving for hours, she asked the time. Nobody answered.

"You cannot tell me what time it is?" she asked again.

All she got was another slap on her face. "Silence!"

"I need some water. And I really need to go to the bathroom." Nobody answered. Her eyelids were slowly giving in again, as she was too drained both physically and mentally to stay awake. Not a second later, she got slapped again.

"DON'T!" one of the agents screamed at her.

"I need to go to the bathroom," she pleaded.

"Yeah, bathroom, pfft! If you need to go, go. You are going to shit yourself anyway. But don't worry, this will all be over in a few days."

8:45 AM

Offices of Hamilton & Hamilton

Patrick was typing away when a startled young woman walked into the offices. They looked at each other through the glass wall, each puzzled about the presence of the other.

"Who are you? What happened to you? And what happened to the bathroom?" she asked, standing in the doorway of the conference room, taken by Patrick's bruised cheek and neck as well as the bandages around his wrists. "What is going on?"

"What time is it?" Patrick asked, turning his attention back to his article.

"I'll call security," she said, turning around.

"No, wait! Please! Tell me what time it is," he asked without taking his eyes off the screen.

"It's just past 8:45," she answered, not happy her inquiries were ignored. "Who are you? And how did you get in?"

Patrick again did not answer. "I need Internet access to get this out," he demanded instead, nodding toward the article on his screen.

The young woman leaned against the doorframe, crossing her arms. "As soon as you tell me what is going on, and not a second before."

"Give me five minutes, and I will tell you whatever you want to know. For now, I urgently need to get this to my boss," Patrick pleaded.

The young woman did not know what to do. "What happened here?" she asked again, eyeing him suspiciously, still considering calling security.

"Please," Patrick pleaded. "Five minutes."

Hesitantly, she walked over to the dry-erase board. "This is the guest Wi-Fi password," she told him, writing it on the board. "You have five minutes, not a second more."

Patrick nodded, too busy to even thank her.

10:46 AM (ART)
Dieter's Bedroom

Dieter had asked for breakfast to be served in his room, but it was just sitting on one of the side tables, untouched, getting cold. He had thought it might be a good idea to eat something, but as it turned out, he was too nervous to do so. He was haunted by the horrific scenes of his nightmare popping into his thoughts over and over, all the suffering, all the screams. He could not help but think of Susan and what she must be going through. His right leg was rapidly moving up and down, a nervous tic fueled by his inner turmoil. *Come on, Patrick. Get that damn article online already.* The deadline was rapidly approaching; just a little over an hour was left. He again questioned the feasibility of his Plan B, fueled by worry about its potentially dire consequences. Was it the right thing to do? It was the *only* thing to do, the only scenario he could think of where everyone may survive. Except ....

8:51 AM (EST)
Offices of Hamilton & Hamilton

The article could have been more polished, but Patrick was content when he finally hit the send button. He called his boss and alerted him to his email, expressing once more the urgency of the matter. Dave acknowledged receiving the write-up and promised to have someone prep it for publication right away. To Patrick's dismay, he also reiterated the dependency of its publication on the missing evidence.

"Listen, Dave, I need you to come through here for me. I would not send this to you if not every word was true," Patrick stated his case once more. "I know the paper's reputation is at stake. But so is mine, and you know I would never risk either on just a hunch. You know me better than that. For heaven's sake, lives are at stake here."

"Unfortunately, so often lives are. Don't make this harder than it already is. You know how this works."

"You have the two lists," Patrick protested.

"And these are quite the story. But your article is not about these lists. It is about an accusation of a highly prominent figure that needs to be backed up with evidence. Isn't that why you are on the Cayman Islands in the first place?"

"You have the two in Long Island, and you have, you know .... How many more bodies do you need?"

Dave let out a long sigh. "You are not hearing me, Patrick. Get me these contracts."

"Listen, Dave, I would never—" Patrick stopped himself. "At least do it for Sarah. She sure deserves justice."

"As soon as I have the evidence," Dave replied coldly, and then hung up.

The young woman emerged from the breakroom and again entered the conference room, serving Patrick a welcome cup of coffee. She sat down in a chair on the other side of the table.

"You don't look happy," she noticed.

Patrick did not respond. He just sat in his seat, thinking, somewhat resigned, gently squeezing his lower lips between his thumb and index finger.

"By the way, I'm Avery."

"Patrick," he replied, absentmindedly.

"Now that you seem to be done with your work …"

"Ah yes, the promised explanation." As obliged, he dove right into his story. "I am here regarding some Yamaguchi papers."

"Oh my God!" Avery shot up from her seat. "I did not expect a Caucasian man. Shouldn't you be at the International Cayman Bank, like in"—Avery checked her watch—"nine minutes?"

"International Cayman Bank?"

"Yes, to retrieve the Yamaguchi contracts from the safe deposit box. I talked to your boss's assistant just yesterday. For whatever reason, he suddenly thinks they are safer with him. Do you know what is happening?"

Patrick's eyes opened wide as he was shaking his head in disbelief. He had cornered Alfonso with proof threatening his very existence, put him through a terrible car crash, roughed him up, and even threatened to kill him. Despite everything, the old lawyer had played his cunning game, loyal to his client through and through. As astonishing as this was, what Patrick just heard was even more so.

"Well, I was told to meet Alfonso here," he played along.

"No, no! You are mistaken. The appointment is at the bank, 9 a.m. sharp, when they open, and my boss is not the kind of person who likes to wait."

"Are you sure? I could have sworn—"

"Yes, I am sure. Come on, you need to go."

"I'd better, then," Patrick responded, getting up, "as he is the only one with access to the safe deposit box."

"Exactly. Go now."

"Well, Avery, in that case, you better drive me."

The young woman looked him up and down. "Do you at least have a clean shirt?"

34

9:07 AM (EST)

International Cayman Bank, Cayman Islands

The International Cayman Bank was located inside a beautiful, solid rock, stand-alone structure, built at a time when pirates on windjammers were threatening law and order. The building was immaculately maintained, with much attention given to the preservation of the old Caribbean architecture. One would have the sense of being projected back in time if it were not for the latest security technology. Various cameras, bulletproof windows, and a controlled-access entrance were well integrated despite contrasting with the overall look.

"He is already here," Avery pointed at the black Bentley in front of the bank.

"Wait for me here, will you? If you see him, call me on this number right away, okay?" he instructed Avery.

"What is going on?" she asked.

"Nothing. It's just in case I miss him in there," Patrick grinned at her.

"It is not a big place. You will see him."

"Still. Please ..."

She handed him a tie she had brought from the office. "You

won't get far in there without this."

Patrick was thankful Avery had pulled a fresh shirt from Alfonso's office closet. It did not fit, of course. It was too loose, yet the sleeves and length were much too short, Patrick found as he struggled to tuck it into his pants. The jacket handed to him was a leftover from Alfonso's brother, who was thankfully closer to Patrick's stature. Even then, it did not fit either, but it would do if left open in the front. Most important, the ensemble covered his injured wrists as well as the bruises around his neck. Some of Avery's makeup took care of the wounds on his face.

Patrick entered the bank and was immediately greeted by one of its employees. He charmed her with a fake interest in a security deposit box and a desire to check out the facilities. The receptionist made a phone call while Patrick kept an eye out for Alfonso. Not a minute later, a banker walked through one of the many bulletproof glass doors.

"I will need two forms of identification," she requested. Patrick handed over his passport and driver's license, and with the necessary formalities out of the way, he was ushered through a metal detector. The banker then signaled her co-worker behind another security window to call the elevator. They entered the cabin as soon as the doors opened. There were no buttons to push, yet the elevator soon started to descend. The ride down took longer than anticipated, the cabin lowering deeper and deeper underground. When the doors finally opened again, they were welcomed by an armed security guard.

"Good morning, Jim," the young lady greeted him.

"Good morning," he nodded back, swiping his badge through a card reader, and then gesturing for the employee to do the same.

Patrick noticed the expensive marble floors, complemented with stainless steel and translucent glass walls, all dimly lit. The main door opened, as signaled by a strip of small green lights above. Patrick could not quite make out the size of the facility but was astonished by the length of the various corridors. It was much larger than the small building above let one imagine, and so quiet one could have heard a pin drop. There still was no sign of Alfonso or his Japanese friend.

"We have various sections down here, all completely separated from each other. Every inch is under surveillance, except our privacy rooms, of course, where our clients transfer their valuables in and out of the deposit boxes. And just so you know, no two parties are ever allowed in one section at the same time," the bank employee proudly pointed out. "To access your safe deposit, clearance from a security specialist in an office above is required, given only after a successfully passed retina scan. Each box is equipped with two locks. An accompanying bank employee opens the first and will then leave the room. The section door will close, and once secured, you can retrieve the box by unlocking the second lock with your key. The door will not open again till your box is safely back in its place. As you can see, security is our top priority. Everything is state-of-the-art."

Patrick nodded in pure astonishment. "Impressive. But I will need a bigger box than those. Can I see one of those rooms?"

"Unfortunately, this is the only one I am authorized to show. However, the other sections are all quite similar." No sooner had she spoken than a small red light started to blink and a subtle beep warned of the closing doors. "We currently have clients in one of our other sections. It looks like they are now leaving. We will have to wait," the employee smiled.

Patrick quietly nodded while staring at the red light above the door, anxious for it to turn back to green. A good minute later, the doors finally opened again. Patrick immediately dashed back to the elevator.

"Do you have any questions?" the employee asked, trying to keep up with him.

"No, you explained everything nicely," he smiled back. The elevator made its way up, and as soon as his phone picked up a network, it started to ring. There was no need to answer the call.

"Unfortunately, the box size you are looking for is currently unavailable, but we do have a size that is slightly—"

The elevator doors opened, and Patrick hurried out of the bank, leaving the puzzled woman behind. Running toward Avery, he signaled her to move into the passenger seat, then jumped into her 1966 Mustang and started the engine.

"Where did they go?" he shouted.

"What is going on?" she responded.

"Tell me where they went!"

9:18 AM

Abandoned Warehouse

The door opened, and someone Susan had not seen before entered. As he walked into the light, she noticed a crooked face riddled with deep scars. Susan wondered what terrible injuries this man must have suffered.

"Nice to make your acquaintance, Ms. Sobchak. I am in charge of, let's just say, special operations, and I understand we are going to do some business together," he introduced himself with an accent as equally heavy as the rest of the team's.

All Susan could do was to stare at his deformed face.

"I have this effect on people, I know," he explained, waiting for her to say something.

She did not.

"Very well then, it's okay if you do not want to talk. I prefer it this way. But you will scream," he continued, looking at her swollen eye. "Now look at that. That just makes me angry. They promised not to start without me." Then, with the attention, respect, and grace of a conductor guiding his orchestra through a symphony, the scar-riddled man set up a tripod, put a video camera on top, and ceremonially placed various objects on the table in front of her. When finished, he closed his eyes and took in a deep whiff of the electrifying atmosphere. "I love those moments before I start my work," he mused, then produced an old photograph and held it so Susan could see it.

"You see, this is Klaus. Look how handsome he was. This person strapped to the chair is one of ours, may peace be upon him. And look what is on the table. The medical bag of Dr. Mengele. Did you know my great-grandmother and her sister were in Auschwitz? They were twins. Oh, what this man did to them. Now, pay close attention to the instruments next to the bag. Right here.

Do you see?" he asked as he pointed at the picture. With an elegant gesture, he presented his prepared workspace. "May I introduce you to the same line of instruments Klaus used on our friends?"

9:25 AM

International Cayman Bank

"They just left. Did you not see them inside the bank?" Avery asked, wondering.

"Where did they go?" Patrick shouted. "WHERE DID THEY GO?"

"Down this road, toward the airport."

Patrick stepped on the gas. It took only a minute till Avery spotted the beefed-up Bentley Continental GT with its heavily tinted windows, a sportier car than the Maybach, customized for even greater horsepower. Alfonso's expensive taste seemed to extend to his collection of cars.

"What is going on?" she asked.

"I'll let you know, but for now we need to keep an eye on your boss."

"No! This is my car, and he is my boss. Tell me."

"Alfonso is in danger. So please, help me keep an eye on him." Avery could not wrap her head around what was happening, and Patrick was not surprised she was freaking out.

"I'll call the cops," she said while handling her phone, about to dial the emergency services.

"No, don't! They will do more harm than good. I am here to protect him," he lied. "Everything will be okay."

"So, you are not here for the documents?"

"I am, but also to make sure nothing happens to your boss," Patrick lied again. "He is in danger for the very reason Yamaguchi wants his contracts."

Avery looked at him, and hesitantly put the phone down. "What in the world is going on?" she asked again.

Without answering, Patrick followed the black car at a safe

distance. At the next roundabout, the Bentley kept going around in circles. Patrick recognized the evasive tactic. As he did not want to give himself away just yet, he drove into the roundabout as one normally would, but the Bentley immediately showed up behind them, its acceleration perfectly timed to crash into the rear of the old car.

"Did he just hit us?" Avery shouted. Then they got hit again. It was clear it was not Alfonso driving the sporty vehicle.

"WHAT THE HELL? DO SOMETHING!" she screamed. At a disadvantage in the lower-powered car, he took the first exit. The Bentley immediately disappeared in another direction. Patrick did a 180 back through the intersection to follow the two, but they were already gone, nowhere to be seen. He slowed and asked Avery to keep her eyes on the side streets. They scanned every corner they passed. Suddenly, Patrick saw the aggressive front of the GT in his back mirror, approaching at a high speed. In a barrage of curse words, he immediately stepped on the pedal again, but despite the 120 horsepower engine of the classic, its acceleration was no match for the larger car's speed.

"Hold on," Patrick warned Avery. A second later, the Bentley again crashed into them, jolting their automobile forward.

Avery screamed again. "MY MUSTANG! What the heck?!" The Bentley kept slowing, accelerating, and crashing into their rear. Patrick had the pedal to the floor, flying down the street, desperate to keep the car under control, and an eye on his rearview mirrors. Once or twice the impact caused them to swerve, but he managed to correct his line and avoid worse.

"Make it stop!" Avery pleaded.

"I know what I am doing," Patrick responded.

"Do you?"

"Hold on!"

"WHAT DO YOU THINK I HAVE BEEN DOING ALL THIS TIME?" Avery was screaming.

The Bentley was again accelerating toward them when, just before impact, Patrick pulled the handbrake, locked his tires, and drifted into one of the smaller side streets.

The move took Hironori by surprise. With a reflex, he yanked the steering wheel around, but it was too late. People on the sidewalk, already alerted by the commotion, started running from the rapidly approaching car, screaming. The Bentley, with an enormously loud bang, crashed right through the patio into the coffee shop on the corner of the intersection. Tables, chairs, and broken glass flew everywhere. The shop's heavy neon sign thundered through the car's windshield, coming to a halt just inches shy of Alfonso. As white as a sheet, he stared at the massive piece of metal and broken neon tubes in front of his eyes. Hironori was equally enraged. With spinning tires, he backed into the street, the g-force catapulting the marquee off the hood.

"STOP IT!" Alfonso screamed at Hironori. "STOP!"

But the assassin yanked the gear stick into drive and accelerated as hard as he could. The Bentley shot forward, racing down the road to catch up with the bright red car.

+ + +

It gave Patrick nothing more than a moment to breathe. To his dismay, the Bentley soon appeared behind them again. He had a feeling the Mustang would not be able to handle another strong hit. With no other solution at hand, again timing his move to perfection, Patrick executed another handbrake turn to avoid the charging, horsepower-rich behemoth. This time, Hironori did not crash but overshot the intersection. It only took him seconds to be right on their tail again.

Avery sat in her seat, scared out of her mind. "You wrecked my car. YOU FREAKING WRECKED IT!" she screamed.

"*They* did!" Patrick replied calmly, focusing on yet another sharp turn and another, not allowing his Japanese counterpart to crash into them again. He was unable to shake him off, however. Then, at the next intersection, Patrick spotted a narrow pedestrian passageway between two buildings, leading into the bulbous end of a cul-de-sac behind. He stepped on the accelerator. It took Avery a second to realize what he was up to.

"ARE YOU CRAZY? YOU ARE GOING TO KILL US!" She frantically shouted at Patrick. "STOP ... STOP THE CAR!" Patrick gaged the opening as just wide enough. At a dizzying speed, the horn blasting and without any regard for cross traffic, they shot through the intersection, right into the passage. The car violently jolted around. Both side mirrors were immediately ripped off and flew through the air, and so did pieces of the fender and headlights. With a short but deafening sound, the metal on each side scraped along the walls. It was obvious that the Bentley not far behind would not fit.

+ + +

Hironori cursed, hitting the brakes of the heavy car. Through the broken windshield, he did not see the narrow opening till Patrick shot right through it. Next to him, Alfonso, his eyes closed and fingers clawed into the dashboard, was mumbling a prayer in anticipation of the impact. The heavy car screeched into the intersection, Hironori desperate to turn. The sideways impact on the curb ripped the tires right off the rims, launching the vehicle into the air and flipping it around before smashing it into the storefront.

Inside the upside-down wreck, Hironori hit his fist onto the steering wheel. "Damn, damn, damn!"

+ + +

Patrick saw the crash in his rearview mirror and hit the brakes, then put the car in reverse.

"What are you doing?" Avery asked, still shaking. "Let's get out of here!"

"We can't," Patrick insisted. "The documents are in that car."

"Wait a second. You are not the guy who was sent from Japan, are you? That man with Alfonso is. What is going on? Who are you?"

"You are right. But once the documents are gone, your boss will be too. And I have to protect him." Avery decided again to call the authorities. Patrick had a feeling she would not accept any more excuses, so he snatched the phone out of her hands and threw it out the window. She looked at him in disbelief, now even more scared. She desperately tried to get out of the car, but the passenger door was too mangled to open.

"LET ME OUT!" she shouted. There was no time. Patrick was still backing up when a car came speeding around the corner, also forcing itself through the narrow opening. He immediately changed gears and shot forward, down the cul-de-sac, into a main street. Hironori was on his tail again, but with the powerful Bentley now out of commission, Patrick fancied his chances. He turned left, and then right, taking over car by car, swerving in and out of traffic. But whatever he tried, the Japanese hit man stayed right on his tail.

11:30 AM (ART)
Estancia de Gobineau

Dieter again looked at his phone. He had waited long enough, maybe longer than he could afford. No call, no article, and only thirty minutes to go. It was painfully obvious that Patrick had failed, and it was time for his Plan B. A wave of excitement overcame the German. Finally, the moment he was waiting for all his life has come. He was about to free himself from the shackles of his family legacy and leave this golden cage once and for all. With a galloping heart, he stashed his wallet into the otherwise empty backpack, grabbed his jacket and hurried, right past his father's master suite, down the stairs into the basement.

+ + +

Inside the high-tech security room, Carlos was standing in front of the many monitors. He observed Dieter leave his room, wondering about the backpack on his shoulders and warm jacket under the arm. Alerted, Carlos got up, locked the door, and turned his attention back to the monitors. He had a feeling Dieter might do something stupid, or smart, but not before his father's passing. His eyes jumped from monitor to monitor, following the German down the stairs into the community room. As there were no cameras in there, he could only imagine what was going on. Carlos took his eyes off the screens and looked at the communication radio in front of him.

+ + +

Dieter carefully rolled the Chagall up into a cardboard tube, but he was not done yet. *As of now, the thing you hate the most, me, and the thing you love the most, this monstrosity, will part with you forever.* He squeezed Dr. Mengele's notorious medical bag into his backpack. Now ready, he could not help but look around the room once more at the despised memorabilia that had unwillingly been part of his entire life.

"Adios, muchachos!" he said out loud while giving a two-finger salute. The smile on his face could not have been bigger. Somewhat in disbelief, he asked himself again if this really was it. Like Patrick and Susan before him, he climbed through the secret opening inside the closet, and then disappeared into the dark tunnel.

9:37 AM (EST)
Streets of George Town

I need an advantage. Something ... Patrick was looking ahead for an opening, desperate to shake off his Japanese nemesis. Minute after minute passed with nothing. He managed to keep a good gap between him and the assassin, still overtaking one car after another. Suddenly, traffic got denser, and the cars ahead slowed dramatically. Patrick immediately crossed the center line onto oncoming traffic.

"WHAT ARE YOU DOING?" Avery screamed again, scared for her life. Just before causing a head-on collision, Patrick hit the brakes, switched back, squeezing in tightly between two cars, then shot forward again, accelerating, taking over car after car, trying to extend his lead. He saw Hironori do the same, following him closely. The Japanese man not only kept up but even gained some ground. At the next opening, Patrick again stepped on the accelerator, rushing by a good number of cars. He waited till the last second to switch back. But traffic in the lane next to him had come to a stop, not leaving any room to do so. He turned his steering wheel the other way, hitting the pavement, taking out potted plants and advertisement boards alike. As soon as the oncoming car had passed, Patrick got back onto the street. He finally seemed to gain some ground. But another car was already approaching fast, less than one hundred yards ahead. With standstill traffic on one side and pedestrians on his other, this time he had nowhere to go. Patrick spotted the cargo port, one of its entry gates just ahead. He was not sure if he could make it, but he hit the gas, flashing his high beams. The driver of the approaching car only marginally slowed. *Is he asleep?* Patrick wondered, but he kept going, the distance between them rapidly closing. At the last possible moment, he ripped the steering wheel around, his tail brushing the oncoming car sideways. Patrick corrected his line, not taking his foot off the accelerator. Their car fishtailed through the entry point, crashing through the barrier and flying by the astonished guard, as it sped toward the shipping containers on the docks. It took a good fifteen seconds till, in his back mirror, he saw Hironori nearly take out the protesting man at the gate. Fifteen seconds was all he needed.

11:38 AM (ART)
Estancia de Gobineau

One last time before crawling out of the well, Dieter checked his PDA for the article, but the website refused to refresh. The reception was just too spotty. "Oh, come on," he mumbled impatiently, holding up his phone in all directions. It took longer than he had the patience for, but the page did finally load. As expected, there was no article. He climbed out and started walking through the forest. Everything was as calm and peaceful as ever, even more than usual as Dieter noticed the absence of the flocks of birds chirping. It was not long before the silence was interrupted by the distinct sound of bullets being chambered. Out of nowhere, he was commanded to get on the ground, and only minutes later, he was presented to the leader of the unit.

"My name is Dieter Heydrich. I am here to hand over my father," he said somewhat proudly, desperate for his plan to work.

The man in front of him, dressed in full fighting gear, stared him up and down. "Is he ready to give himself up?"

"No!" Dieter chuckled at the thought. "He would never do that."

"Well, then, where is he?"

"You will have to go get him."

"Get him?! I am not in the mood for jokes," the commander angrily responded, moving his half-smoked cigar from one corner of his mouth to the other.

"I am not joking."

"Don't you think we would have done so if we could? Those walls are high, the gate sturdy, and from what I hear, the guards mighty capable. Not to speak of the dogs and considerable weaponry in there."

"You are spot on," Dieter replied. "But forget the walls, forget the gate. As for the rest, all you need is the element of surprise."

"Are you serious?"

"I am serious," Dieter calmly replied.

The commander was shaking his head. "Are you trying to lure us into a trap?"

Dieter shook his head. "That would not fit my plans."

"Actually, you are quite right. We can forget everything because now we have all we really need. You! And with you in custody, we will get him," the commander pointed out.

This was exactly what Dieter was afraid of, the very words that could make his plan go sideways. Nonetheless, he pressed on. "I would not bet on it. He is not going to give up, no matter what you do to me."

The commander did not react.

"Wouldn't you rather have him?" Dieter nervously tried to convince him. He got no response. "All you need is to get in unnoticed. The rest should be a piece of cake," Dieter added.

The commander shook his head again. "We are not here to start World War III. Our mission is to take into custody anyone of importance that walks out of this fortress. Mission accomplished! Cuff him and put him in the truck." He underlined his command with a dismissive gesture. "And notify the guys in the Caribbean," he added, then started to walk away.

"Did you see me come out?" Dieter shouted after him.

The commander kept walking.

"There is another way in, one not over the walls or through the gate."

The unit leader stopped, turned, walked back, and stared into Dieter's eyes.

"There is a secret passage through the well down there. It leads directly into the main compound. All that separates you from my father Klaus is this tunnel, and two flights of stairs."

Again, the commander just stared at him, gently chewing his cigar.

"Come on," Dieter pleaded. "We are out of time here."

The man glared at him for a few more seconds.

Dieter summoned all his courage, straightened his shoulders, and squinting his eyes a bit confidently stared right back at the commander. "Maybe I overestimated you." The two men kept staring at each other. "Maybe you are not as witty and tough as your reputation makes us believe." The stare-off continued. "No wonder you could never get my father. What a damn shame!"

Another few seconds passed before the commander turned his head slightly and, without taking his eyes off Dieter's, addressed his second in command. "You stay here. If we are not back in fifteen, shoot him."

35

Abandoned Warehouse

As ceremonially as he had done his work so far, the scarred man checked his watch, took a small vial from his bag, held it into the light, drew its liquid into a syringe, and pressed the plunger till it started to squirt.

"This will make everything so much more enjoyable," he told Susan with a smirk. "For us, of course."

"What ... what ...?"

"I am glad you ask. It's quite an amazing, potent little thing. It will sharpen your senses. An invention of mine, I might add. Every sensation you are about to experience will be exponentially magnified. I can't wait!" In a rather harsh manner, he jammed the syringe into her shoulder and injected the drug. With the adrenaline rush fighting her extreme exhaustion, she was already struggling to keep her mind lucid. Now with the psychedelic drug or whatever it was kicking in, things got worse. With every beat of her heart, the pain in her swollen eye got another jolt.

Estancia de Gobineau

The commander watched his team of six highly trained paramilitary specialists enter the well before him. They then carefully moved up the long, dark tunnel, keeping an eye out for eventual booby traps, all the while setting their own charges. Within minutes, they stepped into the community room. Everything was as described by Dieter. He radioed their progress to the agents outside before commanding his team to get ready for the next phase. They all switched off their night vision equipment, double-checked the silencers, and once again tested the in-ear communication system— all but one, who was busy pushing a tiny camera scope through the rubber soundproofing between the door and floor. Nobody was in sight; everything in the hallway was quiet. Without making a sound, the team moved out of the room and secured the bottom of the stairway, ready to move upstairs. Out of the blue a door opened, just around the corner, by someone humming a song. The commander signaled two of his men to get into position. Seconds later, an unsuspecting, middle-aged, heavy-set woman with a basket full of freshly laundered clothes was snatched. Frightened to her core, she dropped the basket, the sound of its fall alerting the guard upstairs.

"Everything okay down there?"

She was signaled to cooperate. With a silencer on her temple, she quietly nodded, and slowly, the gloved hand pressing on her mouth let go.

"Yes, señor, not to worry. Everything is okay. I just dropped my basket. I am so sorry. Again, not to worry. Don't come down. I just dropped my basket. Don't come down … no need to come down," she responded.

Alerted by the unusual nervousness of the housekeeper, the guard made his way downstairs, the squeaking of the wooden steps alerting the team below, but he suddenly stopped.

"What?" he whispered through the intercom as, in his ear, he had heard the distinct click of an incoming transmission. When his inquiry went unanswered, he continued his careful descent.

Pop! Pop! He never knew what hit him.

Inside the security room, Carlos had been keeping an eye on the monitors. He first thought Dieter just wanted to disappear, which served him just right, but it came as no surprise when a tactical team moved out of the community room and took up position at the base of the stairs.

"Here we go," he said out loud, once again glancing at the radio in front of him. Curious, he moved closer to the monitors when he saw the housekeeper walk out of the laundry room, and even closer when, mere moments later, one of his men in the lobby walked toward the stairs. "God damn it," Carlos cursed, recognizing the guard as none other than his younger cousin. He immediately grabbed the radio and pushed the talk button. He saw his cousin, alerted by the click in his earpiece, stop and press his finger onto it.

"What?" he inquired.

Carlos, with a heavy heart, let go of the radio. His eyes followed the youngster as he made his way down the stairs, knowing full well what was about to happen. It would be only the first of many tough decisions to come. If he couldn't have made such, he should not have applied for the job in the first place. And now with Klaus about to be gone …. In his newfound confidence, he kept his eyes glued to the monitors, watching the assault team step over his relative's dead body and move up the stairs. Carlos smiled.

9:49 AM (EST)
Cargo Harbor, Cayman Islands

"Listen, Avery, when I say NOW, you climb into my seat as fast as you can, okay?" She was too scared to talk but managed to give him a nod.

"Trust me, it's going to be alright. He wants me, not you," he tried to calm her again. Patrick was racing the car down the narrow corridor between piled-up containers, counting the seconds since his last turn. Twelve, thirteen, fourteen …. He knew his pursuer was about to get a visual on them again, so he turned once more, out of sight, and drove the few yards toward the edge of the pier.

"NOW!" He forcefully opened the bent door and got out. "Turn the car around. In a few seconds, you will see him race by. It is your cue to head back to the gate. You'll be safe there." Avery nodded.

"What are you going to do?"

"I am going to finally end all this." Patrick slammed the door shut, ran over to one of the cranes, and hid behind its base. Avery buckled up and, somewhat unnerved by the pier's edge, carefully executed the three-point turn. Patrick counted the seconds again. Sixteen, seventeen, eighteen …. He started to wonder what was happening, as the pursuing car should have passed by now. A few more seconds had gone by when it calmly drove around the corner and lined up right in front of the red classic, all the way up to Avery's bumper. Intimidated, she looked around for Patrick, but he was gone. Hironori menacingly revved his engine and, seconds later, engaged the clutch and started to push her toward the water. She instinctively pressed harder on the brakes, and when her car kept crawling backward, she put it in gear and hit the gas. Her wheels started to spin. It slowed the push, but despite her tires thrusting against the menacing car in a big cloud of smoke, the grip was still not enough. Closing in on the water's edge, she again nervously looked around for Patrick. He had seen her cry for help and was already running toward her, but when he was only halfway there, with a loud pop, one of the Mustang's tires burst. Avery was still frantically pushing the gas pedal, but the grip was gone. Three feet, two feet, one foot … Patrick was too late, yet close enough to hear her muffled screams when the car tilted over the edge, splashing into the ocean right between two cargo ships.

9:51 AM

Abandoned Warehouse

To Susan's dismay, the pulsating pain was not the only side effect of the potion. Everything around her was distorting in all sort of ways.

She was quickly overcome with nausea and only a few seconds later had to throw up the little liquid left in her otherwise empty stomach.

"Now we just have to wait till they are ready," the scar-riddled man informed her. With headphones over his ears, he patiently sat, eyes closed, swaying back and forth to the sounds of Wagner's *Ring of the Nibelungen*, waving his left arm to the music, bathing in these specific moments of anticipation he lived for. Susan knew the worst was yet to come, but she was too exhausted, too drained to even feel fear anymore. At peace with the inevitable conclusion of her short life, death was now nothing more than a welcome relief to whatever was about to happen next.

9:52 AM
Cargo Harbor

When exiting the car, Hironori had not yet seen Patrick charging and was taken off guard when the former SEAL crashed into him. Taking advantage of the briefest of confusion, Patrick squeezed his nemesis between the door and the frame with full force, cracking one or two of the Japanese man's ribs. Hironori's face distorted in pain, but he managed to push back, enough to turn toward Patrick, whose leg was now exposed. With a precise, skillful kick, the martial arts expert hit his knee, right into one of those special trigger points that caused such a thrust of pain. Patrick fell backward onto the floor, cursing. Within a fraction of a second, his only advantage was wasted. Hironori, angry as one could be, pushed the door out of his way and positioned himself above Patrick.

+ + +

Avery was still screaming. For a short moment, the air inside lifted the car back up to near the surface, but then with water gushing in, it was again pulled back down, heavy engine first, deeper and deeper. She tried to open the door but did not have enough strength to fight the ocean's pressure. The water inside was now up to her hips, the cabin filling up fast. She tried to roll down the window, but the handle was bent out of shape from a previous impact and would not budge. She thrusted her elbow against the glass. It did nothing but bruise her arm. She tried smashing it with the car key, but it did not work either. She looked around for anything that might help. There was nothing. Then she remembered something she had once seen on television. She tilted her seat backward, just enough to remove the headrest, and then crashed the two metal holders into the glass. To her relief, it cracked. The ocean's pressure accomplished the rest. A powerful stream of water rushed inside, pushing Avery away from the window, only to be held in place by her seatbelt. She did not manage to catch another breath. This was the now-or-never moment to make her way out, but she was stuck. In her panic, she had forgotten to unbuckle herself. Avery desperately looked for the release mechanism, but everything was dark, and the little she saw, blurry. She tapped around and quickly felt the release button and pressed, but the buckle did not dislodge. She then frantically pulled on the seatbelt; it did not give. She pushed the release button again, but as before, the buckle would not give. Running out of air, she pushed and pushed, and then, out of desperation, pulled on the belt while once more pushing the button. With her hand on the release mechanism, she passed out.

11:53 AM (ART)
Estancia de Gobineau

The team had swiftly moved up the stairs into the lobby one by one, covering each other, then up one more flight of stairs. Knowing the area to be surveilled, they hurried to secure the corridor on the upper floor, surprised by the nonexistent resistance. Once in position in front of the master bedroom, they stormed through the heavy doors. The three guards inside were taken by total surprise. Two were instantly taken out by precise hits, but one managed to jump away from the hailing bullets and, while in the air, returned fire, hastily aiming into the general direction of the assault. One slug went through the upper thigh of one of the charging men, but the solider kept going, taking out the shooter while limping into position, doing his part to secure the room. Klaus, rather clumsily, reached for his handgun and just managed to switch off the safety, but before he could aim, assault rifles were already on him, the red lasers cutting through the rank air, pointing dots at his forehead. Not ready or willing to give himself up, the dying man fired his gun, its bullet narrowly missing the head of one of the attackers.

"We need him alive," the commander shouted, ensuring no one was to pull the trigger, and then turned to the old man. "Try once more and I will roast you over an open flame."

+ + +

The two shots fired had echoed through the entire compound. Carlos cursed. On the monitors, he saw his alerted teams on patrol make their way toward the master bedroom. This time, he hastily picked up his radio.

"All units, code orange, code orange. Unit two, code blue. Unit two, code blue." The patrols, surprised by the orders, asked for confirmation.

"Affirmative. Code orange, code orange. Unit two, code blue," Carlos repeated.

"We heard shots coming from the inside," one responded.

"Do what I tell you," he snapped.

"But sir—"

"The upper floor is secured. Make sure you take care of the outside. Release the dogs into the perimeter." All the guards ran out of the building except unit two, which, as instructed, made their way into the basement. Carlos observed the maneuvers, making sure every single one followed his instructions.

+ + +

The assault team hastily ripped the various tubes from Klaus's body, and then one man hoisted him over his shoulder while another helped his injured colleague. The numerous medical devices triggered all kinds of alarms. Undeterred, they hurried back down the corridor and stairs, the two men in the front scanning their path through their visors, the commander securing the back, their precious cargo and injured solider in between. A guard positioned at the main entrance was taken out as swiftly and silently as his colleague before, the task executed to perfection to avoid slowing the team's pace down to the basement. As she was commanded, the housekeeper was still sitting on the floor, the basket next to her, mumbling prayers, rosary in hand. The team's front man had already pushed down the handle of the community room door when, in his earpiece, he heard the commander's calm voice. "Stop!"

Everyone froze in place, their eyes scanning for possible threats, all except the commander, who looked at the woman sitting uncomfortably on the hard floor.

+ + +

Carlos cursed again. His eyes glued to the monitors, he was closely observing the assault team halting their exit. What was going on? He had been worried the unit sent downstairs would not execute their orders in time, but it only took seconds till the "all ready" notification came through the radio. *Just open the damn door! Open the damn door!* He shouted on the inside. But nothing happened. Despite the hurry, the entire team stood as if frozen in time. He kept his eye on the commander, whose eyes were still on the housekeeper. *What are you looking at?* The commander turned his head toward the camera and, through the monitor, looked directly at him. Anxiously, Carlos awaited their next move.

+ + +

The commander took his eyes off the camera and looked back at the woman. She was staring back at him, her lips nervously moving in quiet prayers. He pointed at the door with a most subtle of head gestures. The housekeeper did not respond, but tightened her grip on the rosary, closed her eyes, and intensified her prayers.

"STING AHEAD, STING AHEAD," the commander

warned his team. Everybody immediately lined up against the wall except the man in front, who knew better than to let go of the door. The breacher stepped forward, and with a fast-setting compound, glued the handle in position, releasing his colleague from the delicate situation. He carefully tied a nylon line around the handle, stepped aside, and with just the slightest pull, opened the door. A huge blast thundered through the halls, causing the entire house to shake. A wave of dust and smoke was rapidly thrust through the corridors up into the lobby. Struggling to see and breathe, the team hurried through the now doorless opening into the debris-riddled community room, and with the cabinet shredded to sawdust, toward the hole in the wall. Suddenly, muzzle flashes lit up the lingering smoke. One of the front men was jolted back by a slug hitting his bulletproof vest. The rest immediately dropped to the floor, covering Klaus. The breacher pulled his remote, paired it with the closest charge inside the tunnel, and hit the red button. The explosion took out the two-man unit ahead of them. After letting the additional dust settle for just a few seconds, the assault team, one by one, swiftly entered the secret passageway. Close to the well, bullets started to fly again, this time from their six. The commander immediately returned fire, covering the exiting team, while steadily backing up himself. He held the position till everyone was safely out, tossed his assault rifle the moment he was given the all-clear, and hurried up the ladder and out of the well. Gasping for fresh air, he let himself fall over the edge and onto the forest floor. The breacher had already been waiting and again pushed the red button on his remote, triggering the entire array of set explosives. The earth started to tremble, and with the high velocity of projectiles, rocks and dust flew out the well, high up into the air, its shockwave rocking everyone nearby.

9:54 AM (EST)
Cargo Harbor

Patrick was holding his throbbing knee. Hironori knew exactly how much pain his paralyzing kick had caused. All he had to do now was to move in for the easy kill. Putting his hands under his clothes to unsheathe his knife, he calmly looked at Patrick on the floor. *Soon, he will be begging for mercy*, he thought, as all his victims had done uncountable times before. Against expectations, Patrick shot up and smashed the Japanese assassin against the car. Hironori's already broken ribs were pushed into his lungs, taking his breath away. Patrick grabbed the wrist of the hand holding the knife and smashed it against the car frame while keeping Hironori's other arm in check, but the Japanese man did not let go of the blade. On the contrary, he pushed back and managed to slowly turn its sharp tip toward Patrick. The former SEAL pressed his entire weight against his opponent's injured torso, hoping the force would worsen the injury of the broken bones, while pushing the knife back as strongly as he could. With eerie strength, his opponent soon had the blade on Patrick's throat, slowly muscling it into Patrick's trachea. The two were staring into each other's fury-filled eyes, Patrick's face strenuously distorted, the Japanese man's stone cold.

"Your woman, she was quite something," Hironori provoked, and he immediately noticed his opponent's face turn dark red as Patrick's anger started to boil over. He let go of Hironori's left arm, put his freed hand on his other one, closed his eyes, and with all the force he could summon, tried to push the blade away from his throat. Hironori's left hand grabbed onto Patrick's neck and pressed it toward the knife, but the trained SEAL managed to stop it from further cutting into him. Both knew they could not keep up the stalemate for long.

"You should have seen the little whore begging before I cut her like a pig. I thought you ought to know before you die," Hironori was laughing.

Patrick, with shaking hands, stared even deeper into his opponent's eyes. "It is not me who is going to die, but you. And the best thing is I do not even have to kill you. Your boss will do that for me. I can only imagine his disappointment."

It was now Patrick who noticed the anger in the Japanese man, but his verbal jab did little to help his struggle. On the contrary, Hironori tensed his muscles even more, while Patrick's were tiring fast. He had to do something. Lightning fast, he turned, keeping his grip on his opponent's wrist. With the knife-holding arm now over his shoulder, Patrick yanked it down with all the force he could summon. The assassin's elbow fractured with a noise so loud it hurt Patrick's eardrum. The knife immediately dropped to the floor. Patrick then turned again, grabbed his opponent's upper arm, and swung the Japanese man around, crashing him into the side of the open door, right onto the pointy top corner of the frame. Hironori's rib cage once again took the brunt of the impact, the metal edge cutting into his already injured sternum. Patrick pushed his body onto his, pressing his opponent further into the metal frame. A few seconds later, the towering Japanese man finally collapsed onto the floor.

Patrick immediately searched the car for the documents. They were nowhere to be found. Most likely still in the Bentley, they were now long gone. With no contracts and sirens approaching fast, it was high time to go after Avery, but just when he was about to jump off the pier, he asked himself if Hironori would really part with items of such importance. Patrick started to tap the assassin down and, on his back, discovered a tight-fitting satchel, nicely hidden underneath his clothes. He retrieved the knife, cut through the leather band to get it off, and opened it.

"BINGO!" Patrick said out loud, looking at dozens of contracts. With the deadline passing, there was no time to gloat in his success. He immediately put the stack on the floor and, struggling with the papers in the slight breeze, started to take pictures with his phone.

"Hands up!" someone shouted at him. Only a few feet away, two policemen were pointing their guns at him. "Down on the ground!" Patrick ignored the order and attached a batch of the pictures to a text message.

"I said, get down on the ground," one of the officers repeated. Patrick was too busy to notice them approach, but he felt the kick into his back, jolting him onto the ground, knocking the phone out of his hand. It slid under the car just before he managed to hit the send button.

"I SAID DOWN ON THE GROUND!"

Patrick dove after the phone but was immediately dragged

away. Another police car arrived. This one had a passenger: Alfonso!

"Oh great," Patrick said out loud, staring into the barrels of the officer's guns. With a sinking heart, he realized it was all over. He had come close, so close, but had failed, letting everyone down. All except one. There still was a chance to save Avery, and he could not give up on her just yet. Maybe, just maybe, she was still alive. He looked at the two officers and then at a jubilant Alfonso exiting the cruiser. Patrick stood up.

"Get down on the ground!" he was told and he again ignored the command.

"My leg hurts. I need to have it stretched out."

"I said, DOWN ON THE GROUND!" Patrick was screamed at, but he again ignored the order. He held on to his aching knee, moving around, all the while shifting closer toward the water. Now at the edge of the pier, to everybody's surprise, he jumped, letting himself fall backward into the harbor. As he fell, bullets flew right above Patrick's head, except one that penetrated deep into his left shoulder.

10:00 AM
Abandoned Warehouse

"Any news from down south?" the old man asked, checking his watch. The guy behind the bright spotlights shook his head.

"Ten o'clock. Time to get started." He gestured to the scarred man, who stopped the music, removed the headphones, and walked over to the video camera. Susan immediately noticed the little red light.

"Which one shall I start with?" he asked her, looking at his collection of tools.

She did not answer.

"It's quite the overkill. You see, one does not need all of these. Those guys back in the sixties—they had no idea what they were doing. But the old man asked me to bring them all, so I did," he explained. "To be honest, it makes me look like a fool, but I believe they want them for theatrics," he continued, pouring some oil into a pan and heating the hotplate. He then picked up a rather rusty dental drill and pushed the power pedal on the floor. A grinding noise cut through the room.

"Please don't," Susan pleaded, eyeing the old instrument, her arms and legs pulling on the ties in a desperate effort to free herself. "Please, please don't," she started to sob. "I'll give you anything you want, but please don't," she begged again.

"QUIET!" the old man shouted. Susan's head was pulled back and secured with a wide leather strap around her forehead, and a metal contraption was pushed inside her mouth.

"Another one of my inventions," the scarred man proudly mentioned, while another man operated a small handle to spread the device apart. "It ensures your cooperation."

Susan again tried to plea, but with her mouth pried open, all she managed were gargling noises.

"So, the begging continues," the scarred man kept grinning, holding the drill right in front of her face. "It will soon stop. It always does."

Susan looked again at the old instrument with eyes as wide open as her mouth. She tried to scream, but the high-pitched noise of the drill overpowered whatever sound she managed to make. At first, Susan felt only the terrible vibrations on her bottom molars, but soon after, like a striking bolt of lightning, pain jolted through her jaw, her gargled screams now overpowering even the sound of the drill. She desperately tried to yank her mouth out of harm's way, but the band around her head did not leave even the slightest wiggle room. Tears started to flow, and her vision blurred.

"STOP!" the old man shouted.

Susan was relieved when the drill was retracted, but the pain lingered.

"REMEMBER," he scolded his executioner, "nice and slow, how it was done to our friends."

The scarred man closed his eyes, just for a few seconds, again taking in the electric atmosphere.

"Nice and slow," the old man repeated. Then, the drill started up again.

Cargo Harbor

During his fall, Patrick had forced himself to take in a big breath of air, but the pain of the hitting bullet knocked it right out of his lungs again. With strong, one-armed strokes he dove deeper and deeper into the increasingly darkening water, the salt stinging his wound, elevating the already intense pain. Only seconds later, he reached the submerged car, managed to open the door, and tried to get Avery out. Patrick reached over her to release the seatbelt, but as before, the buckle would not dislodge. He pushed again, two, three, four times—nothing. Patrick then noticed that Avery, in her panic, had fastened the clip into the passenger side's socket. The belt released right away, and he finally managed to get her out of the car. Now desperate for air, he struggled to pull her upward. From below the surface, he saw the five men above look over the edge. When he finally broke through the water, Patrick took in the breath of his life.

"Avery!" Alfonso shouted. One of the officers jumped into the water, taking the unconscious young woman from Patrick. An alerted crane operator lowered the hook and hoisted the officer, Avery in his arm, onto the tarmac.

Patrick managed to climb up the ladder onto the pier, where he saw two of the police officers frantically working on the unconscious woman. The other two were attending Hironori, while Alfonso was calling for an ambulance. Still out of breath, Patrick sat down and leaned against the rear fender of Hironori's car, exhausted, a puddle of water forming around him from his dripping clothes.

"Wake up, Avery! WAKE UP!" Alfonso shouted.

To everybody's relief, she began to throw up water, followed by heavy coughing. As the commotion had everyone distracted, Patrick leaned over, as well as his injured shoulder would allow, and peeked under the car. His phone was just inches away, lying right behind the back tire. Patrick looked up again. Nobody was paying any attention to him. He scooched over and moved his hand forward to see if he could reach it. With his fingertips, he dragged it toward him, grabbed it, and then sat back up. The screen was cracked, but it lit up, on it a message from his boss. "Great job!" Patrick clicked on the attached link.

"Get the phone away from him. Quick! Get the phone," Alfonso screamed at the officers. Patrick did not care. There it was, on the front page of *The New York Times* website—his article in all its glory, black on white. He could not believe it. Had the falling phone triggered the send button? It couldn't have, as the message was not yet sent. It did not matter anymore, but Patrick finally hit the button to transmit the missing evidence. With all four officers charging at him, he had just about enough time to hold up his phone and grin at the cunning lawyer.

"Too late, my friend. Too late."

36

Cayman Health Hospital, Cayman Islands

Against doctor's orders, Patrick took a walk around the corridors, pushing the IV drip stand ahead of him. He was sick and tired of the hospital bed, too nervous to just lie there. Otherwise he felt good and did not understand why he had not yet been released, but that was the least of his worries. Susan was on his mind constantly. He also had frantically tried to reach Dieter, but his calls remained unanswered, his whereabouts another mystery. Strolling near the emergency room amongst busy people dashing by, his phone started to ring. It was his boss returning his earlier call.

"Thank you for publishing my article," Patrick expressed his appreciation, "and without the documents."

"I wish I could take all the credit, but I got partial confirmation on your story," Dave lied.

The increasingly loud siren of an arriving ambulance prompted Patrick to press the phone to his ear. "Confirmation? What confirmation?"

"It doesn't matter. But I do feel much better now that we have the copies of these contracts, especially since every news outlet has picked up on your story. It's making quite the splash."

"Good. The world needs to know."

"How are you doing?"

"I'll be all right. They removed the bullet from my shoulder blade."

"Any word from Susan or Dieter?"

"I sincerely hope soon. Any word from Japan?" Patrick asked.

"My sources tell me a raid is being prepared. But it will take a day or two till they have their ducks in a row."

"Time we do not want Yamaguchi to have."

"Nothing we can do about that," Dave reasoned, while someone shouted at Patrick to get out of the way. A team of medics rushed by with a gurney. Patrick caught a brief glimpse of the injured woman and wondered if she had been in a bad car accident.

"I also alerted our South America correspondent. He is in touch with his sources down there. I am sure we will hear from him sooner than later."

"Well, let me know the minute something comes across your desk."

"Sure thing, Patrick. Again, excellent work. Congratulations. And feel better soon."

"You can congratulate me once Susan and Dieter are safe."

"You are right," Dave replied.

"Just keep me—" *Was this—no, it couldn't be—SUSAN!* Patrick dropped his phone, ripped the dripline off the bag, and started to run after the medical team that had just passed by him.

"Susan," he shouted down the corridor. "SUSAN!" But just when he had caught up, the doors to the operating unit were shut in front of him, and he was told this was as far as he could go.

"Just tell me if she is going to be okay," he pleaded with a nurse.

"Are you family?"

"I am her friend."

"Sorry, then," he was coldly turned down.

"You are one lucky man," the nurse smiled at Patrick as she changed his bandages.

"Listen, I know you are not allowed to tell me, but …. The woman who was brought in this morning, is she going to be alright?"

The nurse looked around, making sure no one was nearby. She was about to answer when a familiar voice filled the room.

"Yes, she is going to be alright."

Was he dreaming? Or did his medications cause hallucinations? Patrick turned his head and hardly recognized the person entering the room.

"SUSAN!" he shouted. "Thank God!"

She immediately squinted her eyes, placing her right hand onto her head. "Please, not so loud."

"You are okay!" Patrick said, relieved, looking at her swollen face. "Well, are you?"

"Let's just say it could've been much worse. I am good, thanks to a lot of painkillers."

"What happened?"

"They suspected a head injury and worried about brain swelling, but the CT scan thankfully showed none of that. However, I am going to need some major dental work, at least on one of my molars."

"That is good to know. But what I meant …."

Susan carefully sat down on the bed. "I can't remember much. A sting on my neck, then being tied up in a dark room. There was an old guy, and one with lots of scars on his face. There must have been a drill of some kind, and from what I hear, a drug."

"I was worried they would make you pay for Klaus."

"I guess they did, at least for a while."

"Then stopped because they got Klaus."

"It looks like it. How is Dieter doing?" Susan was anxious to know.

So was Patrick. "No update yet. I am curious about what

happened down there. I hope he is okay."

"He saved my life. Again." Susan said while glancing at Patrick's heavily bandaged shoulder. "What happened to you?"

"It's a long story."

"I was just telling him how lucky he was the bullet missed the artery," the nurse informed Susan.

"Artery?" Susan asked concerned.

"Please tell him to stay in bed. He does not want to listen to me, nor any of the doctors."

"I doubt he will to me either," Susan chuckled.

"You need to rest, and I will be back later to check on you again, and God help you if you are not right here, on this mattress, when I do," the nurse cautioned Patrick before exiting the room.

"Shot? Seriously, you were shot?" Susan asked, her eyes wide open.

"Yes, but as I said, it is a long story."

"What about the article?"

Patrick lifted his phone. "Published!"

"How did you get your hands on the contracts?" Susan asked.

"That's a part of the same long story."

Susan got quiet.

"What?" Patrick asked.

"Are we safe now?" she asked hesitantly, as if she dreaded the answer.

"Yamaguchi must know he is done. So should the assassin."

Susan took his hand and laid it between hers. "I don't know how to thank you, Patrick," she choked up. "You risked your life. For me. And I don't even know what to say about Sarah …."

"You don't have to say anything. What happened to Sarah is not your fault."

"We both know I had something to do with it."

37

September 11, 2017—7:45 PM (JST)
Minato-Ku

This time for his mission debrief, Hironori was summoned to Tokyo instead of the syndicate headquarters and Yamaguchi's private residence in Kobe where, over the years, he had gotten to know the entire family, from the youngest to oldest, growing into a trusted friend and companion. The unusual location was not the best of signs. It, therefore, came as no surprise when he was asked to wait. It was all part of the game. The bench he was sitting on was handcrafted in a light-colored wood, shaped into a simple yet elegant form, matching the linear wall panels that could be found throughout the ultramodern estate. Recessed neon lights illuminated the room in a slight green tint. One hour passed, then another, then one more, all the while he was being closely watched through a small camera up in one of the corners. He sat still, staring into nothingness, still struggling to breathe.

While he appeared calm on the outside, thoughts were racing through his mind—about the failed mission, leaving the organization, his loved ones, Akiko and Shin, and above all, the outcome of this meeting. So many before him had walked into his boss's office to only be carried out, terminated for less. Another twenty-five minutes passed before Hironori heard steps echoing through the seemingly endless halls. When Yuzuki entered the small room, he hardly recognized her. He had never seen Yamaguchi's assistant in anything but ultra-conservative outfits. But here in Tokyo, her long, flowing hair was not tamed in a tight bun, and her elegant two-piece was a vibrant, light blue color, the skirt way above her knees, her long legs bare, and the high heels more provocative than the usual flats. The elegant ensemble conveyed a sense of feminine confidence usually not tolerated in the organization's environment of strict traditional structures. Things thankfully seemed to work a bit differently in the capital.

"Hironori, my friend. How are you?" she greeted him with a charming smile.

He responded only with a slight nod.

"It's been a while since I last saw you," she tried to make conversation.

He nodded again, not in the mood for small talk.

"He is ready for you now."

Yuzuki had been fond of Hironori—so much so, she had hoped to become more than just acquaintances, despite their difference in age. But he had never returned as much as a friendly smile to her flirtatious advances, and she herself was too shy to push things further. At night, when she was alone, she had often fantasized about them living together, getting married—about gifting him a healthy baby boy. On some level, she knew her dream was nothing more than a fantasy; nevertheless, it evaporated in bitter disappointment just hours ago when she learned about Hironori's secret. Nevertheless, she managed to find happiness for them.

The two walked up the stairs and down the long corridor, then stopped in front of the main office. Hironori took as deep a breath as he could manage. This was it. Yuzuki sensed the lingering tension and wondered if this meeting had to do with the recent revelation of his newborn son, but she did not dare to ask. When finally told to enter, Hironori found Yamaguchi standing behind his heavy oak desk. His fists were on the table, an angry look on his face, his tattoo-covered torso without a shirt, showing off the inked samurai, a symbol of the clan's strictest of rules: loyalty, honor, and above all, respect, an individual's life secondary to the cause, to be sacrificed for the good of all. Right in front of his boss, centrally showcased, was the notorious and much feared tanto, its blade still covered with the blood of its last victim. Both Hironori and Yuzuki immediately understood the meaning of the not-unexpected setup. Without saying a word, Hironori sat down on the small wooden stool in front of the desk and lowered his head to show the demanded respect. The changed dynamics between the two spoke volumes. Yuzuki, taken by surprise, tried to puzzle together what might had happened from the little bits and pieces picked up over the last few days. Fearing whatever came next, she attempted to excuse herself, but Yamaguchi commanded her to stay.

"This was a close one," the boss said, staring down his subordinate. He lifted his fists and slammed them onto the table. Yuzuki jumped. Yamaguchi then took the tanto off his desk and walked over to his assassin. Hironori kept his eyes on the floor.

"Look at it," his boss commanded, holding up the blade.

Hironori did not obey.

"For years, I could count on you. For years, you have served with the utmost loyalty. For years, you were the very best. By far! But now?"

Hironori did not show the slightest of emotions. Yuzuki could not watch any longer. Scared to her core, she turned her face, struggling to keep herself composed. She was desperate to stop whatever was going on but knew better than interfere.

"Thankfully, the story has sort of a happy ending. My collection is safe," Yamaguchi said and kept staring. "You are the one everyone strives to be. Yet, this entire mission …."

Again, Hironori did not move, but from the corner of his eye he kept a close watch on the blade.

"I cannot tolerate failure, and on any other day—" Yamaguchi tightened his grip on the tanto. "But there is no one like you. And I know you still have it in you, the old you."

Hironori closed his eyes, his thoughts drifting to his loved ones. As he had so many times before, he imagined a little house somewhere in the countryside on a lake surrounded by trees, he and his son sitting on a small dock with fishing poles in their hands. His boss did not notice, but for a split second, the slightest of smiles spread across his assassin's face. Was he a fool to ever believe it could become a reality? He vividly remembered that fateful day when he was kidnapped right out of his local martial arts school and forced into the syndicate, at the tender age of only eight. He never saw his family again. That traumatic experience became the main factor in his decision to leave the organization: to provide his son what he had lost so early on. Despite the heavy weight of Yamaguchi's words, for him there was no going back.

"As you have saved my life more than once, this one time, and ONE TIME ONLY," Yamaguchi screamed angrily, "your failures will be forgiven. You will serve me again with the utmost professionalism, efficiency, and loyalty expected from you!"

Hironori stayed quiet. His boss had expected as much.

"Look at me," he demanded. "LOOK AT ME!"

Hironori hesitantly looked up. In Yamaguchi's face, he saw an expression he had not seen before.

"You left me no choice; you fool."

Hironori looked down again, determined.

"LOOK AT ME!" Yamaguchi screamed again, grabbing Hironori by his hair, forcing his head up.

Yuzuki was horrified. Pressing her lips together, she could not hold back her tears any longer.

"YOU DO AS YOU ARE TOLD!" Yamaguchi screamed frantically, pressing the tanto against Hironori's face, the fresh blood on the blade smearing over his nose and cheek. "You do as you are told, or your blood will wash off this blood." The boss tightened his grip on Hironori's hair. "THIS BLOOD!" He screamed even louder, staring deep into Hironori's eyes. "THE BLOOD OF YOUR LOVER AND YOUR SON."

In an inconceivable act of defiance, Hironori grabbed the wrist of his boss, pushed the tanto out of his face, stood silently before shoving his boss out of the way, and with a blank stare, walked out through the heavy, wooden doors.

Yuzuki, in total despair, gagged, about to throw up. Against her orders, she ran out the room and into her office. Leaning over her desk, she breathed heavily, shaking all over. *Not baby Shin! Not*

Akiko! How could he? The monster! She sat and let her head fall into her hands, failing to compose herself, sobbing away. Never in her wildest dreams had she imagined her boss to be this cruel. Never! Then, as if out of nowhere, her tears stopped. Surprisingly calm, she took the phone from her purse and texted the one person she knew she should not.

38

Berta Strasse 16, Munich, Germany

"I hope the tip is solid. We brought everybody," SWAT team leader Bunke said to his colleague and personal friend.

"You brought everybody because I asked you to. There is a chance we are going to need them all," Police Chief Josef Meckler responded.

"So, how credible is this information?" Bunke dug further.

"The tip came from the most inner circle. I'd say it is as good as it gets."

"Inner circle, huh? Why would someone do that?"

Meckler shrugged his shoulders. "Why should I care?"

"I am just saying … it could be a trap."

"That's why you are here, the top dogs." Meckler again looked through his binoculars to check for any developments, but everything was calm.

"It's kind of ironic," Bunke smiled, "bringing all that cargo right back here to Europe, to Germany of all places, considering its history."

"Well, maybe that is exactly why," Meckler responded. "No one expects it to be here. But I personally don't yet know if it is an ingenious move, or really dumb one."

"It's a thin line on this one."

"Is your team in place?" Meckler inquired.

Bunke nodded. "Snipers in the front and back, all exits covered, and two teams ready to move in."

Meckler radioed for an update. Nothing out of the ordinary had been detected.

"We will soon know how good this tip really is," Bunke followed up on his concern.

"Cargo being there, not being there, I really don't give a crap. All I care about is this going by the book. Make sure you guys don't mess it up. I don't want to have to deal with the consequences."

"Why would it not go by the book?" Bunke responded, a bit annoyed.

"You know what I mean."

"Not really." The SWAT leader gave his friend Meckler a disapproving look. "Just let us know when you want us to move in."

"As the minister is anxious for an update, now is as good a time as any." Meckler went back inside the commando trailer to keep an eye on the many monitors. "Ready?" he radioed.

"Affirmative," Bunke responded.

"Then go!"

Two armored vehicles approached the apartment complex, one from each side of the blocked-off street, and came to a stop just outside the entrance. The teams disembarked and, as quietly as a feline stalking over a pillow, got into position, one team to the left, one to the right of the entry door.

"Alpha team ready."

"Beta ready."

A group of three pushed toward the entrance, two providing cover for the one picking the lock. With the door compromised, both teams dashed into the building and up the stairs. No matter how many operations he had under his belt, Meckler still got nervous in the seconds before a raid. He did not mind. On the contrary, he enjoyed the rising tension; the rush was what he liked about his job. On the monitors, he got a visual on the apartment door, with the teams neatly lined up in the staircase. Everything was going according to plan.

"Again, everyone, mind the cargo," Meckler responded.

"Affirmative," the two team leaders confirmed.

"Whenever you are ready," the SWAT leader gave the go-ahead. The door was breached with one hit of a battering ram and flash grenades rapidly thrown inside. Not a second later, the teams moved in and detained no fewer than seven stunned operatives. Only moments later the "all clear" was announced.

"By the book," Bunke could not help but radio his superior.

7:17 PM

"How long do you need?" Meckler asked the short, bald man with round glasses.

The art expert called on scene could not believe the sheer volume of crates. "It will take days, weeks, to catalog everything."

Meckler nodded. "I understand, but I need to update the minister. How soon can you tell me something?"

"Well, ten to fifteen minutes and we will have a good indication what this is all about," the expert responded, "as long as your men will open a few of these crates for me." He put on white gloves and, with all the care in the world, took out the first painting. With a magnifying glass in hand and corresponding documents on the table, he started his examination, soon to switch his focus to the second and third painting.

"Remarkable!" the expert said, visibly excited. "This is it, the real deal, with a very high degree of certainty. And looking at all these crates, we are standing in front of the biggest find of looted art in history, right here in this apartment."

"Are you sure? You only looked at three."

"Unless these are forgeries of unseen quality, they are legit, and if they are, chances are the others are too," the expert snapped at the police chief. "That is all I can tell you for now."

"Time for me to join the minister for the press conference then," Meckler announced, already on his way out the door.

September 12, 2017—4:07 AM (JST)
Minato-Ku

It was rare but not unprecedented that Yuzuki was called in in the middle of the night. But this time, she already knew what it was all about.

"What is going on?" she asked innocently upon entering her boss's office.

With the push of a button, the heavy wall panels behind Yamaguchi moved to the side, unveiling a large television screen. He lifted the remote and switched to a twenty-four-hour news channel.

"What can you tell me?" he demanded.

Yuzuki stuck to acting innocent. "Are these your paintings?"

"Oh, Yuzuki, what have you done? I just need to know why."

Yuzuki stayed silent.

"Just tell me, my dear. Why?" he asked her again, his voice drenched in deep disappointment.

"Really? You don't know?"

"I need to hear it from you."

Yuzuki straightened her back. "I have never minded the thefts, the drugs, the schemes, or the extortions. I even ignored the many executions. I have kept my mouth shut the countless times the Public Security Intelligence Agency arrested and interrogated me all night long. I even tolerated your unwanted advances to satisfy your perverted pleasures. I knew what I was getting into the second I accepted the position and have always served you loyally without ever questioning anything. But this time—this time you went too far. How could you? A woman! A child! No, a baby! What kind of monster are you?"

"You know what this means?" Yamaguchi asked coldly.

She nodded. "I knew the moment I sent that text."

Her surprising confidence was nothing but a mere conclusion of her broken loyalty. But Yamaguchi knew it did not matter anymore. The first domino had fallen; the rest would follow. Yuzuki, with a surprising determination, walked behind Yamaguchi's desk, picked up the tanto, and confronted her boss head on. He looked at her in pure astonishment as nobody was ever to touch the blade, and no one ever had but him and his father before him. *How dare she?*

"Here," she said, and with her head held high, stretched out both her hands, offering her boss the blade, the sharp end toward her. "Take your revenge. But before you do, you need to know I am at peace. As for you, you will burn for all eternity. Now do what you must."

Yamaguchi was taken by the unexpected show of strength. He took her hand off the blade and placed it on the handle, then did the same with her other, before wrapping his over hers. The move took Yuzuki by surprise. She looked up at her boss, trying to free herself, but her hands were trapped underneath his.

"I will not be a part of this," she pleaded. "This is all you. Do what you must but let go of me." She again tried to free herself.

It started with him gradually strengthening his grip. Little twitches in his eyelids followed, and his hands started to shake, then his head.

"LET GO!" Yuzuki screamed.

A few seconds later, her boss was so entranced his entire body started to quiver.

"You are hurting me," she pleaded with her seemingly possessed opposite. Yuzuki's hands were now in utter pain. Yamaguchi's grip intensified even more, and so did his trembling, then he let out a frantic scream. Terrified, she turned her head away from her boss, but suddenly, everything stopped, and all was quiet again. Wondering what was happening, she looked into Yamaguchi's empty eyes.

"You have betrayed me. YOU, of all people. The one I trusted the most. For this, you will suffer. Not me. YOU WILL!"

Yuzuki saw the growing intensity in his eyes, all the while his grip on the blade tightened again. She did not know why, but she could not help but stare, her eyes meeting the evil in his. Then, with the quickest of motions, Yamaguchi turned the knife and thrusted it into his abdomen. With her hands still involuntarily on the tanto, Yuzuki screamed.

"NO! OH NO!"

Yamaguchi collapsed onto his knees, pulling her down with him. He continued moving the knife, cutting his insides. When his hands finally let go, in her shock, Yuzuki kept hold of the blade, causing it to slide out of Yamaguchi's body.

"I told you, you will suffer," he reminded her while collapsing onto her.

She immediately pushed him off. "You really think you can save your honor by committing seppuku? YOU FOOL!" she shouted at him, tanto still in hand. Then, in her anger, Yuzuki adjusted her hold on the handle and thrust the blade into his chest. "This is for Akiko," she shouted, then stabbed him again. "And this is for little Shin."

Yamaguchi, in agony, looked at her in utter disbelief.

"Your honor! You can shove it …. And do you really think what you just did will haunt me for the rest of my life? Not for a second. As a matter of fact, I could not be prouder right now, and I will make sure the whole world will know you died a coward, killed by a woman." She stabbed him again and again as Yamaguchi groaned in pain. "This time, *your* blood is on this blade, you pathetic man!" she screamed, holding the tanto above his eyes. "Now die in shame." She threw the blade to the side, got up, and walked out of the office, leaving her boss to die alone.

1:39 PM

Watanabe Funeral Home, Shinjuku City, Japan

Hironori stood in silence, dressed in a black suit, white shirt, and black tie, seemingly emotionless, as he watched the body of Akiko, with little Shin in her arms, placed into the crematorium chamber.

"Please come back later to collect the ashes," the funeral director requested, nudging him to leave.

"No," Hironori responded. "I'll wait."

"This will take a while, and the ashes will need to cool down afterward."

"No. Place both inside one urn as soon as possible."

The director shook his head. "This is a very unusual request."

"Do as I say," Hironori insisted.

"Of course," the director bowed. "May I suggest waiting in our lounge? You may be more comfortable there."

+ + +

Yuzuki later heard Hironori stood in front of the ovens for the entire four hours till the cremation was completed. He left with the urn, never to be seen again. She often wondered about him. Years later, rumors would reach her that a group of backpackers, in the remotest of areas, found a small, seemingly abandoned wooden cottage, deep inside a forest, next to an idyllic lake, with a small dock attached. In the otherwise empty interior was an urn, placed on a beautifully crafted pedestal and below the small shrine the pieces of a disassembled Samurai sword. It seemed the place had not been visited in years, yet, to the hikers' astonishment, a fresh lily had just recently been placed in front of the urn.

39

September 16, 2017—10:45 AM (PDT)
Offices of *The New York Times*, Los Angeles

Susan and Patrick walked into *The New York Times* offices and were welcomed with a big round of applause. Everybody stood up and clapped the second they stepped off the elevator. Susan could not hold back her tears from the emotional welcome. Both appreciated the gesture, but neither of them felt like celebrating. Dave noticed, and he quickly ushered them past the flowers, the many hors d'oeuvres, and the champagne bottles into his office. Dave gestured to Susan and Patrick to sit down.

"You have no idea the waves your article has made. Well done, both of you."

Patrick and Susan thanked Dave for the kind words.

"I have to say, it is quite a story," his boss said, shaking his head, still in disbelief. "Every news outlet and talk show host wants you on their show. You are going to be busy."

Patrick, though, did not feel like stepping into the limelight. "I did it for Sarah. Maybe not in the beginning, but …."

Dave's mood rapidly turned somber. "Yes, Sarah. Of course. I am so sorry, Patrick. I would like to express our deepest condolences, from all of us. She was such a wonderful person; you know we all liked her. If there is anything we can do—anything you need—anything."

Patrick was thankful for the offer, but he just nodded in silence. The reality of her death had not really hit him until he went back to her condominium. Her scent was still in the air, and the many pictures reminded him of their happy times together. Despite knowing better, he anticipated her walking through the door at any moment and greeting him with a kiss. That was until the blood stain on the carpet reminded him otherwise.

"And you, Susan, I am very sorry about your grandparents. It must be hard for you, too, especially the way ...."

"Yes, it is. But I feel I did not even know them—the real them. It's like I am grieving for people who never really existed."

Dave responded with an understanding nod.

"Have you heard anything?" Patrick was wondering.

"Actually, I did not want to tell you till after our little celebration out there, but there is news on all fronts. Good and bad."

"Anything on Dieter?" Susan asked anxiously.

"Well ..." Dave seemed to struggle for the right words. "I got notified just minutes ago ... the Bariloche authorities found two bodies in the exact same spot those agents were found in 1960. We have nothing official yet, but—"

"No, not Dieter too!" With all hope for him gone, combined with the dread of what must have happened to him, Susan's energy drained from her body in bitter disappointment. "Are you sure?"

"As I said, it's not official yet, but ... I am so sorry. I wish I had better news."

"You said you do. We could use some," Patrick pressed on.

"The Yamaguchi/Heydrich drug operation was struck down. Hundreds of people were arrested in a synchronized, worldwide police operation. The stolen artwork has been recovered in Germany, of all places, and is currently being cataloged. The wheels are in motion to get them reunited with their rightful owners as quickly as humanly possible. As for Yamaguchi, the coward tried to escape the law by committing an honor suicide, but in the end he was knifed down. Apparently, an inside job."

"Good," was the only word Patrick managed to say, Sarah and

Dieter still on his mind.

Dave looked at the two. "Listen, I know you both have other things on your mind right now. But don't ever forget what you have accomplished. You did well. Really well. The return of the artwork will take a bit of time, but decades-old wounds are healing right now because you brought justice to these people—hundreds of them. You cannot put into words what it means to them."

After contemplating Dave's words, Patrick got up, took Susan by the hand, and dragged her out of the office, through the small crowd, to the table with the many champagne bottles. Dave, taken by surprise, followed. Patrick handed Susan a champagne flute, gave one to his boss, and took one for himself. When Patrick lifted his glass, everybody quieted down.

"Let's celebrate our adventure, and let's celebrate this incredible woman standing right next to me, Susan, my new friend, whose courage and determination are beyond remarkable." The entire team started to clap while he gave a blushing Susan a big hug.

"There are other protagonists that must be acknowledged," he continued, "especially one whose heroism was beyond comprehension: Dieter Heydrich, whose incredible story you will soon hear."

"It truly is an incredible story," Dave added.

"I am just happy and relieved we can put this nightmare behind us now," Susan chimed in.

"Oh, it's not over yet," Patrick smiled.

"Please don't tell me," Susan looked at him, worried. "What?"

"I still have an old pocket watch to return," he smiled. Susan nudged him with her elbow in return.

Patrick noticed his assistant standing without a glass, seemingly not in a celebratory mood. "Here, Eva," he said as he handed her some champagne. "Drink with us. After all, if you had not convinced me to speak to that old lady—"

"Then Sarah would still be alive today," Eva cut him off, lowering the flute.

"Then one of the biggest drug rings would not have been busted, the Nazis would have one more stronghold to spread their message of hate, Japan would be plagued by one more crime syndicate, and the stolen art would never be reunited with its rightful owners. Sarah's death is not your fault, on the contrary. Everybody owes you, and none of this would have happened without you."

Everybody started to clap again. Dave raised his glass. "My friends, above all, let's celebrate Sarah. Without her, this story would not have found its successful end. May she be in our hearts forever."

"To Sarah," Susan raised her glass.

"And to the justice she deserves," Dave added.

Patrick looked at his boss with suspicion written all over his face. "Is this why you published … you know … without the evidence?" he asked him quietly.

His boss returned nothing but a grin. Patrick looked back at Eva. Encouraged by his words, she lifted her glass. "To Sarah!"

Everybody, glasses raised, responded in unison, "To Sarah!"

Epilogue

September 23, 2017—10:02 AM (EDT)
Long Island, New York

Susan marveled once again at the red Klee back on the dining room wall of her grandparents' mansion, where it had so often been the center of conversation and admiration. The house on the beach, now Susan's new home till her grandparents' estate was settled, would certainly not be the same without it. Yet, plans were in the works to have it loaned to the Metropolitan Museum of Art in honor of its original owner

According to her lawyers, her chances of not losing the inheritance were much better than anticipated. Nonetheless, it would take years for the matter to be settled, as questions of jurisdiction, international asset protection, and criminal forfeiture laws, among other complex legalities, would need to be argued. To her surprise, she was also about to inherit the entire von Badenholz estate, including a sizable parcel of land in Germany as well as many valuable items that had been stolen before the building was bombed but were since gradually recovered. She had already decided, with these proceeds, to continue her grandparents' foundation benefiting victims of wars, not to clear the heavily tarnished family name but out of her own goodwill.

Still staring at the painting, Susan was suddenly overcome with an unexpected wave of peace and calm. Not a minute later, her phone rang. She did not recognize the international number but had a feeling what it may be about.

"Ms. Sobchak, this is Amelia. I am one of the nurses at the Medicover Hospital in Warsaw. We met the day before yesterday."

The Day before Yesterday

"She is in room 747. But before you go in there, you must know she is very old, pushing one hundred, and unfortunately in quite poor health. As a matter of fact, she is so weak she has not spoken in days now."

Susan gave the nurse an understanding nod.

"Let's not overwhelm her. It might be better if I wait here," Patrick proposed.

Susan again nodded. "It's probably a good idea."

"Nervous?" he asked.

"A bit, but more out of excitement," she replied. Slowly, Susan opened the door and peeked inside the room. "Elizabeth?"

The frail women on the bed struggled to open her eyes for even the briefest moment.

"Elizabeth, I am Susan Sobchak. You do not know me, but I have something I believe belongs to you." Susan removed the heavy wrapping, then sat on the hospital bed next to the fragile woman and held up the red painting.

"Can you open your eyes?"

Elizabeth did. An immediate jolt of energy transcended through her aged body; her face was suddenly graced with the brightest of smiles. With a noticeable change in demeanor, she even managed to lift her head just enough to get a better look, the unexpected sight bringing back the happiest of memories of times long gone.

Susan held the painting till the old woman closed her eyes

again. She then walked over to the wall, took down the framed photograph of a spring landscape, and put the Klee on the nail. She sat back on the bed, where, in the most tender of gestures, the old woman stretched out her hand for Susan's, who gladly laid it in hers and put her other on top.

"Listen, Elizabeth, I am so sorry this painting was taken from your parents. And I am so sorry I could not bring it back sooner. Please accept my most sincere apology."

The old woman, faintly whispering in her heavy Polish accent, asked what had happened to the Klee. Susan briefly summarized what she knew, while Elizabeth, eyes closed, listened intently.

"My dear, I hope you did not come here to ask for forgiveness," the old woman whispered.

"First and foremost, I am here to put a wrong right because this painting is yours," Susan answered. "But what my grandparents did does weigh on my conscience. They had no right …."

"Listen, my child. There is nothing to forgive. Your grandfather stole it from the thieves who stole it from me, and this is not the worst that could have happened."

"Be that as it may, I have—"

"As a matter of fact, you deserve our admiration. Rumor here has it that you are quite the hero."

Susan affectionately tightened her hold on Elizabeth's hand ever so slightly.

"Can I see it one more time?" asked Elizabeth.

"Just open your eyes. It is right there, on the wall, for you to look at whenever you want to."

Elizabeth gazed at it for quite a while. "I never imagined I would see it again. Look at those colors … those shapes …" The old woman's affection for the painting warmed Susan's heart.

"My dad was always very fond of the work of Paul Klee. He had supported him as long as he could, bought a lot of his work and sponsored many of his exhibitions. On one of the weekends Paul visited us, he asked my dad for permission to paint me. I was so excited, but when I saw the finished portrait, I did not understand. I was so disappointed, so confused by the abstract, as I could not recognize myself in it. Mind you, I was only five back then. 'In time, you will,' Klee had told me. He was right. With age, I did start to see his vision more and more, and I must confess now, he captured me—what is not immediately visible to the naked eye—rather well."

Susan noticed the passion in the old, fragile voice. "You know, I could not help but think this may have been a portrait of you. I just felt it somehow."

"Not many know this very painting was exhibited at the first Bauhaus exhibition in Weimar back in 1923, just weeks after it was painted. It was quite the hit," Elizabeth ended her story proudly. Susan waited in silence for the old woman to catch her breath.

"I already know what you are going to say, my child, but I need you to listen. I'd be honored if you accept this painting as my gift. I cannot think of a more deserving person to have it."

Susan was stunned. "I am sorry, I … I … I cannot accept it. The painting is finally where it belongs. With you."

"Yes, after so many years it has found its way home. But I have no family left, and as mine comes to an end, it is time to ensure the best continuation of its journey. Take it, please, as a thank-you. Not only for bringing this back to me but also for bringing all these paintings back to these families who shared our fate. You more than deserve it."

"I cannot possibly … Elizabeth! It's not right. I just can't."

"It's my final wish. You can, and you will. I am just glad, thanks to God, that I could see it one more time. This is all I could have asked for. Listen carefully as I am not going to beg. Take it back home with you. It's yours."

+ + +

"Please don't tell me," Susan pleaded.

"As you requested, I unfortunately need to notify you that Elizabeth passed about half an hour ago."

Despite the somewhat expected news, Susan was quite shaken. She thanked the nurse for the notification and was about to hang up.

"Listen, I think you ought to know …" the nurse interjected.

"Ought to know?" Susan prompted.

"Well, Elizabeth was hanging on for much longer than … well, people usually do. She just refused to go, like she had some unresolved business. But since you were here—I don't know how to say this. Everything changed. She was suddenly happy—finally at peace."

Thank you

… for reading my novel. I truly hope you enjoyed it. If so, please let other readers know and help them find 'The Second List':

www.thesecondlist.com/review

Written with Deep Gratitude

To my dear friend Russ Abrahams, for making me believe in my storytelling abilities this one fateful evening.

To my dear friend McKinley Marshall, for championing my project and generously and unselfishly sharing her wisdom.

To my teacher and friend Xavier Tachel, for his greatly undervalued philosophical views on God and the world.

To my mom, for her creative influence.

To my daughter Ciena, for all her encouragement and input when nobody else knew what I was up to.

To my daughter Cheyenne, as without her, this story would never have been written.

To my extended family, especially Renate, Barbara, Andreas, Sandra, Simon, Reto, Aline, Levin, and Alena, for bringing so much joy and happiness into my life.

To all my dearest of friends, simply too many to list here.

To the world's great storytellers, with my deepest respect for being such guiding beacons.

And above all, to my wife, Susan, after whom a protagonist in this story is named, as a humble thank-you for all her love, encouragement, and support, without which such a project could never have come to fruition.

About the Author

Max Bridges was born and raised in Switzerland. After successful studies at the renowned Architectural Association School of Architecture, London, and Columbia University, New York, opportunity brought him to Southern California, where he now lives with his wife, two daughters and a dog.

As in any discipline of his creative work, the concept behind is not only present but always paramount—the final product merely a conclusion of its developed narrative. The push into the media of typed words seems nothing more than a logical extension to his already expansive portfolio spanning architecture, design, and photography.

MaxBridgesAuthor.com
Facebook: facebook.com/maxbridgesauthor
Instagram: instagram.com/maxbridgesofficial

Made in the USA
Las Vegas, NV
11 December 2021

37172125R00246